Rave reviews for the novels of Erica Spindler

All Fall Down is "shocking, emotional,
an engrossing read."
—Stella Cameron, author of *Glass Houses*

All Fall Down is "a smooth, fast ride to the end.
Spindler is at the controls, negotiating the curves with
consummate skill."
—John Lutz, author of *Single White Female*

"Spindler's latest moves fast and takes no prisoners.
An intriguing look into the twisted mind of someone
for whom murder is simply a business."
—*Publishers Weekly* on *Cause for Alarm*

"...a compelling tale of kinky sex and murder."
—*Publishers Weekly* on *Shocking Pink*

Shocking Pink is "one of the best,
most frightening novels of the year."
—*Painted Rock Reviews*

"Ms. Spindler spins an amazing tale
of greed and obsession."
—*Rendezvous* on *Fortune*

"Carefully woven plot...enticing characters....
Give yourself plenty of time, and enjoy!"
—*Romantic Times* on *Fortune*

Spindler delivers "a high adventure of love's triumph
over twisted obsession."
—*Publishers Weekly* on *Forbidden Fruit*

"Outstanding! A first-rate romantic thriller."
—*Rendezvous* on *Forbidden Fruit*

Dear Reader,

Thank you for purchasing *Bone Cold*. Those of you familiar with my novels know that my ideas are sparked by real-life occurrences. This story is no exception. A letter from a young fan proved that I can twist even the most innocent events into springboards to terror. I hope you enjoy reading *Bone Cold* as much as I enjoyed writing it.

In closing, the response to last year's offer of an *All Fall Down* commemorative refrigerator magnet was so overwhelming, I'm offering one again. If you'd like to receive a *Bone Cold* magnet,* simply write to me at P.O. Box 8556, Mandeville, LA, 70470-8556 and request one. You may also request one through my Web site: www.ericaspindler.com

Best wishes and happy reading,

*While supplies last

ERICA SPINDLER

BONE COLD

ISBN 1-55166-794-0

BONE COLD

Visit us at www.mirabooks.com

Printed in U.S.A.

For my readers.
Thank you.

I need to thank the following people for their offering of time, expertise and support during the writing of this novel. Without their generosity, *Bone Cold* would not have become the book it is.

Lieutenant Marlon A. Defillo, Commander,
Public Affairs Division,
New Orleans Police Department.

Evan Marshall, The Evan Marshall Literary Agency.

Dianne Moggy and the entire amazing MIRA crew.

And finally, a special acknowledgment
to Rebekah Bevins, my youngest fan,
whose (perfectly innocent) letters sparked
the original idea for this story. Thanks, Bekah!

Prologue

June 1978
Southern California

Terror held thirteen-year-old Harlow Anastasia Grail in a death grip. She huddled in the corner of the dimly lit, windowless room, Timmy cowering beside her, weeping.

The matted carpet smelled faintly of urine, as did the mattress she and Timmy had awakened on hours before. Or had it been days? Harlow didn't know. She had lost all sense of whether it was day or night and of the hours passing. Time had ceased to exist the moment Monica, her father's trusted nurse, had coaxed her and Timmy into a car Harlow hadn't recognized.

He had been waiting inside it. The man Monica called Kurt.

Harlow shuddered, remembering the cold way he had smiled at her. She had known instantly that he meant her and Timmy harm; she had screamed and lunged for the door handle. He had stopped her, holding her fast while Monica injected her with something that had turned her world black.

"I want to go home," Timmy whimpered. "I want my mom."

Harlow drew the boy closer to her side, protectiveness surging through her. It was her fault he was here. She had to take care of him; he was her responsibility. "It's going to be all right. I won't let them hurt you."

From the adjoining room came the sound of a TV news report in progress:

"*—yet in the kidnapping of little Harlow Grail and her friend, Timmy Price. Harlow Grail, daughter of actress Savannah North Grail and Hollywood plastic surgeon Cornelius Grail, was abducted from the stables on the family's estate. The housekeeper's six-year-old son had apparently followed Grail to the stables and was also abducted. Authorities do not believe he was part of the original plot and FBI officials—*"

A crash rent the air, followed by the sound of splintering wood. "Son-of-a-bitch!"

"Kurt, calm dow—"

"I told them what would happen if they went to the cops! Stupid Hollywood assholes! I told them—"

"Kurt, for God's sake, don't—"

The door flew open with such force it crashed against the wall behind it. Kurt stood in the doorway, breathing hard, face white with rage. Monica and the other woman, the one called Sis, hovered behind him. They looked terrified.

"Your parents didn't listen," he said softly, voice vibrating with hatred. "Too bad for you."

"Let us go!" Harlow cried, pulling Timmy closer. The boy clung to her, sobbing, hysterical.

He laughed, the sound cruel. "Spoiled little bitch. If I let you go, how will I get what I want?"

He crossed the room and grabbed Timmy, wrenching him from her.

"Ha'low!" the boy screamed, terrified.

"Leave him alone!" As she scrambled to her feet to help him, Monica and Sis sprang forward, stopping her. Harlow fought them, but they were too strong. Their hands circled her arms, their nails dug into her flesh, holding her fast.

Kurt tossed Timmy onto the dirty cot and held the struggling six-year-old down. "Watch carefully, little princess," he said to her. "See what your parents caused. They didn't listen to me. I warned them not to go to the authorities. I told them what the consequences would be. They did this. Stupid Hollywood assholes."

Laughing, Kurt grabbed a pillow and pressed it over Timmy's face.

"No!" The word, her scream, flew out of her, reverberating off the walls and back. "No!"

Timmy struggled. He clawed at Kurt's hands, his legs flailed wildly at first, then with less force. Harlow watched in horror, a litany of pleas slipping from her lips, tears streaming down her face.

Timmy went still. "No!" Harlow screamed. "Timmy!"

Kurt straightened. He turned and faced her, an evil smile twisting his lips. "Your turn, little princess."

He and Monica dragged her to the kitchen. Harlow told herself to fight, but terror had leeched her of her ability to do more than beg. Monica forced her right hand out over the white porcelain of the chipped and stained sink.

"Ready or not, here I come."

Harlow caught the glint of metal. Some sort of cutters or clippers, she realized, a scream rising in her throat.

He found her hand, closed the cutters over her right pinkie. First came the pain, hot, blinding. Then the *pop* of bone being snapped in two. The white sink turned red.

Harlow's vision blurred, then faded to black.

Pain emanated from Harlow's bandaged hand and up her arm in fiery waves. With each crest, a bitter, steely taste filled her mouth, all but choking her. She bit down hard on her bottom lip to keep from crying aloud. She had to be quiet. Absolutely still. Kurt and the others thought she was asleep, knocked out by the pain medication Monica had given her. The medicine Harlow had only pretended to take.

The wave passed and Harlow experienced a moment's respite from the agony. Tears flooded her eyes, tears of horror. Of hopelessness. With the emotion came another wave of pain. Light-headed, on the verge of passing out, Harlow struggled to breathe. She couldn't pass out now. She couldn't give in to the pain. Or the fear. Not if she wanted to live. Her parents were making the drop tonight. She had heard Kurt talking. He'd told the other two he would let her go when he got the money.

He was a liar. A filthy bastard liar. He'd killed Timmy even though the boy hadn't caused any trouble. Sweet little Timmy. All he had wanted was to go home.

Dirty bastard was going to kill her, too. No matter what he promised. She might be only thirteen, but she wasn't stupid—she had seen all three of their faces.

Harlow eased herself off the cot, careful not to cause the springs to squeak, and crept across the matted carpet to the door. She pressed her ear to it. Kurt was speaking, though Harlow couldn't make out exactly what he was saying. It involved her. And the pickup.

It was happening tonight.

Harlow hurried back to the cot, lay down and closed her eyes. She heard the click of the doorknob being twisted then the soft whoosh of the door opening, of someone crossing to stand beside her.

Once again the door hadn't been locked. Why would they lock it? They thought she was in a deep, drug-induced sleep.

Her visitor bent over the bed and Harlow realized it was the old woman, Sis. Harlow could tell it was her by the way she smelled—of roses and baby powder, sweet scents that only partially masked the gross smell of cigarettes.

Sis leaned closer. Harlow felt the woman's breath on her face and fought to lie perfectly still, to not recoil.

"Sweet lamb," the woman whispered. "It's almost over now. Once Kurt has the money, everything will be all right."

He had left to make the pickup. Time was running out.

"I couldn't stop him before. He was angry…he… Your parents shouldn't have defied him. It's their fault. They're the ones—'' Her voice thickened. "I did the best I could. You have to understand, he…"

You didn't do the best you could. You could have saved Timmy, you old witch. You made such a fuss over him but you didn't do a thing to save him. I hate you.

"I'll be back." The woman pressed a kiss to Harlow's forehead; it was all Harlow could do to keep from screaming. "Sleep sound, little princess. It'll be over soon. I promise."

The woman exited the room, closing the door behind her. Harlow listened intently for the telltale click of the lock turning over.

It didn't come.

She cracked open her eyes. She was alone. Carefully, heart thundering, terrified of making a sound that would alert the old woman, she sat up. Too quickly. Dizziness assailed her and she grabbed the edge of the cot for support. She held herself perfectly still, breathing deeply through her nose, fighting to clear her head.

The dizziness passed, but still she remained motionless. She collected her thoughts. From what she had been able to ascertain over the past few days, she was being kept in a small, relatively isolated house. She hadn't heard sounds of traffic or passersby; nobody had rung the doorbell. In the morning she had heard the twittering of birds and twice at night the lonely howl of a coyote.

What if she couldn't find anyone to help her? What

if she got lost? What if the same coyote she heard howling found her and tore her apart?

Act or die, she reminded herself, trembling. Kurt intended to kill her. At least if she ran she would have a chance.

A chance. Her only chance. Harlow climbed out of the bed, swaying slightly as she stood. She pressed on anyway, creeping toward the door. She inched it open. The room beyond appeared to be empty. The TV was on, sound muted. A cigarette burned in the ashtray on the arm of the easy chair, a curl of acrid-smelling smoke wafting toward the ceiling.

She had to go now. She had to run.

Harlow reacted to the thought, darting toward the front door. She reached it, fumbled with the dead-bolt lock, then grabbed the handle and yanked it open. With a small, involuntary cry, she stumbled out into the dark, starless night. And began to run. Blindly. Sobbing. Across scorched earth, through a thicket. She pitched headlong into a ditch, then clawed her way out and back to her feet.

And onto a deserted road. Hope exploded inside her. *Someone, there had to be someone…*

As the words made their way through her head, a car crested the hill ahead, its headlights slicing through the darkness, pinning her. She stood frozen, trembling, too weak and exhausted to even wave. The lights grew closer; the driver blew his horn.

"Help me," she whispered, dropping to her knees. "Please, help me."

The vehicle screeched to a stop. A door opened. Footsteps sounded on the pavement.

"Don't, Frank," a woman begged. "What if—"

"For God's sake, Donna, I can't just... Oh my God, it's a kid."

"A kid?" The woman emerged from the car. Harlow lifted her head and the woman caught her breath. "Dear Lord, look at her red hair. It's her, the one they're searching for. Little Harlow Grail."

The man made a sound of disbelief, then apprehension. He glanced around them as if suddenly realizing he could be in danger.

"I don't like this," the woman said, obviously frightened. "Let's get out of here."

The man agreed. He scooped Harlow up, his grasp strong but gentle. "It's all right, it's going to be all right," he murmured, starting for his vehicle. "You're going home. You're safe now."

Harlow shuddered and slumped against him, though even as she did, she knew she would never feel safe again.

1

Wednesday, January 10, 2001
New Orleans, Louisiana

"Timmy! No!"

Anna sat bolt upright in bed, drenched in a cold sweat, Timmy's name, her screams, reverberating off the walls of her bedroom.

With a squeak of terror, she dragged the blankets to her chin. She looked wildly around her. When she'd drifted off, her bedside light had been on—she always slept with a light on. Yet her bedroom was dark. The shadows in the corners mocked her, deep and black. What did those shadows hold for her? What could they hide? Who?

Kurt. He was coming for her. To finish what he'd begun twenty-three years ago. To punish her for escaping. For spoiling his plans.

"Ready or not, here I come."

With a cry, Anna scrambled out of bed. She ran from the bedroom to the bathroom, located down the hallway. She raced to the commode, flipped up the seat, bent and threw up. She heaved until she was empty, until she had nothing left to expel but memories.

She yanked off a length of toilet tissue, wiped her mouth, then dropped the tissue into the commode and flushed. Her right hand hurt. It burned, as if Kurt had just done it. Severed her pinkie finger to send to her parents as a warning.

But he hadn't just done it, she reminded herself. It had happened a lifetime ago. She'd been a child, still Harlow Anastasia Grail, little Hollywood princess.

A lifetime ago. A whole other identity ago.

Turning, Anna crossed to the sink and turned on the faucet. Bending, she splashed the icy-cold water on her face, struggling to shake off the nightmare.

She was safe. In her own apartment. Except for her parents, she'd cut all ties to her past. None of her friends or business associates knew who she was. Not even her publisher or literary agent. She was Anna North now. She had been Anna North for twelve years.

Even if Kurt came looking for her, he wouldn't be able to find her.

Anna muttered an oath and flipped off the water. She snatched the hand towel from the ring and dried her face. Kurt wasn't going to come looking for her. Twenty-three years had passed, for heaven's sake. The FBI had been certain the man she'd known as Kurt posed no further threat to her. They believed he had slipped over the border into Mexico. The discovery of Monica's body in the border town of Baja, California, six days after Harlow's escape had supported that belief.

Disgusted with herself, she tossed the hand towel onto the counter. When was she going to get over this? How many years had to pass before she could sleep without a light on? Before nightmares no longer awakened her, night after night?

If only Kurt had been apprehended. She would be able to forget then. She would be able to go on without worrying, without wondering if he thought of her. Her escape had upset the ransom pickup. Did he curse her for spoiling that? Did he wait for the day he would make her pay for spoiling his opportunity at wealth?

She looked at herself in the mirror, expression fierce. She couldn't control her nightmares, but she could control everything else in her life. She would not spend her days—or nights—dodging shadows.

Anna stalked back to her bedroom, grabbed a pair of shorts from her bureau drawer and slipped them on under her nightshirt. If she couldn't sleep, she might as well work. A new story idea had been kicking around the back of her brain and now seemed as good a time as any to start it. But first, she decided, coffee.

She made her way to the kitchen, passing her office—a desk tucked into a corner of the living room—as she did. She flipped on the computer then moved on, past the front door. Out of habit she stopped to check the dead bolt.

As her fingers closed over the lock, someone pounded on the door. With a small cry, Anna jumped back.

"Anna! It's Bill—"

"And Dalton."

"Are you all right?"

Bill Friends and Dalton Ramsey, her neighbors and best friends. Thank goodness.

Hands shaking, she unlocked the door and eased it open. The pair stood in the hallway, expressions anxious. From down the hall she heard the yipping of Judy and Boo, the couple's Heinz 57 mini-mutts. "What in the world…you scared the life out of me."

"We heard you screa—"

"I heard you scream," Bill corrected. "I was on my way back in from—"

"He came and got me." Dalton held up a marble bookend, a miniature of Michelangelo's *David.* "I brought this. Just in case."

Anna brought a hand to her chest, a smile tugging at the corners of her mouth. She could picture fifty-something, mild-mannered Dalton winging a chunk of marble at an intruder. "Just in case of what? That my library needed tidying?"

Bill chuckled; Dalton looked irritated. He sniffed. "For protection, of course."

Against the intruder who would have made his escape by the time her friends had gathered their wits about them, selected a weapon and made their way to her door. Thank goodness she had never actually needed saving.

She bit back a laugh. "And I appreciate your concern." She swung the door wider. "Come on in, I'll make coffee to go with the beignets."

"Beignets?" Dalton repeated innocently. "I don't know what you're talking about."

Anna wagged a finger at him. "Nice try, but I smell them. Your punishment for coming to my aid is having to share."

New Orleans's version of a doughnut, beignets

were fried squares of dough, liberally dusted with powdered sugar. Like everything New Orleans, they were both decadent and addictive.

And definitely not for those, like Dalton, who professed to be watching their weight.

"He made me do it," Dalton said as they stepped into the apartment. He looked accusingly at Bill. "You know *I'd* never suggest such indulgences at two in the morning."

"Right." Bill rolled his eyes. "And whose figure suggests a tendency toward…indulgences?"

The other man looked at Anna for support. Bill was ten years Dalton's junior, trim and athletic. "It's not fair. He eats everything and never gains weight. Me, I eat one little thing and—"

"One little thing? Hah! Ask him about the Fig Newtons and barbeque chips?"

"I was having a bad day. I needed a little pick-me-up. So sue me."

Anna linked her arms through her friends' and nudged them toward the kitchen, the adverse effects of her nightmare melting away. The two men never failed to make her laugh. Nor did it ever cease to amaze her that they were a couple. They reminded her of a peacock and a penguin. Bill was outspoken and often outrageous, Dalton a prim businessman whose meticulous manner tended toward fussiness. Yet as different as they were, they had been together for ten years.

"I don't care who's guilty of the idea," she said as they reached the kitchen. "I'm just grateful for it. A 2:00 a.m. beignet-binge is just what I needed."

Truth was, it was their friendship she was grateful for. She'd met the pair her second week in New Orleans. She had answered an ad for a job at a French Quarter florist shop. Although she hadn't had any experience, she'd always had a flair for arranging and had been in need of a job that would allow her the time—and energy—to pursue her dream of being a novelist.

Dalton had turned out to be the owner of the shop; they had hit it off immediately. He had understood her dreams and applauded her for having the guts to pursue them. And unlike the other potential employers she had interviewed with, he had been comfortable with her need to think of her position at The Perfect Rose as a job, not a career.

Dalton had introduced her to Bill and the two men had taken her under their wing. They'd alerted her to an upcoming vacancy in the French Quarter apartment building they not only lived in, but that Dalton owned, and had given her recommendations for everything from dry cleaners to restaurants and hairstylists. As Anna had come to know them better, she had allowed them to take a real interest in her writing: it had been Bill and Dalton who had cheered her up after every rejection and Bill and Dalton who had cheered her on with each success.

She loved them both and would face the devil himself to keep them safe. They, she believed, would do the same for her.

The devil himself. Kurt.

As if reading her mind, Dalton turned to her,

aghast. "Good Lord, Anna. We never even asked, are you all right?"

"I'm fine." Anna poured milk into a saucepan and set it on the stove to heat. She retrieved three mugs from a cabinet and a tray of frozen coffee cubes from the freezer. "It was just a bad dream."

Bill helped her out, dropping a cube of the frozen cold-brewed coffee concentrate into each mug. "Not another one?" He gave her a quick hug. "Poor Anna."

"It's those sick stories you write," Dalton offered, artfully arranging the beignets on a plate. "They're giving you nightmares."

"Sick stories? Thanks, Dalton."

"Dark, then," Dalton amended. "Twisted. Scary. Better?"

"Much, thank you." She poured the steaming milk into the mugs, then handed each man his café au lait.

They carried the pastries and coffee to her small, bistro-style table, sat and dug in. Dalton was right. Her novels—thrillers—had been described by reviewers with just such adjectives. Also by ones like compelling and gripping. If only she could sell enough copies to make a living writing them.

Nobody was holding her back but herself. That's what her agent said.

"Such a nice, normal-seeming lady." Bill lowered his voice to a horror-flick drawl. "Where *do* her stories come from? Experience? Extracurricular activities? What gothic horrors lurk behind her guileless green eyes?"

Anna pretended to laugh. Bill couldn't know how

close to the truth his playful teasing had come. She had been witness to the darkest depths of the human spirit. She knew from firsthand experience the human animal's capacity for evil.

That knowledge stole her peace of mind and sometimes, like tonight, her sleep as well. It also fueled her imagination, pouring out of her in dark, twisted tales that pitted good against evil.

"Didn't you know?" she asked, keeping her tone light. "All my research is hands-on. So please, don't look in the trunk of my car, and be sure to lock your door at night." She lowered her voice. "If you know what's good for you."

For a split second, the men simply stared at her. Then they laughed. Dalton spoke first. "Very funny, Anna. Especially since that gay couple gets whacked in your new story idea."

"Speaking of," Bill murmured, brushing at the sprinkling of powdered sugar on the table in front of him, "have you heard anything on the new proposal yet?"

"Not yet, but it's only been a couple weeks. You know how slow publishing can be."

Bill snorted in disgust. He worked in advertising and public relations, most of the time he was going ninety-to-nothing, hair on fire. "They wouldn't last two minutes in my business. Crash and burn, big time."

Anna agreed, then yawned. She brought a hand to her mouth, yawning again.

Dalton glanced at his watch. "Good Lord, look at the time! I had no idea it was so—" He turned toward her, expression horrified. "Heavens, Anna! I forgot to tell you. You got another letter from your little fan. The one who lives across Lake Pontchartrain, in Mandeville. It came today to The Perfect Rose."

For a split second Anna didn't know who Dalton was referring to, then she remembered. A few weeks ago she'd received a fan letter from an eleven-year-old local girl named Minnie. It had come through Anna's agent, in a packet with several others.

Though Anna had been disturbed by the thought that her adult novels had been read by a child, she had been charmed by the letter. Anna had been reminded of the girl she had been before the kidnapping, one who had seen the world as a beautiful place filled with smiling faces.

Minnie had promised that if Anna wrote her back she would be her biggest fan forever. She had drawn hearts and daisies over the back of the envelope and printed the letters S.W.A.K.

Sealed with a kiss.

Anna had been so captivated, she had answered the letter personally.

Dalton dug the envelope out of the pocket of his sweat-suit jacket and held it out. Anna frowned. "You brought it with you?"

Bill rolled his eyes. "He grabbed it right after he selected *David* from his weapon collection. It was all I could do to stop him from baking muffins."

Dalton sniffed, expression hurt. "I was trying to help. Next time I won't."

"Don't you pay any attention to Bill," Anna murmured, taking the letter and sending Bill a warning glance. "You know what a tease he is. I appreciate you thinking of me."

Bill motioned to the envelope. Like the previous one, the girl had decorated it with hearts, daisies and a big S.W.A.K. "It came directly to The Perfect Rose, Anna. Not through your agent."

"Directly to The Perfect—" Anna realized her mistake and for a heartbeat of time, couldn't breathe. In her zeal to answer the child, she had forgotten caution. She had grabbed a piece of The Perfect Rose's stationery, dashed off a response and dropped it in the mail.

How could she have been so stupid? So careless?

"Open it," Bill urged. "You know you're curious."

She was curious. She loved to hear that a reader enjoyed one of her stories. It was satisfying in a way nothing else in her life was. But a part of her was repelled, too, by this physical connection to strangers, by the knowledge that through her work strangers had an opening into her head and heart.

Her work provided them a way into her life.

She eased the envelope open, slid out the letter and began to read. Bill and Dalton read with her, each peering over a shoulder.

Dear Miss North,

I was so excited when I received your letter! You're my very favorite author in the whole world—honest! My Kitty thinks you're the best, too. She's gold and white with blue eyes. She's my best friend.

Our favorite foods are pizza and Chee-tos, but

he doesn't let us have them very often. Once, I sneaked a bag and me and Tabitha ate the whole thing. My favorite group is the Backstreet Boys and when he lets me out, I watch *Dawson's Creek.*

I'm so glad you're going to be my friend. It gets lonely here sometimes. I felt bad though, about what you said about me being too young to read your books. I suppose you're right. And if you don't want me to read them, I won't. I promise. He doesn't know I read them anyway and would be very angry if he found out.

He frightens me sometimes.

Your friend and pen pal,
Minnie

Anna reread the last lines three times, a chill moving over her. *He* frightened her. *He* didn't allow her to eat pizza or Chee-tos often.

"Who do you think 'He' is?" Dalton asked. "Her dad?"

"I don't know," Anna murmured, frowning. "He could be her grandfather or an uncle. It's obvious she lives with him."

"It's kind of creepy, if you ask me." Bill made a face. "And what does she mean by 'when he lets her out, she watches *Dawson's Creek*?' It makes her sound like a prisoner, or something."

The three looked at each other. One moment became several; Anna cleared her throat, forcing a laugh. "Come on, guys, I'm the fiction writer here. You two are supposed to be my reality check."

"That's right." Dalton smiled wanly. "What kid ever thinks they get *enough* junk food? In fact, at thirteen, I thought my parents were a couple of ogres. I felt *so* abused."

"Dalton's right," Bill agreed. "Besides, if this guy was as bad as we're making him out to be, he wouldn't allow Minnie to correspond with you."

"Right." Anna made a sound of relief, folded the letter and slid it back into the envelope. "It's 2:00 a.m. and we're overreacting. I think we all need to get some sleep."

"I agree." Bill stood. "But still, Anna, I wish you hadn't answered her on Perfect Rose stationery. Given the types of books you write, who knows what kind of wackos might try to track you down?"

"It's okay," she murmured, rubbing at the goose bumps that crawled up her arms. "What harm could it be for an eleven-year-old girl to know where I work?"

2

"**W**hat are you saying, Anna?" Jaye Arcenaux asked, slurping the last of her Mochasippi up through her straw. "That you think this kid's some sort of stalker or something? That would be so cool."

Jaye, Anna's "little sister," had turned fifteen a couple of weeks ago and now everything was either so "cool," or "totally out there."

Anna arched an eyebrow, amused. "Cool? I hardly think so."

"You know what I mean." She leaned closer. "So, is that what you think?"

"Of course not. All I'm saying is, there was something strange about her letter and I'm not sure I should answer it."

"What do you mean, strange?" Jaye reached across the table to snitch a piece of Anna's chocolate-chip cookie. "Dalton said all three of you got the creeps."

"He's exaggerating. It was late and we were all tired. But it did seem like there was something weird about her home life. I'm a little concerned."

"Now you're talking my area of expertise. I've

seen pretty much every kind of weird home life there is.''

That was true, a fact that broke Anna's heart. She didn't let her feelings show, however. Jaye didn't want her pity, or anyone else's for that matter. Jaye accepted her past for what it was; she expected no less from those around her.

''Actually, I was hoping to get your opinion.'' Anna reached into her purse and drew out the letter, handing it to Jaye. ''I could be reading more into it than is there. After all, concocting trouble is my stock-in-trade.''

While Jaye read the letter, Anna studied the girl. Jaye was strikingly attractive for one so young, with finely sculpted features and large, dark eyes. Until a week ago, when she had shocked Anna by showing up sporting her just-dyed, flame-red hair, she had been a brunette, her tresses a warm mocha color.

Jaye's physical beauty was only marred by the brutal scar that ran diagonally across her mouth. A final gift from her abusive father—in a drunken rage he had thrown a beer bottle at her. It had caught her in the mouth, splitting her lips wide open. The bastard hadn't even gotten her medical attention. By the time the school nurse had taken a look at her mouth the following Monday morning, it had been too late for stitches.

But not too late to call Social Services. Jaye had been on her way to a better life, her father to jail.

A lump formed in Anna's throat and she shifted her gaze. She had become involved with Big Brothers, Big Sisters of America after researching the organization for an element in her second novel. She had interviewed several of the older girls in the program and had been profoundly moved by their stories, ones of need, salvation and affection.

Those girls had reminded her of herself at the same age. She, too, had been troubled and lonely, she, too, had been in desperate need of an anchor in a time of emotional turbulence.

Anna had decided to become a Big Sister herself, figuring she didn't have anything to lose by giving the program a try.

She and Jaye had been "sisters" for two years.

In the course of those two years, they had become close. It hadn't happened easily. At first Jaye, cynical for her age, angry and distrustful from a lifetime of being hurt and lied to, hadn't wanted anything to do with Anna. And she had made her feelings clear.

But Anna had persevered. For two years she had followed through on every promise; she had listened instead of lectured, counseled only when asked and had stuck to her own beliefs, standing up to the girl's every test.

Finally, Jaye had begun to trust. Affection had followed.

That affection was a two-way street. Something Anna hadn't expected going into the program. She had wanted to do something to help someone else, in return she had forged a relationship that filled a place in her life and heart that she hadn't even realized was empty.

Jaye looked up. "You're not imagining things. This guy's bad news."

Anna's stomach sank. "You're sure?"

"You wanted my opinion."

"When you say bad news, what do you mean...that he's—"

"Anything from a major A-hole to a pervert who should be behind bars for life."

A bitter edge crept into Jaye's voice, one that made Anna ache. "That's a pretty broad spectrum."

"I'm not a psychic." Jaye shrugged and handed the letter over. "I think you should write her back."

Anna pursed her lips, less certain than her young friend that she should continue the correspondence. "I'm an adult. She's a child. That makes communicating with her tricky. I don't want an accusation of impropriety to come back from her parents. And I can't very well just ask her about her father."

"You'll think of something to say." Jaye wiped her mouth with her napkin. "This kid needs a friend."

Anna frowned, torn. A part of her, the part that had always played it safe, urged her to toss the letter and forget all about Minnie and her problems. The other part agreed with Jaye. Minnie needed her. And she couldn't turn her back on a child in need.

"Are you going to eat the rest of your cookie?" Jaye asked, interrupting her thoughts.

"It's all yours." Anna slid the plate across the table. "You've been really hungry lately, isn't Fran a good cook?" she asked, referring to Jaye's foster mother.

"Good cook?" Jaye made a face. "She's like the worst cook on the planet. I swear, she must have studied at the Cordon-ralph."

Anna laughed, then sobered. "But she is nice, right?"

Jaye lifted a shoulder. "She's okay, I guess. When she's not riding her broomstick and sacrificing small children and stray dogs under the full moon."

"Very funny, wise apple."

Anna supposed she liked Jaye's new foster mother well enough, but something about her didn't add up. She always seemed to be trying too hard. As if her heart wasn't really into fostering so she had to pretend. Anna had been unsettled from the moment they'd met.

Still, she had been hoping Jaye would like Fran Clausen and her husband, Bob.

They left the CC's coffeehouse minutes later, making their way out onto the French Quarter sidewalk. "So, how is everything going?" Anna asked.

"School or home?"

"Either. Both."

"School's okay. So's home."

"Next time, don't bog me down with so many details. I'm overwhelmed."

The girl grinned. "Sarcasm, Anna? Cool."

Anna laughed and they continued to make their way along the busy sidewalk, pausing occasionally to ogle a store's display. Anna enjoyed the scents, sounds and sights that were the French Quarter: a blending of the mostly old and sometimes new, of the garish and elegant, the delectable and offensive. Populated by both tourists and locals, street performers and street people, the place had captivated Anna on sight.

"Look at that," Jaye murmured, stopping to peer in at a display of faux-fur jackets in a shop's window. She pointed to a zebra-print coat in a bomber style. "Is that cool or what?"

"It is," Anna agreed. "You want to try it on?"

She shook her head. "Only if they're giving it away. Besides, it wouldn't go with my hair."

Anna glanced at Jaye. "I'm finally getting used to you being a redhead. The best part is that we look like sisters now."

Jaye flushed, pleased. They continued on their way. After a couple of moments, Jaye glanced at Anna. "Did I tell you about that creep who was following me?"

Anna stopped and looked at her friend, alarmed. "Someone was following you?"

"Yeah. But I gave him the slip."

"When did this happen? Where?"

"The other day. I was on my way home from school."

"What did he look like? Was it just that once or has he followed you before?"

"I didn't get that good a look at him. From what I did see, he was just another old pervert." Jaye shrugged again. "It's no big deal."

"It's a very big deal. Did you tell your foster mom? Did she call—"

"Geez, Anna, get a grip. If I'd known you were going to flip out, I wouldn't have told you. "

Anna took a deep breath. If she overreacted, Jaye would clam up. And that was the last thing she wanted. Jaye was a street-savvy kid, not an innocent who would be easily tricked by a stranger. She had even lived on the street for a time, a fact that never failed to make Anna shudder.

"Sorry for getting so intense," she murmured. "Old people are such worrywarts."

"You're not old," Jaye countered.

"Old enough to insist that if you see this guy again you'll tell me and we'll go to the police. Agreed?"

Jaye hesitated, then nodded. "Agreed."

3

Detective Quentin Malone entered Shannon's Tavern, calling a greeting to a couple of his fellow officers. For many New Orleanians, Thursday night represented the official kickoff of the weekend festivities. Bars, restaurants and clubs all over the Crescent City benefited from the laissez les bon temps rouler attitude of the city's residents, and Shannon's Tavern was no different.

Located in the area of the city called the Irish Channel—named for the Irish immigrants who had settled there—Shannon's catered to a working-class, local crowd. And to cops. The Seventh District of the New Orleans Police Department had adopted Shannon's as their own.

Shannon McDougall, the tavern's proprietor and namesake, a former bricklayer with hands the size and shape of meat hooks, had no problem with that. Cops kept the rougher crowd away. They kept the drugs, brawls and hookers out of his place and out on the street. As a way of thanking the boys in blue, he refused to allow any of the more seasoned officers to pay for anything. The rookies, however, were a different story. Just as in the force, the new kids on the block had to earn their stripes. Even so, tips were welcome from anyone and many a first of the month, green could be seen passing from a grateful detective or lieutenant's hand to McDougall's apron pocket.

Quentin definitely fell into the seasoned category. At thirty-seven he was a sixteen-year veteran of the force and a detective first grade. He was also a part of a NOPD family dynasty: his grandfather, father, three uncles and one aunt had been cops; of his six siblings only two had opted out of police work, Patrick who had become a number cruncher, and Shauna, the baby of the brood, who was studying art in college.

Quentin strolled toward the bar for a beer. He was waylaid by the barmaid, a perky twenty-three-year-old with super-short, spiky blond hair. She had made it plain she would love to go out with him, but Quentin had no desire to date a girl the same age as his kid sister. Something about that just felt a little weird.

"Hey, Malone." She smiled up at him. "Haven't seen you in a while."

"I've been around." He bent and kissed her cheek. "You doing okay, Suki?"

"Can't complain. Tips have been good." She glanced toward a group making their way to one of the tables. "Gotta go. Talk later?"

"Sure."

She started off then looked back over her shoulder at him. "John Jr. was in. He asked me to tell you to call your mother."

Quentin laughed. John Jr. was the oldest of the Malone brood and had appointed himself caretaker of the family. If any of the siblings had a problem, they went to John Jr. If any one of them had an issue with another member of the family, they went to John Jr. And conversely, if John Jr. perceived there to be problem in the family, he took matters into his own hands. Obviously, Quentin had missed one too many of his mother's Sunday dinners.

"Message received, Suki. Thanks."

Quentin crossed to the bar. Shannon had already drawn the draft; he slid it across the counter. "On the house."

"Thanks, Shannon. You seen Terry tonight?" he asked, referring to his partner Terry Landry.

"He's here." The older man jerked his thumb toward the back room of the bar. "Last I saw, he was breaking a new rack. Seemed a little off tonight, you know what I mean?"

Quentin nodded. He did indeed know what Shannon meant. His partner was going through a tough time. His wife of twelve years had recently kicked him out, claiming him impossible to live with.

Quentin didn't doubt that was true. Because of the job, no cop was easy to live with. Terry, with his hard-partying ways and hair-trigger temper would be more difficult than most.

But even with his faults, Terry was a good father and a devoted husband. He loved his family and as far as Quentin was concerned, that counted for a lot.

Terry had taken the breakup hard. He was angry and hurt; he missed his two kids. He was drinking too much and sleeping too little, his behavior had become erratic. Partnering with him had become a tightrope walk.

But the way Quentin figured it, Terry had been there for him lots of times, now it was his turn. Partners stuck together.

Quentin motioned in the direction of the back room. "Think I might go lend a little aid and expertise. Wouldn't want Terry to lose his rent."

Shannon chuckled, shook his head and moved down the bar to serve another customer.

Quentin made his way through the still sparsely filled room. An hour from now it'd be standing room only, music blaring from the jukebox, a fine haze of cigarette smoke hanging above the crowd, a dozen or more couples gyrating on the makeshift dance floor. But for now, bar to back room was a clear shot.

Until Louanne Price stepped directly in his path, stopping his forward progress. The woman had the face of an angel and the body of one of Hugh Hefner's bunnies, and many a man had fallen adoringly at her feet. Problem was, any man in the vicinity of Louanne's feet would likely be kicked square in the gut. Or even lower.

That was the kind of woman Louanne was. And life was too short for a kick in the balls. Even if preceded by a trip to paradise.

She moved nearer Quentin, not stopping until her body brushed his. She stood on tiptoe, laid her hands on his shoulders and leaned into him. "Malone, sweetie, what am I going to have to do to get you to share some of that fine Irish sugar with me?"

He flashed her a quick smile. "Aw, Louanne," he drawled. "You know Dickey'd kick my butt if I so much as wagged my tail in your direction." Dickey was her father and an NOPD sergeant. "I'll just have to lust after you from afar."

"That would be a crime, I think. And you're a cop, sworn to uphold the law." She threaded her fingers through his hair. "He wouldn't have to know. It could be our little secret."

Quentin set her away from him, feigning regret. It wasn't that he didn't enjoy aggressive women, he had certainly been friendly with a number of them. It was Louanne's sly edge, her easy dishonesty that turned him off.

"Sorry, babe. You know there aren't any secrets in the NOPD. At least ones that everybody doesn't know. Catch you later."

Quentin walked away without a backward glance. He found Terry just where Shannon had promised, a pool cue in his hand and a cigarette dangling from his lips. He looked up at Quentin, eyes glazed from drink.

Terry had been here awhile already.

"'Bout time you got your ass down here. Night's half over already."

"Only if you've already drunk so much you're going to be out cold an hour from now." Quentin sauntered into the room. He pulled a chair from one of the tables, swung it around and straddled it. "Covered for you with the captain."

Terry lined up his shot, drew back on the cue then followed through. The ball sailed into the pocket. "Where was I? The john?"

"You went to see Penny. To talk."

"That bitch? No thank you."

Quentin cringed. He'd known Penny Landry for ten years and she was many things, bitch not among them. Terry hurt, he was angry and bitter, but still Quentin couldn't let it pass. Some things just weren't right.

He took a swallow of his beer, working to keep his demeanor casual. "Seems to me she's doing what she feels she has to. For herself and the kids."

Terry missed his shot and swore. His opponent, a man Quentin had seen run a table many a time, smiled and stepped up to shoot.

Terry downed the last of his beer, then glared at Quentin. "Whose side you on, partner?"

"I didn't know I had to take sides."

"Damn right you do."

"Penny's a friend." Quentin met the other man's gaze evenly. "I don't know if I can do that."

Terry flushed. "This is just f'cking wonderful. Outstanding. My best friend's telling me he—"

"Eight in the corner."

They turned and watched as the other player nailed the shot.

"Rerack?" he asked.

"Screw it. The table's yours." Terry looked at Quentin. "I need a drink."

The last thing his partner needed was another drink. But stating the obvious would serve no purpose but anger the other man. They left the pool room and headed out front.

In the twenty or so minutes he'd been in back, the crowd in the bar had doubled. Quentin saw a number of their fellow officers, his brothers Percy and Spencer among them. They caught sight of him and started over.

"What do you say we get out of here and go grab some grub? I'll ask Percy and Spencer along."

"Hell no." Terry's words slurred. "The night's young. Ripe with possibil... Hey now, who do we have here?"

Quentin shifted his gaze in the direction Terry indicated. A woman in a spandex minidress was shaking it on the floor. She wore her bottle-enhanced red hair long, in a mass of tousled waves. As she danced, she moved her fingers through it, her gold bangle bracelets jangling as she did. It wasn't clear if she was dancing with one man, several or just putting on a show for them all.

And a show it was; a number of bar patrons had already gathered around to watch. Quentin and Terry joined them.

After a moment, Quentin glanced at his partner. "I don't know, Terry, she looks—"

"She looks good. Damn good."

What Quentin had been about to say was, this woman didn't look the type to be messed with. She didn't look like the type who would go around with cops, except on the sly. Not exactly a rich bitch, but a climber. One of those women who valued prestige, position and Armani suits.

She would choose to hang out with the guys who could give her those. A cop could not. Tonight, obviously, she'd gone slumming.

His brothers made it across the bar. Percy spoke first. "What's happening, big bro? Hey, Terry."

Quentin glanced at his brothers. The family resemblance between the two brothers was marked: both possessed the trademark Malone blue eyes and dark, curly hair. Percy, however, had yet to grow into his lanky six foot three frame and Spencer, the street-brawler, had the profile of a prize fighter who had taken one too many pops to the nose. "Currently I'm trying to stop my partner from making an ass of himself."

The younger Malones followed Quentin's gaze. Percy grinned. "She's hot, no doubt about it. You feel like being burned, Terror?" he asked, using the nickname Terry had earned his first year on the force. "Spencer here went down in flames ten minutes ago."

"No comment," Spencer muttered, sending his brother an irritated glance.

Terry smoothed back his hair. "Watch a professional at work, fellas."

The three Malone brothers hooted. "I don't know," Quentin called after him, "you've been out of circulation awhile."

Terry glanced back at the other men, his grin cocky. "Once a lady-killer, always a lady-killer."

Even three sheets to the wind, Terry was indeed, a lady-killer. Tall and lanky, with the dark hair, eyes and patois-on-demand of his Cajun ancestors, Terry cut a damn dashing figure. Quentin gave him a better than fifty-fifty chance.

His friend sauntered over to the woman and began

swaying with her to the music, moving in close. She turned her back to him, not missing a beat of the music.

Terry glanced over. Quentin grinned and mimicked a plane going down with his right hand. Percy and Spencer chuckled.

Terry didn't give up. He tried again. Again she made it clear she wasn't interested, this time more pointedly.

The third time, she didn't waste time on subtlety. She stopped dancing, looked him squarely in the eyes and told him to get lost. As she spun away, she shook her spandex-encased hips, as if taunting Terry with what he couldn't have.

Far from deterred, Terry swaggered back to his friends. "She wants me. No doubt about it."

The three men howled. Spencer leaned toward Terry. "First round—woman one, The Terror zip."

Quentin shook his head. "Give it up, partner. The lady's not interested."

Terry laughed. "She's playing hard to get. You just watch, she'll come around."

"Yeah, she'll come around, all right. To slapping your face." Percy looked at Quentin. "Why don't you give her a try, bro. Turn that legendary smile of yours on her."

"No thanks." Quentin took a swallow of his beer. "I like my ego intact, thank you."

"Yeah, right." Spencer looked at Terry. "You ever hear the story about cute little Miss Davis? She was Quentin's English teacher his senior year of high school."

"Oh, please," Quentin muttered. "Not this story again."

Terry sank onto a bar stool, signaling Shannon for another drink. "I don't believe I have. Fill me in."

"Well," Spencer continued, "seems big bro here didn't spend enough time in class cracking the books and had earned himself a big fat F."

"Things looked grim," Percy embellished. "Not graduating with his class. Summer school. Dad kicking his ass. The whole bit."

Terry yawned. "Is this story actually going somewhere?"

The two younger brothers grinned. "Rumor has it," Spencer said, "that after a couple of private meetings with pretty Miss Davis, that F jumped to a C. Just like magic."

"Some magic. He used that devil smile on her, the one that—"

"Devil smile? Give me a break." Quentin rolled his eyes.

Ignoring Quentin, Spencer picked up where Percy had left off. "Even though he won't talk, he used more than the smile, my men. Trust me."

"That true, partner?" Terry lifted his eyebrows. "You sweet-talk yourself into a diploma?"

Quentin scowled at the three, annoyed at his brothers for bringing up that story and with himself for being such a screwup. It was damn embarrassing to be a grown man best known for his high school conquests with the opposite sex. "Grow up, boys. Get a life."

The men hooted in amusement; the night progressed. And as it did, Terry's determination to score with the redhead grew. As did her determination that he not.

To Quentin it seemed as if the woman was making a game out of teasing Terry. Out of taunting him. She danced with every guy who asked her, sometimes two at a time—everyone but his partner. It was as if she wanted to see how far she could push him.

Not much farther, Quentin realized as his friend's mood shifted from cocky to angry and belligerent.

Quentin saw trouble ahead.

It came sooner than later.

"Excuse me?" the redhead said loudly, swinging to face Terry. "Do you have a problem?"

"Yeah, baby," he slurred, "I have a problem. The guy you're dancing with is a stiff. Come on over here and get a taste of a real man."

Quentin tensed as the other man flushed and curled his hands into fists. The woman laid a hand on her dance partner's arm and raked her gaze scathingly over Terry. "In your dreams, loser. Got that? Not now, not ever. Get lost."

Terry's mouth curled into a sneer and Quentin muttered an oath. He nudged his brother Spencer, who was in a conversation with Shannon. "We may have trouble. Get Percy." He started for the dance floor.

"You heard the lady," the woman's dance partner said, stepping forward. "She's not interested. Beat it."

Terry ignored the man, his full attention—and fury—focused on the woman. "What did you call me?'' he asked, loud enough to be heard across the bar. A ripple moved through the crowd.

"You heard me, cop." She held up her right hand, shaping thumb and forefinger into an L. "Loser. With a capital L."

Terry went berserk, lunging for the woman's dance partner. Quentin saw it coming and sprang forward, throwing himself between the two men.

Blinded by rage, Terry threw a punch; it clipped Quentin's shoulder. Percy and Spencer grabbed Terry. He fought them, cursing them for holding him back, taking a swing at Percy when he half freed himself.

In the end, it took all three Malones to drag Terry out to the alley behind the bar.

The frigid night air seemed to shock some sense into him and the fight drained out of him. He slumped against the alley wall. Quentin motioned his brothers back inside.

Alone, Quentin faced his partner. "Get ahold of yourself, Terry. This is Shannon's place, for God's sake. You're a cop. What were you thinking?"

"I wasn't." Terry dragged a hand across his face. "It was that chick. She really got under my skin."

"That's no excuse, man. Forget her. She's not worth it."

Terry's eyes became glassy and he quickly averted them. "In there, when she... I kept thinking about Penny. About her kicking me out. She called me...she called me a lose—"

He choked the word back, then muttered an oath.

"It's tough, Terry. I know." He laid a hand on his

partner's shoulder. "What do you say we get out of here? Who needs it?"

"So I can do what?" he asked. "Go home? I don't have a home anymore. Remember? Penny took my home away from me. She took my kids."

"Penny's not the enemy, Terry. And you're not going to get her back by treating her like she is. You do want her back, right?"

His partner looked at him. "What do you think? Of course I want her back. I love her."

"Then show her. Try a little romance. Candy and flowers. Take her to dinner. Or some sappy chick flick. Pretend you like it. For her."

"That's right," Terry muttered, lips screwing into a sneer, "the mighty Malone knows everything about women. And now, it seems he knows everything about my woman."

Quentin ignored the sarcasm, chalking it up to Terry's marital problems and his having had too much to drink. "Hardly. We're not talking rocket science here. Raging like a bull and calling names doesn't soften a woman's heart. Remember the song? Try a little tenderness."

Terry's face twisted with bitterness. "What's going on here, *partner?* All those times my wife asked you over for dinner, what was that all about?" He leaned toward Quentin, eyes alight with fury. "While I was choking down her leftover meat loaf, what were you enjoying?"

Quentin hung on to his temper. "You're going to regret that comment in the morning," he said softly, tone deadly. "And because you're going through a hard time, I'll let it pass. This once. Do it again and I won't be so forgiving. You got that?''

Terry crumpled. "I'm a screwup, man. A total screwup. A loser, like that chick said. Like my old lady always told me I would be. A worthless nothing."

"That's bullshit and you know it. You're drunk and feeling sorry for yourself. Just don't turn it on me, partner. I'm on your side."

He pulled himself together. "I'm going back in there. I don't want that cocktease or anybody else to think she's won."

The rest of the evening passed in a blur. The crowd grew bigger and rowdier, the redhead apparently grew bored and decided to take her goodies elsewhere and everyone seemed to forget the altercation between her and Terry. At the height of the night's revelry Quentin lost sight of Terry, not hooking up with him again until they closed the place at 2:00 a.m.

"Shannon," Terry said, clapping the bartender on the back, "I'm sorry, man. I shouldn't have—" He weaved on his feet; Quentin grabbed his arm to steady him. "—shouldn't have started nothin' in your place."

"It's okay, Ter." The big man waved off his apologies. "You're going through a lot of crap right now. You just needed to let off a little steam."

"No 'scuse, man. None." He shrugged free of Quentin's grasp, swaying dangerously. He dipped his hand into a trouser pocket and pulled out a bill. He pressed it into Shannon's hand. "No 'scuse. Take it, it's my 'pology."

Quentin glanced at the bill in Shannon's hand, then

looked at Terry in shock. *A fifty? Where the hell had Terry gotten that?*

Shannon must have been wondering the same thing because his eyebrows shot up in question a moment before he stuffed the bill into his apron pocket.

Quentin turned to his brothers who had hung around to help him get Terry home. "What do you say we get soon-to-be Sleeping Beauty out of here?"

Terry could hardly walk. With his brothers' help, Quentin got him outside and poured into his Bronco. He handed Percy Terry's keys. "See you there."

"Yeah. Quent?"

He met his youngest brother's vivid blue eyes. "That was a fifty Terry gave Shannon."

Quentin frowned. "I saw."

"That's a lot of money to be throwing around."

"No joke." Especially for a cop who was supporting a family—at two separate residences. Unless that cop was on the take.

Terry was not. Quentin would stake his life on it.

"Forget about it, Percy." Quentin saw the question in his brother's eyes and turned away. "I'm beat, let's get this over with."

The insistent scream of the phone dragged Quentin from a deep sleep. Muttering an oath, he answered it. "Malone here."

"Rise and shine, sweetheart," the desk officer drawled. "Time to go to work."

Quentin muttered another oath. A call from the precinct this time of night meant only one thing. "Where?" he managed to say, voice thick with sleep.

"In the alley behind Shannon's Tavern."

The response jump started his brain. He sat up. "Did you say Shannon's Tavern?"

"That I did. Female. Caucasian. Dead."

Shit. "You don't have to sound so damn cheerful about it. What are you, some sort of ghoul?"

"What can I say? I love my work."

He glanced at his watch, calculating how long it would take him to get to the scene. "You call Landry yet?"

"He's next."

"I'll take care of it."

"Good luck."

She had that right. Quentin hung up and dialed his partner.

4

The scene resembled dozens of others Quentin had worked over the years. The seasons changed, the location, the number dead and amount of blood. The aura of tragedy did not. The smell of death. The perverted destruction of life that screamed so loudly no amount of small talk or tasteless one-liners could block it out.

This one stood out only because its location struck so close to home. A homicide was definitely not the kind of publicity a bar owner needed. And it'd been a quiet night murder-wise in New Orleans; Quentin figured this stiff would be page-one news. Too bad for Shannon.

Quentin swung out of his Bronco. The pavement was wet. The air damp and cold. To-the-bone cold. Quentin glanced up at the black, starless sky and shrugged deeper into his jacket. A lot of the locals complained about August in New Orleans. As far as he was concerned, hellfire hot beat out cold and damp as the grave any day.

But then, he'd spent too much time around the dead.

He flashed his shield at the uniform guarding the perimeter, then ducked under the yellow tape.

"Damn cold night to die," the officer said, huddling deeper into his coat, obviously miserable.

Quentin didn't comment. He crossed to the first officer, a rookie who hung out with his brother Percy. "Hey, Mitch."

"Detective." He shifted from his right foot to his left. "Man, it's cold."

"As a witch's tit." Quentin roamed his gaze over the area. "I'm the first."

"Yup. Johnny on the spot."

"Touch anything?"

"Nope. Checked her pulse and ID. Called it in."

"Good. What've we got?"

"Female. Caucasian. According to her driver's license, name was Nancy Kent. Looks like he raped her first."

Quentin looked at the rookie. "Medical examiner's on his way?"

Mitch nodded.

"Who found her?"

"Garbage collector." Mitch jerked his thumb in the direction of the Dumpster. Two legs poked out from behind the far side of the Dumpster, which obscured the rest of the body. They were fish-belly white against the dark pavement. One foot was bare, the other encased in a strappy, high-heeled pump.

The hair on the back of Quentin's neck prickled.

"Got the driver's name and employee number,"

Mitch continued. "He had to finish his route. Said he knew the drill, found a body once before. About ten years ago."

"I'm going to take a look. My partner gets here, send him over."

Quentin approached slowly, scanning the ground before him, left to right. Finally, with a sense of inevitability, he brought his gaze to the victim. She lay faceup on the pavement, eyes open, legs spread. Her black mini dress had been shoved up over her hips, her black G-string panties ripped half off. Her long red hair spread in a tangle around and over her face, partially covering her mouth, open to a silent scream.

The woman from the bar. The one who had refused Terry's advances.

"Damn." He muttered the word on an expelled breath, a cloud forming behind it.

He turned at the sound of footsteps. Terry approached, his face as pale as the one at the pavement below. "Evidence team just pulled up." He rubbed his hands together. "Could this creep have picked a crappier night to—"

"We have to talk. Now."

Terry's gaze moved past Quentin's to the victim. A sound slipped past his lips; it reminded Quentin of one a small, trapped animal might make. He returned his gaze to Quentin's. "Oh, shit."

"You've got that right, partner," he said grimly. "And it's about to hit the fan."

5

Two hours later, Quentin tapped on his captain's open office door. Captain O'Shay, a trim, sharp-eyed brunette, glanced up. She didn't look happy to see them so early in the morning. Beside him Terry shifted nervously. This meeting could go one of two ways: bad or worse. Captain O'Shay didn't approve of her detectives participating in drunken brawls—or of them having altercations with women who turned up dead hours later.

"Got a minute?" Quentin asked, flashing her a quick smile. If he had hoped to disarm her he saw immediately that he'd been wasting his energy. Patti O'Shay had fought her way up through the ranks of mostly male, sometimes misogynist and often chauvinist officers, earning rank of captain through brilliant police work, single-minded determination and the ability to go toe-to-toe with some of the best bullshitters around. There wasn't a captain on the force tougher than Patti O'Shay.

"We've got a potential situation," Quentin said.

She frowned and waved them into her office. Her

gaze flicked to Terry, then back to Quentin. "You two look like hell."

Not quite the opening they were hoping for. "We were at Shannon's last night."

"Surprise, surprise." She folded her hands on the desk in front of her. "That's where that girl was found."

"Correct. In the alley behind the bar."

"Fill me in."

"Her name was Nancy Kent." Terry cleared his throat. "Twenty-six years old. Recently divorced. A party girl. Had come into some serious cash with her divorce settlement. Apparently, she was flashing it around last night."

Quentin took over. "M.E. places time of death somewhere between one-thirty and three."

Captain O'Shay seemed to digest that piece of information. "That means Kent was killed either while the bar was still open or within an hour of closing. By that time of night the crowd should have thinned considerably."

"Not last night, Captain," Terry said. "At one-thirty the party was still in full swing. Shannon had to force the diehards out at two. Threatened to call the cops."

She ignored his snicker—a third of those diehards had been cops—and turned to Quentin. "What about Shannon?" she asked.

"Questioned him," Quentin answered. "He was pretty shaken up. Didn't hear or see anything. Same for Suki and Paula, the two waitresses who closed with him."

"Any chance Shannon's our guy?"

"No way. Besides, he has an alibi. Until closing, he never got out from behind the bar. After closing, he was with Suki and Paula. They all walked out together."

Terry chimed in. "Usually Shannon takes the trash to the Dumpster while the girls clean the bar, but last night each of the girls grabbed a bag, then they all walked out together."

"What time was that?" she asked.

"Between 3:00 and 3:10 a.m."

"And none of them saw anything?"

She sounded incredulous and Quentin stepped in. "The alley's poorly lit. The three were exhausted and anxious to get home and Suki and Paula were sniping at each other over some split tips. The vic was obscured behind and in the shadow of the Dumpster."

Captain O'Shay hesitated, then nodded. "What about cause of death?"

"Pending a complete autopsy, M.E. called it suffocation."

The captain's eyebrows shot up. "Suffocation? In an alley?"

"Yeah, unusual. She was definitely raped first. Signs of bruising and tearing on and around the labia. Bruises on her inner thighs as well."

"The evidence team find anything?"

"A few hairs, some fiber. Scraped under her nails."

Terry shifted in his seat. He looked ill.

"What about her ex?" The captain looked directly at Terry.

"An old guy," Terry replied, voice shaky. "Broke

down, blubbering like a baby when we told him. Still loved her, he said. Hoped she'd come back to him.''

''Sounds like he had motive.''

''But no opportunity.'' Quentin shook his head. ''When Terry said older, he meant *old*. An oxygen tank, wheelchair, full-time nurse. The whole deal.''

''Old but very rich,'' Terry added. ''Old Metairie address. New Orleans country club. The whole bit. Bet it never occurred to her that she'd go first.''

Captain O'Shay glanced sharply at him. ''Any boy-friends?''

''None that her ex knew of,'' he answered quickly. ''We'll keep asking around.''

''So what's this about a potential situation?''

She looked directly at Terry once more. He shifted uncomfortably under her direct gaze. ''Like we said, we were there last night. At Shannon's. The vic was really carrying on, dancing in a real sexual way. Putting on a show, if you know what I mean?''

The captain's eyebrows shot up once more. ''No, I'm not sure I do.''

Quentin glanced at his partner. Going down the ''she asked for it'' avenue was not going to work with Patti O'Shay. In fact, it would do little but piss her off.

Terry realized his mistake and quickly changed tack. He cleared his throat. ''All I'm trying to say is that...I came on to her. More than once.''

''And she wasn't interested.''

''Yeah.'' He flushed slightly. ''I'd had a little too much to drink and...and—'' He fumbled around for something that would paint him in a more sympathetic light.

When he came up blank, the captain filled the break. "And you didn't take no for an answer."

"Like I said, I'd had a little too much to drink."

Captain O'Shay stood and came around the desk. She perched on its edge, looking down at her detective, forcing him to look up at her. "And you think that makes bad behavior acceptable?"

He squirmed under her withering gaze. "No, Captain."

"I'm glad we agree on that, Detective. What happened next?"

"I pushed too hard. Me and the vic exchanged words, the guy she was with and I almost came to blows."

The captain didn't look happy. "Almost?"

"Malone saved my ass."

She shifted her gaze to Quentin's. He nodded and she crossed to the window, looked out at the cold bright day. Without turning she said. "Write it up. All of it. Both of you."

"Yes, Captain."

She turned then. "I know you're having some trouble in your personal life, Detective Landry. Do you need a leave of absence until it's straightened out?"

He shot to his feet. "No way, Captain! I'd go crazy if I couldn't work."

She hesitated a moment, then inclined her head. "All right. But I don't want to see a repeat of last night's behavior. I will not allow you to drag this department through the muck with you. Is that understood?"

"Yes, Captain."

"Good. One more item. I'm giving the case to Johnson and Walden."

"Those disc jockey wanna-bes?"

"That's bullshit, Captain."

Detectives Johnson and Walden took never-ending ribbing about the similarity of their names to New Orleans homegrown, premier radio personalities Walton and Johnson. The deejays were creative, innovative and funny as hell. The two detectives, on the other hand, were not only distinctly unfunny, but a couple of dull bulbs.

"Landry" she continued as if they hadn't spoken, "you're off. Malone, you'll assist."

"Assist?" Quentin leaped to his feet. "Captain O'Shay, with all due respect—"

"Conflict of interest," she said crisply, cutting him off. "Hours before Nancy Kent was raped and murdered one of my detectives had a heated argument with her. A very public argument. That makes him a suspect. Automatically."

She looked from one man to the other. "How wise of me would it be to let that detective work the investigation? Or to let that detective's partner serve as lead man on the case? I think you'll agree, it wouldn't be wise at all."

"And once Terry is cleared of all suspicion?" Quentin asked.

"Then, hopefully, the case will be solved. If not, we'll talk."

But don't get your hopes up. "Is that all?"

"Landry, you're excused. Malone, I need to speak with you privately." When Terry had closed the door behind him, she met Quentin's eyes. "The way Landry said, that's the way it went down, right?"

"Absolutely."

"And after the incident with the woman, what happened?"

"We partied. I drove him home just after 2:00 a.m."

"He was unable to drive?"

"He was fall-down, stinking drunk."

"And you're one hundred percent certain your partner is innocent of this crime?"

"Yes, dammit!" Quentin looked away, then back. "No way did Terry do this. Besides, Terry could hardly walk let alone overpower and murder a woman."

She was quiet a moment, then she nodded. "I agree with your assessment, Malone, but I'll be watching him. I'm not going to let one of my detectives fall apart on the job."

"He's okay, Captain. He—"

"He's not okay," she corrected, tone curt. "And you know it. Don't let him take you down with him, Malone."

She returned to her desk, signaling that they were through. Quentin crossed to the door, stopping and looking back at her when he reached it. "Aunt Patti?" She looked up. "Tell Uncle Sammy I said hello."

"Tell him yourself." A smile touched her mouth, softening her face. "And call my sister. I hear from John Jr. that you've been neglecting her."

With a chuckle and a small salute, Malone agreed.

6

A headache held Dr. Benjamin Walker's cranium in a vise. He struggled beyond the pain to focus as the patient sitting across from him described his ambivalent feelings about the recent death of his mother. Ben had been working with this man three months; in that time he'd only begun to scratch the surface of the damage done by the man's horrific childhood.

"It's not right, Dr. Walker. She was my mother. And she's gone. Gone." The man wrung his hands. "Shouldn't I feel something at her passing?"

"What do you think you should be feeling, Rick?"

The man lifted his bloodshot gaze to Ben's. "Grief. Regret. Fury. I don't know, but something for God's sake!"

Ben jumped on the last. "Fury? That's a strong emotion, Rick. One of the strongest."

His patient stared blankly at him. "Fury? I didn't say that."

"You did."

"I couldn't. I loved my mother."

"Actually, it's quite understandable that you might be angry. Even furious."

"Really?" The man looked relieved. "Because she's gone?"

"Could be that. Maybe in part." Ben folded his hands in his lap, schooling his features to neutrality. "Could be other things as well."

"What things? What are you suggesting?"

"Think about it, Rick. You tell me what things."

Ben sat back, waiting, silent. Giving his patient time to consider the question, then to fill the quiet that screamed to be broken. Someday, he believed, Rick Richardson would fill that quiet. And the noise would be deafening. Frightening. Ben had glimpsed a simmering rage in this man, a rage directed at women. It had emerged in the recounting of a routine argument with his wife; his attitude toward his boss, who happened to be a woman; in word choice; body language; subtle shifts in facial expressions when talking about women.

Ben suspected the true source of Rick Richardson's pain and rage was his controlling and abusive mother. A fact his patient was as yet unwilling—and unable—to admit. Now that she had passed, with nothing resolved between them, those feelings of rage most probably would worsen. They could turn inward. Or outward.

Either way, Ben feared they were in for some rough sessions ahead.

"She was a good mother, Dr. Walker," Rick said suddenly, tone defensive. "A very good mother."

"Was she?"

Rick shot to his feet, fists clenched at his sides, vein popping in his forehead. "What the hell is that supposed to mean! You didn't know her! You don't know anything about our relationship or the kind of person she was!"

"I know what you've told me," Ben murmured. "And I'd really like to know more."

Rick stared at him a moment, then jerked his gaze away. "I don't want to talk about her right now."

Ben watched as his patient began to prowl the room. "Why not?" he asked.

Rick whirled to face Ben. "Because I don't. Isn't that good enough for you? Why do you have to pick at me like that? Pick, pick pick. Just like my wife. Just like my moth—fuck."

"Did your mother pick at you?"

He flushed. "I said, I don't want to talk about her."

"Fine. We have a few minutes left, you tell me what you do want to talk about."

Predictably, his patient chose the less emotionally charged subject of his job. While he talked, he continued to prowl about the room. Ben followed the man's movements; as he did he caught a glimpse of himself in the antique, three-by-five-foot gilt-framed mirror that hung directly across the room from him. The mirror had been an outrageous indulgence, a recent gift to himself to celebrate taking on his twenty-fifth patient.

Twenty-fifth patient. Eighteen months ago he had been with a thriving psychiatry group in Atlanta, a partnership offer on the table. He had chucked it all to follow his elderly mother to New Orleans.

Her move had been a shock. She had just picked up and gone, insisting afterward that it had been his idea. Ultimately, Ben had seen her behavior as a blessing—and a wake-up call.

His mother's bizarre behavior had forced him to slow down and take a long look at her. When he had, he'd realized something was wrong with her, something more than absentmindedness. Test results had proved him right—she had been suffering with the early stages of Alzheimer's disease.

The realization had stunned him. It had made him feel as if he'd been an inattentive, ungrateful son— and a fool as well. He was a doctor, for God's sake! He should have seen what was happening to her before she'd gotten so far gone. For years she had confused people and events; she had forgotten appointments and special occasions. But then many people forgot things.

At least that's what he had told himself. Until her behavior had forced him to face the truth.

Six months after arriving in New Orleans, Ben had convinced her she would be happier—and safer—living in a semi-independent living facility.

"I fantasized about dying again."

Ben sat up straighter, instantly one hundred percent focused on his patient, annoyed with himself for having let his mind wander. "Tell me about it, Rick."

"There's nothing to tell."

"If that was true, you wouldn't have mentioned it. Did you fantasize about ending your own life? Or did you simply picture the world without you?"

"I just...faded away. I was there, then gone."

A trickle of relief moved through Ben. No clinician worth his salt took a patient's thoughts of death or dying lightly. However, as such thoughts went, fading away set off far fewer alarms. Also, Rick had experienced similar fantasies before, always during times of great emotional stress.

"And how did that make you feel?" Ben asked.

"Angry." Rick stopped pacing. He looked at Ben, his handsome face twisted with some strong emotion, though Ben wasn't sure whether pain or fury. "Nobody seemed to notice or care. They went right on with the party."

The party. Life. Ben understood. He leaned forward in his seat. "I think it's interesting that in many ways this fantasy mirrors your feelings about your mother's death. Your ambivalence and anger. Your isolation. Think about that this week. We'll talk about it during your next session."

Ben stood, signaling that their time was up. He walked Rick to the office door, wished him a good week and said good-night.

He watched his patient exit the waiting room, then returned to his desk, smiling with anticipation. Rick had been his last patient of the day. After he reviewed the notes from their session and straightened up his desk, the weekend was his.

He planned to spend all of it working on his book, a nonfiction tome on the effects of early-childhood trauma—particularly physical, mental and sexual abuse—on personality.

The idea for the book had been born during his first year as a practicing clinician, from the hours he had volunteered at the free clinic in Atlanta. The idea had solidified the following year, when he'd joined the Peachtree Road Psychiatry group. The patient demographic couldn't have been more different than that of the free clinic's, yet he saw the same manifestations of childhood trauma on the personalities of individuals from both groups.

He had realized two things. The first was that child abuse crossed all social, economic and racial lines. The second was that the effects of that abuse could be seen in a predictable pattern of adult pathologies. He had begun researching the work of scholars in the field and immersing himself in the case studies of other clinicians.

Only after that research had begun to stack up and take shape had Ben realized he wanted to write a book on the subject. He wasn't breaking any new ground, his certainly wouldn't be the first book detailing the adult pathologies of childhood trauma and it wouldn't be the last. It would, he hoped, be the first written for the masses, one that spoke to Jane and John Q. Reader. His ultimate goal: to educate and to heal.

Once begun, the book had become his obsession, one he devoted as much time to as he could.

On his way out of the office, Ben once more caught sight of himself in the rippled glass of the antique mirror. It was a flickering glance and he stopped, startled. For a fraction of a second, he had looked like someone else.

Like who, for God's sake? Ben gave his head a shake. The man in the moon? Rick Richardson?

Ben thought of his patient, of his dashing good

looks. Benjamin Walker look like Rick Richardson? In his dreams. Ben studied his reflection. Medium height and build. Medium-brown hair, brown eyes. Glasses that made him look as bookish as he was.

He would never be a lady-killer. He would never make women swoon. Or drool. Or faint.

Which was okay. That wasn't what he was about.

Smart. Steady. A good son. Someday, when he found the right woman, a faithful husband and a devoted father.

He was comfortable in his own skin, with the man Ben Walker had become, the choices he had made, his life.

With a wry grin, he snapped off the office light and stepped into the waiting room, locking his office door behind him.

His was a one-person outfit; he didn't even employ a receptionist. He didn't need one. He made his own appointments, an answering service picked up his calls when he was in session and a computer program helped him with his bookkeeping. As of yet, his contact with insurance companies had been minimal. He was totally self-sufficient. A far cry from the Atlanta group with its plush offices and staff of twenty.

Truth was, he didn't miss it. This was where he belonged.

He supposed as he became busier, he would require an employee. A part of him, a big part, would regret that day. His office was located in half of a Garden District double; the other half served as his residence. It was cozy. Intimate and homey. The inclusion of another would change that.

But change, he acknowledged, was an unavoidable, intrinsic part of life.

Ben crossed to the coffee table to straighten the magazines, only then did he notice the manila envelope propped against one of the sofa cushions. He picked it up. His name had been printed neatly in the upper left-hand corner of the otherwise unmarked envelope.

Curious, he opened it. Inside he found a hardcover suspense novel by Anna North, an author he didn't recognize. As he turned the book over in his hands, a note fluttered to the floor. Short and cryptic, it read:

Tomorrow. 3 p.m. E! Entertainment Network.

Ben drew his eyebrows together, intrigued. Who had left this for him? Why had they left it?

He flipped through the book, but found nothing to indicate an answer to either of those questions. It seemed logical to assume one of his patients had either brought the book for him and forgotten to mention it or had dropped it off while he was in session.

Ben thought back. He had seen six patients today. He ticked off each in his head and saw no reason any of them would have left the book. *If* one of them left it. Anyone could have come in while he was in session and left the package.

Still, the question was, Why?

A mystery, he thought, a smile tugging at the corners of his mouth. One to read. And one to solve.

He would begin tomorrow at three, by tuning in to E!

7

Just after 2:00 p.m., Anna arrived home from her half-day shift at The Perfect Rose. She shivered and glanced up at the gray sky, wishing the sunshine predicted by the Channel 6 meteorologist that morning would make its promised appearance. Winter had only just begun and she was already ready for it to end.

After her lunch with Jaye on Thursday, Anna had returned to work, unsettled by Jaye's revelation that somebody had been following her. She had even considered calling Jaye's foster mom or the police, then had rejected the thought. First off, Jaye would have been furious with her, and secondly the girl had agreed they would go to the police if she saw the man again. Although not completely comfortable with her decision, Anna had decided that for now she would let it drop.

Anna retrieved her keys from her purse. In addition to her concerns about Jaye's safety, she had been preoccupied with thoughts of Minnie and the discomfiting "He" of the girl's letter.

Deciding that Jaye had been right about Minnie

needing a friend, Anna had responded to the child's letter. She had kept it light and chatty, working in a couple of subtle queries about Minnie's parents, about her relationship with them. Now she hoped they had been subtle enough. She worried that Minnie's folks would see right through them.

And come down on her like a ton of bricks.

Anna opened the gate to her apartment building's courtyard, pausing to wave at old Mr. Badeaux from across the street. A neighborhood character, Alphonse Badeaux spent most of his days on the front steps of his shotgun double with his ancient, one-eyed bulldog, Mr. Bingle.

Alphonse, a two-time widower, chatted with everyone who came, went or passed his front steps. Anna had learned that if she needed to know anything about anyone on this or the immediately surrounding blocks, Alphonse was her man.

"You got a package today," he called to her, standing then moseying over. "Saw the man deliver it. Don't know who it's from, though. None of my business."

She fought a smile at that. "Did they toss it over the gate?" If no one in the building was available to buzz a delivery in, packages were often thrown over the courtyard gate. That practice worked out well except when it rained unexpectedly. Considering how often that happened in New Orleans, Anna had received a number of soggy packages.

"Nope." He scratched his head. "Somebody buzzed him in. Came and went in about four minutes. Don't know who, though. None of my business."

"Thank you, Alphonse. I'll look for it." She glanced across the street to where the old bulldog lolled on the porch steps. "You and Mr. Bingle been feeling okay?"

"Pretty good." He ran a hand across his face, skin leathery and lined from age and years exposed to the south Louisiana sun. "Don't like the cold, though. Goes down deep, into my bones."

"I know what you mean," she agreed. "It's so damp."

He nodded and jerked a thumb toward his dog. "Doesn't seem to bother Mr. Bingle. Cold or hot, wet or dry, old Bingle doesn't seem to notice the difference."

The dog lifted his head and looked at them with his one good eye. Anna smiled and touched her neighbor's arm. "Come up for a hot chocolate one day. If I do say so myself, I make a pretty mean cup of the stuff."

"That's mighty sweet of you, Miss Anna. I'd like that. You watch out for that package, now."

She told him she would, then let herself in through the gate, locking it behind her.

Like many of the old buildings in the French Quarter, or Vieux Carré, hers had been built around a central courtyard. In days gone by, the courtyards, with their brick walls and lush vegetation, had offered New Orleanians a respite from the stifling heat of summer; today, they served as an oasis from the city that lay beyond their vine-covered walls.

Anna made her way up the narrow staircase to the second floor. As her neighbor had warned, a padded mailing envelope sat propped against her door. She retrieved it, unlocked her apartment and stepped inside. After dropping her purse on the entryway table, she took a closer look at the package. It was addressed to her but unmarked in any other way. No return address, postmark or shipper's label.

Odd, Anna thought. She tore open the envelope and drew out a videotape marked Interview, Savannah Grail.

Her mother. Anna smiled. *Of course.* Last time they'd spoken, her mother had mentioned that her agent had called about a couple of opportunities. This must have been one of those.

Anna turned on the TV, popped in the tape, then wandered to the kitchen for a glass of water and a handful of crackers. Her mother missed working. She missed the limelight, the adulation of fans. She missed being a *star*.

Although, she hadn't been one for a long time now. For a while after the kidnapping, her mother's already waning career had been revived. It hadn't lasted. She had already been forty-five at the time, the age when Hollywood's sex symbols began metamorphosing into movie moms. Those roles went to Oscar-caliber actresses. Something her mother had never been, not even at the zenith of her acting career.

The sad fact was, her mother had now reached an age where, save for an occasional television commercial or local theater production, there simply wasn't any work to be had.

It had been hard for her mother to accept, though she had survived. When her marriage to Anna's father had ended, she'd left southern California and moved back to her hometown, Charleston, South Carolina.

There, she was still a star, still *the* Savannah North—the part she had been born to play.

Smiling with anticipation, Anna settled on the floor in front of the TV and pressed the play button. A moment later the screen was filled with her mother, gorgeous in a peacock-blue silk suit and diamonds.

Anna smiled and munched on her goldfish-shaped crackers, watching as her mother came to life before the camera, preening for the interviewer, every bit the celebrity. She was still so beautiful, Anna thought. Still the flame-haired, green-eyed bombshell that the American public—particularly the male public—had loved to ogle.

The interviewer went to work. He remained unseen. From growing up around cameras and taping, Anna knew it would be easy to piece in the interviewer later. Many taped interviews were done exactly that way.

The man questioned her mother about her work: about being a screen goddess: about the movies and television series she had starred in. They talked about the Hollywood of the fifties, about the stars of the day, Savannah's romantic conquests.

Then the interview changed directions. The videographer began to question Savannah about her personal life: her divorce, her move back to Charleston and her only child, little Harlow Grail.

Anna straightened at the mention of her own name, a knot forming in the pit of her stomach. The interviewer pressed on despite the wrinkle of discomfort that marred her mother's forehead. He discussed the "tragic" kidnapping, its aftermath on Savannah's marriage, their family, on Harlow's psyche.

Anna studied her mother's reactions to the questions, acknowledging the interviewer's skill. He alternated between adulatory and accusing, admiring and suspicious, seeming to know not only which of her mother's buttons to push, but when to push them. He went so far as to comment on the way her career had profited by the tragedy.

The last infuriated Anna. She saw through the man's manipulation to what he was attempting to do. Obviously her mother did not. She folded like a house of cards, becoming apologetic and defensive.

He used her discomfort to his advantage, moving in for the kill. "It's just tragic," he murmured, "that Harlow never overcame her kidnapping. She had such strength and courage, it must hurt you terribly to have watched her disappear into obscurity. I can only imagine how angry and...helpless you must feel."

"Harlow has certainly *not* disappeared," she said proudly, jumping to her daughter's defense. "She's a novelist, living in New Orleans. And quite a successful novelist, I might add. Her first two thrillers received rave reviews."

Anna's heart began to thunder; she felt ill. In one fell swoop her mother had revealed not only her occupation but her city of residence as well.

"A mystery novelist?" the interviewer murmured. "I'm surprised I hadn't heard this before. It seems the name Harlow Grail alone would have made her a bestseller."

"She's taken a pseudonym. After what she lived through, she prefers to avoid the spotlight. I'm sure you understand."

The interviewer made a sound of sympathy. To Anna's ears it sounded false. "Oh, I do. Completely. But surely you can tell us a little more? After all, the story of Harlow's nightmare ordeal and daring escape held all of America captivated for seventy-two hours. We feared for her, then cheered for her. She was, and still is, one of our heroes. Could you at least share a title with us?"

"I wish I could, but—"

"What about her publisher? Is it Doubleday? Cheshire House?" He saw by her expression that the last had been correct. "Cheshire House publishes some big names in suspense. Would Harlow be one of those?"

Anna hit the pause button, struggling to catch her breath. She felt as if she had been struck in the chest by a baseball, one speeding off a professional's bat.

Blood pounding in her ears, she stared at the television, at the frozen image of her mother. Her mother had revealed everything about Anna but her new name and phone number: her city of residence, occupation and the kind of books she wrote. She supposed she should be grateful her mother hadn't mentioned The Perfect Rose or announced her street address.

Calm down. Don't panic. Assess the damage.

Anna breathed through her nose, ticking off the facts in her head. New Orleans was a big city, one with a large community of writers. Nothing in her publisher's materials revealed the city in which she lived, including her author bio. Cheshire House published quite a number of mysteries and suspense novels; her mother hadn't mentioned the exact month her book was scheduled to appear.

Or had she? Anna glanced down at the remote control, still clutched in her hand. Without giving herself time to reconsider and chicken out, she hit the play button.

The video advanced. Her mother looked distressed, near tears. The interviewer wrapped the segment; a moment later the television screen went to black.

Black save for the crudely executed white words that flashed onto the screen:

Surprise, princess.
E! Today at three.

8

Saturday, January 13
3:10 p.m.

Saturday at three sneaked up on Ben, so much so that he missed the first ten minutes of the E! program, one about unsolved Hollywood mysteries. He sank back against the sofa cushions, exhausted. He'd fallen asleep at his research last night and, although he only had a vague recollection of doing so, he'd stumbled to his bed sometime during the night. He had awakened just before dawn, lying horizontally across the bed, completely dressed and feeling as if he had spent hours out howling at the moon instead of slumped over a desk.

The show cut to commercial break. As it did, the narrator urged viewers to stay tuned. Up next: Fairy Tale Turned Nightmare: The Harlow Anastasia Grail Kidnapping.

Ben leaned forward in his seat, instantly alert. The Grail kidnapping was one of those cases that resurfaced in the media every few years. It possessed all the elements to make its appeal timeless: beautiful people with Hollywood connections, wealth, children in danger, both a tragic and triumphant ending, an unsolved mystery.

The narrator returned, briefly recounting the tale of the little Hollywood princess and the day she and her friend had disappeared from the stable on the Grail's Beverly Hills estate. The show recounted the story in news clips from the time and in dramatic reenactments—including one of Harlow Grail's daring escape.

Ben hung on every word. He realized he was holding his breath and released it slowly. Whatever happened to her? he wondered. After enduring such an ordeal, what had she become? How had the horror of those three days affected the person she was today? The choices she'd made and the relationships she'd forged?

Even as the questions filtered through his brain, the show switched to a recent interview with Savannah Grail. Minutes later, the show's focus shifted to another mystery.

Ben flipped off the TV and sat back, intrigued. Harlow Grail's story would be an incredible addition to his book. She had survived an experience few did; that experience had no doubt shaped the rest of her life. Inclusion of her story would not only enrich his book, it would make it newsworthy.

He drew his eyebrows together, reviewing what he had learned from the program. Savannah Grail had indicated that her daughter lived in New Orleans, that she was a suspense novelist, published in hardcover by Cheshire House. She had revealed that her daugh-

ter wrote under a pseudonym and fiercely guarded her
privacy.

Ben stood and crossed to his desk. There he found
the book that had been left for him the day before.
The spine listed the publisher as Cheshire House, the
author as Anna North.

Of course. North had been Savannah Grail's
maiden name, a fact he hadn't remembered until it
had been mentioned on the show just now. Anna was
a diminutive of both Anastasia and Savannah. Obviously then, Anna North the novelist was little Harlow
Grail, the kidnapped Hollywood princess.

Ben frowned down at the novel in his hands, puz-
zled. Which of his patients had left the book for him?
Why had they left it?

He would simply ask, he decided. Starting with the
six patients he had seen the day before.

9

The sun finally made its promised appearance and cold, harsh light spilled across Anna's kitchen table. She sat, staring blindly across the room as the phone screamed to be answered.

She didn't make a move toward it and the machine finally picked up. She had turned the recorder's volume all the way down so she wouldn't know who was calling. She couldn't face another person's surprised disbelief.

She had already talked to her mother. And father. She had talked to a half-dozen friends. Her agent and editor. They had all been sent a copy of her latest book and a note urging them to tune into E! today at three. One after another they had expressed their disbelief over learning that she was Harlow Grail, the kidnapped Hollywood princess. Again and again she had been asked to explain why she hadn't told them.

Some, like her editor, had been delighted by the news. Now, the woman had gushed, they had the perfect promotional hook to send her upcoming book straight onto the bestseller lists. Her agent, on the other hand, had been furious at her for having kept something so important from him. How could he adequately represent her when he didn't even know who she was?

Anna brought a hand to her mouth. Who had done this to her? Why had they done it?

A knock sounded on her front door, followed by Dalton's voice. "It's us," he called out. "Dalton and Bill."

Anna dragged herself to her feet, went to the door and opened it. Her friends stood on the other side, both grinning from ear to ear.

"We tried to call—"

"First the line was busy, busy, busy—"

"Then you didn't answer."

"You saw," she said. "The show on E!"

"Of course we did, you naughty, naughty girl." Dalton wagged a finger at her. "And here Bill and I thought we knew you."

"She's an open book," Bill murmured, moving across the threshold. "That's what we thought. Then we got your note about the show today."

Dalton closed the door behind them. "Cute, Anna. But you could have just told us."

Anna couldn't speak. She couldn't form the words for the fear choking her. The despair.

She turned her back to her friends and brought her shaking hands to her mouth. *Whoever had done this not only knew where she lived but who all the important people in her life were. Dear God, who could know so much about her?*

"Anna?" Dalton murmured. "What's wrong?"

"I didn't send you that note," she managed to say, voice choked with tears. "I wish I had."

"I don't understand. If not you, who?"

"I don't know." She turned to face her friends once more. "But I think...I'm afraid—"

Kurt. He'd found her.

"I think I'd better sit down."

She turned and crossed to the couch, then sank onto it. They followed her, each taking a seat beside her, Dalton on her right, Bill on her left. Neither pressed her to speak, which she appreciated. She hated losing control in front of others and struggled to regain it.

When she had, she told them about her past—her parents and her idyllic, star-kissed childhood, then about the kidnapping, the horror of Timmy's murder and her last-minute escape.

She rubbed her arms, at the gooseflesh that raced up them. "After the kidnapping my life changed," she murmured, looking back, aching at the memories. "I changed. I didn't feel safe anymore. I wasn't so...open as I had been. I didn't trust. I was...afraid."

Her friends were silent, no doubt digesting all that she had told them. After a moment, Dalton cleared his throat. "You mean he killed that little boy...in front of you?"

Her eyes filled with tears even as her head flooded with images—of Timmy struggling while Kurt held the pillow over his face, his arms flailing and body jerking. Then of him going deathly still.

A sound rose in her throat, and she choked it back. One of remembered horror. And pain. It still hurt, almost more than she could bear.

She found her voice. "And then he came after me."

"Your finger."

She nodded and Bill curled his hand around hers. "No wonder you're frightened, Anna. How awful."

"You two weren't the only ones who received a note about the E! program." She drew in a deep, fortifying breath, acknowledging that she was afraid. "Nearly everyone in my life got one, my mother and father, friends, agent and editor." She explained about coming home to find the package containing the tape of her mother's interview, the same one that had been incorporated into the story about the Hollywood mysteries. "The tape ended with a message urging me to watch the E! program."

"You don't think your mother—"

"No." Anna shook her head, acknowledging hurt at her mother's part in this. Acknowledging a feeling of betrayal. The truth was, neither her mother nor father fully understood her fear of exposure.

"About a year ago, my mother was contacted by an independent videographer. He was putting together a series he called *Screen Goddesses of the Fifties.* He wanted to include her. She gave the interview and never heard from him again. Until indirectly, today."

Dalton bristled. "That doesn't explain how she could have revealed so much about you during that interview. Really!"

Anna glanced down at her hands, then back at her friends. "It's done now. And she's not the enemy. She's not the one who wishes me—"

She bit the word back, but it hung in the air between them.

Harm. Someone wished her harm.

For several moments they were silent, then Dalton hugged her. "My poor sweet Anna. You're being forced out."

Bill drew his eyebrows together. "By any chance, does your mother remember the videographer's name?"

Anna shook her head. "But she took his card. She's going to look for it."

"I tell you what," Bill murmured. "I have a couple of friends in television production. How about I give them a call, see if one of them can find out who E! acquired the piece from. With a little luck, I can track down where they got the footage of your mother."

"Thank you," she said, reaching a hand across to his. "That would be so...it would really help."

"Do you have any idea who could be behind this?"

"No, I—" Anna shifted her gaze to Dalton, struggling to form the words, knowing how ludicrous they would sound. "As you know, Kurt was never caught. But the FBI insisted he wasn't a threat—"

"You think that Kurt person is behind this, don't you?"

"I know it sounds crazy, but I...do you think it could be?"

Dalton pulled her closer, shooting a narrow-eyed glance at the other man. "It's highly improbable, I should think."

"That's right," Bill agreed. "Why would Kurt come after you now? So much time has passed."

"Unfinished business," she whispered. "To get even with me for screwing up his plans."

Again her friends fell silent. This time, Bill spoke first. "Let's think this through, Anna. I understand your fears and why you would feel threatened by this man. But why would he want to force you out?"

"That's right," Dalton spoke up. "If Kurt wanted some sort of revenge, why not just have it? Kidnap you again? Kill you?"

"Thanks a lot, Dalton." She forced a weak smile. "Remind me to have burglar bars installed."

Bill frowned. "Kurt coming after you simply doesn't make sense, Anna. Look at the facts. Twenty-three years have passed. This Kurt has no doubt gone on to other crimes. He may be imprisoned. Or dead."

She rubbed her fingers over her deformed hand. "I want to believe it, but…I have this awful feeling he's found me."

"You have to go to the police." Dalton looked at Bill for affirmation. He got it and returned his gaze to Anna's. "The sooner the better."

"The police," she repeated. "And what do I tell them? That someone is sending cryptic notes and copies of my novels to my friends? Come on, I'd be laughed out of the place."

"No, you go to them with your suspicions. With your past and the recent turn of events, I hardly think they'll laugh."

"I agree," Bill said. "If nothing else, it'll serve as a kind of heads-up. What do you have to lose?"

Truth was, she didn't have a lot of confidence in

the police—or in the FBI. If not for their bumbling, she believed Timmy would be alive today.

But Anna didn't tell them that. Instead, she murmured, "I'll think about it. Okay?"

"Promise me," Dalton said, tone fierce. "I don't want anything to happen to you."

"All right, I'll think about it. I promise."

They talked a while more, then after Anna assured them she would be fine alone, they stood to leave.

On his way out the door, Bill stopped and looked over his shoulder at her. "How did Jaye take the news?" he asked. "She can be so sensitive."

Anna froze. Amazingly, until that moment, she hadn't thought of Jaye. And from the calls she'd received, it seemed all the important people in her life had been contacted. Had Jaye?

She swallowed hard, a sick feeling in the pit of her stomach. Jaye, whose trust had been so hard to win. Jaye, who had been lied to by everyone she had ever loved or trusted. Jaye, who would perceive Anna's secret as a lie and yet another betrayal in a life filled with them.

Anna said goodbye to her friends and ran for the phone. She checked the answering machine, found her young friend had not called and quickly dialed her number.

Jaye refused to come to the phone.

Devastated, Anna told Jaye's foster mother that she was coming over. It was imperative that she speak with the girl as soon as possible.

Anna flew to Jaye's, making it to her mid-city neighborhood in record time. The entire way she gripped the steering wheel tightly and repeated a prayer in her head that it was going to be okay, that she could make Jaye understand why she had kept her past a secret from her.

But she saw right away that she couldn't make Jaye understand, that she couldn't make it okay. "I can explain, Jaye."

"There's nothing to explain." Jaye hiked up her chin. "I trusted you and you lied to me."

"I didn't." At the girl's disgusted snort, Anna reached a hand out. The sun had begun to set and dusk closed around them as they stood on the porch. "Please, listen to me, Jaye. That person, Harlow Grail, that's not who I am. She doesn't exist anymore. I left her behind when I moved down here. I told you who I am, Anna North."

Jaye hugged herself against the cold. "That... bullshit! Anna North is only a part of who you are."

"I changed my name, I moved. I left behind everybody but my parents—"

"Adults always do that, don't they? Justify what they do even when it's wrong. Insist that it's the *juvenile* who's not thinking clearly."

"That's not what's going on here. I'm trying to tell you, trying to make you see why—"

"Why you lied to me. I'm only fifteen and I know how screwed up that is." Her disdain made Anna cringe. "*'You've got to face the past to overcome it.'* How many times have I heard that? How many times did I hear *you* say it?"

"I didn't lie." Anna shook her head. "I'm Anna

North now. Harlow Grail only exists in people's memories. I left her—''

''You haven't left her behind!'' Jaye cried. ''You can't. I know because a day doesn't go by that I don't think about my dad and the things he did.'' She tipped her chin up, struggling, Anna saw, not to cry. ''If you had really left Harlow Grail behind, you wouldn't be working so hard to hide from her.''

She was right, dammit. How did someone so young know so much? Even as Anna wondered, she knew. *With pain came insight.*

''Our situations aren't the same.''

Jaye stiffened, spots of bright color dotting her cheeks. ''Oh, I see. My opinion and feelings don't matter. Because I'm just a stupid kid.''

''No, they're different because your dad's in jail. She held up her mutilated hand. ''The man who did this to me was never caught. I'm not hiding from my past. I'm hiding from him. I'm afraid.''

Jaye's expression softened and for a moment Anna thought she may have convinced her friend. The moment passed and Jaye shook her head. ''Real friends are one hundred percent honest with each other. I have been. But you…I don't even know who you are.''

''I'm sorry, Jaye. Forgive me.'' She reached a hand out to the girl. ''Please.''

''No.'' Jaye's eyes flooded with tears and she took a step backward. ''You lied to me. I can't be your friend anymore. I won't.''

She turned and ran inside, slamming the door behind her. The sound reverberated through Anna, final and heartbreaking.

10

Wednesday, January 17
The French Quarter

For the next four days Anna had called Jaye every day, at least twice. Each time, the girl had refused to take her call.

Anna missed her. Their falling-out had left a big hole in her life and her heart. Bill and Dalton believed Jaye would relent in time, that before long she would call Anna and everything would be all right.

Anna hoped they were right. But she knew Jaye. She understood her. When it came to relationships, if someone hurt Jaye, she cut them out of her life, swiftly and brutally. The girl had developed the tactic as protection against the kind of hurt she had suffered as a youngster.

Anna had never thought Jaye would feel compelled to use the tactic with her.

Sighing, Anna stepped through The Perfect Rose's front door. Dalton had beat her in this morning. He stood behind the register, counting the cash in the drawer.

"Sorry I'm late," she called, slipping out of her jacket and heading for the workroom.

He looked up and smiled. "Good morning."

"What's good about it?"

"I take it Jaye still refuses to speak to you?"

"You take it right." She hung her jacket on the hook on the back of the door, then slipped her apron on. "Her foster mother's starting to get annoyed with my calls. Today she very firmly told me that Jaye would call when she was ready to talk to me. Then she hung up."

He frowned. "Charming. I take it she's not your ally in this?"

"Hardly." Anna made her way to the register. "It seems everyone thinks I'm the enemy."

"Jaye'll come around. If you're missing her this much, think how much she's missing you."

Anna thought more about how she had unintentionally hurt her friend. She changed the subject. "My agent called this morning, that's why I'm a little late."

"Finally! Are they taking the new book?"

"They want it—" she held up a hand to stop his congratulations "—but only on their terms."

"Their terms? What does that mean?"

"It means, they want it only if I'll let them publicize it and me as they see fit. It seems they think Harlow Grail has the ability to sell a lot more books than Anna North."

"I don't understand." He drew his eyebrows together. "Your new story doesn't have anything to do with your kidnapping experience."

"Apparently, my past is a hook that'll get me a mother lode of media coverage." A bitter edge crept into her voice. "As my agent explained, my book's just another suspense novel. What makes it special is that Harlow Grail, kidnapped Hollywood princess, wrote it.''

''I'm sorry, Anna. That really sucks.''

''It gets worse. If I won't go along with their promotion plans, they're dropping me. I'm not profitable enough for them.''

''They want a home run or nothing.''

''Apparently so.'' She began counting the cash in the bank bag, grateful to have something to do with her hands. ''My agent wants me to agree. He doesn't understand my hesitation. Most authors, he said, would kill for the offer of a big push and lots of promotion. Besides, the cat's out of the bag now and the world hasn't come to an end.''

''Nice guy. Understanding.''

''I used to think he was on my side. Now I see he's on whichever side the money's on.''

Dalton gave her a quick hug. ''What are you going to do?''

''I don't know yet. I want to take the offer. I worked so hard to get published. You know how hard I worked. You know how much…how much writing means to me.'' Tears stung her eyes and she fought them back. ''But I can't imagine going on TV and radio and…talking about what happened to me. I can't imagine opening my personal life to strangers. I know what kind of people are out there, Dalton. I *know*.'' She pressed her fist to her chest. ''And I can't expose myself that way, I know I can't.''

''And if you don't—''

''I lose everything I've worked for.'' A lump

formed in her throat and she swallowed past it. "It's so unfair."

He kissed her on the cheek. "I'm here for you if you need me."

"I know." She leaned into him, resting her cheek against his shoulder. "And believe me, I appreciate it."

The bell above the shop door jingled and Bill strode in. In his navy, double-breasted suit and crisp white shirt he looked like a banker.

"Caught in the act," he teased. "And to think I trusted you both."

Anna stepped out of Dalton's arms and smiled affectionately at her friend. "I'd steal him from you in a heartbeat, if I thought I had a chance."

Bill brought a hand to his chest in mock heartbreak. "And here I thought you wanted me."

She laughed and shook her head, grateful for her friends. "What are you doing here so early this morning? And looking so—"

"Boring?" he filled in, glancing down at himself in disgust. "I'm meeting with the group financing our new Art in the Park event. For some reason they're more comfortable giving money to men wearing blue suits. Go figure." He crossed to the counter. He shifted his gaze to Dalton. "Did you give her the letter yet?"

Anna looked over her shoulder at Dalton—and caught him signaling Bill to shut up. She frowned. "What letter, Dalton?"

"Don't be mad. It came yesterday, while you were at lunch."

"It's from your little fan," Bill offered, rubbing his hands together. "The saga continues."

Dalton sent Bill an annoyed glance, then pulled an envelope out of his front apron pocket. He held it out to her. "I know how her last letter troubled you. And you were so down yesterday...I didn't want to make your day worse. I was going to give it to you first thing this morning, but—"

"I didn't give you the chance. It's okay, Dalton." She took the letter, feeling both hopeful and apprehensive. She had been thinking a lot about Minnie, she had reread her letters a dozen times. She had come to believe that the girl was an abductee.

Anna had grown so concerned she had called a friend who worked for Social Services. She had explained the situation and read her friend the letters. Although the other woman had thought the situation suspicious and had been sympathetic to Anna's concern, without something concrete to go on, a witness or even the girl's written claim of abuse, her hands were tied.

Anna swallowed hard and lowered her gaze to the envelope. She hoped this correspondence proved her wrong. She hoped that after she read it she'd feel like a reactionary idiot. She feared she wouldn't.

"Are you going to open it?" Bill asked.

She nodded and ripped open the envelope.

The letter began in much the same way as the others had, with a greeting and a sentence or two of chitchat about Tabitha, Anna's books and small occurrences in Minnie's days. But this time, it took a frightening turn:

He's planning something bad. I don't know what, but I'm afraid. For you. And another one. Another girl. I'll try to find out more.

Anna reread those few lines, her heart in her throat. "Dear God." She lifted her gaze to her friend's. "He's going to do it again."

The two men exchanged concerned glances. "Do what, Anna?"

"Another girl." She handed Dalton the letter, her hand shaking. "I think he's planning to abduct another girl."

Bill peered over Dalton's shoulder so that he, too, could read the letter. He whistled when he finished. "I don't like the way that sounds."

"Neither do I." Dalton frowned. "What are you going to do?"

Anna was silent a moment, considering her options. There were few. She came to a decision, the only one that made any sense. She slipped off her apron and crossed to the workroom to retrieve her jacket. She pulled it on, then met her friends' concerned gazes. "You'll have to hold down the fort for a while. I'm going to the police."

Forty minutes later, Anna was shaking hands with Detective Quentin Malone. "Have a seat." He motioned to the chair in front of his desk. "I apologize for the wait. We're short-staffed today. Half the force is down with the flu.''

She slipped out of her coat and sat. "So the desk officer explained. He also informed me that you would take my statement but another detective would follow up later.''

"I'm usually assigned to the Seventh.'' He sat and folded his hands on the desk in front of him. "My partner and I are filling in here today.''

"And you just happened to be the lucky one who got me.''

"Yes, ma'am, that's me.'' He slid his gaze over her, then smiled, the curving of his lips slow and suggestive. "Lucky.''

She would just bet he was. Tall, broad-shouldered and strikingly good-looking, she had no doubt that this man was never without willing female companionship. And by the way he was sizing her up, he expected her to jump for the bait as well.

Sorry, stud. Not this century. Men who thought they were God's gift to the female sex were not her cup of tea. Having grown up around the film industry, she had spent more time with that kind of man than she cared to recall. She found them to be cocky, arrogant and narcissistic, more interested in looking at their own reflection that into their lover's eyes.

"Considering the lack of available manpower, I'm glad I wasn't here to report a murder.''

"I'm glad too. Murders are bad. The less of 'em the better.''

She frowned, slightly off balance. "Are you trying to be funny?"

"And failing. Obviously." He flashed her another smile, one she was certain was meant to send her pulse racing, and took a small, spiral-bound notebook from his breast pocket. "Why don't you tell me what brought you in today?"

So she did. Anna explained how she had received a fan letter from Minnie, then about her reply and the two letters she had received from the girl since.

She opened her purse and handed the letters to him. He scanned them while she spoke. "Something's not right with this child's situation. At first I was concerned but now, with this last letter, I'm frightened."

"And that's why you're here? Because you're frightened?"

"For her, yes. And now, for the other girl Minnie referred to in the letter."

He looked up, waiting, expression giving nothing of his thoughts away. She made a sound of frustration. "I think Minnie is an abductee. I think the man she refers to as 'He' is her abductor. And I believe he's planning to snatch another girl."

For a heartbeat of time he was silent, then he leaned back in his chair. The springs creaked. "You're reading a lot into these letters. Ms. North. This Minnie never comes right out and says she's being held against her will or is in any kind of danger."

"She doesn't have to. Read the letters, read between the lines. It's all there."

"You're a suspense writer, isn't that correct?"

"Yes, but what does that have to do with—"

"This kind of story is your stock-in-trade."

Anna felt angry heat flood her cheeks. "You think I'm making this up? What, do you think I'm doing research here?"

"I didn't say that." He leaned forward once more, gaze unflinchingly on hers. "I have another theory about these letters. One I wonder if you've considered."

She stiffened. "Go on."

"Has it ever occurred to you that these letters could be some sort of a scam?"

"A scam?" she repeated. "What do you mean?"

"I mean, maybe an eleven-year-old girl didn't write these letters. Maybe Minnie is some wacko fan trying to yank your chain. Playing some sort of sick game with you?" He paused for effect. "Or pretending to be Minnie in an attempt to get close to you?"

A chill raced down Anna's spine. She shook it off. "That's ludicrous."

"Is it?" He cocked an eyebrow. "You write dark suspense novels. There are a lot of sick people out there, one of them, for whatever reason, could have fixated on you or your stories. It happens."

Her hands began to shake, and she folded them in her lap so he wouldn't see. She tipped up her chin. "I'm not buying any of this."

"You should." He leaned toward her. "Considering your personal history, you should not only buy it, but you should take it very seriously."

She stiffened. "Excuse me, but what do you know about my—"

"Think about it, Ms. North. With your history, the sick game becomes sicker. Your obsession with children in jeopardy makes you an easy mark for—"

"Obsession with children in jeopardy? Excuse me, I don't think so. And just what do *you* know about my personal history?"

He sat back. "Sorry, ma'am, but even big dumb cops like me can put two and two together. You're the novelist Anna North. You write suspense novels for Cheshire House. You're a green-eyed redhead of approximately thirty-six and you reside in New Orleans." He motioned her hands, clasped in her lap. "And you're missing your right pinkie finger."

She felt exposed and ridiculous. And was angry that she did. Angry with him for toying with her. He had known her full identity this entire time, yet he hadn't let on until now. The macho jerk. She would write him into her next novel—as a bumbling buffoon who did not get the girl and ended up waxed.

She sent him her frostiest stare. "And sometimes, big dumb cops watch E!"

He flashed her a quick "aw-shucks" smile, closed his spiral and slid it back into his breast pocket. "Actually, studying famous unsolved crimes is a hobby of mine. Yours is one of the ones that interests me."

"I'm flattered," she muttered, anything but. "Solve it yet?"

"No, ma'am, but you'll be the first to know when

I do.'' He handed her the letters and stood, signaling the end to their meeting.

She followed him to his feet, furious. "I won't hold my breath.''

Instead of being offended, he looked amused. Which only made her angrier. "You're wrong, you know. The person who wrote these letters is a child. You only have to look at them to know. And even if an adult could have successfully feigned this hand-writing, which I don't believe they could, the person who wrote these thinks like a child. And that child's in danger.''

"I'm sorry, I don't see it that way.''

"So, you're not going to do anything about this?'' Anna said, disgusted. "Not even follow up on the P.O. box or phone number?''

"No, I'm not. However, Detective Lautrelle might feel differently. He's expected back tomorrow, I'll give him a full report.''

"An unbiased one, I've no doubt.''

He ignored her sarcasm. "Of course. I advise you to be careful right now, Ms. North. Report anything out of the ordinary. Anyone out of the ordinary. Be cautious about new people who enter your life.'' He paused. "You didn't respond to these letters using your home address, did you?''

Instead, she had responded using an address she could be accessed at six days a week. How could she have been so stupid? "My home address?'' she re-peated, sidestepping the truth, not wanting to admit to

this insufferable know-it-all how careless she had
been. "No, I did not."

"Good." He handed her Detective Lautrelle's card.
"Anything comes up, give Lautrelle a call. He'll be
able to help you out."

She pocketed the card without looking at it. She
crossed to the cubicle's opening, stopping and looking
back at him when she reached it. "You know, Detective Malone, after meeting you it doesn't surprise me
that there are so many famous unsolved crimes."

11

Quentin watched Anna North walk away, half-amused, half-awed. Harlow Grail, in his office. Who would have thought it?

He had been fourteen when she'd been kidnapped and remembered sitting with his father and uncles and listening to them talk about the case. He remembered the newscasts, remembered staring at Harlow Grail's image on TV and in the newspaper and thinking her about the prettiest thing he had ever seen.

He had fantasized solving the case and being a big Hollywood hero, and when she had escaped he had cheered for her—even as he'd listened to his father and uncles say that something about the case just didn't add up.

Like it had the rest of the country, the Grail kidnapping had continued to fascinate him. Hers had been the first of many unsolved cases he had studied over the years.

"Hey, partner." Terry ambled over to stand beside him. He motioned in the direction Anna North had gone. "Who was the dish?"

"Name's Anna North."

"She kill anybody?"

Quentin glanced at his partner from the corners of his eyes. "Only on paper. She's a suspense novelist."

"No joke? So, what'd she want with you? She gonna make you the hero in her next book?"

Remembering the way she had looked at him, Quentin doubted that. A victim, maybe. One who died a bloody and gruesome death. "Yeah," he murmured, "something like that."

Terry motioned the front desk. "We got our walking papers. LaPinto and Erickson just straggled in."

Quentin glanced over. "They don't look too good."

"I say we get while the getting's good."

Quentin agreed. They signed out, then stepped out into the gray, chilly day. Terry shivered and zipped his leather jacket. "I'm getting pretty fucking sick of this cold. This is New Orleans, for Christ's sake."

"It could be worse," Quentin murmured, looking up at the sky. "It could snow."

"Bite your tongue, Malone. Remember the last time it snowed? A couple snowflakes and this town goes nuts. We'd be working around the clock."

They reached his Bronco and Quentin unlocked the doors. After they had climbed in and buckled up, Terry turned to him. "So what did the redhead want? She really going to write you into her next book?"

Quentin grimaced. "With the way our meeting went, only if I get whacked right off the bat."

The other man laughed. "No doubt about it, you're a charmer." He angled toward Quentin. "So, if she's not going to make you her next hero, what'd she want?"

"She's been getting some disturbing letters from a fan."

"No joke? Threats?"

"Not to her, no. Supposedly this fan's a kid. An eleven-year-old girl."

"Supposedly?"

"I've got my doubts." Quentin filled his partner in. "Ms. North believes the child's in danger. I'll fill in Lautrelle when he's back to work. He can follow up if he thinks there's anything there."

Terry leaned his head against the rest and closed his eyes. "After getting a look at her, my mind's made up. I'm putting in for transfer to the Eighth. Maybe they'll give me Lautrelle's caseload."

"Give it up, Terror. No way you'd even get to first base. She's way out of your league, partner."

Terry smiled but didn't open his eyes. "You so sure about that? I've nailed way classier broads than her before."

"Nailed? Broad?" Quentin laughed. "Yeah, I'm sure."

Quentin crossed Poydras Street, heading uptown. "How'd it go with PID yesterday?" The Public Integrity Division was the NOPD's version of Internal Affairs. Terry had been called in for questioning about the Kent murder the day after her murder, then again yesterday.

"They asked me a shitload of questions about Nancy's murder, then let me go. Thanks in no small part to your statement. I appreciate it, man."

"I only told it the way I saw it." He glanced at his

partner and grinned. "What's the deal? You and the deceased on a first-name basis now?"

"After the past week? We're practically family."

They drove in silence until they reached the Seventh. Quentin parked the Bronco; they climbed out of the vehicle and headed into the building. After signing in, they parted company. On his way through the squad room, Johnson called him over.

"What's up?"

He tossed a manila folder across the desk. "Take a look."

"The Kent homicide?" He flipped open the folder. "What've we got?"

"Official cause of death was suffocation. Raped first."

Quentin scanned the medical examiner's report. Other than tearing and bruising to the labia, she was relatively unmarked. A few abrasions to the back of her head, legs and arms and that was it.

"Weird," he murmured.

"What?"

"She didn't put up much of a fight."

"Think she knew the guy?"

"Yeah, maybe. They get much from under her nails?"

"Nada. Got the blood test back. Our guy's O-positive. Like nearly half the population of New Orleans."

"Not me," Quentin murmured, flipping forward in the report. "I'm A-positive." He stopped, frowning. "You and Walden didn't interview any women from the bar that night?"

"The waitresses. We focused on the guys. Why?"

"Think about it, Johnson. You've got this gorgeous woman monopolizing every available guy in the bar with her exhibitionist antics. Basically, she's cutting in on every other woman's chance of making a connection. Right?"

"Right." The other detective scratched his head. "So?"

"So, you have some pretty pissed-off chicks. And what happens when somebody pisses you off?"

"You punch 'em in the face?"

"Not in this case." He answered his own question. "In this case, you can't take your eyes off them. The other ladies at that bar were watching every move Nancy Kent made. Keeping count of the men she danced with and for how long. They're who we have to talk to."

Johnson nodded. "You've got a point, Malone."

Quentin stood. "I'll pay a visit to Shannon this afternoon, get a list of names. Start making calls."

"By George," Johnson said in an attempt at a British accent but coming off as a mentally challenged Cajun, "I think he's got a plan."

12

Ben stopped outside the florist shop's door. The sign above it proclaimed this The Perfect Rose.

Anna North's workplace.

She hadn't been difficult to track down. She had dedicated her last book to the Big Brothers, Big Sisters of America and her "Little Sister" Jaye. The local B.B.B.S.A. director was an acquaintance of his; he had contacted her and she had suggested he reach Anna through The Perfect Rose.

Ben cleared his throat. He probably should have called first. It would have been the proper thing to do. But refusing him over the phone would have been too easy. And he didn't want to make refusing him easy. He wanted her to agree to let him interview her for his book.

Wanted it rather desperately.

He had thought a lot about Anna North since seeing the *Unsolved Hollywood Mysteries* segment on E! He had read her novels. Had read between the lines and learned a great deal from her stories. He had put that information together with what he knew about her past and present in an attempt to anticipate how she would react to his having found her. She would be angry with him. If he understood her as well as he thought he did, his showing up would frighten her. She fiercely protected her privacy out of fear. She would most probably react like a cornered animal.

He would win her over.

Ben took a deep breath and pushed through the door. She appeared at the workroom doorway; he recognized her by the glorious mane of red hair, so like her mother's.

"Good morning," he said, smiling and crossing to the service counter.

She returned his smile. "How can I help you?"

The moment of truth. "I'm Benjamin Walker." He held out his hand. "Dr. Benjamin Walker."

She looked surprised, but took his hand. "Nice to meet you."

"Likewise."

"So, what can I do for you today? We have some really nice hydrangeas in. From California. And our roses are always—"

"Perfect?" He smiled. "Actually, I'm here to see you."

"Me?"

"First let me say that I'm a fan of your work."

"My work?" she repeated. "Oh, you mean the arrangements. I'm sorry, but I can't take credit for them, though I wish I could. Dalton Ramsey is both the owner of The Perfect Rose and the artistic force behind its creations."

"You misunderstand, Anna. I'm a fan of your novels."

The blood drained from her face. "My nov— How did you—"

"Justine Blank is an acquaintance of mine. She told me how I could reach you."

Anna looked confused. And upset. He hurried to reassure her. "I'm a psychologist and quite harmless, as Justine knows. My specialty is the effect of childhood trauma on adult personality and behavior. Your case has always interested me and when I learned you were both Harlow Grail and the author Anna North, I took a chance on coming by here. I hope you'll agree to speak with me."

She seemed to absorb that information. Some of the color had returned to her cheeks, but not much. "This past Saturday you saw the special on unsolved Hollywood mysteries and put two and two together?"

"Yes. And I saw your dedication to the B.B.B.S.A. in *Killing Me Softly*. I figured Justine would be able to tell me how I could get in touch with you. I was right."

She looked away, then back at him. He saw now that she was angry. "My *case*, as you call it, has interested a lot of people. But I'm not interested. In fact, I've done everything I could to forget it. Now, if you don't mind, I have work to do."

"Please, Ms. North, hear me out."

"I don't think so." She folded her arms across her chest. "I'm a private person, Dr. Walker. By hunting me down like a prize in a child's treasure hunt, you've invaded my privacy. I don't appreciate that."

"It frightens you, I understand."

She frowned. "I didn't say it frightened me."

"You didn't have to. Of course it does. You lived

through a nightmare. You were snatched by a stranger and held against your will. Control of your life was taken away. Control of your body. You were physically assaulted and forced to helplessly watch a friend be killed.

"The ordeal left you with a very real sense of the sickness and evil in the world. You hide from the public because of that knowledge. Because you promised yourself you would never put yourself in that position again. You promised yourself that you would never offer some stranger the opportunity to take your life away from you again.

"So you changed your name. Left your past behind. Anonymity makes you feel safe. And my showing up here today makes you feel anything but safe."

"How do you know this about me?" she managed to say after several moments, voice shaking. "We've never met."

"But I know about your past. I've read your novels." He pressed a business card into her cold hand. "I'm writing a book on the effects of childhood trauma on personality. I'd like to interview you for it. The inclusion of your story, how your ordeal has shaped you and your life, would greatly enhance the book."

She opened her mouth; to refuse, he knew. He saw it in her eyes. In the tightness around her mouth. He didn't give her a chance to refuse. "Just think about it. Please. That's all I ask."

Without another word, he turned and quickly left the shop.

13

For Anna, the next twenty-four hours crawled by. She had found herself on edge, constantly looking over her shoulder, scanning the faces in the crowd, searching for the one that didn't fit. She'd noticed each groan and creak of her old building, had heard each footfall in the hallway outside her door.

Sleep had eluded her. She'd tossed and turned, remembering the past and worrying that somehow it had caught up with her. When she had managed to drift off, she'd awakened terrified, a scream and Timmy's name on her lips. Timmy's name, not Kurt's.

A fact she found odd and somehow more frightening.

Anna was uncertain who she blamed more for her state of mind: Ben Walker for having found her so easily or Detective Malone for planting the seed of doubt about Minnie's letters.

She'd decided on a combination of the two but focused the majority of her irritation on Detective Malone. Because until him, she had taken Minnie's letters at face value.

Anna muttered an oath and stepped out of her morning shower. Damn Malone for making her jumpier than she already was. For scaring the life out of her yet being unwilling to do a thing to help. She shook her head. Minnie wasn't some obsessed fan playing a sick game with her, she was a child. She thought like one; she wrote like one. And she needed Anna's help.

And help Anna would give her, NOPD or no NOPD.

Anna checked the time, then dried off and dressed. She didn't have to be in to The Perfect Rose until noon. That gave her three full hours to do a little investigative work of her own.

She found her shoes, stepped into them and tied the laces. The night before, she had called the number Minnie had given in her first letter. A man had answered. That had been a disappointment. She had hoped to reach Minnie directly. Undaunted, she had taken a deep breath and asked for the girl.

The man had been silent for a full fifteen seconds, then had hung up on her without saying a word. It was then that Anna had known for certain that Minnie needed her.

In the hopes of the child answering, Anna had called back a half-dozen times, including twice this morning, but had gotten no answer. Today, she planned to drive across the lake to Mandeville—a bedroom community on the north shore of Lake Pontchartrain—to check out where Minnie lived. Once there, she would decide what to do next.

An hour later she saw that there was little she

would be able to do with this address. It belonged not to a residence, but a mail and copy store.

Anna double-checked the number, then went inside. She smiled at the man behind the counter and introduced herself. "I'm a writer and I've been corresponding with a fan. She claimed this as her return address." Anna handed him an envelope. "I've responded so I know she's received my letters, but now I wonder how that can be."

The man, who turned out to be the store owner, handed the envelope back, smiling. "Actually, one of the advantages of renting a mailbox from us instead of the post office is that you get a street address instead of a P.O. box number."

"You're saying, this person rents a box from you?"

He smiled again. "That's correct. You see, a street address suggests permanence. Permanence equals solvency. Commitment. Believe it or not, a street address helps when applying for a job or credit. There are other advantages to using our box service. For one, you can receive shipments from carriers who won't deliver to a P.O. box, Federal Express for one. Also, we offer other features, like a forwarding service. For an additional charge, of course."

Obviously, this guy believed in his business. She worked to hide her disappointment. "It sounds like a great service."

"It is." From the way he was looking at her, he was ready to sign her up. "Let me get you some information."

Before she could refuse, he had retrieved a flyer

from under the counter. "Just in case you should ever need one."

She thanked him, slipped the flyer into her pocket and returned the conversation to the reason for her visit. "I really need to get in touch with the girl who wrote this letter. Is there any way I can get her actual address from you?"

"Sorry." A customer entered the store and the man's gaze drifted toward the door, then back to her. "I can't give that out."

"Not even if it's an emergency?"

"We guarantee our clients full privacy. Short of a court order, that is."

"Look—" she lowered her voice, pleading "—it's *really* important that I find out who's renting that box."

"Can't do it. Sorry."

She lowered her voice more. "I know this sounds crazy, but a little girl's in danger. Couldn't you bend the rules just this once? Please?"

His expression went from helpful to annoyed. Obviously, he didn't buy the kid-in-danger scenario. She tried again anyway. "Please? I promise, this is a matter of life and death. An eleven-year-old girl—"

"No," he said sharply. "I will not make an exception. Now, if you'll excuse me, I have a customer."

Anna left the store, frustrated, fired by renewed annoyance with Detective Quentin Malone's lackadaisical attitude. If Malone had been the one demanding the box owner's address, he would have gotten it. No pleading necessary. She was certain of that.

What did she do now?

The name, she realized. Minnie went by the surname Swell, an unusual name for this part of the country.

Jo and Diane. At the Green Briar Shoppe.

Of course. Jo Burris and Diane Cimo knew almost everybody on the North Shore. If anyone by that name had passed through their boutique, they would remember.

Anna climbed into her car and drove across Highway 22 and onto the service road. Anna had met the two women when she had wandered into the boutique on her first visit to the North Shore. Warm, fun-loving and outgoing, Jo and Diane had made her feel as welcome as an old friend. An hour and a half later, Anna had exited the store with two outfits she couldn't afford and two new friends worth more than any amount of money.

Jo's shop was located in an aging strip mall on the service road just a couple of minutes from what had become the hub of Mandeville. Anna parked in front of the store, climbed out of her car and went inside. The bell above the door tinkled, and Jo, a gorgeous woman of an indeterminate age, looked up from the box she was unpacking.

She smiled warmly. "Anna, I was just thinking about you." She spoke in a honeyed drawl that Anna didn't doubt had sent many a man's pulse racing. "We've gotten the prettiest things in." She held up the rose-colored chenille sweater she was unpacking. "With your hair, honey, no man could resist."

Anna laughed, took the sweater and held it against her while she stood in front of a mirror. She gazed at her reflection, then made a sound of regret and handed it back. "It would, Jo. If only I could afford it."

"You could put it on layaway, pay just a little every week." Jo's bangle bracelets clicked together as she refolded the sweater. "It would look so good on you."

Anna didn't weaken, though she longed to try the sweater on. Instead, she turned the conversation to the reason for her visit.

"Swell," Jo repeated, drawing her eyebrows together in thought. After a moment she shook her head. "Sorry, Anna honey, I just don't recognize that name."

It had been a long shot, Anna knew, but still she was disappointed. "How about the name Minnie?" she asked. "Hear anybody talk about a girl named Minnie?"

Again Jo shook her head. "But Diane might have. Or one of our customers. We can ask around, if it's important?"

"It is, Jo. Really important." They chatted a few minutes more, during which Anna avoided Jo's not-so-subtle curiosity about the reason finding Minnie Swell was so important. After quickly flipping through the racks, oohing and aahing over several things and promising to come back and shop when she had more time, she left—no closer to helping Minnie than she had been first thing that morning.

When Anna arrived at work fifty minutes later, she found several messages waiting for her, two from her agent and one from Dr. Ben Walker. She returned her agent's call right away. "Hey, Will, what's up?"

"They've upped their offer."

Her stomach dropped to her toes. "What did you say?"

"You heard me, Madeline called this morning and upped Cheshire House's offer on the new proposal."

"But why would they up their offer?" she asked. "I haven't even officially refused—"

"I'd called, expressed your concerns, pointed out what a monumental personal sacrifice they were asking you to make." He made a sound of satisfaction. "I love it when a plan comes together."

Anna swallowed hard, heart thundering in her chest. "Will," she murmured, "the issue isn't the money. It was never the money."

"Anna, they're offering fifty thousand."

For the second time in five minutes, Anna's stomach took a tumble. "Say that again."

He repeated the figure and she laid her hand on Dalton's arm for support. She knew that figure was a far cry from the multimillion-dollar advances the brand-name authors pulled in per book, but it was a quantum leap from the twelve-thousand-dollar advance she had received for her last.

"How much?" Dalton whispered, nearly dancing with excitement.

Propping the phone to her ear with her shoulder, she opened and closed her hands five times. He brought his to his chest in mock heart failure.

"Same contract stipulations," her agent continued.

"A full tour and no-holds-barred publicity campaign."

Her soaring spirits took a nosedive. "They won't budge on that?"

"Not even a millimeter." At her silence, he rushed to add, "Think about it, Anna. Think about what this could mean to your career. We're talking bestseller lists. Name recognition. An advertising budget. Then, if this book sells as they expect it will, the publishing stratosphere. Now, think what you stand to lose if you turn this offer down. With your present numbers it's not going to be easy to sell you to another house. You'll be regarded as a bad bet and a money loser."

His words hurt. That he could spit them at her so matter-of-factly, with no regard for her feelings, hurt more. "I thought you believed in my work," she said, voice thick.

"I do. But in this market it takes more than a great story to sell books. It takes a hook. And you've got that, Anna. Use it. Don't throw this opportunity away."

"I hear what you're saying, but I…I can't do this." She shook her head. "I know I can't."

"Why are you sabotaging yourself this way?" His tone took on an unpleasant edge. "Don't you see? This is a once-in-a-lifetime opportunity, you can't throw it away."

"I don't want to, but—"

"I'll go back to the table. I can get you more money than this. I'll get you a guaranteed publicity budget. Cover and title approval. Right now they see you as a potential gold mine, and if you agree to go along with their plans—''

"Will! Stop and listen to what I'm saying. I want to, but I can't. I can't do it!''

For a long, uncomfortable moment, her agent said nothing. When he finally spoke, his tone was bitter but resigned. "Is that your final decision?''

"Yes," she managed to say, all but choking on the words. "It is.''

"You're the boss." He paused. "If I were you, Anna, I'd consider getting some professional help with this problem. And it is a problem, even if you don't see it that way.''

He hung up and Anna was left with the dead receiver pressed to her ear. Struggling to keep ahold of the despair careening through her, she returned the phone to its base unit. She wasn't a fool. Along with a new publisher, she would be looking for a new agent as well.

Starting over. She would be starting over, after how hard she had worked. How she had struggled.

"Did he hang up on you?'' Dalton demanded, already knowing the answer, outraged. "I never liked him, Anna. And neither did Bill. He's an arrogant little prick.''

She tried to smile but failed miserably.

"I never told you this," Dalton continued, "but on several occasions he was quite rude to me on the phone." Her friend lowered his voice. "Not only is he an officious A-hole, but a homophobe as well. I'm certain of it.''

But he was a good agent, she thought. One well

respected in the publishing community. And one who knew how to sell books.

The shop door opened and a woman entered. Dalton glanced at her, then back at Anna. "Are you going to be all right?"

When she nodded, he gave her shoulders a quick squeeze, then hurried to help the customer.

The phone rang and she snatched it up, hoping it was Will, calling back to apologize. "The Perfect Rose."

"Anna, it's Ben Walker. But wait! Before you hang up, please just listen to me."

Anna curved her fingers around the portable phone, a part of her wanting to slam the phone in his ear just as Will had slammed it in hers. But having just been on the receiving end of that humiliating experience she couldn't do it. "Go ahead," she said. "But make it quick, I'm working."

"I'm sorry," he said. "For intruding on your life the way I did. It was inappropriate and insensitive. I knew how you would react but in my zeal to interview you, I forged ahead anyway. Please accept my apology."

She felt moderately appeased, but only moderately. "I prefer not to be reminded of the past. I've moved on."

"But you haven't, Anna. Don't you see that? If you're so afraid of the past you have to hide from it, it's not your past. It's your present."

Jaye had said almost the same thing to her. As had her father, the other day on the phone. And just a few minutes ago, her agent.

Get some professional help with this problem. And it is a problem, even if you don't see it that way.

Who better to help her than a doctor with a specialty in childhood trauma? Who more knowledgeable than a doctor writing a book on the subject?

Do it, Anna. What do you have left to lose?

"Tell me again," she murmured. "Why were you so eager to talk to me?"

"Just meet with me. I'll tell you about me, my practice, this project. No strings. If you're uncomfortable or simply not interested, I won't bother you again. I promise."

She heard the excitement in his voice; felt a corresponding excitement within herself. Still she hesitated. One moment became two became several. What *did* she have to lose? she wondered. She had already lost Jaye, her anonymity and her publishing career. What was left?

"Okay," she murmured, "I'll meet with you. How about tonight at five, the Café du Monde. First one to arrive gets a table."

14

Anna arrived at the Café du Monde early. Located on Jackson Square in the French Quarter, the Café du Monde had exactly one food item on its menu—beignets. That one item had made this unassuming little café a New Orleans legend. No tourist's visit to the Crescent City was complete without at least one stop for the decadent squares of fried dough. New Orleanians themselves were not immune to the call of the café and actually turned up their noses at beignets from any other source. After all, the best was the best and with perfection so close, why settle for less?

Anna took a seat outside despite the chill, choosing a table along the sidewalk facing St. Peter Street. She loved this time of day, the early-evening rush of businesspeople heading home, the subtle shift from light to dark, day to night, frenzied to unhurried.

Anna ordered a café au lait and sat back to wait, using the minutes to people watch. She scanned the faces that passed, noticing body language and expressions, catching bits and snatches of conversations, filing the information, the impressions away for a time when they would emerge in a scene or in one of her characters.

People both fascinated and frightened her. They were a constant source of joy, curiosity and bedevilment. Was that the way a psychologist thought of his patients? Anna wondered. Was that the way Dr. Walker thought?

She shivered suddenly, grateful for the arrival of her steaming mug of coffee. She curled her hands around the mug, admitting to herself that she was nervous. She had seen a number of shrinks in the years after her kidnapping. The last time she had been sixteen and an emotional wreck—depressed, wary and distrustful of others, constantly on edge. Her parents, their marriage in tatters, had forced her to go. She needed someone to talk to, they had insisted. Someone to share her deepest, darkest thoughts with. Someone who would understand and help Anna put her feelings into perspective.

But the woman hadn't understood. How could she have? The worst thing that she'd ever lived through, Anna had decided, was a bad hair day. The therapist had been condescending, her probing questions unsympathetic and intrusive.

Anna had been resentful, angry at her parents for forcing her to see the woman. When they had finally agreed to let her call it quits to the therapy, she had vowed she would never again subject herself to that kind of mental assault and battery.

Then what the hell was she doing here? Anna wondered. She glanced at her watch and saw that the doctor was ten minutes late already. Why not bolt? Just stand up and walk away?

Why not? By being late, he had given her the opportunity. She could leave and not even feel guilty about it. She grabbed her purse and dug out her wallet to pay for her coffee. She realized with a sense of shock that her hands were shaking.

"Sorry I'm late." Ben Walker came up from behind her and slipped into the chair across from hers. "I couldn't find my keys. I had them this morning, then they were gone. This morning," he continued, loosening his tie. "What a nightmare. The alarm never went off and I overslept. Which isn't surprising considering I was on the Internet doing research most of the night." He laughed. "I swear, it's a good thing I didn't go into teaching. I'd be a Disney cliché, the absentminded profess…"

His words trailed off as he took in her expression, the open wallet in her hands, the two dollars on the table beside her half-full coffee cup. His face fell. "How late am I?"

"Not too," she answered, feeling somewhat calmed by his self-deprecating manner. How could she be intimidated by such a self-proclaimed bumbler?

She pulled a deep breath in through her nose, feeling a little like a kid caught with her hand in the cookie jar. "Actually, I was having second thoughts about our meeting. My experiences with shrinks haven't been all that great."

"You have friends who are shrinks?"

She drew her eyebrows together. "I don't follow. What does that—"

"So, you do?"

"No, but—"

"How about family members? A boyfriend?" She answered in the negative again and he arched his eyebrows. "Oh, you mean you've had a doctor-patient relationship with a shrink?"

"Yes, several." She tilted her chin up slightly. "When I was much younger."

"After the kidnapping?"

"That should be pretty obvious." Her chin inched up another millimeter. "After the kidnapping, yes."

The waiter arrived. Ben ordered a café au lait and plate of beignets, then turned back to her, never missing a beat. "That's not the kind of relationship I'm proposing. Not at all."

"No?" She arched an eyebrow. "Exactly what sort of relationship are you proposing?"

"Author and author. Interviewer and interviewee. Maybe, eventually and if I'm lucky, friend and friend."

A smile tugged at the corners of her mouth, and Anna realized with a sense of shock that she liked him. She realized, too, that all thoughts of leaving had disappeared. She closed her wallet and returned it to her purse. "You're good."

He laughed, thanked her and leaned forward, expression earnest. "But I mean it. Look, Anna, I'm not trying to head-shrink you. I'm hoping you will simply and honestly talk to me about your life, your feelings, the choices you've made and why."

"I assure you," she murmured dryly, "that my life story will make anything but fascinating reading."

"You're wrong about that. To me, it will be. To the people who pick up this book, it will be." He sobered. "Let me tell you a little about myself and my practice, then maybe you'll see why I'm so interested in interviewing you."

He began by telling her about himself, his upbringing and schooling. He was an only child, raised by a single mother—whom he adored. He had been the result of a brief dalliance with a man his mother refused to speak of, and other than one uncle, he'd had no family. He remembered little of his early childhood other than that they had moved around a good bit.

"Without friends and much family, it was a lonely childhood. Then I started school. I loved it. Excelled at it. Learning and books became my constant companions. It didn't even matter if I had to change schools, because I never had to leave behind the opportunity to learn."

Anna propped her chin on her fist, totally into his story, the sound of his voice melodic and soothing. "Why psychology?" she asked.

"I wanted to help people but I can't stand the sight of blood." He grinned. "That's only partly true, however. People fascinate me. Why they do what they do. What makes them tick. How events can profoundly affect a person's life."

She had to admit, as a writer, she was fascinated with the same things. That fascination translated into fully rounded characters imbued with both strengths and weaknesses, characters whose sometimes tragic pasts had far-reaching present-day consequences. "Why childhood trauma?"

"That's where it all begins, isn't it? Our childhoods. Those first, formative years that in essence influence every year that comes after." He took a swallow of his coffee. "In my first year of practice, I consulted on a fascinating case. The woman suffered from disassociative identity disorder—"

"What?"

"Disassociative identity disorder, or DID. It's the new name for multiple personality disorder."

Anna thought for a moment, trying to recall what she knew about the disorder, realizing she knew little. She told him so.

His mouth thinned. "DID is the result of repeated horrific and sadistic abuse in early childhood. In an attempt to protect itself from the unthinkable and unendurable, the psyche splits, forming a whole new personality, one equipped to handle whatever the situation."

He paused. "In the case I consulted on, the woman had eighteen separate and distinct personalities and each performed a specific function within the system."

Silence fell between them. Anna searched for a quick comeback but came up empty. She picked up her coffee and drained the last of the beverage, gaze focused on the sprinkling of powdered sugar on the Formica tabletop in front of her.

After a moment, she cleared her throat and looked up.

And found Ben's gaze on her deformed hand, his

expression strange. She stiffened and dropped her hands to her lap. "You know who I am, so you know I wasn't born with a four-fingered hand." He didn't reply and she cleared her throat again. "Ben?"

He shuddered, blinked and met her eyes. "What?"

"My hand. You were staring."

He looked surprised. Then embarrassed. "Was I? I'm sorry, I didn't realize. I get started talking about my work and sometimes I...get lost in my own thoughts. It's that absentminded-professor thing again. I really am sorry."

She waved the apology off. "It's all right. I've pretty much learned to live with it."

"With your deformity? Or with people staring?"

"Truthfully? Living with four fingers is a lot easier than dealing with people's curiosity."

"You mean their rudeness."

"Sometimes, yes."

They both relaxed and Ben talked more, about that DID case and others he'd read about. Anna propped her chin on her fist as she listened, hanging on to every word.

"I can see why you're so interested in the subject," she murmured after a moment. "It's fascinating."

"It would make good material for one of your novels."

"Are you a mind reader?" She shook her head, a smile tugging at her mouth. "I was just thinking the same thing."

"I tell you what, you help me with my book, I'll help you with one of yours."

She opened her mouth to agree—and to ask him

for help with her own personal problem—but found herself asking him about his practice instead. As he answered, she only half listened, using the moments to try to figure out why she had hesitated. She liked him. He was funny and smart. Down-to-earth and straightforward in a way she hadn't expected. She believed in what he was doing, that it could help others. She believed that if she asked, he could help her.

So why couldn't she bring herself to agree to be interviewed?

"Something's holding you back?"

"Yes."

"If this will help you decide, I hope my book will not only educate the public of the far-reaching effects of child abuse but also help heal adult survivors of child abuse. I'm a great believer in the curative power of knowledge. Knowledge brings understanding and acceptance, only then can healing begin."

"Physician heal thyself?"

"In a way." He leaned forward, expression earnest. "Actually, there is something to that. We all have the power to heal ourselves, especially in the area of mental illness. We just need help accessing that power."

"And that's where you, the trained professional, come in?"

"Exactly. And self-help books."

"Like yours."

"Exactly." He fiddled with his napkin. "Tell me what I can say to sway you in my favor."

She looked away for a moment, then back at him. "I'm not sure there's anything you can say. I don't talk about my past much. I don't like to think about it.''

"But you dream about it, Anna? I know you do. It's right there. At the edge of your consciousness, constantly poking at you. Whispering in your ear, influencing your every move. That's a dangerous place for it to be. It's an unhappy one.''

She stared at him, stunned. Uncomfortable. ''I could tell you that wasn't true.''

"But you won't. Because you're an honest person.''

She laughed suddenly, surprising herself. ''Know-it-all.''

"What can I say? I'm a smart guy.'' A dimple appeared beside his mouth. ''Cute, too. In a bookish sort of way.''

He was cute, she decided. Smart and funny. She liked intellectual men. Especially ones with a sense of humor.

Ben Walker was the kind of guy she enjoyed spending time with.

She dropped her hands to her lap. ''I'm still a little confused about how you came to find me.''

"My friend at the BBBSA—''

"No, before that. You just tuned into the E! special and...what?''

Ben glanced down at his hands, then back up at her. ''I had a copy of *Killing Me Softly* on my desk and things just fell into place.'' He laced his fingers together. ''I've been interested in your story since I was a kid and it occurred to me while I was watching the show, that the inclusion of your story in my book would be perfect. Your trauma was unique, unlike anything else I presently have.''

''And where else could you find a kidnapped Hollywood princess?''

His expression grew solemn. ''Most kidnapped kids never return home, Anna. You're an exception.''

Timmy hadn't made it home. A lump formed in her throat. *She'd been the lucky one.*

''What do you say? It'll be painless, I promise.''

She doubted that. Just thinking about it had her stomach in knots. ''I'll think about it. I really will.''

He looked let down. ''Often it's the first step that's the hardest. Not to push you, of course.''

She smiled, liking him more with each passing minute. ''I know. But I do need a little time. I hope you're not too disappointed.''

''I'm a big boy, I can handle it.''

They stood and exited the café. ''I'm going this way,'' she said, pointing in the direction of St. Louis Cathedral. ''How about you?''

''I'm parked at Jax Brewery.''

''Then this is goodbye.'' She stuffed her hands into her pockets and shivered as the cold wind wrapped around her legs.

''It is. For now.'' He bent and brushed his lips against her cheek. ''I enjoyed talking, Anna. Call me.''

Without waiting for her reply, he turned and walked away.

15

Ben lay on his bed, alone in the dark. He breathed slowly and deeply through his nose, the warm compress across his forehead cooling quickly. Too quickly.

The headache that had dogged his day had returned during his meeting with Anna, growing in intensity as their minutes together had ticked past. Still, it hadn't been too bad until he'd reached his car.

He had managed to unlock the car door and fall into the vehicle. How he had made it home, he didn't know. But he had. Obviously, for here he was.

Ben closed his eyes, the pill the doctor prescribed bringing a whisper of sweet, merciful relief. He thought of Anna, of their meeting, of the way it had ended. She had watched him walk away. He had been intensely aware of her gaze on his back and had given in to the urge and had glanced around—to find her staring after him, a hand to the cheek he'd kissed, her expression both surprised and pleased. Or so he had wanted to believe.

Ben reviewed their conversation, both the highs and

the lows. She had been openly interested in his work. Her enthusiasm had been contagious and he had found himself opening up, sharing more than he usually did. They'd gotten along well, he thought.

His self-satisfaction evaporated. Then she had caught him staring at her deformed hand. It had been upsetting to her, though she had handled it well. He had been truthful with her when he'd said he hadn't even realized he was doing it. That he had blanked out.

All his life he had suffered from lost moments like those. And like his chronic headaches, those moments had become more frequent in the past months. Concerned, he had discussed both with his physician, who had ordered a battery of tests, including a CAT scan and MRI.

The tests had turned up nothing abnormal, much to Ben's relief. He had feared the worst, of course.

His doctor had questioned Ben at length about his eating and drinking habits and also the stress in his life, of which he'd had plenty this past year, what with his mother's rapidly disintegrating condition and the changes in his life that had occurred because of it.

In the end, the physician had recommended that Ben lay off caffeine and suggested meditation, yoga or another exercise regime as a way to reduce stress. Ben had followed the doctor's orders and had experienced an improvement in his condition. But only a slight one.

Ben dragged his attention away from that disconcerting thought, focusing on another, equally disquieting: Anna hadn't agreed to be included in his book. He had pushed too hard. Had scared her off.

He hadn't been truthful with her.

The pressure in his skull intensified and Ben groaned. He had always gone by the adage that honesty was the best policy; as a therapist he saw firsthand the destruction dishonesty wrought in people's lives and relationships, and steered his patients toward total emotional honesty.

So why hadn't he told Anna the truth about how he had come to be watching E! that Saturday afternoon? Instead, he had led her to believe it had been a coincidence, that he had already been a fan of her novels.

He had been afraid if he told her the truth, she would bolt.

She had bolted anyway.

If his head didn't hurt so bad, he would kick himself for being such a jerk. He liked her. She was smart, with a subtle sense of humor and an emotional integrity he didn't see in many people these days. She deserved his honesty.

And if he was completely honest with himself, he liked her in a way that had nothing to do with his book.

Suddenly, miraculously, his pain was gone. Ben made a sound of surprise and relief, plucked the compress from his forehead and sat up. He smiled, then laughed, feeling as if he had once again faced the devil—and fought him off.

He would call Anna, Ben decided. He would ask

her to dinner and over a sumptuous, five-course meal come clean: about the package that had been left for him and his feelings.

Where they went from there remained to be seen.

16

After leaving the Café du Monde, Anna had gone to mass at the cathedral. The doors had been open, the church bells ringing, and on a whim she had slipped inside and let the welcoming arms of the church enfold her.

The familiar ritual had both reassured her and lent a clarity to her thoughts. Now she left feeling centered. Warmed and ready to face whatever new curve life threw her.

Jaye would come around. She would find a new publisher. A new agent. In the end, nothing would come of the show on E! except an increased feeling of independence.

Despite the chill, Anna took a roundabout route home. She wandered past familiar shops and restaurants, ducking down residential side streets, each as recognizable to her as the back of her hand. Once she reached her apartment, her thoughts would be interrupted. There'd be dinner to prepare, the answering machine to check, mail to sift through.

For now, these few minutes, she didn't want to

think of anything but Ben. Their meeting. She had liked him. Enjoyed his company. Been fascinated by his work, the things he'd had to say about it.

She brought a hand to her cheek, to the spot where he'd brushed his mouth against her skin. It had been a bold move. Romantic. The kind of gesture meant to steal a woman's breath. To force intimacy.

In those ways, it had worked. She had experienced a tickle of excitement, a small but heady rush of pleasure. Of *what if?*

But it had taken her aback as well. Because it had seemed so out of character for the man she thought Ben Walker to be.

Anna frowned. She had only just met him, shared no more than an hour of conversation, that hardly made her an expert on his character. Still, in some strange way, she felt as if she *did* know him.

Anna shivered and huddled deeper into her coat. Fully dark now, the temperature had begun to careen toward the expected low of thirty-eight. Not too terribly cold until factoring in the humidity. The wet cold seeped through outer garments, clothes and skin, going clear to the bone.

Enough mooning, she decided, shivering again. Time to go home.

Less than ten minutes later, Anna stepped into her apartment. She tossed her mail on the small entryway table, slipped out of her coat and hung it up. Still chilled, she hurried to the kitchen to fix a cup of hot tea, pausing at the thermostat to kick up the heat a notch.

While waiting for the water to boil, she listened to

her messages. Her mother had phoned—she had found the videographer's business card, and just as she had recalled, he had one of those silly names: Peter Peters. Dalton had called as well, wondering how her meeting with Ben had gone; her dentist's office had left a reminder about her appointment the following day.

The last message was from Jaye's foster mother, requesting that Anna call. Surprised, Anna did so immediately.

The woman picked up on the second ring. "Fran, Anna North. You called?"

"Yes," the woman said, sounding frazzled. "I was wondering, is Jaye with you?"

"I haven't seen or spoken to her." Anna frowned. "Didn't she come home from school?"

"No. I wasn't concerned at first, she sometimes stops at a friend's or goes to the library. But she knows the rules, unless she has permission to stay out, she's due home at five-thirty for supper."

Anna glanced at her watch. It was nearly eight and dark already.

"I'm sure she simply went to a friend's after school and lost track of time," Fran said, "but as her legal guardian, it's my responsibility to know where she is."

Anna frowned. *Her legal responsibility. Not because she cared. Or was truly concerned.*

Anna scolded herself for her thoughts. Fran and Bob Clausen had been good to Jaye.

"Do you have any idea who she might be with?" the woman asked. "I'm afraid I'm at a loss."

"I tell you what," Anna offered, "I'll call around and see if I can locate her. I'll call you back."

Ten minutes later, Anna had eliminated all the possibilities. She'd talked to Jennifer, Tiffany, Carol and Sarah—Jaye's closest friends. None had seen her, not in school or after, a fact that deeply worried Anna.

"Did I tell you about the creep who was following me?"

At the memory, a flicker of panic burst to life inside her. Anna shook her head and dialed Fran in the hope that Jaye had returned. She had not and Anna filled the woman in on what she had learned and her plan to check out all Jaye's favorite hangouts.

"Did Jaye tell you she was followed home from school the other day?"

For a moment the other woman was silent. "No," she said finally, "this is the first I'm hearing about it."

"Jaye wasn't overly concerned but now—"

"Let's not jump to conclusions, Anna. She'll probably walk through the door any moment."

Anna hoped so. After promising to keep in touch, she grabbed her purse and car keys and headed out.

At ten-thirty she gave up. Not because she was tired, but because she was flat out of ideas. She had tried the arcade and Rock 'n Bowl, two CC's coffeehouses and even the library—all the places Jaye frequented either alone or with her friends. Nobody had seen her all day. *Fourteen hours.* Too long for a fifteen-year-old to be unaccounted for. Too much could happen to a teenage girl in that amount of time. Most of it bad.

Panicking in earnest now, Anna hung a left on Carrollton Avenue, heading toward the Clausens'. Surely Jaye had arrived home by now. Safe and sound, pouting because the Clausens had administered an appropriate punishment. Sure, Anna thought. Jaye had been in some sort of pique and decided to skip school. Maybe her friends had even been in on it and had been covering for her.

Though Jaye hadn't behaved in such an irresponsible fashion in a long while, it wasn't out of the realm of possibility. She was a teenager, after all.

Fran Clausen opened the door before Anna knocked. Her face fell. "You didn't find her, did you?"

Anna shook her head. "I'd hoped she would have shown up here by now."

"She hasn't," Bob Clausen said from the doorway to her right, his voice gruff. "And she won't either."

Anna turned to face him. He was a big man, well over six feet, with rough, uneven features. "Excuse me?"

"She's run off."

Anna made a sound of dismay and shifted her gaze to the other woman. "Fran, has something happened that I don't know about?"

The woman opened her mouth; her husband answered for her. "Surely you're not surprised? She's done it before."

"But she's grown up so much since then. She's taken a long look at herself and what she wants out of life. She knows that running away isn't going to get it for her."

Anna looked from the wife to the husband. "Did Fran tell you that a man followed Jaye home from school?"

He rolled his eyes. "That sounds like nonsense to me. If she had really been followed, she would have told us about it."

"I didn't believe she had run away at first either," Fran murmured. "But after you talked to her friends and learned she hadn't been to school..."

Bob Clausen snorted with disgust. "A cat can't change its spots. Once a self-absorbed, selfish little snot, always one."

Anna stiffened, cheeks burning. "Jaye's neither self-absorbed nor selfish, thank you very much."

"Bob didn't mean that." The other woman wrung her hands. "But you didn't live with her, Anna. She was very strong-willed, oftentimes defiant. When she made up her mind about something, she did it, consequences be damned."

Anna held on to her temper, but just barely. "You have the kind of childhood Jaye had, you sure as hell better be strong-willed. If you're not, you don't make it. Period."

The Clausens exchanged glances. Bob opened his mouth to retort, then snapped it shut. Without a word, he turned on his heel and returned to the den and the television show he had been watching.

Fran watched him go, then turned back to Anna. "We'll call you if she shows up or...or if we hear anything."

In other words, scram. Anna decided she would do just that—after she did a little more digging. Something about this whole thing just didn't feel right to her. It didn't make sense.

"Would you mind if I took a peek at Jaye's room?" she asked.

"Her room?" Fran glanced toward the den, though Anna was uncertain if she was worried that her husband was listening or if she was looking for his moral support. "Why?"

"I guess I just want to…see for myself that she's gone." She lowered her voice. "Please, Fran. It would really mean a lot to me."

The other woman hesitated a moment, then relented. "All right. I suppose it won't hurt."

Fran led the way, waiting outside in the hallway while Anna went into Jaye's room. Like so many teenagers' private domains, this one looked like a small hurricane had struck.

Anna picked her way to the center of the room and stopped, emotion overwhelming her. It smelled like Jaye, like the light, girlish perfume she favored. Across the chair in the corner was the tangerine-colored sweater Jaye had worn the last time they'd gotten together, on her nightstand sat three empty Diet Coke cans and a stack of CDs. Anna crossed to them and flipped through the pile, a lump in her throat. Anna recognized several as Jaye's favorites. If she had run away, why hadn't she taken any of them? Jaye owned a portable CD player; she rarely went anywhere without it.

Anywhere but school. Personal CD players had been outlawed at the beginning of the term. Jaye had been incensed and had written an outraged letter to the school administration.

Anna glanced at the floor. There at the foot of the bed lay a library book, three bright-colored scrunchies, a candy-bar wrapper and the Dr. Marten shoes she'd used her own money to buy.

She loved those Docs. She had saved up four months to get them, gone without all luxuries, even the Mochasippis she claimed she couldn't live without.

Anna swallowed hard and moved her gaze over the room and its contents, searching for something that would convince and reassure her. Or an irrefutable something that would send her into a total panic.

She found it tucked under Jaye's mattress: a slim, tin box full of mementos. Jaye's mother's wedding ring. A photograph of her mother as well as a snapshot of the woman holding baby Jaye in her arms. Jaye's birth certificate and the two poems she had written last year that had been published in her school's annual literary magazine.

A picture of the two of them, pink-cheeked and smiling, arms around each other's shoulders.

Anna picked the photo up, tears pricking the back of her eyes. She remembered the day this had been taken, remembered it clearly. It had been shortly after she and Jaye had really become friends, after the last of Jaye's walls had come tumbling down. The spring day had been beautiful, bright and sweet and kissed by the heat of the sun. They had gone to the zoo and spent the day laughing at the animals' randy springtime antics, eating junk food and simply enjoying each other's company.

Aching at the memory, Anna carefully laid the snapshot back in the box. *No way Jaye would have willingly left all these things behind. They represented everything about her past that she wanted to remember.*

With the realization, fear speared through her. Real and icy cold. *If Jaye hadn't run away, where was she at ten-thirty on a school night?*

Anna fitted the lid back onto the box, scooped it up and carried it out to where Fran Clausen waited. "Did you see this?" she asked the woman.

"That?" She looked at the box, her expression uneasy. "What is it?"

"Jaye's memento box." Anna removed the lid and showed the woman the box's contents. "It was tucked under her mattress."

Fran made a fluttery, nervous gesture. "So?"

"So, no way would Jaye have knowingly left these things behind. She didn't run away, Fran. Something's happened to her."

The woman paled. "I find it hard to believe—"

"Did she have a bag with her this morning?"

"Just her book bag, but—"

"I didn't see any of her textbooks in her room. Why would she run away and take her textbooks but leave this? If she had planned to run away, wouldn't she have filled her book bag with the things she would need, clothes and shoes, her toothbrush, her mementos? Come on, Fran, she wouldn't run away with *nothing*. She wouldn't."

"For God's sake!" Bob Clausen roared, stepping into the hallway. "Stop badgering my wife!"

Anna faced him, heart hammering. "I'm not trying to badger her. I just want her to see—"

"Accept the fact that Jaye's gone and leave us be."

"Have you talked to Paula?" Anna asked, referring to Paula Perez, Jaye's social worker. "I think she needs to be told Jaye's—"

"We've already talked to her. She thinks Jaye's run away. In fact, she came to that conclusion before we did. If Jaye's not home by midnight, Paula's reporting her missing to the authorities."

"But she didn't know about this," Anna said, motioning to the box of keepsakes. "She couldn't have because you didn't even know."

"Call and tell her. I don't give a flip."

"Yes," Anna said softly as he began to turn away. "It does seem as if you don't give a flip."

Bob Clausen froze. He turned slowly to face her. "What did you say?"

Anna hiked up her chin, hiding how intimidated she felt. Bob was built like a mountain and right now he looked as if he would enjoy throttling her.

"You're Jaye's foster parents. I find it...odd that you're not more concerned about her."

His face mottled. "How dare you waltz in here and lecture us! How dare you suggest—"

"Bob," his wife begged. "Please."

He ignored her and took a threatening step toward Anna. "Don't you get it? *We've* been through this before. You haven't. Girls like Jaye don't hang around. The minute something doesn't go their way, they're history. They leave without a word to the people who cared for them. Period.''

He took another step toward Anna; she instinctively backed up. "I'd like you to leave now."

Anna looked beseechingly at the other woman. "Please, Fran...I know Jaye. She's my friend and...she wouldn't do this. I know it."

The woman backed away, expression closed. "If we hear anything from her, we'll call you."

"Thank you." Anna tightened her grip on Jaye's keepsake box, unwilling to let it go—although she wasn't quite sure why. "May I keep this for her?"

"In this situation we're supposed to turn all of Jaye's belongings over to Social Services."

Anna swallowed hard. That sounded so ominous. So final. As if they were discussing the belongings of someone who had passed. "Please. I'll make sure Paula gets it. I promise I will."

The woman hesitated a moment more, then agreed. The Clausens walked Anna to the door, standing guard and watching as she walked away, box clutched to her chest. When Anna reached her car she glanced back to see Fran and her husband exchanging furtive glances.

In that moment, Anna was filled with dread. It stole her ability to move or think; in that moment, she was incapable even of unlocking her car and climbing inside.

As she stood there frozen, gaze fixed on the couple, a single question kept playing in her head: What had happened to Jaye?

17

Jaye awakened with a groan. Her head and back ached and her mouth felt dry and dirty, like the inside of a ditch after a month with no rain. She moaned and rolled onto her side. A sour smell filled her head and she opened her eyes.

And remembered. Walking to the bus stop. Looking over her shoulder for the old pervert. Grinning because she had given him the slip. Or so she had thought. In the next moment she had found herself being dragged behind an azalea hedge before something was forced over her nose and mouth. She remembered her terror. The silent scream that sounded in her head.

Her world going black.

Jaye scrambled into a sitting position, heart racing, breath coming in small gasps. She darted her gaze around the dimly lit room, seeing at once that she was alone.

Jaye breathed deeply through her nose to calm herself, her survivor instincts kicking in. *Stay cool. Figure it out.*

She was sitting on a foldout cot. The mattress was bare, soiled from use. Jaye pressed her lips together to keep them from trembling. The only other piece of furniture in the room was a folding lawn chair, one of those flimsy aluminum and nylon web ones. Located against the far left wall was a single sink and commode. Beside the toilet sat a roll of toilet paper, on the sink a new toothbrush, tube of toothpaste and a towel.

Jaye choked back a sound of despair and shifted her gaze. The plaster walls were cracked, what was left of the faded wallpaper water-stained and peeling. The room's one window had been boarded over, slivers of dim light peeked around the edges of the crudely nailed one-by-fours. Directly across the room from the window lay the door.

Jaye scooted off the cot and tiptoed to the door. She reached cautiously for the knob. Her hand shook. She remembered a horror flick she had seen a couple of weeks before. In it a girl in a similar position had tried to escape; as her fingers had closed over the knob, it had become a writhing snake.

That had been a movie. This nightmare was for real. And she had to find a way out.

Swallowing hard, Jaye grasped the knob. It was cool, smooth and unyielding against her palm, and she let out a breath she hadn't realized she was holding. Saying a silent prayer, Jaye twisted it.

The knob didn't budge. Tears flooded her eyes and she blinked them back, scolding herself for hoping for a miracle. What kind of kidnapper would have left the door unlocked? The criminal equivalent of Dopey?

She would just have to find another way out, the hard way. She lowered her gaze, noticing what she hadn't before: that one of the door's panels had been replaced with a pet door.

Jaye knelt and examined it. It looked to be newly installed, unmarred by even one scuff mark. She pushed against the panel, finding it latched from the outside. Jaye pressed harder, felt it begin to give, then drew back, frustrated. She could kick it open, but she couldn't fit through the opening, so what was the point?

She stood and turned to face the boarded-over window. She crossed to it and pressed her face close to the cracks between the boards, hoping to get an idea of where she was. She saw immediately that it was night, that the light seeping around the edges of the boards was artificial, provided by a nearby street lamp. She couldn't place anything else.

But she could hear—the muffled sound of traffic and music, of people talking.

People! Someone who would hear her call out and come looking. Or contact the police.

"Help!" she called, excited. She pounded on the boards. She screamed again and again, pausing between cries to listen. The conversations from somewhere beyond her prison didn't change tempo. No one came looking for her. No one answered her cries for help.

They couldn't hear her. They were too far away.

Frantic now, she turned and raced to the door and began to pound, kick and scream. Her voice grew hoarse, her hands sore and arms weak. Still she cried out, until her pleas became feeble mewls of despair.

Finally, exhausted, she sank to the floor and sobbed.

18

Friday, January 19
The French Quarter

Her name had been Evelyn Parker. She'd been beautiful, well liked, fun-loving. A regular of the downtown club scene. She'd worked as a hygienist for an uptown dentist and had resided in the area of the city called the Bywater.

She had died on her twenty-fourth birthday.

"Hell of a thing, getting whacked on your birthday, eh, Malone?" This came from Sam Tardo, one of the evidence collection team. "And don't touch anything, we haven't done the body yet."

Quentin grunted in response to the other officer and squatted beside Evelyn Parker. He moved his gaze over the victim, looking for something that might have been missed: a button or scrap of paper, spots of blood, a footprint.

"You thinking what I'm thinking?" Terry asked, stooping to get a better look.

Nancy Kent. "Yeah." Quentin frowned. Evelyn Parker was a beautiful strawberry blonde; she had been out clubbing the night of her death. It looked as if she had been raped, then suffocated. And like

Nancy Kent, Evelyn Parker had been found in an alley behind a club.

"Captain's going to be pissed." Johnson rolled his shoulders. "Like it's our fault or something."

"Who found her?" Quentin asked.

"Jogger."

Quentin looked up, frowning. "What's a jogger doing in an alley?"

"Chick runs early. Brings her golden retriever along. For protection, she says. Anyway, at the alley entrance the dog goes nuts. She decides to check it out and gets more than she bargained for."

"Walden take her statement?"

"Yeah." Johnson jerked his thumb in the direction of the club. "He's with the bar owner now. So, where've you guys been? Me and Walden practically have this thing solved already."

"Kiss my ass, Sleeping Beauty." Terry made a sound of disgust. "Didn't you hear? While you and Walden were snug in your beds, me and Malone were in the Desire. Drug-related triple homicide."

A downtown housing project, the Desire was the most dangerous piece of real estate in New Orleans. Life expectancy for a cop who wandered in alone was slim to none. Life expectancy for the folks who lived there wasn't much better.

"Lucky you." The other officer shrugged deeper into his coat. "I'll take a French Quarter alley over the Desire any day."

Walden called to his partner from the bar doorway. Johnson excused himself, and Quentin returned his attention to the victim. Unlike Kent, this woman had put up a good fight. There were contusions around her face, neck and chest. She had been wearing skintight jeans and from the looks of them and the twisted position of her body, the perp had had a hard time holding her down and getting them off. They were bunched around her knees; her panties torn away.

Quentin glanced at Terry to comment on the jeans, but swallowed the words, noticing for the first time how tired his friend looked. How bloodshot his eyes were. How quiet he had been.

Quentin frowned. He and his partner had been at the Desire for the past few hours, before that Quentin had been home, sleeping. Where, he wondered, had his partner been? "You okay?" Quentin asked.

"As well as can be expected with no home to go to and no sleep." He rubbed his eyes and swore. "I'm getting damn sick of this shit."

The evidence team moved in and they stood to give them room to work. There wasn't much left for them to do here anyway. Next step was sorting through the physical evidence, immersing themselves in Evelyn Parker's life and the night of her death.

Quentin drew his eyebrows together. He looked at Terry. "I don't think she was raped, Ter. No way could this perp have penetrated her with those jeans around her knees. So unless he took the time to try to get her jeans back up, I think he gave up and just killed her."

"Goodbye DNA."

"Exactly." They started out of the alley. "Which will make the likelihood of linking the cases with physical evidence a lot more difficult."

"Near impossible." For a moment, Terry was silent. "Which doesn't help me out." He swore. "I hope they don't try to pin this shit on me."

Quentin stopped and looked at his partner. "Why would they?"

"Because of Nancy Kent, of course."

"But you were cleared."

Terry shoved his hands into his jacket pockets, mouth twisting with bitterness. "Yeah, but this changes everything. They're going to revisit every suspect from the original homicide. You know that. Expect us to be called in the minute we hit headquarters. Shit."

Quentin hoped his partner was wrong, but admitted he probably wasn't. "When the captain asks where you were last night, what are you going to tell her, Ter?"

"The truth. That I was at my crappy-ass apartment. Alone and nursing a bourbon. Before that, I was with Penny."

They exited the alley and angled toward their vehicles, parked side by side along the curb. "Any progress convincing her to let you move back in?"

"Move back in?" Terry laughed, the sound bitter. "What? And ruin her good time? Life's a party for her. She's fucking one guy after another, apparently making up for time lost married to me."

It wasn't just his partner's ugly words that stunned Quentin, but their tone as well. The venom behind them. "No way," Quentin said softly, thinking of his friend's wife. Quentin couldn't picture the woman he knew her to be—a devoted wife and conscientious mother—sleeping around.

"Hell of a thing," Terry said, all but spitting the words. "She won't let me, her husband, near her, but she'll share her goodies with every Tom, Dick or Harry who comes around."

"You got any proof, Ter? That sure doesn't sound like the Penny I know."

"I've got proof all right. Alex told me she's been out a lot at night, that Grandma Stockwell's been sitting for them. He said it's really late when she gets home."

"That's it?" Quentin unlocked his car door. "That's your proof? Alex, who's six? Pretty flimsy, Detective."

"Why else would she be out at night? What else would keep her out so late?" He balled his hands into fists. "She's my wife, goddammit! She belongs at home with our kids."

"She could be visiting with a girlfriend. Or at the show. You don't know for sure that she's with other men."

"I know. I just do." Terry swung to face Quentin. "You've got to talk to her, Malone. She likes you. She respects your opinion." His friend's voice took on a desperate edge. "Please, talk to her. Convince her to take me back."

When Quentin hesitated, Terry took a step toward him, expression pleading. "You've got to help me out, buddy. You've got to make her see it's the right thing to do. The best thing for the kids." He glanced over his shoulder, then back at Quentin. "I gotta be honest, I don't know how much longer I can go on this way.''

''All right,'' Quentin said. ''Against my better judgment, I'll do it.''

19

Friday, January 19
Central Business District

Twenty-four hours passed with no word from Jaye. With each hour, Anna grew more certain that Jaye had not run away. And more certain that the Clausens were not the caring, concerned foster parents she had once hoped them to be. In fact, as Anna had replayed her conversation with the couple in her head and had recalled their expressions, tones of voice and body language, she had become convinced that they were hiding something.

What she was thinking frightened her to the core.

Desperate, Anna had decided to pay a visit to Paula Perez, Jaye's caseworker. Anna poked her head through the doorway of the woman's windowless, closet-size cubicle. "Knock, knock."

The woman looked up and smiled. "Anna, come in."

"The receptionist wasn't at her desk, so I came on back. Is this a good time?"

Paula motioned the top of her desk—every available inch was covered with case files, memos, textbooks and court reports. "Here at Social Services there's no such thing as a good time. Or a bad one. Have a seat."

Anna did as the woman invited, clutching Jaye's memento box to her chest. "I came to talk about Jaye."

"I figured. There's been no word yet, Anna."

"I know." Anna lowered her gaze to the box, then returned it to the social worker. "I wanted you to see this. It's Jaye's."

She handed it over. The other woman opened the container and leafed through its contents. After a moment, she looked back up at Anna. "How did you get this?"

"From the Clausens, the night Jaye disappeared."

"I'll have to keep it. As a ward of the state—"

"I know. But I was afraid…" She drew in a deep breath. "I was afraid if I didn't take the box, it might disappear."

Paula drew her eyebrows together. "I don't understand."

"The contents of that box are proof Jaye didn't run away."

"We went over this on the phone, Anna. I know you don't want to accept—"

"She wouldn't leave these things behind, Paula. She wouldn't! They represent her history. They're all she has of her past."

"Jaye's a smart girl, Anna. She knows that anything she leaves behind gets sent to us for safekeeping. She also knows we have no time limit on storage of her things. She shows up for them ten years from now, and they're here for her."

Undaunted by that logic, Anna tried another tack. "If Jaye had planned to run away, why not fill her book bag with food and clothes? Why pack it with textbooks? Why leave her music behind? It doesn't make sense."

"Fran and Bob called just this morning. Seems quite a number of food items are missing from their pantry.

"So they say."

Paula stiffened, her cheeks growing red. "What's that supposed to mean, Anna?"

"It means, maybe Fran and Bob aren't telling the whole truth. Something's fishy about—"

"For God's sake!" Paula stood and glared down at Anna. "These are nice people. People who have been foster parents for nearly twenty years. They are very highly thought of by everyone, including me. How dare you come in here and suggest them guilty of some sort of…criminal activity."

Anna got to her feet. "All I ask is that you dig a little deeper into Jaye's disappearance. Question the Clausens more thoroughly, call the police—"

"I have contacted the police, I reported Jaye missing, just as I'm required to by law."

"I know Jaye, Paula. She wouldn't do this. She wouldn't. Something's happened to her." Anna leaned forward. "She told me a man followed her home from school. Maybe if you told the police—"

"Fran passed that information to me and I passed it to the authorities." The woman let out a tight-sounding breath. "You may not know Jaye as well as you think you do. She's a complex child, one capable of unexpected and troubling behavior. That may be difficult for you to hear, but it's true."

"I know about her past. That she's run away a half-dozen times. That she attacked one of her teachers. That she tried to take her own life. But she's grown so much in the past two years. Emotionally. Spiritual—"

The social worker held up a hand, stopping her. "Before you say another word, Anna, I want you to ask yourself how much your own guilty conscience is contributing to your refusal to accept that Jaye's run away."

"My guilty conscience?" she repeated. "What do I have to feel—"

"I understand you two fought recently. That she felt you betrayed her. That by keeping the truth about your past from her, you lied to her."

"That has nothing to do with this."

"Doesn't it? Have you considered that she ran specifically because you hurt her? Just as she ran so many other times in her life? That the emotional growth you saw in her, growth based on trust, was shattered by what she perceived as you lying to her?"

A denial raced to Anna's lips, choked back by the lump of tears that formed in her throat. "I didn't mean to hurt her," she finally managed to say. "I tried to explain about my past and why I kept it from her."

"I know," Paula said softly. "I understand. But I'm not a hurting teenager who's been betrayed by everyone she ever loved and trusted."

Guilt overwhelmed her. As did regret. And despair.

"I didn't mean to hurt her," she said again. "I love Jaye."

The social worker's expression softened. She picked up the box and held it out to Anna. "Keep it for now. I think she would like you to be the one holding it for her."

Anna took the box, turned and walked away. As she left the building, Anna prayed that Jaye was all right. Safe and warm. She prayed that she really had run away and that she would come to her senses and return home soon.

20

Friday, January 19
Seventh District Station

Quentin spotted Anna North the moment he entered the precinct. She stood across the crowded room from him, a slim box clutched to her chest. Her face was in profile, her stance and what he could see of her expression conveyed unease, which was not unusual as few civilians visited the cops under happy circumstances.

He tilted his head, studying her. What was it about Anna North that drew his gaze as if she were a burst of color in a black-and-white day? Sure, she was a looker. But there were probably a half-dozen equally gorgeous women in the room, and his gaze hadn't been drawn to them.

Nor was it her clothes, nothing more outstanding than a brilliant blue sweater, black jeans and deep brown leather jacket. Nor even her red hair, as bright and shiny as a new penny.

So what was it?

A sudden smile tugged at the corners of his mouth. It had been obvious at their last meeting that Anna North had not been impressed with his detecting skills. She certainly wouldn't be happy to be paired with him again.

He liked nothing quite as well as a challenge. Especially such an attractive one. It was a character flaw, he acknowledged that. But what the hell.

He sauntered over to the desk officer. "Morning, Violet," he murmured, leaning against the counter. "I must say, you're looking mighty inviting this morning."

Violet DuPre, a fifty-something woman with enough sass to face down even the cockiest the NOPD had to offer, swept her gaze over him. "Can the crap and sell it to somebody else, Malone. What do you want?"

"That's what I like about you, Violet. You're so susceptible to my charms." He rested an elbow on the counter and leaned his face to hers. "What's with the redhead? She waiting for someone special?"

"We all are, toots. Unfortunately, the good Lord don't always send the choicest cut." She grinned. "That one asked to speak with a detective."

"She didn't request me by name?"

"Sorry, Romeo. Better luck next time."

"You've got the wrong idea, doll. That one's been in before, touting some crazy story about alien abductions. I pulled her while filling in over at the Eighth. I'd hate to have one of my fellow officers be forced to deal with that."

Her full mouth lifted in a smirk. "That's real generous of you, Detective Malone."

"That's me, always thinking of others."

She shook her head, expression disgusted. "You

know, Malone, I'd think since another girl died last night you'd have more to do this morning than worry about alien abductions.''

He straightened, sending her a wicked grin. ''You're selling me short, babe. Got that covered, too.'' And he did. He had interviewed a half-dozen bartenders, gotten the descriptions, names and when possible, the addresses of the men Evelyn Parker had spent time with the night of her death. He'd spoken with her family and had paid a visit to a couple of her friends and co-workers. Using the information he'd gleaned, he had begun piecing together a time line of her last evening alive. And it wasn't even lunchtime yet.

He leaned closer to the other officer. ''So Violet, most gorgeous one, anything you can do to help me out?''

She shook her head and reached for the phone, a smile twitching at the corners of her mouth. ''Actually, since you two have a history, I'm thinking I ought to assign her to you. For expediency's sake.''

''You're a peach, no doubt about it.''

She snorted with disgust. ''No self-respectin' black woman's gonna be no peach. Save that for those wimpy white girls. And you might want to lose that tie. It's not so cool, stud.''

He laughed and blew her a kiss. ''I'll take that under advisement. See you around.''

Quentin crossed the room, aware of Violet watching him, no doubt smirking with amusement.

''Ms. North,'' Quentin drawled. ''What brings you down to my neck of the woods?

She turned, a subtle expression of dismay crossing her features. Obviously, she had hoped their paths would never cross again. "I needed to speak with a detective—"

"That would be me."

She glanced toward Violet—and found her smiling at them—then back at him. "I see you got lucky again. And here I thought they might assign me a different detective. Me being in a different precinct and all."

"Computers." He lifted a shoulder. "Once you're in the system with one of us, you can't get away."

"Like a fish with a hook in its mouth."

He laughed. "Follow me."

He led her through the busy squad room to his desk and motioned her to take a seat. When she had, he perched on the desk's edge, directly in front of her. "How's the writing coming?"

"Very well, thank you." She crossed her legs. "Nice tie. Colorful."

He looked at it and grinned. "Thanks."

"It's not every grown man who can carry off a tie printed with crawfish and bottles of hot sauce."

"You didn't miss the Mardi Gras masks, did you?" He leaned toward her. As he did he caught the scent of flowers, a little sweet, a little spicy. Like her, he thought, a ripple of awareness moving over him.

"How could I, Detective? They're purple and gold." She arched an eyebrow. "The tie, is it a homicide thing? A way to inject a little levity into what's a grim job?"

"Naw, dawlin'," he murmured, slipping into a Cajun patois. "It's a N'awlins thing. Laissez les bon temps rouler."

For a moment she was silent, then she made a sound of irritation. "Are you at all interested in what brought me in today? Or did you want to spend the day chatting about your tie?"

"You brought it up, sugar." He plucked his spiral and pen from his breast pocket. "How can I help you, Ms. North?"

"A friend of mine is missing. Actually, she's my little sister."

"Little sister?"

"I'm a Big Brothers, Big Sisters of America volunteer. Jaye's been my little sister for two years."

He asked the girl's full name, her age, where she lived, who she lived with, jotting the information down. That done, he looked up. "When did she go missing?"

"Thursday morning she left for school at the regular time. She had her purse and backpack. She told her foster mother goodbye and no one's seen or heard from her since."

Anna smoothed her hands over the lid of the box in her lap. "That night I called her friends, checked all her regular haunts. No one had seen her all day."

"What about her foster parents? Why aren't they sitting where you are now? And what about Social Services? She's a ward of the state and as such—"

"They think she's run away. If you check police records, I'm sure you'll find they reported it. You see—" she smoothed her hands over the box again "—she's been in the foster system for years and has had a pretty tough time. She's bolted from foster homes in the past.''

"How many times?''

She didn't blink. ''Six.''

He made several notes in his spiral, then met Anna North's eyes once more. ''But you don't think that's the case now?''

She leaned forward. ''I know it's not. Look at what I found under her mattress.'' She opened the box and passed it over. ''Jaye's a kid who's had a lot more bad in her life than good. She's lost everyone and everything she's ever loved, beginning with her mother. The contents of this box represent everything that's tangible about the good in her past. It's all she has. She wouldn't leave it behind.''

He sifted through the contents. ''Is that all?''

"No. A week ago she mentioned that some guy followed her home from school.''

"Did she report it?''

Anna sighed. ''No.''

"Was it an isolated occurrence or did it happen mare than once?''

"I don't know.... She only told me about the one incident.''

"That's not much to get excited about.''

"But she left that morning with a book bag filled with textbooks! If she had planned to run away, wouldn't she have filled her bag with clothes, toiletries and her keepsakes? She left other things of importance to her behind as well. Her CDs and player for one. It doesn't make sense.''

"Her friends don't know anything? Could she have stashed clothes and toiletries with one of them?"

"I don't think so. I've hounded her friends. They're not lying about not having heard from her, because they're scared. I see the fear in their eyes. Besides, that doesn't account for this box of mementos."

Quentin shuffled through the items once more, admitting that he couldn't find fault with her logic. This girl had obviously held on to some of these items for a long time. According to what Anna had told him, the girl kept the box under her mattress, indicating that she coveted its contents.

"I know Jaye, Detective Malone." Her voice thickened and she cleared it. "I know she didn't run away. I know it."

He closed the box and handed it back. "So you suspect...what? That she was kidnapped? Some sort of foul play?"

Her eyes flooded with tears. "Yes," she managed to say. "I wish to God I didn't. I wish she had run away. At least then...she—"

The last came out choked and Quentin waited while she struggled to get a grip on her emotions. "I've done all I can," she continued softly. "I've contacted her friends and cruised her hangouts. I don't know what else I can do, so here I am."

Quentin stood, went around the desk and sat. He tossed his spiral onto the desk beside him. "I'm going to pass something by you, Ms. North, just for the sake of argument. Two days ago you were in to see me. You had received some letters from a fan and were concerned that this fan, a child, was in danger."

"Her name's Minnie, but yes, that's right."

"In fact, you not only believed Minnie was in danger, but some other, yet unknown girl as well."

"That's right, but I don't see where that has anything—"

"How old is Minnie? According to her letters?"

"Eleven."

"And how old is Jaye?"

"Fifteen."

"And how old were you when you were kidnapped?"

Anna shot to her feet, cheeks flaming. "I see where you're going with this and you're wrong!"

He ignored her outburst. "Could it be that you're preoccupied with the idea of young girls in danger?"

"No. Look—" She brought a hand to her head, then dropped it. "Jaye's gone. If she purposely ran away, she left without some things of great importance to her. Her foster parents...they didn't act right, Detective Malone. Their behavior varied between nonchalance and anger at my interference. I sensed they were...hiding something."

"Whoa. Are you suggesting that the foster parents might be responsible for Jaye's disappearance?"

She tipped up her chin. "Something's not right about their reaction to Jaye's disappearance. Please, won't you talk to them? I'm so afraid for Jaye."

Quentin didn't reply, instead used the moment to silently recount what she had told him. On the one hand, this kid had a history of running away, on the other he bought the theory that she wouldn't have knowingly left her box of keepsakes behind.

He stood. "I'll look into it."

She made a sound of surprise. "You will?"

"I'll check out Jaye's file, talk to her caseworker. I'll speak with her foster parents, check their record. Will that make you feel better?"

"Immensely." She let out a shaky-sounding breath. "Thank you."

He walked her out of the squad room, told her he would be in touch and watched her walk away, acknowledging that she intrigued him. Because of her past and what she had lived through. Because she was a writer.

He narrowed his eyes in thought. Twice in three days she had been in with half-baked theories and over-the-top suspicions. Were her books getting to her? Was her past? Or were her concerns and feelings of danger justified?

Terry sauntered over. He smacked his lips. "There's just something about a redhead that starts my motor running."

Quentin turned to his partner in disbelief. "For God's sake, Terry, do you ever pause a moment to think before you open your mouth?"

"What?" He held his hands palms up, the picture of innocence. "All I said was, redheads get me going."

"That's right. You and at least one other guy out there."

His friend paled. "Oh man, I didn't mean—"

"Of course you didn't." Quentin glanced over his shoulder. "But you know as well as I do that there are some folks around here who have no sense of humor."

"The captain being one." Terry made a sound of frustration. "She took a big chunk out of my ass already this morning."

They turned and headed for Quentin's desk. "What about?"

"She just needed something to chew on, I was it."

Good old Aunt Patti. She was the biggest ball buster on the force. And she was not about to let one of her detectives go to wrack and ruin, not easily anyway.

"How'd it go with PID?"

"Went okay. Would have gone better if I'd been home in bed with Penny. Those A-holes refused to call Jack Daniel's an alibi."

Quentin sat behind his desk. "Captain was pissed about you being at the scene last night."

"Oh, yeah." Terry slouched in a chair. "I'm to steer clear of anything that might be even remotely related to the Kent and Parker homicides. It really burns my ass, too."

He had expected as much. "The evidence will clear you."

"Yeah. Though from what I hear, they didn't get much from the Parker scene. You called it right-on. She wasn't raped. Those jeans served as a kind of chastity belt."

"But he killed her anyway." Quentin frowned. "Why redheads?"

"Because his mother was a redhead. Or an Irish setter bit him when he was a kid. Or he's part bull and red sets him off. Who knows?'' Terry rubbed the side of his jaw. ''Besides, you might be barking up the wrong tree with that. Some would have called Evelyn Parker a blonde.''

''Hey, Malone,'' Johnson called. ''Captain wants to see us. Bring your notes on Parker and Kent.''

''This really sucks.'' Terry got to his feet. ''I feel like the kid who didn't get picked for the team. Or a freakin' leper.''

Quentin stood, pocketing his spiral. ''It'll blow over.''

''Keep me posted.''

''Don't worry.'' He gave his partner's shoulder a squeeze. ''I have the feeling we're going to need your help on this one.''

Quentin followed Walden and Johnson into their captain's office, closing the door behind them, aware of Terry watching them. He muttered an oath and crossed to his aunt's desk. He laid his palms on its top, bent and looked her dead in the eyes.

''I want Terry on the team. He's a good cop.''

''Was a good cop,'' she corrected. ''He's falling apart. And he's under suspicion. Can't do it.''

''Under suspicion, what a load of crap. And you know it. No way Landry had anything—''

She cut him off. ''I've made my decision. Now, unless you'd like to join your partner outside, I suggest you shut up and sit down. Do you get me, Detective?''

He did but instead of taking a seat, he stood, resting against the door frame.

''What do we have?'' the captain asked, folding her

hands on the desk in front of her, tone brisk, confrontation forgotten.

"Victim's name was Evelyn Parker," Johnson offered. "Twenty-four, Caucasian, a looker. Worked uptown. Lived in the Bywater."

"Liked to party," Walden added. "Same as Kent. Was out partying the night of her death."

"Got all this already," the captain murmured. "We got anything to go on? Leads? Theories?" She arched an eyebrow. "A good guess?"

Quentin jumped in. "In my mind, the red hair's the thing that links them. What we need to figure out is why this guy's going after redheads."

"Red hair?" Johnson looked at Quentin. "We've got a bottle-dyed burgundy and a blonde."

"A strawberry blonde," Quentin corrected. "A kind of red."

Walden shook his head. "Both women were out clubbing the night of their deaths, both were big party girls. To my mind, that's what links them."

Quentin looked at the other man. "The clubs are *how* he finds them, not why he chooses them."

"Who've you talked to?" Captain O'Shay asked.

"More like, who haven't we talked to." Johnson filled the captain in. "We've got some good leads. So far no crossovers from the night of the first murder. But just because we haven't got 'em yet doesn't mean they're not there."

Quentin spoke up. "My feeling is this guy interacts with the women publicly though not excessively. He's careful not to call attention to himself. He buys her a drink, asks her to dance a time or two. But somebody saw him with her, someone will remember.''

''These girls are being killed in alleys.'' The captain moved her gaze between the three detectives. ''So what's he smothering them with? Not a bed pillow.''

''His hand?'' Walden offered.

''Tough when you got a fighter like Evelyn Parker,'' Quentin said. ''Unless he's got some damn big hands. Plus, you'd have more bruising of the nose and mouth.''

''A plastic bag then. From a dry cleaner's. Or even a kitchen trash bag, right from the box. Easy to carry in a jacket pocket.''

''There hasn't been any trace plastic found at the scene. Seems like there would have been, considering the asphalt surface underneath both victims' heads.'' Johnson looked at Walden. ''Search of the Dumpsters around the scene turn up anything of that nature?''

''Not from Kent's scene. The evidence crew is still sifting through the stuff from Parker's.'' Walden scratched his head. ''Usually, when a bag's used it's left on the victim. Getting it off can get complicated and the perp risks leaving more evidence in the process.''

''Maybe we've got a savvy killer here,'' the captain offered. ''One concerned about latent prints. He kills the girl, then pockets the murder weapon, disposing of it when he's a safe distance from the scene.''

''Simple is better. We need to operate under the assumption that this one's not stupid.''

Johnson snickered. ''You mean he didn't flunk out of Dumb Fuck 101? Too bad for us.''

"If he's not stupid, he's wearing gloves, so he's not worried about prints. Besides, as cold as it's been, nobody would have thought twice about a guy wearing gloves. Not even the victims."

Quentin drew his eyebrows together. "Here's a simple theory. It's cold out. He uses his coat."

"What about trace evidence? There'd be fibers for sure. More fiber evidence than we've gotten, that's for damn certain."

Quentin pushed away from the door. "What about a leather coat?"

The occupants of the room fell silent. They exchanged glances. "He has it with him all the time," Quentin said. "The weather's cold so nobody thinks twice. It's pliable but not porous. It's also nonfibrous and easy to clean. And the best part is, he walks away wearing the murder weapon."

"It works for me," Johnson offered. "But so does the plastic bag theory. It's too convenient not to follow up on."

Walden nodded. "Ditto. It makes more sense than a guy who carries around a bed pillow."

Captain O'Shay leaned back in her chair. "I want this thing solved. Two such similar deaths in such a short space of time has sent the media into a feeding frenzy. They're already speculating about when and where number three's going to happen. Chief Pennington's crawling all over my frame and let me tell you, it's damn uncomfortable."

Johnson cleared his throat. Walden coughed and Quentin narrowed his eyes. "We've got plenty to go on, Captain. We'll close this quick. I guarantee it."

"See that you do," she said. "And keep me in the know."

Johnson and Walden got to their feet and joined Quentin at the door.

The captain stopped Quentin. "Malone?"

He looked back at his aunt. "Not a word to Landry. He's totally out of the loop. Do you understand?"

He frowned. Something in her expression made him uneasy. *What did they have on his partner that they weren't saying?* "You want to tell me what's going on?"

"Can't. Not yet." She arched her eyebrows. "Can you cooperate? Or you want off the case? I'll understand if—"

"I'll cooperate," he snapped. "But I'll tell you right now, I think it's a crock of shit. Terry's clean."

21

Friday, January 19
The French Quarter, 3:00 p.m.

Anna sat in front of her computer, the glowing screen blank. Over the past two hours she had written and discarded a dozen paragraphs, unhappy with every word she had written.

Usually she cherished the afternoons she didn't work at The Perfect Rose, time she set aside for her writing. Usually, she made the most of every moment.

Today, she couldn't concentrate. She was plagued by thoughts of her earlier meeting with Detective Malone, her worries about Jaye, her continuing stalemate with her agent and publisher.

Today? she thought in disgust. Truth was, she hadn't written one good page since her editor had delivered her strings-attached offer. What was the point? If she refused their offer, she wouldn't have a publisher—or most probably, an agent—so why rush to write another book?

Tears of frustration pricked the back of her eyes, and she muttered an oath. She would *not* cry over this. If she was going to cry, she would cry for Jaye. Or

Minnie. They needed her. They mattered. Not something as trivial as her publishing career.

Trivial? Her books, her publishing career mattered. They were important to her.

But not as important as Jaye. As finding out what had happened to her. The good news was, Detective Malone had promised to look into Jaye's disappearance. Anna didn't believe he was convinced something was amiss with her friend's foster parents, nor that Jaye had fallen in harm's way, but at least he would check it out.

Anna propped her chin on her fist, recalling their conversation. Their bantering. What had *that* been all about? Sure, he was a gorgeous-looking man, with one of those quicksilver, rakish smiles, the kind that could melt a woman's heart and good sense. If a woman liked that swaggering, macho type.

She didn't. Period. So where had all that nauseating sexual sparring come from? She'd been there about Jaye, for heaven's sake. What was wrong with her?

Anna told herself to get a grip and dragged her gaze back to the computer screen. She wrote one sentence, then two. The sentences mounted, creating paragraphs.

Of pure, uninspired drivel.

With a sound of frustration, she deleted them. Dear Lord, would she ever write again?

The phone rang and she grabbed for it like a lifeline. "Hello?"

"Anna, Ben Walker."

At the sound of his voice, Anna experienced a rush of pleasure—and a twinge of guilt. She hadn't thought about him or their discussion since Jaye had disappeared. Although understandable, she felt bad about it anyway. "Ben," she murmured. "Hello."

"How are you?"

"I'm fine. Feeling a little guilty. I was supposed to call you, wasn't I?"

"Don't worry about it."

She made a sound of regret. "A lot's happened in the past couple of days and truthfully, I haven't had a chance to really think about our conversation." She filled him in about Jaye, her fears and even her trip to NOPD headquarters.

"Good God, Anna, is there anything I can do?"

"Not unless you can tell me where Jaye is. At least the detective promised to look into it for me. Not that he bought my story."

He was silent a moment, then cleared his throat. "Call me if you need anything, even if only someone to vent your frustrations on. Don't hesitate, no matter the time of day or night."

"Or night? Geez, considering how much I've actually slept the last few nights, making that offer's risky."

"On call night and day, that's me, Dr. Johnny-on-the-Spot." He sobered. "But I mean it, Anna. Anything at all, call me."

She thanked him again and silence fell between them. After a moment, he broke it. "Got a question. You haven't ruled me or my offer out have you?"

She liked his straightforward approach and smiled. "No. Definitely not."

"Good. Because I was hoping you'd go to dinner with me."

"Dinner?" she repeated, surprised.

"Yes. Tonight." He paused. "No pressure about anything. Just you, me, a bottle of wine and a really good meal. What do you think?"

She didn't hesitate. After the few days she'd just had, the idea of a low-key meal with an interesting man sounded better than good. It sounded perfect.

Three hours later, Anna arrived at Arnaud's, a fine old New Orleans restaurant in the Creole tradition. They had arranged to meet at the restaurant and Ben was already there, waiting for her on the sidewalk. He wore a navy blue suit, white shirt and garnet-colored tie. He looked cold.

He crossed to the curb and opened the cab door for her, helping her out. "You could have waited inside," she murmured apologetically. "It's freezing out here."

"I didn't want to give you even a moment to change your mind." Smiling, he tucked her hand into the crook of his arm. "Shall we?"

He led her inside; the maître d' had their table ready, one along the wall of leaded-glass windows that faced the street. "I love Arnaud's," she murmured. "Besides the food being wonderful, it's one of the prettiest dining rooms in town."

"It's lovely but—never mind."

"No, tell me." She smoothed her napkin across her lap. "But what?"

"I was going to say, I wouldn't know because I

can't take my eyes off you. You're beautiful, Anna.'' He turned red. "I can't believe I said that. How hokey.''

"I think it was sweet." She reached across the table and lightly touched his hand. "Thank you, Ben."

Their waiter arrived, introduced himself, took their drink orders, then disappeared. They chatted about the menu while they waited for their drinks, swapping food stories—a favorite pastime of any New Orleanian worth his salt.

"How's the book going?" she asked after the waiter brought their drinks and took their food orders.

"Oh no you don't." Ben wagged a finger at her. "Last time I did all the talking. This time it's your turn." He smiled. "How's *your* writing going?"

Anna thought of the dozen or so paragraphs she had written—and deleted—earlier that day. "It's not," she murmured, taking a sip of her wine. "Currently, I'm without a contract. And soon, without a publisher as well."

"How can that be? Your books are terrific. Every bit as good as Sue Grafton's or Mary Higgins Clark's."

She thanked him, pleased at the compliment, then explained. "They think my past is just the hook they need to catapult me onto the bestseller lists. They've made a more than generous offer, and I want to take it, but…"

"What?" he prompted when her voice trailed off. "Are they difficult to work with?"

"Not at all. I like my editor very much and as a

group, they've done a terrific job packaging my stories.''

''So what's the problem?''

She lowered her gaze to her hands, clutched tightly in her lap. ''They only want me if they can capitalize on my past. If I take their offer, I'll have to tour. I'll do TV, radio, newspaper. My editor thought they might even be able to get me on one of the big morning shows, *Today* or *Good Morning America.*''

''And the thought terrifies you.''

''God, yes.'' She met his eyes. ''I want to accept, but I can't imagine fulfilling my part of the agreement. Going on TV and radio and talking about not only my books but my past? Exposing myself to any nut who might...'' She shuddered. ''Help me, Ben. Tell me what to do.''

''About their offer?'' He laughed without humor. ''You already know what you have to do, you just don't like the answer.''

''Damn,'' she muttered. ''I was afraid you were going to say that. No miracle cure, Doc?''

''Sorry,'' he said softly, tone sympathetic. ''You're not ready. And you know it. You're not emotionally able to do what your publisher wants.''

''Why is this happening to me?'' She fisted her fingers, frustrated. ''Everything was going so well. My writing, my life...everything.''

''Was it?''

''What do you mean?''

''Nothing's really changed about your life, Anna. You've simply been presented with a choice.''

''One that totally sucks, if you ask me.''

"Not from their point of view. No doubt they think they're being extremely fair. From what you've said, your publisher is offering you not only a lot more money than before, but the kind of opportunity most writers only dream of."

"You sound like my agent," she muttered.

"Sorry about that." He leaned toward her. "The fact is, at this point your fear is stronger than your longing to continue being published. And that fear is understandable, considering your past. But it isn't necessarily rational. And it's not healthy."

She picked up her wine and sipped, shocked to realize her hands were shaking. "So you think I should just buck up, face my fears and do it? Agree to their offer?"

"I didn't say that. I think your fears can be overcome by working with a good therapist. Not, as your agent and editor seem to think, through sheer determination. That's a recipe for disaster."

Silence fell between them as their first course was delivered, seafood gumbo for him and shrimp Arnaud for her.

"I know you're leery of therapists, Anna," he murmured, dipping his spoon into the thick, savory soup. "But what about working with a group of other people who are in a similar boat? I facilitate a fear group on Thursday evenings, you could come check us out, see if it's something you feel you'd benefit from. If you didn't feel comfortable working with me, there are a number of such groups in the area. I could check around, do a little research for you, recommend a few."

A group? Of other people like her? Would she be able to open up in front of them any better than she could to other strangers? Could it help her?

He searched her gaze. "How do you feel about that?"

"Apprehensive." She caught her bottom lip between her teeth. "Nervous about the idea. Curious."

"Good." He smiled. "That's a start."

"Do you need an answer now?"

"Absolutely not. Take all the time you need. This has to be a decision you come to willingly, Anna. Not under pressure."

Willingly? A nice concept, but one her mystery terrorist—as she had come to think of him—had stolen from her.

"If you decide to give us a try, let me know right away. Group is an intimate forum. One that relies on a high level of trust between the participants. If you want to sit in, I'll have to introduce the idea to the group, tell them a little about you and, basically, get their permission to allow you in."

She liked the sound of that and told him so. She also promised to let him know the minute she decided she wanted to participate.

From there, they concentrated on their meal, which was every bit as fabulous as Anna had expected. While they ate, Ben told stories about the different places he had lived, but from time to time Anna caught her attention wandering to Jaye and Detective Malone's promise.

When he poked around the Clausens' past, what would he find? Jaye, she prayed. Safe and sound.

"Anna? Are you all right?"

She blinked, jostled out of her thoughts by Ben's question. She smiled apologetically at him. "Sorry. I guess the last few days are catching up with me."

"No problem. Is there anything I can do to help?"

"Just keep putting up with me, okay?"

He agreed, and for the remainder of their meal Anna kept her attention focused on her dinner companion.

The bill paid, they stood to leave the restaurant. Before Anna could ask the maître d' to call a cab for her, Ben offered to drive her. "That's silly, I'm only a few blocks from here and it's out of your way."

"But I asked you to dinner. Any gentleman worth that title sees his date safely home."

She hesitated only a moment, then agreed. "All right."

Only a handful of minutes later, Ben double-parked in front of her building, climbed out of the vehicle and came around to open her door. He helped her out and walked her to the courtyard gate. There, they faced one another. "I had a really nice time, Ben. Thanks." Her lips lifted. "Actually, tonight was just what I needed."

He reached out and lightly touched her cheek, then dropped his hand. "I'm feeling a little guilty right now," he murmured, voice deepening. "You see, I had an ulterior motive for asking you to dinner tonight."

Ben had expressed his interest in her in subtle ways all evening. Had he decided to abandon subtlety for a more direct approach?

If he had, how would she feel?

Her cheeks warmed and her pulse began to race. She searched his expression. His face lay half in shadow, half in the light cast by a neighbor's porch light, transforming his looks from that of mild-mannered doctor to mysterious stranger.

Stranger. A man she hardly knew. One whose intentions she couldn't be certain of.

A shiver of excitement and apprehension moved over her. She held her breath, waiting.

"I need to come clean with you about something," Ben continued. "And I hope you won't be too angry with me."

Anna drew her eyebrows together, confused. What he'd just said didn't jibe with her train of thought, not at all. Just what kind of "ulterior motives" concerning their date had he had?

Ben caught her hands. "At our last meeting, I wasn't quite honest with you."

Obviously not the kind she'd thought he'd had. She stared at him a moment, then giggled.

He looked surprised by her reaction, then hurt. "What did I say?"

"I thought... Your ulterior motive—" She giggled again.

It took a half second for her words to sink in, then a slow smile crept across his face. "I like to think I have a little more finesse than that, Anna."

"I'm glad to know you do. I would have hated having to write you off as not only a creep, but a bumbling creep as well."

"So I take it your answer would have been no?"

She ignored his question, as much in an effort at coquetry as because she didn't know herself. "Perhaps we should get back to this ulterior motive of yours?"

"Look at me, I've put it off all night and here we are, saying good-night and I'm still fumbling around."

"Just tell me. I'll bet I can take it."

"All right." He let out a long breath, a cloud of steam following on the frigid night air. "Remember when I said that I just happened to tune into E! that Saturday the Hollywood mysteries show aired?"

She nodded, a chill sensation starting at the back of her neck and spreading outward from there.

"That wasn't true. And it wasn't true that I was already a fan of your novels. I'd never even heard of Anna North until the day before the show aired."

Her lips were numb, she realized. Not from the cold, from apprehension. From what she knew was coming next. "So, how...when did you—"

"The evening before the E! special, I found a package in my waiting room. It contained a copy of—"

"My last book and a note telling you to tune into E! the next day. Dear God." She brought a hand to her mouth. *How far-reaching was her tormentor's campaign of terror? What was he after? And why had Ben been included?*

"That's...yes." He swore under his breath. "I see how upset you are, and I'm sorry. I'm certain one of my patients left the package for me, but I don't know which one or why. I called the six patients I saw that Friday, all six denied having left it."

One of his patients. The videographer. She sucked in a deep breath, excited. "Do you have a patient named Peter Peters?"

He repeated the name, then shook his head. "No."

"You're certain? No one named anything even remotely like Peter Peters?"

"I'm certain." He frowned, concerned. "Why?"

"Because you weren't the only one who received that package. In fact, everyone of importance in my life received one. My parents, best friends, agent and editor…my little sister, Jaye."

She hugged herself and stomped her feet to keep warm, strangely grateful for the cold, for the diversion it provided. "You weren't the only E! viewer who was able to put two and two together and figure out that Anna North is none other than Harlow Grail."

This time it was he who searched her gaze, his filled with regret. "Before then, who knew?"

"Just my parents. I'd worked hard to put my past behind me. To disassociate myself from the kidnapped Hollywood princess."

He let out a long breath. "I'm sorry, Anna. To have been exposed that way must have been very upsetting for you."

Suddenly, she was angry. Furious. "It was worse than *upsetting*, Dr. Walker. It was a shock. I was terrified." She hiked up her chin. "Why didn't you tell me the truth up front?"

"Because I figured you'd be spooked. That you would erroneously believe you were in danger from some nutcase patient of mine. No way would you have talked to me then."

"Considerate, Ben. Thank you."

"Please." He caught her hands again. "I never thought you in any danger, you have to believe me. Therapy can elicit obsessive and sometimes bizarre behavior in patients. The process can bring out anger, bitterness and even rage. These emotions are often turned onto the therapist. That's why I believed the focus of this was me."

She eased her hands from his and hugged herself. "Why are you telling me now? We could have gone on forever without me knowing the truth."

"Because I'm neither a liar nor one of those people who can bend the truth and go righteously on their way." He paused. "And because I like you."

The last took a little of the blow out of her anger and she pulled her coat closely around her. "Why you?" she asked. "There's a twisted kind of logic in my friends receiving the package, but how do you fit in?"

"I don't know. It still makes sense that it's one of my patients doing this. I'll help you find out who, Anna. And why." For the second time that night he reached out and lightly touched her cheek. His fingers were as cold as ice. "Together, we can figure this out. I promise we will."

22

Jaye awakened from a deep sleep. Frightened, she lay stone still, listening. For what had awakened her. For the quiet whoosh of the pet door swinging shut or the creak of a floorboard outside her prison door. Those things had awakened her before.

Her captor came to her in the dead of night. He passed provisions through the pet door—food and drink for the day, fresh towels—never speaking. She had learned after the first day that if she left her garbage and any remnants of her meal just inside the pet door, he would take them away.

His silent presence frightened her. She had heard him on the floors below, moving about, coming and going. She had heard him breathing on the other side of the door. As if listening. And waiting.

For what? Jaye wondered, hugging herself. What did he want with her? He hadn't touched her. Yet, anyway. But he would. And then what would she do?

Fear choked her, and she struggled to breathe past it. Jaye dragged the single blanket to her chin. Her hands screamed protest at the small movement—they were cut and torn from her daily clawing and tugging at the boards on the windows, black and blue from pounding against the door.

She wanted to go home. She wanted to see Anna, her foster parents and her friends. She wanted to wake up in her own bed, surrounded by her own things.

She didn't want to be scared anymore.

A sound slipped from her lips, small and helpless. Then another and another. Jaye strangled the fourth back, not wanting him to hear her. Not wanting him to know how frightened—how vulnerable—she really was.

But he knew. He knew everything.

No! He couldn't see inside her head or her heart. She wouldn't let him.

Jaye swallowed hard and sat up, focusing her thoughts on what *she knew.* On the things she could control. Unless she had somehow lost track of time, she had been held in this room for three days. She had deduced that her prison was some sort of attic room, several stories above the street. At times she heard the distant sounds of jazz, at others the rhythmic sound of taps striking the sidewalk. On several occasions she'd thought she caught a whiff of frying seafood and shrimp boil.

The combination of those things had led her to believe that she was being held in the French Quarter, in a building located away from the busy hub of Bourbon Street or Jackson Square. Perhaps on the fringe between the commercial and residential areas of the Quarter.

That was good news. She hadn't been taken far

from home or the people who were searching for her. Surely by now the police were involved. Social Services. Anna.

A lump formed in Jaye's throat at the thought of her friend. She regretted their fight. She wished with all her heart that she could take back the things she had said. She wished she could have one more day with her.

The thought brought fear and helplessness rushing back, and Jaye fought them, refocusing herself on what she had to do to survive. The way Anna must have, all those years ago. If Anna had given in to her fear back then, she would have died. Like that little boy.

After her and Anna's fight, Jaye had done some research on Anna's kidnapping. It hadn't been difficult, even in New Orleans the story had been front-page news. Jaye had been horrified by the recounting of the boy's murder, the description of how the kidnapper had held Harlow down and snapped off her finger.

Jaye could hardly fathom the terror and pain Anna must have overcome to escape with her life. She had been in awe of her. But unforgiving.

She forgave now. Now she understood.

Jaye closed her eyes. She breathed deeply, drawing strength from thoughts of her friend. What did she know about her captor? Jaye asked herself. She had seen his hands. They were strong-looking, though not overly large. The dusting of hair on their backs and on his forearms was dark. She deduced he was a dark-haired man of medium height, somewhere between the ages of thirty and fifty.

He had planned well for this, that was obvious. The pet door had been recently installed, the window freshly boarded. He had considered her every need ahead of time—toilet and facial tissue, soap and other toiletries, a change of clothes, though she hadn't touched them.

That meant he was careful, that he thought things through. That, most probably, he had preselected her. No doubt it had been he who had been following her, the old pervert as she had called him. Following and watching, learning her schedule and when she was most vulnerable, waiting for the right moment to snatch her.

But why *her?* What about her fulfilled his twisted needs? She wasn't wealthy, so ransom wasn't his motive. So, he must want her for something else. Something…awful. And sick. Jaye swallowed hard. She wasn't naive. She knew what happened to kids who were abducted. She wished to God she didn't.

Suddenly, Jaye became aware of a rustling from the other side of the door. The sound was small, somehow hesitant. Different from the ones she had heard before. A lump in her throat, Jaye turned her gaze toward the locked door.

"Hello? Are you there?"

The voice, though slightly raspy, belonged to a girl. Jaye froze. She looked toward the door. *Another girl? Could it really be?*

She climbed off the cot and crept toward the door,

heart thundering. It could be some sort of trick. It could be her helpless imagination playing with her.

The child spoke again. Her voice shook. "Are you...I don't have much time. If he...finds out, he'll be angry with me."

"I'm here," Jaye said, eyes flooding with tears. She had never been so grateful for anything as she was to hear this girl's voice. "Open the door. Let me out."

"I can't. It's locked. He has the key."

Jaye swallowed the despair that rushed up inside her. "Can you get it? Please, you have to help me."

"I can't...I—" The girl whimpered, obviously frightened. "I just came to... He wants you to be quiet. He's getting angry with you. And when he gets that way he...scares me. He—"

Jaye grabbed the doorknob and shook it. "Help me. Let me out!"

The child on the other side of the door whimpered again and Jaye sensed her backing away from the door. "You have to be quiet," she whispered. "You don't understand. You don't know."

"Who are you?" Jaye shook the knob again, voice rising in terror and frustration. "Where am I? Why is he doing this to me?"

"I shouldn't have come! He'll know...he'll... find..."

The girl's voice faded away and Jaye pounded on the door, desperate. "Don't go! Please don't... Don't leave me."

Silence answered her. She was alone again.

23

Anna awakened groggy from another night of tossing and turning. She had been exhausted and should have slept well, but instead had found her dreams plagued by images of children playing a dangerous game of hide-and-seek with an unseen monster, one who always lurked just beyond Anna's field of vision.

She climbed out of bed and slipped into her old chenille robe and fuzzy slippers. She crossed to the French doors that led to her narrow balcony. The day was bright and crisp-looking, the sky a brilliant, cloudless blue.

Huddled in their coats, Dalton and Bill sat at a table in the courtyard below. Steam rose from their mugs of coffee; between them sat a plate of what looked to be croissants and fruit. Smiling to herself, Anna cracked open the door and poked her head out.

"Morning, boys," she called. "Have you lost your minds? It's freezing out there!"

Dalton twisted to look up at her, patting his mouth with a napkin as he did. "The weather guy promised a warming trend. It's supposed to reach fifty today."

"A regular heat wave," Anna said, shivering. "Don't forget the cocoa butter."

"It's all mind over matter." Bill motioned her. "Come join us. We have an extra croissant and plenty of fruit."

"As much as I love you guys, I value warmth more. In other words, no way and get a grip."

Dalton pouted. "But we want to hear about your date."

"Then come up. I'll make café au lait."

She ducked back inside, not bothering to latch the French door. She hurried to the bathroom, brushed her teeth, then went to the kitchen to get the coffee started.

Just as the she dropped the frozen coffee cubes into the mugs, she heard her friends at the door.

She let them in and they tripped over one another in their rush to get inside, shedding their coats and rubbing their hands together.

"Mother of God, it's cold out there!"

"I've lost feeling in my hands."

Anna arched an eyebrow, taking their coats. "What happened to mind over matter?"

"It froze its ass," Bill replied, irritated. "I'm sick of this weather. This is New Orleans, for God's sake. Southern Louisiana. Practically the tropics."

Dalton gave his partner a brief, conciliatory hug. "Forgive him, Anna. He's on a tear. You know how much he loves dining al fresco."

"And wearing short-shorts. What's the point of having Buns of Steel if I can't show them off?" Bill handed her the plate of fruit and pastries. "Think about it. We live through July and August so we can avoid this freeze-ours-butts-off crapola. How fair is that?''

Dalton agreed. ''It could almost bring one to violence.''

''Exactly.'' Bill rubbed his hands together. ''A killer who only strikes when it's cold.''

Dalton flapped his hands, all but dancing with excitement. ''It starts out as a game. Or out of boredom. It escalates until people are dropping left and right.''

''Like flies.'' Bill clapped his hands together. ''You should use this, Anna. It's good.''

Anna poured the steaming milk into the mugs, a smile tugging at the corners of her mouth. ''Inspired stuff, guys. Keep those ideas coming. I need all the help I can get these days.''

They carried their coffees to her kitchen table and sat. For a moment, they sipped their drinks in silence.

''How was the date?'' Dalton asked, curving his hands around the mug.

''It wasn't a da—'' She bit the words back, because it most certainly had been a date. So why had her immediate response been a denial?

Because it hadn't felt like a date.

She shook her head, picking at the croissant. ''It was fine. Really good.''

Bill and Dalton looked at one another, then returned their gazes to her, expressions expectant. ''Tell us every juicy detail.''

She told them instead about the surprise revelation Ben had sprung on her when he'd driven her home.

Dalton let out a long breath. "Damnation and blue-berries."

"No joke." She pushed away the plate and what was left of the croissant. "He's certain one of his patients is behind it. But he hasn't a clue which one or why."

"Did you give him the name your mother—"

"Yes. He doesn't have a patient named anything remotely similar to Peter Peters." She let out her breath in a frustrated huff. "He promised to find out who had left the package."

"A regular hero." Dalton brought the mug to his lips. "I enjoy that in a man."

"Thank you." Bill blew his partner a kiss, then turned back to Anna. "Do you like him?"

She didn't hesitate. "I do. He's nice."

Her friends groaned and she frowned at them. "Nice is good. It's fine."

"Hot's better."

"Much better."

She laughed and shook her head; silence fell between them. From the corners of her eyes, Anna saw Bill nudge Dalton. The man shot him a dirty look and mouthed something that she guessed to be a warning.

Anna frowned. "You two look like a couple of cats who swallowed canaries. What's up?"

The men exchanged glances.

"We didn't want to upset you."

"We know how distressed you've been about Jaye."

"The last thing you needed was another one of those letters—"

"From your little fan."

Anna's stomach clenched. "When did it come?"

"Just yesterday afternoon," Dalton said. "I could have brought it after work—"

"But you had that date last night and—"

"We didn't want to ruin it."

"I appreciate your concern, boys, but I'm not made of whipped cream. Hand it over."

"I think Dalton left it at The Perfect Rose," Bill offered, not meeting her gaze. "In fact, I'm certain of it."

"Nice try, but I know better." She held a hand out. "Give it to me. Now, please."

Dalton looked sheepish as he dug the letter out of his back pocket. He handed it to her. "You're not mad, are you?"

"Not if you and your cohort in crime promise to stop trying to protect me. Otherwise, I'm furious." She moved her gaze between the two men. "Agreed?"

They did, though she didn't really believe they would stick to their promise. She figured she would cross that bridge when she came to it. For this moment she had another, much more distressing bridge to cross.

Anna opened the envelope, a knot of apprehension in the pit of her stomach. Her hands shook, and she wished she could scrawl *Return To Sender* across the front and put Minnie and her disturbing letters out of her mind forever.

She couldn't do that. Minnie needed her, and although Anna didn't know how she was going to help the child, she couldn't stop trying. She couldn't abandon her.

Anna drew the single sheet of lined paper from the envelope and began to read:

Dearest Anna,

So much has happened since I wrote last. He knows we've been communicating. Whether he just found out or knew all along, I'm not sure. If he knew all along, why did he allow it? What does he have planned?

I'm afraid he means to hurt me. Or the other one. The one who's been crying.

Be careful, Anna. Promise me. And I promise to be careful, too.

As she always did, Minnie decorated the envelope with hearts and daisies and the letters S.W.A.K.

"My God, Anna," Bill murmured, laying a hand on her arm. "You look like you've seen a ghost. What did she say?"

Silently, Anna handed the letter over. Both her friends read it, then met her gaze.

"Do you think this is for real?" Dalton asked her.

"Well, sure. I mean...don't you?"

"At first I did, but now...I don't know." Dalton looked at Bill. "That detective could be right, Anna. This could be a sick prank. It's a little over the top."

"I agree," Bill murmured. "If this mysterious 'He' of the letters knows you've been corresponding and is angry about it, why let it continue? And if this child really is a prisoner, how is she able to write and send letters anyway?''

"And why would *you* be in danger, Anna?" Dalton shook his head, a frown marring his handsome face. "That's just too much for me to swallow."

Bill concurred. "And if this man recently kidnapped a child from this area, why haven't we heard anything about it?"

"Right," Dalton concurred. "Kids don't go missing without an alarm being sounded. It's just not making sense anymore." He gentled his voice. "I'm sorry, Anna."

Anna looked from one to the other of them, considering their argument, realizing they were right. It *was* over the top now—just too much.

Someone had deliberately set out to try to terrify her. And she had fallen for it, hook, line and sinker.

Just the way he—or she—had wanted her to. Just the way they had known she would. Because of her past.

She crumpled the letter and tossed it onto the table. "I feel like an idiot. A total patsy. My God, I went to the police about this."

"Don't do this to yourself, Anna! Bill and I fell for it, too."

"But you weren't the target. You weren't a victim. Again."

Dalton stood, came around the table and gave her a hug. "At least it's over, Anna. You can put it out of your mind and focus on other things."

"Like Jaye and my nonexistent writing career. Gee whiz, I'm thrilled."

"Please don't be upset," they said in unison. "We hate it when you're upset."

"That's why we want you to come out with us tonight."

"We're going to Tipitina's."

"Tonight's zydeco night."

"The Zydeco Kings—"

"Straight from Thibodaux—"

"Are playing. And it's Saturday night. So, why not?"

"I don't know, guys." She shook her head. "I'm really not in the mood—"

"That's exactly why you must come! It'll lift your spirits." Dalton grabbed her hands. "You're a stabilizing influence on us, Anna. If you're with us we won't drink or eat as much. We'll get home before dawn."

"You can invite your doctor friend. And if you do, I solemnly swear not to grab his butt."

Anna laughed, she couldn't help herself. "I love you guys."

"Does that mean you'll come? Please."

She capitulated. "Yes, that means I'll come."

24

At 7:00 p.m. sharp, Bill and Dalton knocked on her apartment door. Anna sashayed out, feeling sassy, sexy and more than ready for a night out with her friends. She deserved it, she had decided. For tonight, she would put everything that had happened in the past days out of her mind. She had even taken Bill's suggestion and invited Ben to join them.

"Couldn't your handsome doctor make it?" Dalton asked as if reading her mind.

"He's going to try." She locked her apartment door, dropped her keys into her purse and turned to face her friends. "He had several late appointments."

"His loss," Bill murmured, taking in her tight blue jeans, soft black sweater and leather jacket. "You look good enough to eat tonight, darlin'."

"Thank you very much, kind sir." She laughed and then the threesome linked arms. "It sucks, however, that the two nicest and best-looking guys I know are gay. Doubly sucky is the fact that they also happen to be the two men I spend the most time with."

"All the more reason to fais do-do," Dalton teased.

"Or cha-cha-cha," Bill added, his smile devilish. "Maybe tonight's your night for a trip to paradise."

Anna laughed with them, but she had no plans of cha-cha-chaing with anybody tonight. Not Ben—if he even showed—or anybody else. Casual sex was definitely not her style.

The three exited the building and started toward Tipitina's. The club, a famous fixture on the local music scene, was located only a dozen or so blocks from their apartment. Though cold, they chose to walk instead of cab, warmed by each other's company and the night's many possibilities.

Tipitina's was in full swing when they arrived. The Zydeco Kings drew crowds wherever they played, and particularly on a weekend night in the French Quarter. The crowd was a mix of locals and tourists, ranging in age from those barely of legal age to those one step from the grave—and everything in between.

Bill spotted some folks he knew from the arts council and they headed that way. They had a table, to which they added more chairs. Some friends of theirs from the neighborhood joined them, they brought some friends of their own. They dragged over another table, then added more chairs.

For the first hour Anna watched diligently for Ben. After that, she gave up, accepting that he wasn't going to show. Although disappointed, she let herself be pulled into the carnival-like atmosphere of the night.

The beer flowed. The music poured forth, a toe-tapping combination of guitar, washboard and harmonica. In true New Orleans fashion, Anna and her friends ate and drank too much, laughed often and too loudly. Anna's group became loud, then rowdy. She found herself having more fun than she'd had in ages, dancing with one partner after another, laughing until her sides ached.

Anna returned to the table, hot, out of breath. "Water," she gasped as she sank onto the chair beside Dalton, fanning herself. She grabbed her glass and downed it.

Dalton slid her his. "No sign of the good doctor yet?"

"Nope." She sighed and eased against the chair back. "I've been watching."

He cocked an eyebrow. "I see that."

She glared at him. "I have. In between dips and twirls."

"Mmm. It's probably for the best anyway."

She took a swallow of Dalton's water. "Yeah? And why's that?"

"Because," Dalton murmured, "there's an incredibly good-looking guy staring at you right now. A real stud."

"Me?" she said, twisting in her seat. "Where?"

"Over there." He pointed. "But wait, don't look yet. You don't want to appear too eager."

She looked anyway. All she could see was a sea of bodies. She turned back to her friend, pouting. "He's probably looking at *you*, Dalton. In this town, it seems like the best-looking guys are always gay."

"No such luck this time, my sweet. This one's one hundred percent hetero, unless my gaydar's gone haywire. He's looking again... Uh-oh he's coming this way. Be still my heart, this one's a wet dream."

"Coming this way?" She craned her neck to see around a couple who had decided to two-step directly in her line of vision. "Are you sure—"

The man twirled the woman; the crowd parted. Her heart stopped.

Detective Malone.

And he most definitely was heading her way.

She swallowed hard as she watched him approach, unable to tear her gaze away. *Dear God, Dalton was right. In his blue jeans and chambray shirt, he really was a wet dream.*

Anna decided that she had danced one too many two-steps and downed one too many Abita beers.

"Hello, Anna," he said, stopping beside her table.

"Detective Malone," she replied, her voice sounding high and nervous to her own ears. *What the hell was wrong with her?*

"Call me Quentin." He flashed her a quick smile. "Or just Malone, like everybody else."

Dalton nudged her. "You going to introduce me to your friend, Anna?"

Her cheeks warmed. "Of course. Dalton, this is Detective Quentin Malone. The detective I told you about."

"Oh, *that* detective." Dalton smiled and held out a hand. "Anna didn't tell me you were a stud."

Quentin shook his hand, apparently unfazed. "I'm sorry to hear that."

"If you ask her to dance, maybe she'll give you the opportunity to prove your stuff. If you're lucky."

"Dalton!" She glared at her friend, irritated. "I

suggest you switch to something nonalcoholic or go home and sleep it off.''

Quentin ignored her comment and held out his hand. ''I'd love the opportunity to prove my stuff. Dance with me, Anna?''

She opened her mouth to refuse but found herself being pushed to her feet by Dalton. As he did, he whispered ''Paradise,'' in her ear.

''Funny guy,'' Quentin murmured, drawing her into his arms. ''A good friend?''

''Yes.'' She met his gaze and tipped up her chin, challenging him to make some crack about gays.

He didn't. Instead, he drew her a little closer. ''You smell good.''

''Cool it, Casanova,'' she murmured. ''If Dalton hadn't all but dragged me to my feet, we wouldn't be dancing right now.''

''I'll have to thank him later.''

He swung her around and their thighs brushed. Her pulse jumped, and she frowned. ''Save it. I promise you, tonight is definitely *not* your lucky night.''

''Aw, cher,'' he murmured in a Cajun patois, pressing his mouth close to her ear, ''you're breaking my heart.''

His breath stirred against her ear, warm, sensual. She steeled herself against the small flame of arousal it ignited inside her. ''Sorry, Detective. Devastating as that patented charm might be to other women, it's not working on me.''

''Really?'' He lowered his voice to a husky caress. ''I thought it was working quite well.''

He was right, dammit. She met his gaze, feigning

cool irritation. "Actually, I find overconfident men a bore. I suggest you go lasso a malleable, willing little thing who'll buy your shtick, because it's wasted on me."

She made a move to break away; he brought their joined hands to his heart. "Aw, cher, cut a good ol' Cajun boy some slack. Dance with me."

"With a name like Quentin Malone, I doubt you have a Cajun bone in your body. More like a good dose of Irish blarney."

He laughed and drew her back into his arms. "You misjudge me, Anna."

"Dalton said you'd been watching me. Why?"

"Why do you think?"

"Don't play games with me, Detective. And don't feed me a line about me being the most beautiful woman in the room. I'm not naive or self-deluded enough to buy that."

His smile faded. "Maybe I thought you needed protecting."

"From whom? Dalton?" She made a sound of derision. "Please."

The hand at her waist tightened. "From the kind of man who comes to a place like this to hunt. A predator looking for a woman like you, shaking it on the dance floor, uninhibited. Oblivious to his attention. Waiting."

"As far I know, you were the only one watching me."

"But I'm one of the good guys."

"How do I know that?" She tipped up her chin,

angry at his attempt to frighten her. "Because you wear a badge?"

"Yeah, because I wear a badge."

"Sorry if that doesn't inspire my confidence." She broke free of his grasp, suddenly more than angry. Suddenly, she was furious. "And what's that supposed to mean, 'shaking it on the dance floor'? What are you saying? That I'm loose? Some sort of a cocktease?"

"I didn't mean that. Look, Anna, two women are dead. Both redheads. Both spent the last night of their lives out with friends, having a good time. Nothing wrong about that. Nothing except they caught the attention of someone they shouldn't have. Someone who was watching."

Gooseflesh crawled up her arms. She shook the sensation off and faced him, cheeks on fire. "Are you trying to scare me?"

"Yes. Because people who are scared are careful."

For a single moment, she couldn't find her voice. Her thoughts flooded with the things she would say if she could speak. And with memories. Ones she wished she could forget. Ones of a trusting thirteen-year-old girl and an innocent six-year-old boy.

"Sometimes being careful means shit," she said softly, voice shaking. "Sometimes being a target has nothing to do with anything but being in the wrong place at the wrong time. I'm fine, Detective Malone. Leave me alone."

She turned and walked away, dodging two-stepping couples, earning a number of curious—and annoyed—glances. He didn't do as she requested, however, and caught up with her at the edge of the dance floor.

Hand to her elbow, he turned her to face him. "I'm sorry if I upset you."

"Well, you did. Now, for the second time, leave me alone."

She broke free of his grasp and crossed to Dalton. "I'm going home. Please hand me my purse."

"Anna?" He shifted his gaze to Malone, expression confused. "I don't understand. What's wro—"

"I have this effect on women," Malone said. "Big feet, big mouth. The curse of the Malone clan."

Anna didn't smile. She held her hand out. "My purse, Dalton. And jacket. Please."

Dalton handed it to her. "I'll grab Bill and we'll all go."

"No need. You to stay and have fun." She bent and kissed his cheek. "Tell Bill I said good-night. I'll see you in the morning."

Dalton hesitated and once more Malone stepped in. "Don't worry, I'll take her home. Just give me a minute to let my partner know what's going on."

She looked disbelievingly at him. "No, you won't take me home. This is good-night."

She walked away. He followed her. "I know you're angry at me, but don't be stupid. Women are dying."

She wouldn't be afraid. She wouldn't allow him to make her afraid. The French Quarter was her home. She had dozens of friends who lived between the bar and her apartment building. Because of her past, there were already too many areas of her life where she harbored fear. But not here. Here she felt safe.

"Look, Detective, I relieve you of all responsibility for my safety. In fact, I insist. Good night."

She marched toward the bar's front entrance, Malone on her heels.

"Let me call you a cab."

"No."

"Anna, this is no joking matter. There's a killer out there."

"And a rapist and crook and a...a kidnapper." She fought for an even breath. "But I can't live in fear. This is my home. I live a dozen blocks from here. Between here and there are the residences of several friends, ones I could call on in case of emergency. In addition, I've walked through the Quarter alone hundreds of times, never with any problem—" She could see by his set features that her argument was falling on deaf ears.

She tried another tack. "Fine. All right, I give up." She sighed with feigned exasperation. "Walk me home if it'll help you sleep. Go tell your partner, I'll wait here." She frowned. "Just don't take too long. I'm liable to take off."

He looked relieved. "Great. I'll be right back." He started off, then stopped and looked back over his shoulder. "Promise you won't bolt?"

She held up two fingers. "Scout's honor."

The moment he disappeared into the crowd, she turned and ducked out the door. She smiled at her own ingenuity, only feeling the tiniest prickle of guilt at having tricked him. After all, he was the one who had forced his company on her.

Besides, she had never been a Scout.

Anna walked quickly, certain that the moment Malone discovered her gone, he would try to catch up with her. She frowned. What a pushy, overbearing man. No doubt that obstinate and dogged determination made him a good cop. It also made him annoying as hell.

She hugged her leather jacket tighter around her, cold without Dalton and Bill's company. The French Quarter streets—their sounds, sights and smells—were familiar. Comfortable.

Usually. But not tonight. It had rained while she had been in Tipitina's, one of those cold, drenching downpours that sent all but the hardiest—and most foolhardy—in for the night. The deserted sidewalks were glassy and slick; the dampness seeming to seep through the soles of her shoes, chilling her.

She turned onto Jackson Square. The storefronts around the Square were dark, closed up tight for the night. She glanced at her watch, noting that it was after one already, much later than she had thought.

Two women were dead. Both redheads. Both killed after a night out clubbing with friends.

Anna muttered an oath and hugged herself tighter. Damn Detective Malone for frightening her. Damn him for forcing himself into her evening and ruining it. She was fine. Safe and in no danger at all.

Still, her thoughts turned to those two women. She had read about them in the *Times-Picayune.* The newspaper hadn't mentioned the color of their hair. It hadn't made a point of the fact that the two had been out dancing the night of their deaths.

It had made a point of how they had died.

Raped. Then suffocated.

Anna shivered. Suddenly, the silence seemed forced. The deserted streets unnatural. The work of movie magic. Her low-heeled mules made a soft slapping sound with each step, a far cry from the heavier footfalls behind her.

Behind her.

Anna's heart skipped a beat. She scolded herself for her overactive imagination. She cursed Quentin Malone for planting the seed of terror in her brain.

She increased her pace anyway, anxious to get home.

The pace of the footfalls behind her increased as well.

She stopped. Silence surrounded her. Heart hammering, she forced herself to peek over her shoulder. The sidewalk behind her appeared deserted. She moved her gaze. The shadows around the Square and the shops' doorways were dark and deep. Threatening.

A squeak of terror rose in her throat and she swallowed it, struggling to get a grip on herself. On her imagination. She began to walk, at a comfortable pace at first, then faster, acutely aware of the increasing speed of the footfalls behind her.

Two women were dead. Both redheads.

Truly frightened now, she broke into a run. She cut through the back of the Square, past the cathedral, its hulking shadow spilling across the sidewalk before her. She ducked onto St. Ann, then Royal, heading for the residential area of the French Quarter.

Still he followed.

Her slip-on shoes slowed her. She kicked them off,

stumbling as she did, crying out as something sharp bit into the tender underside of her foot. Her breath came in short, heavy gasps. Her heart thundered. The gasping and pounding filled her head and she struggled to hear past them but couldn't.

She was almost home. Only four more blocks. To her left lay a narrow side street, one that ran between the rear of two rows of buildings. A shortcut home. Taking it would slice her trip in half. She had done it a thousand times.

Without pausing for further thought, she darted down the street. The darkness closed in on her as she careened ahead, all her energy focused on her forward movement.

From behind her came the sound of a tin can skittering across the pavement.

He had found her.

Now, she was alone with him.

Dear heaven. Instead of losing her shadow, she had virtually lured him into what amounted to an alley.

Fear rose like bile from the pit of her stomach, gagging her. Stealing all rational thought. She plunged forward, stumbling again. Again losing precious seconds. In her mind's eye, she could see him on her heels, gaining on her, arms out.

The bogeyman had emerged from his hiding place in the shadows.

The end of the alley in sight now, she bolted for it.

And ran smack-dab into Quentin Malone. His arms went around her and she cried out in relief and clung to him, all but sobbing.

He searched her gaze, the amusement she had always seen in his gone. "My God, Anna, what's wrong?"

She fought to find the breath to speak. "Follow…someone was…"

He drew away from her. "Someone was following you? Where?"

"There." She pointed down the side street. "And before."

"Stay here. Let me take a loo—"

"No! Don't leave me."

"Anna, I have to." He set her away from him. "You're safe here, stand in the light. I'll be right back."

She did as he suggested and stood under the streetlight, hugging herself, unable to stop her teeth from chattering—though not from the cold night air, from another, much more frightening kind of chill.

Malone returned after a couple minutes, though to Anna it seemed an eternity. "Alley's empty," he said without preamble. "I didn't see anything that looked out of the ordinary. Are you certain someone was following you?"

"Yes." She hugged herself tighter. "I heard… him."

"Go on."

"Because it was so quiet, I…I noticed his footsteps."

"When did you first become aware of them?"

"Just after I…left Tips."

He looked at her long and evenly, as if weighing her every word, every nuance of her voice. With a small nod, he shifted his gaze. "I'll walk you the rest of the way home."

This time she didn't argue, but instead fell into step beside him, acknowledging to herself that she had never been more grateful for anyone's company in her life.

"Your teeth are chattering."

"I'm cold. It's the bare feet."

He lowered his gaze. And made a sound of surprise. "You're not wearing any shoes."

"I kicked them off…somewhere. Back there."

"I'll find them."

"No. Forget them. I just…I want to go home."

He hesitated, frowning. "I could carry you."

"No, please…it's not necessary. Really."

He looked like he wanted to argue with her, but didn't. Instead he glanced down at her, then ahead again. "Tell me exactly what happened."

She did, beginning with her noticing the rain-slicked sidewalks and ending with landing in his arms.

"Are you certain you were followed into the alley?"

She didn't hesitate. "Yes. As I neared the end of the alleyway there was a clattering sound behind me, like a tin can being kicked out of the way."

"But you didn't hear the footsteps."

She shook her head. "I was running and between my pounding heart and ragged breathing, I couldn't hear anything else."

He hesitated a moment, as if considering different scenarios. "Could it have been me you heard behind you?"

She stopped and looked at him. "Excuse me?"

"When I realized you'd bolted from Tipitina's, I asked your friend Dalton the route you would have taken home and headed out. Did you take St. Peter to St. Ann?" She nodded. "Maybe until you darted down the alley, the footfalls you heard were mine."

"What about the tin can?"

"A cat digging through a Dumpster."

They began walking again. *Had she allowed Malone's comments to get to her? Had her imagination run so far and so fast that she had literally fabricated the whole incident?*

"I don't know," she murmured. "I was so frightened and it's not like me to...to go off the deep end that way."

Except at night. When the nightmares visited. When Kurt came to call.

"Is that your building?" he asked, indicating the one just ahead.

She said that it was, then winced as she stepped on something sharp. "Ouch. Wait."

She grabbed his arm for support, then looked at the bottom of her foot. It was bleeding. She lifted her eyes to his, light-headed. "It must have been glass. A...big piece."

"Let me take a look."

He did, muttered an oath and lifted her into his arms. She squealed, surprised. "Malone! Put me down!"

"Not a chance." He closed the remaining distance to her building. "I should have done this two blocks ago."

"I feel silly. What if someone sees this?"

"They'll think we're newlyweds. Besides, it's not every day I get to help a damsel in distress."

"But you're a cop."

He grinned. "Yeah, but my specialty is dead people. You got a key for this place?"

She rummaged in her purse for her key ring and handed it to him. "The round one's for the courtyard gate, the square for my apartment."

Within minutes she was sitting on the edge of her bathtub, her foot on a towel in Malone's lap. He'd already called the Eighth District Station, explained what had happened and asked them to send a couple of uniforms to check out the scene. He also requested that they ask a few question at Tips.

Now his attention was focused on the bottom of her foot. "Yup," he murmured, "it's glass. Looks like it was once part of an Abita Beer bottle. That's the French Quarter for you."

She felt the blood drain from her face. "Do you think I need...stitches?"

Her voice shook and he looked at her in concern. "Please tell me you're *not* going to pass out."

"I'll try not to." She caught her bottom lip between her teeth. "I really don't do well with blood. Ever since—" She sucked in a deep, fortifying breath. "You know."

"I can guess." He stood, went to the sink and soaked a washcloth, then returned and gently rinsed her foot. His touch gentle, he probed the wound. "Doesn't look too deep. I think you can do without a trip to the emergency room."

She let out a pent-up breath, one she hadn't even realized she was holding. "Thank you."

"You're welcome." He got to his feet and went to the medicine cabinet. "I need antiseptic, sterile gauze, tape and tweezers. Have any of those things?"

She directed him and within moments he was performing his brand of bathroom surgery on her. "Okay, doll," he murmured, "bite on a nail, this might sting."

He came at her with the tweezers. Anna squeezed her eyes shut and held her breath, waiting for the sting. It came and a whimper escaped her clenched teeth.

"Got it. Want to see? It's a nice-size chunk."

"God, no." She averted her head, just to insure she didn't peek by accident. "I'd faint for sure."

"Thanks for the warning. Now hold on, here comes the bad part."

He wasn't joking. She came off her seat as he flushed the wound with antiseptic. It burned like hellfire. "Hey, go easy on that stuff!"

"Sorry, babe. Worst is over, I promise."

He grinned up at her, expression boyish, and her heart did this funny little thing—like a flip-flop or side step. She assured herself that the sensation was relief. Not awareness. Not attraction. Not one of those irrational sexual things that could get a girl in a world of trouble.

"You make a pretty good doctor," she said, forcing lightness into her tone. "Maybe you missed your calling?"

Malone laughed. "Hardly. I had enough trouble

getting through the schooling I needed to make detective first grade.'' He quickly and deftly wrapped and taped her foot. ''You have any ibuprofen?''

''In the cabinet.''

He retrieved the bottle and shook out a couple of the blue caplets, bringing them to her with a glass of water. ''You'll be sore for a while,'' he said as she took the caplets, then washed them down with the water. ''I'd suggest forgoing Tipitina's for now.''

''Maybe forever.'' She eased to her feet, wincing as she put pressure on the injured one. ''My dancing days are over.''

''Just take a cab next time, cher. Or bring a date.''

''I tried that,'' she murmured, taking a cautious step toward the doorway. ''He didn't show.''

''I can't say I'm unhappy about that.'' He smiled at her. ''It's not often I get to play doctor.''

Her heart did that jumpy thing again. Only this time she couldn't put it off to anything but what it was. Pure animal attraction. She cocked an eyebrow. ''Why do I find *that* hard to believe?''

''Because you're a cynic?''

''Yeah, right. Come on, I'll walk you to the door.''

''Actually, I suggest you stay off your feet.'' His eyes crinkled at the corners. ''If you'd like, I could tuck you into bed?''

Would she like him to? Yes. Would it be wise? Lord, no. Quentin Malone anywhere near her bed was definitely not a good idea. The man oozed more charm than a snake-oil salesman.

''I don't think so,'' she replied. ''But that was a good try.''

"Glad you think so. I'll try again."

She ignored that—and the realization that she hoped he would.

They reached her door. "Thanks for everything, Malone. I'm really...I'm grateful."

"NOPD, at your service."

"Tonight was way above and beyond the call of duty," she murmured, opening the door. "The truth is...you might have saved...without you, who knows what would have happened."

"I'm going to follow up on this, Anna. I'll let you know if I come up with anything." He paused at the door. "By the way, I looked into Jaye Arcenaux's foster parents for you."

Anna's mouth went dry. "And?"

"Nothing out of the ordinary materialized. In fact the Clausens seem about as true blue, apple pie as they come."

A lump formed in her throat. A part of her felt relief, another despair. "Are you sure?"

"As certain as I can be. They've been foster parents to more than a dozen kids. I checked around, talked to a few of their former kids. They had nothing but good things to say about the couple, and according to Social Services' records, most of their fosters turned out okay."

"Any of them run away?"

"I checked that, too, Anna. Yeah. And the ones who ran away turned up later. Alive and well." His expression turned sympathetic. "It looks like your friend really did run away. And if she did, my bet is she'll turn up sometime. They usually do."

"I wish I could believe that," Anna whispered. "I want to. It sure beats the alternative."

"Yeah, it does." He reached up and trailed a thumb lightly across her cheekbone. "I'll be in touch. Sleep well, Anna."

25

Saturday, January 20
The deep of the night

Jaye awakened to the sound of weeping. The sound echoed through the stillness, hollow and hopeless. The weeping of a lost soul. Another, just like herself.

The girl who had come to the door.

Jaye climbed out of bed and tiptoed to the door. She pressed her ear to the wood, aching for the other girl. Hurting for her. Understanding.

Jaye was certain that the other girl was also a prisoner. She wondered if their captor ever allowed the girl outside. If she ever had the opportunity to play in the park or go to a movie. She wondered if she had been snatched from the street, as Jaye had been.

How long had she been with this monster? Months? Years?

Sorrow rose up in Jaye. For herself. For the other lost soul. She brought her hands to the door, pressing her palms against its rigid surface. "Hello," she called out softly, then louder. "It's me. Upstairs. Stop crying, come talk to me."

The weeping ceased. Silence ensued. Moments ticked past. Jaye called out again. "Come upstairs. I'll talk to you. We'll have each other. We can be friends.''

Jaye waited. Seconds became what seemed like hours. Still Jaye waited. And prayed, heart thundering against the wall of her chest. Finally, she tried again. "Please," she called. "Please come and talk to me."

Somewhere in the house a door slammed, final and deafening. Jaye closed her eyes and sagged against the door. The other girl wasn't going to come. A whimper slipped past Jaye's lips; hopelessness choked her.

Alone. She was still alone.

Sudden laughter shattered the quiet. The sound broke through her thoughts and loosened the monster's grip on her. She wasn't going to give up the way the other girl had. She would never stop trying to escape, would never stop trying to beat him.

The laughter came again. The laughter of a group on the sidewalk below.

Below her window. A group of people who could help her.

If she could get their attention.

Jaye scrambled to the window and threw herself against the boards. She pounded on them like a madwoman, screaming and clawing at them. The cuts on the tips of her fingers opened and began to bleed.

The blood ran down her fingers, sticky and wet. Sobbing, Jaye yanked a piece of peeling wallpaper from the wall and wiped the blood on it. It mixed with her tears, streaking across the faded floral design, creating a web of spidery-looking lines. Like the handwriting of an old woman.

Handwriting. Of course.

She stared at the lines. Her tears dried. Her hands began to shake. She moved her gaze over the wall, looking for an area of loose paper.

She found one and carefully peeled it away. The paper, fragile with age, crumbled. Undaunted, she tried again. Then again, working the paper at the edges, slowly pulling it up and away from the wall.

She ended up with an irregular-shaped piece, slightly smaller than a sheaf of notebook paper. Her wounds had already begun to close, and she squeezed the tip of her right index finger, reopening it. She forced the blood to form a bead, then using the blood, began writing a message on the scrap of wallpaper. Minutes passed. When the first finger began to throb painfully, she switched to another. She repeated the process until she had scrawled:

Help me. I'm a prisoner. J. Arcenaux.

The building was old. The fit of window to frame poor. Maybe, just maybe, she could poke the paper through the slim opening between window and frame.

But first she had to worm her hand through a space between two boards. She managed to do it, though the position was agony; the process slow. Her hand and fingers cramped and sweat beaded her upper lip and the small of her back. She inched the paper forward until it fell away from her, away from the window.

Only then did Jaye realize she was crying. Silent tears of hope. And hopelessness.

She freed her hand and sank to the floor. She drew her knees to her chest and rested her forehead against

them. And prayed. That someone would find the note
and take it to the NOPD. That the police would mount
a search for her and she would be rescued.

It had to happen that way. It had to.

26

Sunday, January 21
The French Quarter

Anna awakened with a hangover. Not an alcohol-induced hangover—though she had drunk more than her usual quota—but an emotional one. She didn't want to move, didn't want to climb out of bed and face the day. Her head and foot throbbed, her eyes felt scratchy and raw, her mood heavy.

She closed her eyes and reviewed the events of the previous night: Her behavior at the bar; what Quentin had said about those other women; how her terror had grown with each step on her way toward home.

What *had* happened last night? she wondered. Had she really been followed from the bar? Or had her imagination taken control of her brain and run away with her?

She wanted to believe the latter. But couldn't. She wasn't prone to hysteria—to have been scared was one thing, to have grown hysterical with fear was another.

The footsteps had stopped and started with hers. If it had been Malone behind her, they wouldn't have— they would have continued.

She grimaced. Unless, of course, she had imagined that, too. She had been under a lot of pressure, stressed out by current events. Malone had planted the seed of fear inside her, it had taken root and become like Mississippi kudzu—growing out of control, gobbling up everything in its path...especially her good sense.

Anna climbed out of bed anyway, the need for coffee stronger than her need to hide under the covers an hour or two more. She winced as she put her weight on her foot, but limped toward the kitchen anyway. St. Louis Cathedral held its last mass at eleven. That gave her plenty of time for coffee, the *Times-Picayune* and a long leisurely shower.

After starting the coffee, she headed downstairs to retrieve the newspaper.

And found Ben on her front steps, preparing to ring her apartment. He cradled several La Madeline bags in his left arm while balancing a beverage tray in the other.

He thought he could stand her up at night and get back into her good graces in the morning? Fat chance. "Ben," she said, tone cool. "What brings you here this morning?"

He turned and looked at her in surprise. "I didn't ring yet, how did you know I was here?"

She brushed by him, bent and retrieved her paper. He understood and flushed.

"I brought cheese and fresh-baked French bread. You haven't eaten, have you?" She didn't reply and he waggled the beverage tray. "Cappuccinos, too. Can I come in?"

"I don't think so. I don't feel very social this morning."

"You're angry with me. About last night."

Anna looked him in the eyes. "It seems to me, Ben, that if you'd wanted to spend time with me, you would have made it to Tipitina's last night. I'm feeling like this morning is too late."

He looked crestfallen. "I wanted to make it. A patient had an emergency…by the time I was free, I figured I'd be pretty crappy company. I didn't want to subject you and your friends to that." He hesitated a moment. "I'm really sorry, Anna. I did want to be with you."

He had big, brown puppy-dog eyes and was looking at her as if she'd just put him out in the cold. She let out her breath in a huff and stepped away from the door. "Oh, all right. But I'm really pissed off."

Obviously seeing right through her, he grinned and stepped into the building's foyer. He moved his gaze over the space, no doubt taking in the ceiling medallion, crown molding, chair rails and high ceilings. "I love these old places. They have so much character."

"I agree. Come on. I need to get off my foot."

He lowered his gaze, saw the bandages, then made a sound of concern. "What happened?"

As they walked up the stairs to her second-floor apartment, she told him. When she had finished, he touched her hand. "I should have been there. This wouldn't have happened."

But then she wouldn't have spent time with Malone.

She had left her apartment door ajar and they entered. "It wasn't your fault, Ben. Kitchen's this way."

A couple of moments later, she tossed the newspaper onto the kitchen table. "Have a seat. I'll get some plates and napkins."

The bags crackled as Ben opened them. "I got Brie, Gouda and herbed cream cheese. I didn't know what you liked best."

She cocked an eyebrow at his obvious attempt at bribery. "You mean, you didn't know just how much trouble you were in?"

He grinned. "Am I that transpar—Anna, did you see this? In the paper?"

She crossed to the table. He spun the paper so she could read the front page. Her eyes went straight to the headline he meant, lower right.

Woman attacked in the French Quarter.

"Oh my God." She sank onto one of the chairs. "This happened last night?"

"Yes." He flipped the paper back around. "She was on her way home from waitressing at the Cat's Meow. He attacked her from behind."

Anna brought a hand to her mouth. "What else does it say?"

He skimmed the article. "She didn't get a look at him. Something frightened him off, but she's not sure what. What time were you followed?"

She thought a minute. "After one. I remember, I looked at my watch."

"This occurred shortly after two. That's what time the club closed."

She swallowed hard, throat tight. "Do you think it could have been the same guy who…followed me?"

"I don't know, but the coincidence…"

He let the thought trail off but it hung in the air between them anyway. *The coincidence seemed too great to ignore.*

"What color was her hair?"

At the question, Ben drew his eyebrows together. "It doesn't say. Why?"

She shook her head. "Never mind. I think I'd better call Malone."

"Malone?" Ben shuddered slightly, as if cold. "Oh, that's right, your knight in shining armor."

She heard an unfamiliar edge in his voice. As if he was jealous. Instead of being flattered, she was annoyed. "If my memory serves, Ben, I invited you out, but you didn't make it. So if you have a problem with Malone seeing me home—"

"A problem?" He blinked and held out the paper cup. "Of course not. Cappuccino?"

The beverage was only lukewarm, but she drank it anyway, enjoying the flavor of espresso and milk at any temperature.

He, too, drank a cool cappuccino. They both chose Brie to complement their French bread and ate in semisilence, chatting about nothing more topical than the weather. When they'd finished, Ben eased his plate away and cleared his throat. "Since we last spoke, I've done some thinking about our mystery man. I wanted to share my thoughts with you."

She sat up straighter. "Go on."

"As you know, I've questioned the six patients I saw the Friday I received the package containing your book and the note about the E! special. All six denied having left the package. Of course, they could be lying. Considering recent events, I really don't expect the guilty party to confess.''

"So what do we do, beat it out of them?''

Her attempt at humor brought a smile to his lips. "We could, but I've come up with another plan. I'm going to put their honesty to the test.''

"And how do you do that?''

"First off, I'm not going to limit my inquiry to the patients I saw that Friday. Any of my patients could have left it while I was in session.'' He glanced down at his hands, folded on the table in front of him, then back up at her. He smiled, the curving of his lips wicked. "I'm going to use psychology on them.''

"I don't understand.''

He leaned forward, eyes bright. "When I asked my patients if they had left a package for me in the waiting room, I didn't say what was in it. So I leave the book in a conspicuous place in my inner office, where my patients will notice it during our sessions. Psychology says the guilty party will be unable to take his eyes off it. I fully expect him to not only repeatedly glance at it, but to comment on it as well.''

She digested that, then nodded. "Sounds good, but...''

"What, Anna? It'll work, I'm sure of it.''

"Are you positive one of your patients is the guilty party? By your own admission, anyone could have come into your office while you were in session and left the package.''

"But why would they? I've thought a lot about this, Anna. Why me? How am I involved in this? I've come to the conclusion that I was a late addition.''

She frowned. "I don't follow."

"This patient, whoever he or she is, started seeing me because of you and their plan, whatever it is. Why I'm involved holds the key to this whole thing."

"Go on."

"Why did they select me? My specialty? Did they hear me speak at a seminar?"

"Your specialty," she said. "It has to be."

"I agree. So how did they find me?" He lifted his coffee cup, saw that it was empty and set it back down. "The Yellow Pages mention my specialty is childhood trauma and certainly our guy could have heard about me by word of mouth, but personally I think it was through a seminar I participated in three months ago. I've called the organizers and requested a list of attendees. It took some convincing, but they agreed. They shipped it out Friday, FedEx. I should have it tomorrow morning."

"You're amazing."

"Thanks." He tipped an imaginary hat. "Sherlock Shrink at your service."

They talked a few minutes more, then Anna walked him out. They stopped at the building's front door. "Thank you, Ben. I feel more positive right now than I have since this whole thing began."

"It's going to be okay, Anna. We'll find out who's doing this to you, and we'll stop him."

Before she could thank him again, he bent and kissed her.

For a split second, Anna froze—taken by surprise, nonplussed. Then she relaxed and kissed him back.

A moment later, he was gone. Anna watched him

walk away, thoughts whirling. She brought a hand to her mouth, still warm from the imprint of his. What in the world, she wondered, had become of her quiet, safe and predictable life?

27

Monday, January 22
9:20 a.m.

As promised by the mental-health seminar organizers, the list of the attendees arrived first thing Monday morning. Ben ripped open the Federal Express envelope and drew out the list of one hundred and fifty-two names.

Aware of the time—his first patient of the day was due in ten minutes—Ben quickly scanned the names, looking for one of his patients or for the name Peter Peters.

The list contained a number of duplicate given names and a few duplicate surnames, but not an exact match.

Damn. He dropped the list onto his desk, admitting disappointment. He had been hoping for an easy, immediate answer. He wasn't going to get it. *They* weren't going to get it.

Anna. He had thought of little but her since their breakfast. He smiled. Kissing her had taken her by surprise. In truth, he had surprised himself.

He liked her a lot. More than was safe or smart.

She could break his heart.

Ben shook his head. He wouldn't think that way.

If they were meant to be together, they would be. Once he'd discovered the identity of Anna's stalker, they would be free to simply get to know one another.

With that in mind, Ben returned his attention to his plan. Everything was set. He had prominently displayed Anna's book on the coffee table in front of the couch, the note about the E! special peeking out from between the pages. The manila envelope both had come in rested on the end table, next to the box of tissues.

The door chimed and Ben glanced at his appointment book. That should be Amy West, a housewife and mother of three who was suffering from depression, the cause rooted in her troubled childhood and unhappy marriage.

Ben stood and crossed to the door to greet her. He didn't expect Amy to be the one. Not only had her depression all but paralyzed her, she didn't fit the psychological profile he had created of Anna's stalker. He believed the man—or woman—who had planned this campaign against her to be both cunning and controlling, highly intelligent, organized and emotionally detached. The person would possess the ability to lie without blinking and because of his or her emotional detachment, have no concern for the feelings of others.

Amy West was nearly the antithesis of that profile.

Even so, he wouldn't take anything for granted. If there was one thing he had learned from his years being a therapist, a patient's true nature only revealed itself over time, and in the end, often ran counter to what he had expected. Nothing about the human psyche surprised him anymore.

28

Quentin stepped into The Perfect Rose. The bell above the door jingled but Anna didn't look his way. She sat on a tall stool behind the counter, staring into space, obviously lost in thought.

Quentin was struck again by her uncomplicated beauty. And by the way looking at her gave him this feeling, this *ahh*. The same kind of feeling he got when he bit into a super-tangy apple or took a deep breath of ice-cold early-morning air.

He'd experienced the *ahh* for the first time while watching her dance at Tips, then again later when he'd bandaged her foot. Her white-tiled bathroom had suddenly seemed too small, the situation unbearably intimate. Unbearable only because the thoughts that had jumped into his head had been out of the question.

If she had given him the smallest sign, he would have had her in bed, to hell with what was appropriate.

As if sensing his presence, she shifted her gaze and looked directly at him. Her expression registered surprise and he thought, pleasure.

"Hi, doll."

"I was going to call you this morning."

"Yeah? Why didn't you?"

"Got sidetracked." She indicated the bag he carried under his left arm. "What's in the bag?"

"For you." He handed it to her, a smile twitching at the corners of his mouth.

She peeked inside, then returned her gaze to his. "My shoes? You went back for my shoes?"

"I have sisters, I know how women are about their shoes." He leaned against the service counter. "So, why were you going to call me? Couldn't put me out of your mind? Wanted to repay me for saving your foot by making me a home-cooked meal?"

"Try again."

"You read about the attack on the woman in the French Quarter and you were worried it might have been the same guy who followed you?"

He heard her indrawn breath. "Yes. Was…was she a redhead?"

"No."

"Thank God. Do you—"

"Think it might have been the same guy who followed you?"

"Yes."

"Could have been. I can't be certain either way, though I doubt it. A couple of witnesses from the Cat's Meow claim to have seen a guy watching her all night. One of them claims to have seen him hanging around after the bar closed."

"So he couldn't be the same one who followed me?"

"If their reports are accurate, no."

"I don't know why that makes me feel so relieved, but it does." She laughed nervously. "I had a little trouble sleeping last night."

"I'll bet." He swept his gaze over her. "How do you feel now, light of day and all that?"

"Okay." She drew in a slow, careful breath. "The guy who attacked that woman, do you think he's the one who killed those other two?"

"I don't think so. The MO's different. This woman was working, not partying. And she wasn't a redhead."

"Maybe he's...he's changed his MO," she offered. "Maybe the first two women being redheads was a coincidence."

"Maybe, Anna, but—"

His words were cut off as Dalton and Bill returned from having coffee. They came through the shop's entrance laughing. Their laughter died when they saw him.

Quentin smiled. "Hello."

Dalton turned to Bill. "It's him. The man who saved our Anna. Our hero."

Beaming, Bill strode forward. He held out his hand. "Bill Friends. I'm forever in your debt."

"We'll never let her walk home alone again, Detective." Dalton looked at her, expression solemn. "Never, Anna."

Quentin shook Bill's hand, then Dalton's. "Quentin Malone. Good to meet you."

"Any luck catching the creep who was following Anna?" Bill asked.

"Sorry to say, no. And to be honest with you, we probably won't. We simply don't have enough to go on."

Silence fell over them. After a moment, Quentin checked his watch. "I've got to get back to work." He smiled at her. "Bad guys to catch and all that."

"And all that," she murmured. "I'll walk you to the door."

Although unnecessary, he didn't tell her no. He glanced back at her friends, who were watching him and Anna, speculative gleams in their eyes. "Nice seeing you two."

They replied in kind; a moment later Anna was standing beside him at the door. She hugged herself. "I wanted to thank you again, for the other night."

"No thanks necessary. Really."

"And for the shoes. You know, for bringing them back to me."

"I couldn't wear them." He paused a moment. "They didn't fit."

She laughed, glanced over her shoulder at her friends, then back at Quentin. "If anything comes up, you'll call me?"

"Sure." He smiled. "And you do the same, okay?"

She agreed and he walked away, wishing he had a reason to stay, wishing he didn't have to follow through on the promise he'd made Terry to pay a visit to Penny, his estranged wife.

But he had promised, and he had put it off as long as possible. So long that his excuses for not following through had begun to sound as lame as they were.

So he had called Penny that morning and asked if he could stop by. She had been frazzled from having the two kids home with the flu and she would be happy, she said, to have an adult to talk to.

Quentin crossed the sidewalk to his Bronco, parked in a red zone, climbed in and fired up the engine. Terry and Penny's home was located in a part of the city called Lakeview, an area built primarily in the 1940s and '50s. Shady, green and almost exclusively residential, the area boasted the best public schools in New Orleans. Catering to middle-class families, Lakeview was one of the few affordable "nice" places to raise kids in the city.

Quentin enjoyed the fifteen-minute drive, purposely not rehearsing what he would say to Penny. Because of his relationship with Terry, he and the woman were good friends. He had been there through their courtship, had stood up at their wedding and was godfather to their oldest child. Not only would she see through a canned speech, but he believed he owed her better than that.

Penny was standing at her front door when he pulled up in front of the two-story stucco home. She saw him, waved and stepped outside.

He pulled his vehicle to a stop and climbed out. Moments later she was hugging him tightly.

"I was glad you called," she said. "I've been missing you."

He drew away from her, experiencing regret. At having neglected her. At the reason for his visit today. He searched her gaze. With her soft brown hair and eyes, creamy skin and curvy figure, she was a very pretty woman, a fact even the fatigue lines around her eyes and mouth couldn't hide.

"How are you doing?"

"Hanging in there." She motioned inside. "Come on in. I just brewed a pot of coffee." She held a finger to her lips. "The kids are sleeping, thank God, so keep your voice low."

He followed her into the kitchen. It was in a state of disarray—the way his mother's kitchen had often been.

"Have a seat. You still take your coffee sweet?"

"The sweeter the better."

She laughed. "I was taking about your coffee, Malone. Not your women."

He smiled. "I said sweet, Penny. Not hot."

She laughed again and set the coffee in front of him, then sat down herself. It had always been this way between them, comfortable, easy. He had liked her from the first moment Terry had introduced them.

"Speaking of, how's your love life?"

Anna's image popped into his head, and his lips tipped up. "What love life? I hang out with cops and criminals all day."

"Yeah, sure." Her smile faded. "How's Terry?"

He lifted a shoulder. "You know Terry."

"Yeah," she said, bitterness creeping into her tone, "I know Terry."

This wasn't going to go well, he acknowledged. Penny was hurting and unhappy. She was angry at her husband. But he had promised his friend he would speak to her, and he would.

"Penny," he began, "I didn't stop by today only to see how you were doing."

She looked away, then back. "Terry sent you."

Quentin leaned toward her. "He's miserable without you, Penny. He's miserable without the kids. He wants to come home."

A short, brittle-sounding laugh bubbled to her lips. "He's just miserable, Malone. It has nothing to do with me or the kids."

Quentin reached across the table and caught her hand. "He loves you, Pen. I know he does. Since you kicked him out, he's been…crazy. Unhappy. Drinking too much, not sleeping. I've never seen him this way."

Her eyes flooded with tears. "Lucky you."

"Pen—"

"No." She pushed her chair away from the table, stood and crossed to the sink and the window that faced the winter-bare backyard. She stared out at the stark day, not speaking.

Finally, she turned and faced him, her expression naked with pain. "I used to tell myself all those things. That Terry loved me and the kids. That we were better off with him. I told myself that I should be grateful that he was a hard worker and a good provider. That I should stick by him because I'd made a promise before God and that I should forgive him because he'd had a shitty childhood."

She sucked in a broken-sounding breath. "I can't tell myself those things anymore. We're not better off with him here, Quentin. He's not good for me or the kids. And I don't believe God wants that for me or the children.'' She brought a hand to her mouth, then dropped it. She looked him dead in the eyes. ''He's self-destructing, Malone. And I can't stop him. And I don't want him to do it in front of Matti and Alex.''

Quentin frowned. ''Self-destructing, Pen? Don't you think that's a bit of an overstatement? Sure, he's going through a tough time, but—''

''But nothing,'' she snapped, cheeks flaming. ''Stop making excuses for him, Malone. They're not helping him, they're not helping me. Yeah, he's going through a tough time, but aren't we all? Yeah, he had a troubled childhood. So, do something about it. He's an adult, not a child. An adult with responsibilities, a family to take care. He needs to start acting like one.''

Her anger seemed to evaporate, leaving her looking young and vulnerable. ''I can't fight his demons anymore. I wish I could, but I can't.''

Quentin stood and went to her. He drew her against his chest and held her for a long time. Finally, he eased her away and searched her gaze. ''What do you know about his mother, Pen? I know almost nothing except that it was bad between them, really bad.''

Penny's eyes flooded with tears. ''I hate her, even though I only saw her a couple of times. Because she did this to him, because she made him...hate himself.''

''But...what did she do, Penny? How did she—''

''Hurt him so deeply? I don't know the details, Terry wouldn't talk about her. He wouldn't allow her to have anything to do with the kids. He didn't even allow them to keep the cards she sent.''

Penny let out a long breath. ''I know she ridiculed

him constantly. Tore him down. Told him he wasn't any good, that she wished she'd never had him. That she should have gotten rid of him, things like that.''

Told that enough, a kid began to believe it. Quentin swallowed hard. It explained a lot. "I'm sorry, Penny."

"Me, too. Damn sorry. I—"

"Mom!"

The cry had come from Matti, her youngest. Penny glanced in the direction of the doorway, then back at Quentin. "I've got to go."

He caught her arm. "I've got to ask you one more thing, because I promised Terry I would. Are you seeing anybody? Going out at all? Alex told Terry—"

She made a sound of disbelief. "Are you asking if I'm dating? Please, when would I have time to go out? Between homework and ball practice and vomiting kids?"

She freed her arm from his grasp, obviously hurt that he'd asked. "Get real, Malone. Terry was the one who'd always had time for that. Not me. And please, tell Terry I said so."

29

Monday, January 22
9:00 p.m.

Ben arrived home late that evening. The day had been hectic. Not only had he had back-to-back appointments, he had given up his lunch to fit in a patient in crisis then, though exhausted, had picked up Popeye's spicy fried chicken—his mother's favorite—and gone to the nursing home to have dinner with her as promised.

Ben sighed, fumbling for his keys. His plan to trap Anna's stalker had come up empty. Not one patient had given the book more than a cursory glance.

He refused to be discouraged. No, he hadn't caught his prey, but he had eliminated seven patients from his list of suspects. That was good news. It was a step forward. Tomorrow he would eliminate several more.

Ben unlocked the front door, stepped inside, then stopped, the hair on the back of his neck prickling.

Something felt wrong. He moved his gaze over the foyer, the parlor to his right and toward the dining room beyond. He frowned. The pocket door that separated the two rooms was closed. Light streamed from beneath it.

He never closed that door.

Heart thundering, he started toward the parlor, moving slowly, his rubber-soled shoes silent on the wooden floor. He crossed to the fireplace, took the log iron from the rack, then closed the distance to the door.

He eased it open. The door slid silently back. Log iron at the ready, he stepped through the opening.

The room was empty. Nothing appeared out of place.

A sound came from the back of the house. A low murmur, like voices. The hair on the back of his neck prickled again. *Stop playing Rambo, Benjamin. Call the cops.*

He started forward instead, adrenaline fed blood pumping crazily through his veins.

The sounds emanated from his bedroom. He reached the door, took a deep breath, grasped the knob and stepped inside.

The bedroom appeared empty. The television was on. Tuned to the Discovery Channel. Ben lowered the log iron, a self-conscious laugh rushing to his lips. He didn't remember leaving the set on, but that didn't mean he hadn't. He often played it while dressing, using it more for background noise than as entertainment. He crossed to the set, flipped it off and turned around.

His smile died. On the bed lay a large manila envelope, his name scrawled neatly in the upper left corner.

Ben stared at the envelope, a knot of apprehension

in his throat. He didn't want to look at it. Didn't want to touch it.

He couldn't not.

He crossed to the bed, retrieved the envelope and opened it. Inside was an eight-by-ten, black-and-white photograph of him and Anna at the Café du Monde. The attached note was short and to the point:

I knew you'd like her.
  I'll be watching.

Ben's hands began to shake and he slipped the photo and note back into the envelope. He should call the police. Call Anna.

His head began to hurt and he brought a hand to his temple. No. If he involved the authorities, the first thing they'd want would be a list of his patients, which he couldn't give them. They would insist on speaking with Anna, who already didn't like or trust the police. She would be upset. Frightened.

Their breakfast together had been so good. Their kiss had been…exciting. He hadn't felt about another woman the way he felt about Anna, not ever. He didn't want to lose her.

She seemed to feel the same about him.

So why this? Why now?

He sank onto the bed, exhausted, headache intense, a burning sensation behind his eyes. He told himself to go fetch a couple of the tablets his doctor had prescribed, but lay back against the mattress and stared blindly up at the ceiling instead.

Who was doing this? Why was he doing it?

He groaned and laid his arm across his eyes. And tonight, how had this person gotten in? When he arrived home, his front door had been locked. What about the back door? he wondered. What about the windows? He needed to check them, although he would be surprised if he found any of them open. Living in metropolitan Atlanta had turned him into a fanatic about personal security.

His keys. The ones that had gone missing for twenty-four hours.

Ben sat up. Of course. The day they had disappeared he'd had them in the morning, had locked up his house then walked next door to the office. Once inside, he had tossed them on his desk. The same as he did every morning.

When he had gone to collect them, they had been gone.

Only to resurface twenty-four hours later. He had tripped over them. Literally.

He hadn't dropped them, the way he had assumed. Or brushed them off his desk and onto the floor. A patient—the same one who had broken in today, the same one who had left Anna's book and note about the E! program—had stolen them, made copies, then returned the keys two days later.

Ben's vision blurred, then cleared, a sign that his headache was making a move from excruciating to unbearable. He dragged himself off the bed, unwilling to give in to the pain, unwilling to let go of this mystery. Gritting his teeth, he went to each window then the back door. He checked to make sure each was secured—and to make certain his theory was correct and that he hadn't simply left one of them open.

He hadn't. Headache tablets in hand, he went to the phone. He called an all-night locksmith, then sat down to wait. When the locksmith had come and gone, he would collect his appointment book from his office. The book would tell him which of his patients had been in the day his keys had gone missing. It would tell him if any of those same patients had been in twenty-four hours later. His sick friend might have just outfoxed himself.

He was going to find out who was doing this and stop them in their tracks.

Or die trying.

30

Tuesday, January 23
1:00 a.m.

A quiet tapping awakened Jaye. She knew from the depth of the darkness and the silence that it was the deepest part of the night. The tapping came again, followed by a cat's meow.

"Shh, Tabby. I think she's sleeping."

Jaye scrambled off the bed and hurried toward the door. "No," she whispered when she reached it. "I'm awake. Don't go."

For a moment, no sound came from the other side of the door. Then the other girl said, "I came to see if you're okay."

"I am, but please don't leave." She pressed closer to the door. "Stay and talk to me."

"I don't know." The girl's voice quivered. "He would be very angry if he knew I was here."

"He won't find out," Jaye said quickly. "I'll be quiet. I promise."

The girl hesitated, then acquiesced. "Okay. But we have to be really quiet."

Jaye promised. She knelt down in front of the pet door. "Tell me your name."

"Minnie. And my kitty's name is Tabitha. She's my best friend."

Jaye digested that. "Tabitha's a pretty name. What kind of cat is she?"

"A tabby. Her eyes are green. She has long, soft fur."

Jaye smiled. "How old are you, Minnie?"

"Eleven. Tabitha's two."

Jaye pressed closer. She heard the cat purring. "My name's Jaye. I'm fifteen."

"I know. He told me."

A chill raced up Jaye's spine, with it a feeling of dread. "Who is he, Minnie? Your dad or—"

"He's Adam. I don't know his last name."

"How long have you been with him?"

"A long time," the girl replied, sounding confused. "Forever, I think."

Not forever, Jaye knew. This Adam had kidnapped Minnie, just as he had kidnapped her. "We have to work together, Minnie. I have friends who live near here. You help me get out of this room, and I'll get us away from him."

"I can't. He would be very angry. He would hurt Tabitha. He's hurt…my friends before."

Jaye squeezed her eyes shut. "You could go home, Minnie." Her voice shook, and she worked to steady it. She sensed that Minnie would be more likely to have confidence in her if she sounded confident herself. "I'd make sure you got to go home."

"Home," she repeated, her whisper almost inaudible. "I don't remember home."

Hatred rose up in Jaye, sudden and swift. For this

monster who would steal a child away from her family. With the hatred came a fierce determination to free them both and make him pay.

Certain that revealing her thoughts would send the other girl running, Jaye kept them hidden. "Tell me more about you, Minnie. Do you go to school?"

She didn't, but she did know how to read and write. That question led to others and before long, Jaye had what she thought was a good picture of the girl on the other side of the door. She was a timid girl, fair-haired and slight. She was a prisoner here and had been for some time, perhaps since she had been five or six years old.

Jaye told Minnie about herself, her life, the people she missed most. She told her about Anna.

Minnie began to cry.

"Don't cry," Jaye said quickly. "Whatever I said, I'll stop. I didn't mean to make you—"

"It's not you. It's... He made me do it, Jaye. He made me write those letters. And now it's...it's my fault you're here. It's all my fault!"

Her voice rose, and Jaye tried to quiet her. She didn't want Minnie to awaken Adam. She didn't want to be alone again. "What are you talking about, Minnie? What letters?"

"The ones to your friend Anna. He made me do it. He said he would hurt Tabitha if I disobeyed."

Jaye stiffened, alarmed. "Anna? I don't understand."

But then she did. The fan letters Anna had received from that kid. The little girl.

Minnie.

Please God, no.

A shuffling sound came from the other side of the door. When Minnie spoke, it sounded as if she had pressed her mouth to the pet door. "Your Anna's in danger. He talks about her all the time. He has these...plans. I listened."

Minnie's voice lowered even more, almost as if it was fading away. Jaye pressed her ear to the door, straining to hear. "That's why he kidnapped you, Jaye. To get to Anna."

A wave of icy-cold fear washed over Jaye. She thought of the fight with Anna, of the awful things she had said to her friend. Regret swamped her. Guilt.

All along, Anna had been right to be afraid. She had been right to keep her real identity a secret.

Jaye should have listened. A real friend would have. She should have put herself in Anna's shoes and tried to understand. But she hadn't.

Now, in a strange way, she was in Anna's shoes.

She had to warn her friend. She had to find a way to help her.

"Minnie?" she whispered. "What's he planning to do to Anna? You've got to tell me. We've got to find a way to help her."

Only silence answered her and Jaye realized with a sense of loss that the other girl had gone.

31

Tuesday, January 23
7:00 p.m.

Anna arrived home after a long, extremely busy day at The Perfect Rose. Typically, Tuesdays were slow, but this Tuesday had been an exception. When she hadn't been taking orders, she'd been helping Dalton fill them, adding bows, filling balloons and writing gift enclosures.

Frazzled, his fingers aching, Dalton had left her to close up shop. She had shooed him off, certain the last hour of the day would be dead slow. She had planned to straighten the shop, readying it for the next day. Instead, two frantic husbands had rushed in, one in search of flowers for his wife's birthday, the other for an anniversary.

Luckily, they'd both wanted roses—which she had been able to handle—though the two orders had eaten up her hour. She had stayed after, knowing that if tomorrow proved as busy as today, she and Dalton were going to need an orderly space in which to work.

Anna unlocked her apartment door and stepped inside. She was hungry. And tired. And feeling about as low as a snake's belly.

Today, her agent had called. Cheshire House had made one last offer. It had been a good one, slightly better than before. They had wanted an answer immediately.

Her answer had been no.

Sighing, Anna tossed her keys onto the entryway table. She had wanted to accept—had wanted to with all her heart—but in good conscience she had been forced to refuse. No way in hell would she have been able to follow through on the publicity they proposed. She couldn't do it. Period.

The hopelessness of it had her feeling depressed. She planned to grab a sandwich and sit at her computer. She was hoping that getting back to work would lift her spirits. If she could just compose a good page or two, she knew she could rekindle her excitement about writing.

After changing into leggings and a big sweater, Anna headed to the kitchen. She glanced at the answering machine, noting that she had no messages, flipped on the radio and headed to the refrigerator.

The ''Mardi Gras Mambo'' filled her tiny kitchen, and Anna hummed under her breath as she collected her favorite sandwich fixings.

Turkey, she decided, loading up her arms. Lots of veggies and mayo. Big dill pickle. Maybe some chips. She set the ingredients on the counter, then returned for the pitcher of water, lifting it off the shelf.

Then she saw it. On a glass dessert plate topped with a red heart-shaped doily sat a finger. A pinkie finger.

Her heart rushed to her throat, a scream with it.

Anna took a step backward, the pitcher slipping from her fingers and crashing to the floor. Cold water sprayed her ankles and feet.

Kurt.

He'd found her.

Hysteria rose up in her; she turned and ran. Out of her apartment and into hall, next door to Dalton and Bill's apartment.

She pounded on the door, sobbing, calling their names. *Please be home. Please…please—*

They were, and thirty minutes later she sat huddled beside Dalton on his couch, his arm protectively circling her shoulders. When she had been coherent enough to tell her friends what had happened, they had called Malone. Right now he and Bill were in her apartment, checking out the situation.

Anna drew in a shaky breath and Dalton squeezed her shoulders. "It's going to be okay, Anna."

He didn't sound convinced. His voice shook slightly, and Anna wished she could reassure him. But she couldn't find the words.

Kurt had found her. He had been inside her apartment.

He meant to kill her.

She shuddered and pressed herself closer to Dalton's side. "I'm scared."

"I know." He let out a long breath. "I am, too."

Malone returned then, plate, doily and finger bagged and marked. Anna shifted her gaze from it to Bill, he trailed behind Malone, pale as a ghost. She swallowed hard. "Was it… I mean, could you tell who—"

"It's a fake," Malone interrupted, crossing to her. "A good one. A prosthesis."

He laid the bag on the table and Anna averted her gaze. Fake or not, looking at it made her feel ill.

Malone squatted down in front of her, blocking her view of the bagged finger and forcing her to look directly into his eyes. "Anna, when you got home, was your front door locked?"

She thought a moment, then nodded. "The dead bolt slid back, just like always. I walked inside and dropped my keys on the entryway table."

"And nothing seemed out of place to you? You didn't get the sense that something was wrong?"

She shook her head. "No. Nothing."

"Did you know your balcony door was unlocked?"

"Are you certain?" She frowned. "That can't be right."

"It was," Bill confirmed. "I saw it with my own eyes."

"The other morning," Dalton murmured, "when Bill and I were breakfasting on the patio. You called to us from the balcony. Could you have forgotten to relock the door?"

She supposed she could have, but it would have been totally out of character. She rubbed her forehead. "I don't remember if I did or not."

"All the other windows were locked," Malone said. "I didn't see any sign of a forced entry."

"You think he got in that way?"

"He could have." Malone took his spiral from his jacket pocket, then looked her in the eyes. "There's another possibility. Does anyone else have a key to your apartment?"

"Just Dalton."

Malone looked at him and Dalton flushed. "I own the building, so actually I have the master key to everyone's apartment."

"But that doesn't mean he would ever use it," Anna said, coming to her friend's defense. "Besides, Dalton and Bill are my friends, they'd never try to—"

"Of course they wouldn't," Malone murmured, turning his gaze back to her. "What about former boyfriends or live-ins?"

Their eyes met; her cheeks heated. Though completely appropriate, his question felt too intimate. It left her feeling exposed. "No, none."

"Any roommates at all?" She shook her head, and he jotted her response in his notebook. "Do you have any idea who could have been behind this?"

His question hit her squarely in the chest; she felt herself beginning to fall apart and squeezed her hands into fists, fighting hysteria off. "Kurt."

"Kurt? You don't mean the man who kidnapped you twenty-three years ago?"

"Yes, I do. He's found me, I know it."

Malone glanced at her friends, then cleared his throat. "Do you have any proof of this?"

She laughed, the sound sharp and humorless. "What more proof do I need than what...happened tonight?"

Malone fell silent a moment. When he spoke his tone was gentle, his words careful. "It's understandable you would feel that way, Anna. But it's much more likely that someone else has singled you out this way. Someone who knows your story and has become fixated on it and you.''

"Great,'' she whispered. "You're saying I have more than one psycho after me. Some girls have all the luck.''

A smile tugged at his mouth, though she knew not because her situation amused him. "Here's the deal.'' He looked at Dalton and Bill, then back at Anna. "It's most likely someone in your life now. A friend or acquaintance. A business associate. A regular customer at The Perfect Rose or someone else who plays a part in the periphery of your life.''

He moved his gaze between the three again. "This stunt shows a high level of planning and determination. It also exhibits familiarity and expertise. Now, think. Does anybody you know come to mind?''

Anna twisted her fingers together. "No. Except for Kurt. I can't imagine who would have done this to me.''

She looked at Dalton, then Bill for confirmation. Both shook their heads. "Nobody I know comes to mind, Detective Malone,'' Bill murmured. "I wish someone did.''

Dalton echoed his partner. Malone frowned. "I'll be blunt with you. Best-case scenario, you're dealing with someone with a twisted sense of humor. Someone who's getting his kicks out of terrorizing you. He's doing it from afar, in secret, that's part of the thrill. You're in little physical danger from him because he doesn't want a face-to-face confrontation. He doesn't have the guts for one.''

"And the worst-case scenario?'' she asked, working to keep her voice steady.

"Worst-case, you're dealing with someone whose sickness is much more dangerous. Terrorizing you from afar is only the beginning of his plans. His campaign of terror is going to escalate in intensity. He means you physical harm."

"Lord almighty," Dalton murmured.

Bill sat down hard. "I think I need a drink."

Anna felt faint. "What should I...do?"

"First thing you can do is help me do my job. Has anything unusual happened in your life? Anything out of the ordinary? Any new people? Any run-ins with anybody?"

"No run-ins, but—"

Malone's gaze sharpened. "But what?"

"It started a little over a week ago," Anna explained, feeling foolish for not having told him about this before. "There was a package waiting for me, no return address. It contained an interview my mother gave an independent videographer. The interview that ended up as part of the E! *Unsolved Hollywood Mysteries Show*."

"The videographer's name?" Malone asked.

She named him then went on to detail the events as they had unfolded, ending with her most recent conversation with Ben Walker. "He was certain the package had been left by one of his patients, though he didn't know which one or why. I asked about the name Peter Peters, but he doesn't have a patient by that name."

Malone arched an eyebrow. "And this Dr. Walker has no previous connection to you?"

"No. He located me through the B.B.B.S.A. director."

"You confirmed that?"

Anna made a sound of surprise. "No, but I had no reason to suspect...I mean, he's a really nice—"

"Guy," Malone supplied, tone dry. "A lot of wackos are."

Her cheeks heated, and she jumped to Ben's defense. "Call him if you'd like. I think you'll find he's *exactly* who and what he says he is."

"I'm sure I will. Do you have his number?"

"No, but his practice is uptown. His full name is Dr. Benjamin Walker. He's a psychologist."

Malone made note of the information. "Anything else?"

"The letters," Dalton said.

"The ones you told me about?" Malone asked. "The ones from the little girl?" She nodded and he frowned. "You think they might be related to tonight's event?"

"I don't know." She looked at her friends for support; they nodded their encouragement. "After the last letter, we figured somebody was playing a sick joke on me. Just like you suggested."

"The letter was over the top," Bill said. "Just way too much to believe."

"Do you still have that letter?"

"I do. I'll—"

"I'll get it for you, Anna." Dalton stood. "Are they in your desk?"

"Yes. Upper right-hand drawer."

A moment later, Dalton returned with the bundle and handed it to Anna. She retrieved the latest letter and gave it to Malone. He glanced at the envelope, then up at her. "She knows where you work?"

Heat stung her cheeks. "I answered the first time on Perfect Rose stationery. I wasn't…thinking."

Malone stared at her a moment more, then returned his attention to Minnie's letter. "Have you received another letter since this one?"

"No." She twisted her fingers together. "Do you think we were right, about it being a hoax?"

"Could be." He pursed his lips as if with thought. "Somebody's playing a game with you, Anna. And not a very nice one."

"I still need that drink. Anybody else?" Bill stood and started for the kitchen. "Mine's going to be a double."

Malone ignored him. "Could I hang on to this?"

"Sure. Would you like the others as well?"

Malone said he would and she gave them to him. He slipped the bundle into his jacket's inside breast pocket. "Anything else I should know about?"

"I don't think so." Anna looked at Dalton in question. He shook his head. "No, nothing."

"Okay, then." Malone stood. "I'm going to call this in. Order an evidence collection team to the sight. Dust for fingerprints."

"You think you might find something?" she asked, cringing at the hopefulness in her tone.

"Truthfully? No, but there's always a chance. I'll be in touch."

32

Quentin stopped on the sidewalk outside Anna's building and glanced up at her brightly lit windows. He frowned. What was going on with her? Obviously, she had been singled out by a wacko, no doubt because of her books or her past.

But how dangerous a wacko was he? Would he take his campaign of psychological terror to the next level? And what part did this Dr. Walker play in the scenario? She had jumped to his defense quickly—and heatedly. They hadn't known each other but a matter of days, what part could the man play in her life already?

That shouldn't matter to Quentin, but it did. He experienced a small but vicious stab of jealousy. Of possessiveness. He was attracted to Anna North. In a big way. She intrigued him. And he flat didn't like the idea of her being involved with somebody else.

Perhaps he would pay a surprise late-night visit to Dr. Benjamin Walker.

As he gazed at the window, Anna appeared. She stood in the rectangle of light, looking down at him.

Their gazes met. Seconds ticked past. Neither moved. Quentin felt a pull, a tug, one from the pit of his gut. And in the small space of time, as he stood in the puddle of light from her window, he imagined crossing to her gate and walking through it. He imagined climbing the stairs to her apartment, striding through her front door and taking her into his arms. And to her bed.

She lifted a hand in a small gesture of recognition, then shut the blind, cutting him off from the light. And from the vivid image of the two of them together, making love.

With a small shake of his head, he turned and crossed to his Bronco, parked half on the sidewalk so as to not block the narrow French Quarter street.

Quentin climbed in, started the vehicle and pulled away from the curb, thoughts shifting to the events of the past week. They settled on his visit with Penny.

He had watched her walk away, then had let himself out, feeling like a heel. For doing something he had known beforehand that he shouldn't. For saying something to her that he'd known in his gut was wrong, for upsetting her when she was already in a bad situation.

Penny had said Terry had been out of control for a long time. That he was self-destructing. Why didn't he see it? Did Quentin, as Penny had suggested, have a rose-colored view of his friend?

Quentin frowned. No. Terry had been fine until his marriage had fallen apart. Sure he drank too much sometimes, stayed out late. It went with the job. A guy had to find a way to let go of the stress, the ugliness a cop dealt with on a daily basis. Some of the guys did it through their families, some through church or chicks, some used drink. Others just turned mean. And some, oddly, didn't seem to need any coping mechanism at all. The job seemed to have no effect on them whatsoever.

Quentin dialed the station. The desk officer on night duty picked up. "Hey, Brad, Malone here. I need you to get me an address, a shrink named Benjamin Walker. Residence not practice, he's probably located uptown."

"Got it. Constance Street. Office and residence."

The desk officer gave him the address and Malone thanked him. "Everything quiet there?"

"As a tomb, Malone. Keep warm."

"You too." Quentin hung up. He crossed Canal Street, passing Canal Place and Saks Fifth Avenue. Terry would calm down once he settled into his situation. Once he admitted to himself that Penny wasn't going to change her mind. His weird mood swings and erratic behavior would even out. The old Terry would be back.

And once Nancy Kent and Evelyn Parker's killer had been apprehended they would all relax.

The media had had a field day with the killings. One irresponsible journalist had even referred to the killer as the Bourbon Street Butcher. Tourists were getting nervous; the public was demanding action and Chief Pennington wanted answers—yesterday.

Quentin frowned. The thing was, nobody seemed to have seen anything, even though both women had spent the last night of their lives surrounded by people. Bar personnel and patrons had been questioned, the men identified as having danced with the two women had been brought in, their stories investigated. Not one good suspect had emerged from among them.

Quentin drew to a stop at Lee Circle. The monument to General Robert E. Lee at its center glowed ghostly white in the darkness, illuminated by several spotlights at its base. Malone stared at it a moment, then returned his gaze to the road ahead. He and his team had revisited every unsolved rape of the past two years, any with a similar MO had been checked out: they'd reinterviewed victims, cross-checked blood types and other evidence found at the scenes.

And uncovered nothing.

Quentin flexed his fingers on the steering wheel, frustrated. He'd been at Shannon's the night Nancy Kent was murdered. By virtue of that, he had been one of the last to see her alive. The murderer had been there that night, Quentin believed that. Watching her, more than likely dancing with her. Quentin had probably seen him. It bothered the hell out of him.

The light changed and he started forward. Both the victims had been robbed. The first victim had been a wealthy young woman, flashing around big bills that last night of her life. Her wallet had been empty when she was found.

Suddenly, the image of Terry handing Shannon a fifty-dollar bill filled Quentin's head. It affected him like a blow and he pulled his vehicle to the side of the road.

Dear Jesus. What was he thinking?

That Terry had killed her? That the fifty-dollar bill

had been Nancy Kent's? Quentin shook his head in disbelief. Terry didn't have murder in him, no way. Besides, they had been together at Shannon's the entire evening. And by the time they had parted company, Terry had been so stinking drunk, he'd hardly been able to walk, let alone commit a murder. Jesus, what was wrong with him? How could he have considered, even for a moment, the possibility that Terry could do that?

Quentin pulled back onto the road. He reached Ben Walker's address within minutes, rolling to a stop in front of the house, a traditional New Orleans double. No light shone from Dr. Walker's windows; the driveway was empty. Quentin glanced at his watch, noting that it was after eleven. His lips lifted. It'd be a shame to wake the doctor up. A damn shame.

Quentin killed the engine, climbed out and headed up the walk. He rang the bell, waited, then rang again. No dog barked, no light snapped on. He knocked loudly, still got no response and went around back. He found the back of the house as dark as the front. He climbed the steps to the rear door, knocked, waited, then repeated the process.

Interesting, he thought, turning and heading back to his vehicle. After eleven on a weeknight and the doctor was out. Apparently the man was a night animal.

Maybe Anna had called him? Perhaps the doctor had gone to comfort her?

Not liking the thought, he discounted it. He'd pay another call on the psychologist in the morning, he decided.

Quentin climbed into his Bronco, started it up and pointed it toward St. Charles Avenue. His mind wandered as he drove the quiet streets, under the canopy of centuries-old oak trees and turn-of-the-century mansions, Loyola and Tulane Universities, all as familiar to him as the back of his hand.

He lived in a small house in an area of the city called the Riverbend, literally where the Mississippi River took a bend and two of the city's great boulevards, St. Charles and Carrollton Avenues met and dead-ended at River Road.

His was a mixed community that catered to young families, working couples and the university crowd, a neighborhood consisting of restored bungalows, doubles and cottages, all in various stages of repair.

Quentin rolled down his street and into his driveway, pulling to a stop under the carport. He shut off the engine, climbed out then stopped dead, a memory flying into his head, taking his breath.

That night at Shannon's, he and Terry had not been together the entire time. He had lost sight of his partner for an hour or more shortly after Terry's run-in with Nancy Kent.

33

The next morning, Quentin climbed Dr. Benjamin Walker's front steps. He moved slowly, taking in the structure's freshly painted exterior and neat though bare gardens, all details he had not noticed the night before. The right side of the double served as the doctor's residence, the left his office. Quentin knew this by the shiny brass plate mounted on the door.

He crossed the narrow porch to the man's residence and rang the bell. Once, then again. Early morning, not even seven, there was an excellent chance he would awaken the psychologist, especially since the man had been out late the night before.

Quentin smiled to himself. He wanted to catch the man unawares, wanted his full attention and cooperation. If he waited until Ben Walker began seeing patients, he would have to settle for being worked in.

From the other side of the door came the sound of footsteps, then the dead bolt being turned. The door swung open; it appeared to Quentin as if the man on the other side had just gotten out of the shower. He had a towel looped around his neck and his hair was wet. From inside came the strains of classical music.

"Benjamin Walker?" Quentin held up his shield. "Detective Malone, NOPD."

The man looked genuinely taken aback. "You're looking for Dr. Benjamin Walker?"

"That's right." He pocketed his shield. "It looks like I disturbed your morning routine. I apologize."

"No problem." He wiped his hands on the towel. "How can I help you?"

"There was an incident last night involving Anna North, and I understa—"

"Anna? Is she all right?"

"May I come in?"

"Of course."

The doctor stepped away from the door and Quentin followed the man inside, through the foyer and into a front parlor. He knew immediately by the spartan interior that Ben Walker was single, had no children and little family. The pieces of furniture were few, though they appeared to be good quality. Little in the way of art or family photos graced the walls; however, several mirrors hung in the parlor, giving the room a fractured, fun-house appearance.

Ben motioned him to take a seat, then took one himself. "Tell me about Anna. Is she all right?"

"Except for being shaken up, she's fine." Quentin looked the other man directly in the eyes, hoping to unnerve him. "Someone played a nasty little trick on her. Entered her apartment and left a pinkie finger in the refrigerator for her. She found it when she got home.''

He paled. "Poor Anna. She must have been terrified. Who's...I mean, do you know—''

"It was a fake.''

"Thank God.'' The man drew his eyebrows together, as if thinking something over, then looked at Quentin. "There's something I have to show you. I'll be right back.''

He returned several moments later with a manila envelope. He handed it to Quentin. "Take a look.''

Quentin opened the envelope. It contained a note and a photograph of the doctor and Anna sitting together at the Café du Monde. He read the note, then returned his gaze to Ben's. "When did you receive this?''

"Two evenings ago. I came home to find someone had been in my home. They'd left that on my bed.''

Quentin narrowed his eyes, unsettled by this newest turn of events. "What do you think it means, Doctor?''

"I don't know. Obviously, whoever took this photo followed me. Or Anna. They're playing some sort of twisted game with me. With us.''

"Actually, that's why I'm here.''

Ben stiffened slightly. "Is that so?''

"Anna tells me you believe one of your patients is responsible for the books and tapes that were sent to her and her friends.''

"It seems likely,'' he murmured, tone careful. "After all, I received the package though I had no previous connection to Anna."

"Except through your work."

"Pardon?"

"Your area of expertise."

"Yes. Although there are a number of psychologists in this area who fit that criteria."

"Then why you, Doctor?"

"I wish I knew that, Detective. If I did, I might be able to determine who was responsible."

"Might?"

"I'm a psychologist, not a swami."

"I need a list of your patients."

"You know as well as I that I can't give that to you."

"One of them means Anna North harm."

"We don't know that, not for sure."

"Don't we? Last night he broke into her apartment and left her a rather gruesome gift. One meant to terrify her."

"I can't do it." He stood, signaling their meeting had come to an end. "I'm sorry."

Quentin followed him to his feet. "Are you really?"

"There's a code of professional conduct I have to live by, Detective. Same as you. If you know someone is guilty but can't prove it, what do you? Do you beat a confession out of him? Plant evidence to frame him? Or do you adhere to your oath to uphold the law?"

Quentin narrowed his eyes, unmoved by the man's impassioned speech. "So what are you saying, Dr.

Walker? That you know one of your patients is guilty?''

''Practicing the art of double-talk, Detective?''

Quentin smiled grimly. ''A cop's stock-in-trade.'' He indicated the photo. ''May I keep this?''

''Fine. I do have a request, however. Anna doesn't know about this yet and I'd like to tell her myself. I was afraid... I didn't want to frighten her.'' As if realizing how ridiculous he sounded in light of what had occurred the previous evening, he flushed. ''I'll contact her immediately.''

''Do that. Otherwise, no promises.'' Quentin handed Ben one of his cards. ''You'll call if you change your mind?''

''Of course.'' He took the card and they started for the door.

''What's with the mirrors?'' Quentin asked, noticing several more. ''They the windows to the soul or something?''

''That's the eyes.'' Ben glanced at him. ''Actually, I don't know why I like them, but I do. I started collecting them several years ago and have nearly twenty now.''

''Interesting hobby. What are you going to do when you run out of room to hang them?''

''I don't know. Move, I guess.'' They reached the door and Ben opened it. ''I'm sorry I wasn't more help. Truly.''

''Me, too. Truly.'' Quentin stepped onto the porch, then stopped and turned back to the doctor. ''By the way, I tried to reach you late last night. After I left Anna's. You must have been out.''

Ben blinked. "I was home all night."

"I rang the bell and knocked. Front and back."

"I'm a heavy sleeper, Detective Malone."

"Funny, your car wasn't in the driveway."

The shrink bristled. "Are you accusing me of something, Detective?''

"Not at all. Just an observation."

"When possible, I park on the street. That way in the morning the driveway is available for my patients and I don't have to move the car." He indicated the row of cars parked on the street outside. ''Mine's the silver Taurus.''

"That's good planning, Dr. Walker."

"Thank you." He glanced at his watch. "I hate to cut this short, but if you don't have any further questions, I have a patient in thirty minutes."

"I appreciate you taking the time to talk to me." Quentin thanked him again, turned and walked away. When he reached his vehicle, he glanced back at the doctor. Why had he taken such a dislike to the man? he wondered. He had been pleasant enough, as helpful as he felt he could be.

Not helpful enough. Too pleasant. The kind of man a woman like Anna could fall for. A professional man.

"Was there something else, Detective?'' he called.

"Yeah." Quentin drew his eyebrows together. "I'd make certain the batteries in your smoke detector are fresh, you being such a heavy sleeper. You never know when something unexpected is going to happen.''

34

Friday, January 26
3:30 a.m.

"Minnie," Jaye called softly, crouching beside the pet door. "Are you awake? Come talk to me, I can't sleep."

Silence answered her and Jaye sat back to wait. Over the past nights she and Minnie had become secret friends. Minnie came to her in the dead of night, always while he slept. Jaye had never tried calling her before. But she was feeling particularly anxious tonight, lonely and on edge. She needed someone to talk to; she needed Minnie.

Jaye rubbed her arms, chilled. Minnie was the most fearful and timid person she had ever known. Everything, every sound, suggestion or request frightened her. Jaye felt her hatred growing for their captor and what he had done to the younger girl.

Jaye wondered sometimes about Minnie's folks, if they still looked for their daughter. Jaye assumed Minnie had been kidnapped as a little girl and wondered how her family would feel about getting her back so many years later? Would they still want her?

She and Minnie would find out sooner than later,

because they were going to escape. And Jaye was going to see to it that Minnie got home.

Home.

Hopelessness settled over her. Over the past days, she had come to realize that no one was looking for her. Since she had run away before, no doubt everyone thought she had done it again. Even Anna, because of their fight.

Jaye leaned her forehead against her prison door, a sigh escaping her. If only she could go back in time. If only she could take back the hateful things she had said to Anna. If not for their fight, Anna would have looked for her. She wouldn't have rested until Jaye had been found.

Despair rose up in her and she called for her friend again. "Minnie, please... Can you hear—"

"I'm here," the girl whispered. "Are you all right?"

"I'm okay." She swallowed hard. "I was just thinking about my friend Anna."

"Don't think about her," Minnie said. "It'll make you sad."

"But how do I stop? I'm so worried about her. And I just...I want to see her again."

"Maybe you will. Someday."

"Is that what you do?" Jaye persisted, pressing closer to the door. She could hear Minnie breathing and Tabitha purring. "Just not think about the people you love?"

"It works. And pretty soon...you just forget."

Jaye's eyes burned with unshed tears. "But I don't want to forget, Minnie. I just want to go home."

"But...if you go, I'll be alone again. I don't want you to go, Jaye. Besides Tabitha, you're my only friend."

"I won't leave without you, Min. We'll go together."

"That's not true. You will go without me. She did. She said she wouldn't, but she did."

Jaye's breath caught. "Who? How did she escape? Was she here, in this house?"

"Her. Another girl. I...don't remember her name. I don't remember any of it."

"You have to, Minnie. You're just scared. Try. Maybe it...it might help us." Minnie was silent, and Jaye pressed on. "Please, Minnie. If you could remember—"

"I told you, I can't remember!" Her voice rose. "I won't!"

Jaye's heart began to thunder; she bent her head closer to the door. When Minnie got upset, she ran away. "I'm sorry, Minnie. It's okay. You don't have to remember if don't want to. But listen to me, I promise I won't go without you. Not ever."

The other girl let out a shuddering breath. "You really wouldn't leave me behind?"

"I really wouldn't."

"I want to believe you, but I'm afraid."

"I know, Min. But you have to trust me. When I escape, I'm bringing you with me."

Minnie calmed and they talked for a while, about what they would do when they were free, where they would go. Jaye assured Minnie they would stay together, and though she didn't know how she would keep her word, she promised herself that she would.

But she needed Minnie's help.

"Minnie," Jaye whispered, "you have to find us a way out of here. There has to be some—"

"I can't. He'll find out and be angry. I don't like it when he's angry."

"But what will it matter if we're gone? He won't be able to hurt us then. Right, Min?"

"I...guess so. He...he hides the key to your door. He won't let me see where."

"Maybe there's another way." Jaye gentled her tone. "You could go without me. Get help and send them back for—"

"I won't go without you. I won't!"

"I know there's a phone because I've heard it ringing. When he's asleep or out somewhere, call 911. They'll come, they have to. It's a law. You have to do this, Minnie. You—"

"Oh no! He's coming!"

Jaye froze. "Are you sure? Maybe it's only—"

"Yes, he's..." Minnie moaned. "Oh God, he knows I'm here. What's he going to do to... I can't stop him. I—"

"Get away from the door!"

The man's voice boomed through the darkness and terrified, Jaye scrambled backward.

He laughed, the sound the personification of evil. "Not so brave now, are you? *Minnie*," he mocked, *"you have to find us a way out of here. I'll take you with me, I promise."* He lowered his voice to a threatening growl. "Like I would let you take her anywhere. She's mine. A part of me." His voice lifted, taking on a teasing quality. "We're inseparable, Jaye. And she's not going anywhere. But then, neither are you."

"What do you want with me?" Jaye cried, marshaling her courage. "What do you want with Anna?"

"That's for me to know and you to find out. Though it won't be long now."

Jaye shuddered and inched farther away from the door. *Minnie, where are you? Are you all right?*

As if reading her thoughts, he said, "Minnie's scurried off, the little mouse. Afraid of everything, even her own shadow." He laughed again. "Did you really think she could help you? Did you think anyone could? Are you really so stupid?"

Jaye heard him insert a key into the lock and a cry rose up in her. She inched backward, looking from side to side, for something to protect herself with, for someplace to hide.

But instead of her captor coming through the door, the pet hatch swung open. A paper fluttered to the floor.

Heart in her throat, Jaye inched toward it. A cry flew to her mouth when she saw what it was.

The note she had written in blood.

"You will cooperate with me in every way or I'll hurt Minnie. Do you understand?" She whimpered that she did and he continued. "The time has nearly come. The time for your friend Anna and I to meet."

"No! Please! Leave Anna alone. She hasn't done anything to you."

''What do *you* know of Anna's sins? Nothing!'' His voice rose, becoming high, unnatural-sounding. Frightening. ''You're just a stupid little nobody.''

The pet door swung open again. A tube of lipstick dropped to the floor, followed by a sheet of paper.

''Seal it with a kiss,'' he ordered. ''Then pass it back.''

It was a letter, Jaye saw. To Anna. Her heart stopped. A letter to Anna from her youngest fan, written in childish handwriting. Minnie's handwriting.

He meant to trick Anna. To lure her out of hiding and into his trap. He was going to hurt her. Maybe kill her.

''No!'' she shouted, hugging herself. ''I won't do it! You're a monster and I won't help you hurt my friend!''

''Cooperate or Minnie dies.'' He paused a moment, letting his words sink in. ''Seal it with a kiss. Do it now.''

Trembling with the force of her despair, she applied the bloodred lipstick, then pressed her lips to the paper and passed it back.

''Don't do this,'' she begged. ''Let me and Minnie go. Leave Anna alone. Please—''

He cut her off, amusement in his tone. ''Did you know? You just sealed Anna's letter with a kill.''

35

Anna stared at the letter, at the bloodred kiss at the bottom, her hands beginning to shake. *Dear God, it couldn't be. Not Jaye, please not Jaye.*

Anna bent and dug her purse out from under the sales counter. She snatched out her wallet, ripped it open and frantically flipped through the photos until she found the one she sought—a close-up of Jaye, her expression dreamy, the light filtering across her face, highlighting the diagonal scar across her mouth.

The scar on the lip print matched Jaye's.

A sound of denial escaped Anna. One of fear. For Jaye. And Minnie.

"I'm back, Anna darling," Dalton announced, entering the shop. He shrugged out of his coat and laid it over his arm. "Lunch was absolutely divine. The roasted-duck salad was as good as any I've ever—" He stopped short. "My God, Anna, what's happened now?"

His question bordered on comical. It seemed her life had become a series of bizarre calamities.

She wasn't laughing. She was terrified.

"It's Jaye," she whispered. "He has her."

"Who has her?"

"The man from Minnie's letters." A knot of tears formed in her throat and she held out the letter.

Dalton crossed to the counter and took it out of her hand. He immediately saw what she had and the color drained from his face. "You were right," he said. "About Minnie and the man from her letters. You were right about Jaye not running away. Lord Almighty, what do you think he—"

He didn't finish the thought, he didn't have to. *What was Jaye being forced to endure?*

Dalton looked ill. "What are you going to do? I think we'd better—"

"Call Malone. I'm calling Malone now."

Thirty minutes later, Anna and Malone, armed with the letter and a picture of Jaye, were halfway across the Lake Pontchartrain Causeway, on their way to Mandeville.

Luckily, her call had caught Malone in; he had come immediately. He'd taken one look at the lip print and photo and asked her if she would like to take a ride across the lake. Anna had jumped at the offer—waiting around to hear what he found would have been agony.

After Malone's initial round of questions, they had hardly spoken. It seemed to Anna there was nothing to say. She sat, her gaze fixed on the road ahead, hands clenched tightly in her lap.

He reached across the seat and covered her hands

with one of his own. "There is good news here, Anna. There is."

Sudden tears stung her eyes, but she met his anyway. Defiantly. "And what would that be? That Jaye's in the hands of some maniac or perver—"

She choked on the words and fought to regain her composure. When she had, she continued. "She's been missing since the eighteenth and no one's been looking for her. You can't imagine how that feels. How afraid for her I am."

"*You've* been looking for her, Anna." He squeezed her hands, then brought his back to the steering wheel. "You never let her go. You never gave up."

"Didn't I? I could have done more. I should have."

He glanced at her out of the corners of his eyes, expression sympathetic. "And what would that have been? You went to Jaye's foster parents, her social worker, the police. You talked to her friends, followed every lead. What else, Anna?"

She looked away, knowing he was right—and that her efforts hadn't been enough. "I went on with my life," she whispered. "I shouldn't have. I…I feel so guilty."

"I know. But you need to let it go. It's not helping her." He glanced back at her. "So, how about that good news? You look like you could use it about now."

"An understatement." She looked at him. "A big one."

One corner of his mouth lifted. "The good news

is, we have a lead. Something to go on. Something concrete.''

"I'm overwhelmed."

He arched an eyebrow at her sarcasm. "Compare where we are right now to yesterday at this time. Hell, to this morning. Every solved case begins with one lead, Anna." He held up his right index finger. "One, that's all. If everything goes our way, the mailbox guy will roll over and the address he gives us will lead directly to Jaye."

"And if it doesn't?"

"We'll keep trying." They exited the Causeway; he turned and looked directly at her. "I won't give up on this, Anna. We're going to find Jaye, if not today, another day. I promise you we will."

The manager of the Mail & Copy store, under police pressure, did, indeed, roll over. The box was rented to one Adam Furst of Lake Street in Madisonville.

Madisonville was a small community located five miles west of Mandeville. A charming enclave on the Tchefuncte River, in recent years Madisonville had become a trendy area of renovated Victorian cottages, seafood restaurants, coffeehouses and million-dollar homes built along the riverfront.

Adam Furst's address, however, led to none of those. It led to a ramshackle-looking double on a street that had yet to be discovered by the yuppies flocking to the "country" from the frenetic pace and crime of New Orleans.

Malone drew his Bronco to a stop in front of the

building. He shut off the engine, then looked at her. "I want you to wait in here." She opened her mouth to protest; he stopped her. "Let me rephrase that, you will wait here. Understood?"

Anna agreed, though grudgingly, and watched as he walked up the overgrown walk to the sagging front porch. He rang the bell, waited, then knocked. He looked back at her, motioning that he meant to walk around the back of the house.

The moment he disappeared from view, she climbed out of the vehicle. No way could she sit back and wait. Jaye might be in that house; if she was, Anna was going to find her.

The porch creaked as she stepped onto it. She crossed to the door, rang the bell then put her ear to the door to listen.

"Can I help you?"

Anna jumped, yelping in surprise. She swung in the direction the question had come, a woman coming up the walk, arms loaded with bags of groceries. A tiny woman with short, flyaway gray hair and arms like toothpicks, she looked about to buckle under her load.

"Here," Anna said, moving forward, "let me give you a hand with those."

"Thanks," the woman said, her tone suspicious. "They are kind of heavy."

Anna took several of the bags, then let the woman assume the lead to the front door. She unlocked it, then glanced back at Anna, eyes narrowed. "Be right back. Don't go anywhere with those groceries."

Anna promised and several moments later the

woman returned for the other bags. She took them, disappeared into the house again, reappearing at the same moment Malone did.

"I thought I told you to stay in the car."

"Who's he?"

The two uttered their questions simultaneously. Anna chose to answer the woman's and ignore Malone's. "Police," she answered. "We're looking for your neighbor, Adam Furst."

The woman made a sound of disgust. "Got ID?"

Malone held out his shield and she inspected it for several moments before nodding and returning her gaze to Anna. "I'm not surprised to see you two, not a bit. That man was a weird one. I always thought he was up to something."

"Thought?" Malone asked. "You don't any-more?"

"He moved out a couple of weeks ago. No word to nobody. Left owing me rent, too."

"Are you the landlord?"

"That's right. This house is the only thing my no-account husband didn't drink away." She crossed herself. "Thanks to Jesus, Mary and Joseph for that."

"What was weird about him?" Anna asked, working to hide how anxious she was.

"Came and went all times of the day and night. Mostly night, though. Sometimes I didn't see him for a week or more. Didn't talk, never had visitors. Kept his blinds closed tight, all the time. Not that I would ever spy on one of my tenants."

"Of course not," Anna said quickly, smiling at the woman.

"Couple times I offered him a beer and tried to start a little conversation, you know? Cut me off, real cold like. Nasty. Made my skin crawl."

Anna rubbed her own arms and the goose bumps that crawled up them.

"When did he move out?" Malone asked. "Can you remember exactly?"

"Sure can." The woman nodded for emphasis. "Day I planned to collect his rent or boot him out. The eighteenth."

The same day Jaye disappeared.

Anna felt the blood drain from her face as she looked at Malone. He met her eyes. She saw that he had also realized the significance of the date.

"He lived alone?" Malone asked.

"Far as I know."

"He didn't have a child with him?" Anna cleared her throat. "A young girl, maybe ten, eleven years old?"

"Never saw a kid with him." The woman squinted up at the bright sky. "Come to think of it, though, I thought I heard a kid crying sometimes. Late at night. Didn't think too much about it till now, you know how sound carries at night. Do you think—"

"I'll need to get into that apartment, Mrs.—"

"Blanchard. Dorothy Blanchard. Though most folks around here call me Dottie."

Malone nodded. "I'll need to get in there this afternoon, Dottie. Me and some other officers."

She smiled broadly, revealing a gold tooth. "Hot damn, you going to dust for prints and stuff?"

"Yes, ma'am. And stuff."

Malone started down the walk; Anna followed after him, hurrying to keep up.

"So what'd Furst do?" Dottie Blanchard called after them. "Kill somebody? Rob a bank? Just what kind of creep was I renting to?"

36

Monday, January 29
10:20 p.m.

Ben awakened to find his mother staring at him the way she did sometimes, her face ashen, her lips a bloodless pink. Although disconcerting, he had learned to ignore such manifestations of her illness. Because Alzheimer's victims floated in and out of cognizance, they were easily startled and upset.

He straightened and the book in his lap slipped to the floor. ''Sorry, Mom,'' he murmured, rolling his shoulders, then reaching for the book. ''I should know better than to try to read to you after such a long day. The sound of my own voice puts me to sleep every time.'' He made a face. ''I can only imagine what it does to my patients.''

''He was here,'' she said suddenly. ''That man.''

Ben came instantly, completely awake. He looked at her. ''Who? What man?''

She shook her head. ''That devil. He was here. While you slept.''

A man was here, in this room, while he slept? He doubted it, though when he fell asleep, he was out cold. Ben narrowed his eyes, studying his mother, seeing real fear in her eyes. "I don't know this man you're talking about. Is he someone you know from here?"

She began to tremble. "No. He's a bad man."

"A bad man," Ben repeated, concerned. "Why is he bad?"

"He wants to hurt you. He wants to hurt me. He said he was going to."

Ben frowned and stood. All visitors were required to check in at the front desk. "You sit tight, Mom. I'm going to have a little talk with the nurse on duty."

"I told him you wouldn't let him hurt me. But he only laughed. He said you couldn't stop him." Growing agitated, she began plucking the front of her robe, picking at a piece of the eyelet. "He's stronger than you, he said. More powerful."

Ben bent and kissed the top of her head, then smiled reassuringly at her, not letting his worry show. "We'll just see about that. Sit tight, I'll be right back."

He left her room and headed for the nurses' station at the end of the hall. He found the nurse and her two aides there, chatting. One had her shoes off and was rubbing her feet.

"Hey, ladies," he said, smiling at the women. "Got a question, has anyone been in to see my mother tonight besides me?"

They looked confused and he smiled again. "I dozed off while I was reading to Mom. She said a guy came into her room while I was asleep and threatened her."

"One of the residents?"

"No. She said he's not someone she knows from here."

The women looked at each other, then Wanda, the R.N., shook her head. "Nobody's been in or out of the facility since eight."

Ben pursed his lips in thought. "How about the past few weeks? She says this man's been in to see her before."

"Let me check the log." Wanda stood, crossed to the desk and took out the logbook. The entries were listed both by the visitor name and resident's name. Several moments passed as she scanned and flipped the pages, going backward in time. "Last week Father Ray was here to see her. Dr. Levine was in the day before that. A couple of teenage girls, volunteers from the Sacred Heart Academy." She flipped a couple more pages, then stopped. "That's two weeks, and other than you, Father Ray, Dr. Levine and the girls, no one's been in to see your mother. Oh, and she had her hair done Monday. Shelley did it."

He drew his eyebrows together. "She's quite upset. In fact, she—"

From down the hall came a crash, then wailing. Ben swung in the direction the sound had come, then looked at Wanda, alarmed. "That's Mom."

Wanda came around the counter in a flash; they both bolted for his mother's room.

They found her on the floor beside her bed, knees to her chest, rocking and weeping. "I tried to stop him!" she cried when she saw Ben. "I tried. See—" She pointed.

Ben looked in the direction she indicated. She had

hurled a vase at the dresser. The crash they'd heard had been the vase connecting with the items on the top of the dresser: her toiletries, framed photos, a porcelain figurine.

He went to her, crouched down and drew her into his arms. She shook with the force of her despair, her body frail and birdlike in his arms.

"I see, Mom," he murmured, voice thick. "It's okay now, sweetheart, everything's going to be okay."

Thirty minutes later, Ben crossed the nursing-home parking lot, heading to his car. He sighed and looked up at the black sky, heart heavy and aching. He hated to see his mother this way, hated to see her failing so fast.

He was losing her. One day in the not so distant future, he would come to see her and she wouldn't recognize him. Her world would be populated by strangers, caregivers and menacing figures like the one tonight.

Why her? he wondered. She had worked so hard her whole life: to give him a good home; a normal childhood despite his having no father; to make sure he felt loved. She had been not only his mother, but his champion and friend as well. She didn't deserve this.

Ben swallowed hard. His uncle had died a few years back and although they hadn't been close, he had been family. When his mother went, he would be alone. No family. No one to call his own.

He thought of Anna suddenly. Her image filled his

head and senses, and a smile touched his mouth. He had called her the other morning, immediately after Detective Malone had left. He'd told her about his home being broken into and about the package that had been left for him.

She had been shaken. Angry. Not so much at him as at the situation. He had promised her he wouldn't rest until he had discovered which of his patients was to blame, he had filled her in on the progress he had made so far.

He hadn't spoken with her since. He missed her.

Ben glanced at his watch and saw with regret that it was too late to call her. He wished it wasn't. He would have liked to talk with her about his mother. His feelings. She would have understood. That's the way she was.

He was falling in love with her. It seemed impossible—they had only known each other a couple weeks. But it was true. It both exhilarated and frightened him, made him feel like running for cover—and walking on air.

He reached his car and saw that someone had tucked a flyer under the driver's-side windshield wiper. Ben yanked it out and stopped short.

Not a flyer. A message:

You're falling in love with her.

She's going to die tonight.

Ben went cold. Fear grabbed him by the throat and he began to sweat.

Not Anna. No, not her.

He unlocked the car and slid inside. Simultaneously, he shoved the key in the ignition and reached for his cell phone. The engine roared to life and he punched in Anna's number.

It rang once. Twice. Three times. Heart thundering, he waited, counting the rings, praying. Anna didn't pick up. Neither did her answering machine.

Something was wrong. Terribly wrong.

She's going to die tonight.

Cursing under his breath, Ben threw the sedan into gear and tore out of the parking lot, the back end fishtailing, spewing gravel. He had to warn her. Protect her. If she wasn't home, he would stand sentinel at her front gate until she returned. He wasn't about to let this maniac harm a hair on her head. And if he did, Ben would rip him apart at the seams. He swore that he would.

37

Anna awakened out of a deep sleep. She opened her eyes, instantly terrified. Her bedside light was off, her bedroom bathed in total darkness. She stared at the room's corners, the darkest and deepest of the shadows, her imagination taking flight and creating monsters with names she knew.

Kurt.

Immobilized by fear, she lay stone still, listening, heart lodged in her throat. The silence deafened. It roared. Marshaling her every ounce of control, she turned her head toward the nightstand and the glowing dial of her alarm clock. Midnight. Almost.

From somewhere in the apartment came a sound. Unrecognizable. Uninvited.

She wasn't alone.

Her terror took shape, settling over her like a leaden blanket, and she struggled to breathe under its suffocating weight. She began to sweat. Her pulse to race. She closed her eyes and forced herself to focus—on pulling air in and pushing it out, with each breath attempting to wrest control of her body from the grip of fear.

Finally, her body responded. As quietly as possible, she shifted onto her side and reached for the bedside phone.

It wasn't there.

She remembered. She had taken a call from Dalton shortly before bed. She had carried the portable into the bathroom and left it there.

A cry rose to her throat. She fought it back, struggling against what she knew was irrational. Tonight was no different than the hundreds of other nights she had awakened certain Kurt had found her.

He hadn't. Like all those other nights, a dream had awakened her. An ugly memory, an old terror. Gone but not forgotten.

Climb out of bed, she told herself. Walk to the bedroom door and through it, retrieve the phone. She would feel safe then, she told herself. She would go back to sleep. Everything would be fine.

Anna slid back the blankets, eased into a sitting position, then swung her legs over the side of the bed. The floor was cold beneath her bare feet and she shivered.

Too cold, she realized. She glanced toward the French doors that led to the balcony and courtyard below. The curtain stirred. She stared at the filmy fabric; the rustling came again, followed by a thread of cold, damp air that slithered across her feet and curled around her ankles.

The French door was open.

With a cry of pure terror she darted for the bedroom

doorway. As she neared it, the door slammed shut and strong arms circled her from behind, one at her middle, one at her throat. He hauled her against his chest and dragged her backward, toward the bed.

The arm at her throat tightened, cutting off her air. She clawed at it, pinpoints of light dancing before her eyes. Weakening from lack of oxygen, she thrashed and kicked out, her attempts feeble at best.

His grip loosened, but even as she gobbled in a lungful of air she found herself being pushed face first onto the bed. In a flash he was on top of her, a hand pressed to the back of her neck, a knee digging into her lower back, immobilizing her. He tore at her nightclothes, as if in a kind of feeding frenzy, making wet guttural sounds as he did.

A litany of pleadings, denials and prayers played through her head, deafening and desperate. He meant to rape her. The way those other women had been raped. Then he was going to kill her. The way those other two women had been killed. Redheads. Just like her.

The back of her gown gave. The ripping sound sawed along her nerve endings. Anna started to sob, the tears bubbling up out of her in increasing intensity. He went for her panties, curling his fingers around the waistband and yanking them away.

In one move, he flipped her over and shoved her legs apart. She saw then that he was masked in one of the pale, expressionless masks favored by the Mardi Gras krewe riders. She sensed his smile, his revelry in her terror, her pain. She felt his pure evil.

"Ready or not," he muttered, "here I come."

Her thoughts went careening back in time. Back twenty-three years. *Timmy lay in an unmoving heap on the cot. Now it was her turn. Kurt turned and started for her, wire cutters in his hand, lips twisted into a cold smile.*

"Ready or not, here I come."

A scream rose in Anna's throat. Dragged from the center of her being, it ripped through her bedroom, echoing off the walls and into the darkness. It was followed by another, then another. Her attacker froze. He shifted his masked face and for the first time looked her directly in the eyes. His were orange. Like a tiger's. Or a devil's.

She screamed again. He leaped off her and was gone, out the way he had come—through the French doors, over the balcony and down.

Still screaming, the sounds ripping from her like a car alarm gone haywire, she scrambled off the bed and raced out of the bedroom and to her front door. Forgetting her nakedness, she yanked it open.

Dalton was there, in the hall outside her door. With a cry, she fell headlong into his arms.

38

Tuesday, January 30
12:45 a.m.

Forty minutes later, Anna sat huddled on her couch, her hands curled around a cup of hot herbal tea, teeth chattering. Dalton sat beside her, Bill hovered protectively behind, both their expressions grim. From her bedroom came the sounds of Malone, a couple of other detectives and the evidence collection team, who had arrived only a few minutes ago. They would dust for fingerprints, Malone had said. Look for any other kind of latent or trace evidence.

Malone had arrived first, within minutes of Dalton's call. Still hysterical, she had relayed what she had been able to, enough to give him the gist of what had happened. He'd called a couple of other detectives from his district and then the evidence team.

Anna looked down at herself. She wore Dalton's sweater and a pair of sweatpants he had dug out of her dresser for her. She glanced toward the doorway to her bedroom where her tattered nightgown lay in an obscene heap. Her panties lay there also, somewhere nearer the bed.

Naked. She had been naked when she ripped open

her bedroom door and stumbled into Dalton's arms. A stranger had torn away her garments. He had touched her. Had tried to take by force the most private part of herself.

She had been saved. Her desperate pleas and prayers had been answered.

But would she ever feel clean—or safe—again?

She shuddered, a small whimper slipping past her lips. As if reading her thoughts, Dalton put his arm around her, squeezing gently. She glanced at him; he didn't speak, he didn't have to. The love and concern in his eyes said everything she needed to know.

Malone emerged from the bedroom, the other detectives with him. Anna met his gaze and a calm slipped over her, a feeling of safety. A feeling that with Malone around, nothing bad could touch her. With the feeling came the longing to stand and move into his arms. And have him hold her.

She would be warm then. She would be safe.

Without breaking eye contact, he crossed to her. He crouched down in front of her, balancing on the balls of his feet, hands resting on his knees. He searched her gaze. "Are you all right?"

She nodded, though she wasn't okay. Not by a long shot.

"Good." He motioned the other detectives. "Agnew and Davis are going to canvas the building and neighborhood, ring doorbells, see if anyone heard or saw anything."

She nodded again, lowering her gaze to his hands, noticing their shape, that is fingers were long, blunt-tipped and immaculately groomed. He had nice hands, she thought. Masculine. Quick, she would bet. Agile.

"Anna?"

She returned her gaze to his, cheeks heating. "I'm sorry, what?"

"He entered your apartment by way of the balcony. I believed he came over the courtyard wall, then scaled the wall to your balcony and its French doors. He broke a pane of glass, reached inside and unlocked the dead bolt."

"So much for all those fancy new locks," Dalton muttered.

Quentin looked at the other man. "You installed the dead bolt?"

"Had them installed," he corrected. "After the finger incident. Actually, I had dead-bolt locks added to every courtyard door in the building."

"And I had my locks changed," Anna whispered. "A lot of good it did me."

Quentin returned his attention to her. "I need to ask you a few questions. Think you're up to that?"

"Yes. I think so."

"Good."

He took his spiral from his jacket pocket. "Let's go through it from the top. Tell me everything you remember, even if you think it's totally irrelevant. Okay?"

She nodded, then began, voice halting. She told him about waking up, being frightened, trying to calm herself, then realizing the French door was open.

"I ran then, toward the door." Her voice began to

shake. "He caught me…he dragged me…back to the…to the—"

Unable to finish, he helped her out. "The bed, Anna?"

"Yes."

Dalton pulled her closer and Bill laid his hands on her shoulders. She let out a trembling breath, tried to continue but found she couldn't. The words lodged painfully in her throat even as the events of the night replayed in her head, like reccurring frames of a horror flick, one she couldn't walk out of.

"Anna," Malone murmured, voice gentle but firm, "look at me. Only at me." She did and as their gazes locked she again experienced a sense of calm move over and through her. "You're safe now," he said. "I'm going to keep you safe. But I need your help. Take a deep breath and talk to me."

She found the words then, though they sometimes tumbled out of her in a garbled rush, other times in a painfully halting crawl. Never taking her gaze off Malone's, she relayed how the man had torn off her clothes, the moment she had realized that he meant to rape her, and how she had screamed.

"You were facedown on the bed the whole time?"

"No, he…he turned me over."

"You saw his face?"

She shook her head. "He was masked. One of those Mardi Gras masks, like the krewe riders wear. But I saw his eyes. They were orange."

Malone frowned. "Orange?"

"I know it sounds crazy, but they were." She

opened her mouth to tell him the rest, then shut it, pressing her trembling lips together.

Ready or not, here I come.

She hadn't said those words aloud in twenty-three years. Not since she had sat across from the FBI agents, a traumatized child clinging to her parents.

"Go on, Anna. Tell me everything."

She took a fortifying breath, then began. "It was Kurt, Quentin. It was him."

Dalton squeezed her hand. "Oh, Anna…honey—"

"It was!" She glanced over her shoulder at Bill, searching for an ally. "It was him. His voice…what he—"

"Excuse me, Detective?"

An expression of frustration on his face, Malone turned toward the bedroom doorway and the team of criminalists. "What?" he snapped.

The other officer looked unconcerned about Malone's obvious ire. "We're done in here. If you don't have anything else, we'll head back to the lab."

"Do that. Call me in the morning."

"Will do." The men headed out, tromping through the center of the living room, not glancing Anna's way.

When they had exited the apartment, Malone turned back to her. "Let's jump forward in time for a moment." He glanced at his notebook and the notes he had taken earlier, then back up at her. "You screamed and your attacker bolted? He darted out onto your bedroom balcony and went over the side?" She nodded and he went on. "Then you ran from your bedroom to your front door. You yanked it open and Dalton was there, waiting. Is that right?''

Before she could answer, Dalton jumped in. ''I wasn't waiting. I'd been out—''

''Walking Judy and Boo,'' Bill offered.

''Our dogs. I opened our apartment door and bent to unleash the babies—''

''And he heard Anna scream.''

''Right.''

Malone shifted his gaze to Bill. ''And where were you?''

''Watching TV.'' He paused. ''Inside.''

''Do you always stay behind when Dalton takes your…babies out?''

Bill stiffened, Anna felt it and glanced apologetically up at him. ''Not typically. But *Mysteries and Scandals* was on and—''

''He loves that show,'' Dalton murmured. ''I didn't mind going out alone. He's done it for me hundreds of times.''

Malone's gaze didn't waver from Bill. ''*Mysteries and Scandals,* that's an E! show, isn't it?''

''It is.'' Bill had grown unnaturally still, and Anna shifted in her seat. ''The best-quality fluff.''

''Cotton candy for your brain.'' Malone smiled and shifted his gaze to Anna. ''Wasn't that the network that ran your mother's interview?''

Anna's heart began to pound. She saw what Malone was doing and didn't like it. Obviously, Dalton did also because his face was flushed with color. ''Are you suggesting that Bill—''

''I'm not suggesting anything,'' Malone murmured,

expression unchanging. "I'm simply trying to get an accurate picture of what happened here tonight. Is that a problem?"

"Of course not," Bill said, though with an edge in his voice. "I love Anna. I'll do anything I can to help."

"As would I," Dalton offered primly.

"I appreciate that." Malone looked at Anna. "I'd like to speak with you privately. Would that be possible?"

She hesitated. "Dalton and Bill are my best friends, there's nothing I can't say in front of them."

"Of course. However, I have to insist." He shifted his gaze to the two men. "You understand, fellas. Don't you?"

They didn't. Clearly. She frowned. "Malone—"

"It's okay, Anna." Dalton squeezed her hands, then released them and stood. "The man's got a job to do. Call us, okay?"

Bill bent and kissed the top of her head. "We're right next door. I can sleep on your couch, it's not a problem."

"Or you can sleep on ours," Dalton offered. "We're here for you, hon."

She thanked them both and watched them go, feeling for all the world like she was being abandoned.

As if reading her thoughts, Malone murmured, "You can call them right back over. I wanted you to feel free to answer my next questions without an audience."

"Why?" she asked defiantly. "Surely you don't

think Dalton or Bill would harm me? Because I can assure you they wouldn't.''

"You're positive of that? You'd bet your life on it?''

She hesitated a fraction of a moment, then heat flooded her cheeks. "Yes. I'd bet my life on it. I want you to leave them alone.''

"Sorry, Anna. Can't do it. Not unless the facts indicate they are just what they seem to be.''

She kept her gaze unwaveringly on his. "They are.''

"So, you're positive it wasn't Bill in your bedroom tonight?''

"Bill?'' The thought brought a hysterical laugh to her lips. "Please.''

"You didn't answer my question, Anna. Are you certain?''

"Yes. Positive.''

"As positive as your mother and father were that your father's nurse wasn't involved in your kidnapping?''

She caught her breath. "Stop trying to scare me.''

"Bill's in good shape. He works out?''

"Yes. And runs.'' She shivered and rubbed his arms. "He was an athlete in college. Track and field.''

"Really? How old is he?''

"Thirty-eight.''

"Not twenty. But still in his prime.''

"You're wrong, Malone.'' She hugged herself. "You are.''

"Think about it, Anna. Dalton was standing in the hall outside your apartment. Why?''

"He was walking Judy and Boo."

"Did you see the dogs? Was he holding their leads?"

She didn't recall. She closed her eyes, trying to remember. Judy and Boo were yippy little things—all bark and no bite. A lot of bark. She didn't recall hearing them, but still that didn't mean they hadn't been there. "I don't know...I was upset. Screaming. I...don't remember."

"When did Bill arrive on the scene?"

"I...a few minutes later."

"How many?"

"I'm not sure...two or three. Five."

"Did Dalton call him?"

She shook her head. "This is a small building, sounds carry."

"Anybody else show up? Other neighbors?"

"A few. Bill shooed them away."

"When did your friends learn the truth about your past?"

"The same day everybody else I know did. They received the note about the E! program and a book."

"Are you certain of that?"

"Yes!" She started to shake. "Why do you ask? What are you thinking?"

"I don't think anything. Yet." He lowered his eyes to his notepad, then returned his attention to her. "What was Bill and Dalton's reaction to learning you were Harlow Grail?"

"They were surprised. Supportive. Concerned for me and what I was going through." She looked directly into his eyes. "I was grateful for their support. I still am."

"I understand." He jotted in his spiral, flipped it shut and tucked it into his pocket. He stood and looked down at her. "You need to be particularly careful, Anna. Make sure all your doors and windows are secure. Don't walk alone at night. Don't become lost in thought, stay aware of your surroundings and what's going on around you."

She tipped her face up to his. "I'm frightened."

"I know." His expression softened. "It's going to be okay."

"Do you have a…a theory about who or—"

"No, not yet." He fell silent a moment. "This could be a random act of violence. Or not."

Anna twisted her fingers together in her lap. "The two women killed…the ones who—" She sucked in a deep breath. "They were both redheads."

"Yes."

"Do you think it could have been him who—"

"Broke in here tonight? The MO's wrong, but I'm not eliminating the possibility."

"Because of my hair."

"Yes."

Silence fell between them and Malone cleared his throat. "I guess that's it. If you want to call someone to come over, I can hang around until—"

"I'm okay." She glanced down at her hands, clasped tightly in her lap, then back up at him. "I can't expect my friends to baby-sit me."

He squatted down in front of her once more and searched her gaze, the expression in his sympathetic.

"You don't have to be strong yet, Anna. Not all at once. Give yourself a little time."

"How long?" Her vision swam. "Twenty-three years, maybe?"

He cupped her cheek in his palm. "I'm sorry, Anna. I am."

His touch was a shock to her system. She tipped her face into his caress, drawn to his warmth, the comfort he offered. For the space of several heartbeats, she didn't speak. Didn't move. She couldn't.

And neither did he.

So subtly that it sneaked up on her, she became aware of the way he smelled, freshly scrubbed and male. She became aware of the way her breathing had begun to quicken, her senses to stir.

Suddenly, her focus shifted. From the horror of the past hours to the possibilities of the next. From the terror of being taken against her will to the pleasure of a consensual joining. To the life-affirming renewal that came from a man and a woman coming together in the most elemental of ways.

She wanted that. To be renewed. Cherished.

She wanted oblivion.

Anna's thoughts stunned her. She couldn't be thinking about sex. Not now, not after the attack she had just suffered.

But she was. She was thinking about making love. About being with this man, about losing herself in shared passion.

Quentin Malone made her feel safe. He made her feel protected. He would make her forget, even if only for an hour, that the bogeyman had come to call on her.

"Anna?"

Her name whispered past his lips. To her it seemed a prayer, a song. An invitation.

She didn't answer. Instead, she cupped his face in her palms and kissed him. Softly at first, then more deeply, with passion.

This was something she had wanted almost from the first time she had laid eyes on him, she realized. Even when she had been furious with him and his refusal to help her, she had been attracted to him. Even then he had called to her on this most basic level.

"Anna..." He broke the contact of their mouths. "You've had a shock. You don't know what you're doing."

"Yes, I do." She laid her fingers against his mouth, warm and damp from hers. "Stay with me tonight, Malone. Be with me."

"Tomorrow you'll regret—"

"Maybe I will." She paused. "Regrets or not, I want this."

In his eyes, she saw the battle raging within him. She respected that. She was glad he hadn't fallen right into bed with her; it said something nice about him. That he was a gentleman. A little old-fashioned. That he had standards.

She liked those things—as long as in the end, he gave in.

Anna brought her mouth to his again, rubbing softly, teasing with the tip of her tongue. She drew away once more, but held his gaze. "I want you, Malone. What I'm feeling isn't about what happened tonight. It's not about fear of being alone. Not only about that anyway." She plunged her fingers into his dark hair. "I want you, Malone."

With a groan, he capitulated. He lifted her off the couch and sat her on his lap so that she straddled him. With a small thrill, she felt that he wanted her as much as she did him.

She moved against his arousal, imitating the love act, her own breath quickening as pleasure speared through her.

He took her mouth, she his. He tore off her sweater, she unbuttoned his chambray shirt. Both found the other's skin—with hands, then mouths and tongues—sighing as they did.

Passion exploded between them. They fell backward, half on the wooden floor, half on the worn Persian rug. They wriggled out of their clothing, unwilling to part to undress.

Making love with Quentin Malone was all Anna had known it would be: exciting, breath-stealing, exhilarating.

His hands and mouth stole her memory. She forget who she was, her past, the future—all that remained was Malone, his body against and inside hers, his quickened breathing, the sound of her name against his lips at the moment of his release.

His name on hers at the same moment.

The moment passed, but still her heart thundered. Anna pressed her face into his shoulder, wondering at the power of what had just occurred between them.

She had been with other men before but none of those experiences had been as moving as this one.

She wondered if it had been the same for him. She hoped so but wasn't deluding herself. Detective Quentin Malone was no stranger to women or sex. He was the kind of man women flocked to, like hummingbirds to nectar.

And she had been simply one of the many.

"Are you all right?" he asked softly.

"Fine," she murmured, keeping her face buried. "Wonderful."

He trailed his fingers through the hair at her nape, his touch incredibly gentle. "Regrets already?"

She shifted so he could see her face. And she his. "No."

He touched her mouth with the tips of his fingers. "I owe you an apology."

"No." She shook her head. "It was me. I initiated—"

"You misunderstand." A smile touched his lips, then faded. "It was...I was so... You overwhelmed me."

Heat stung her cheeks. Not the heat of embarrassment, but of pleasure. *She* had overwhelmed him. She had made him forget, made him lose control. Nothing he could have said would have made her feel more wonderful than she felt now.

"Thank you," she whispered. "I needed that."

He looked confused. "I don't understand."

She snuggled against him. "Never mind."

He wrapped his arm around her, pulling her closer. "Anna?"

"Mmm?"

"About my...loss of control, I'd like the chance to make it up to you."

She lifted her face to his. "You would?"

A slow, sexy smile snaked across his face. "Uh-huh."

"And exactly when were you thinking of making it up to me? Now?"

"Mmm-hmm." He stood and lifted her into his arms. "And all night long."

39

Tuesday, January 30
7:20 a.m.

Quentin's beeper awakened him. Early-morning sun fell across the bed, bright but without warmth. He snatched the annoying instrument off the bedside table, instantly awake. He checked the display, though he would bet a month's salary duty called—no one else would beep him so early in the morning.

He saw he was right and climbed out of bed, careful not to awaken Anna. The bed gave, the floorboard beneath his feet squeaked, and Quentin froze, turning his gaze to Anna. She moaned, stirred then stilled.

Still he watched her. His mouth grew dry, his heartbeat fast. Last night he had told her he thought her beautiful. But what he hadn't told her was, he thought her the most beautiful woman he had ever seen. And that she was too good for him, too smart, too accomplished.

After all, who was he? An Irish-Catholic cop from a neighborhood that boasted far more hoodlums than heroes. A man known more for his sexual prowess with women than anything else.

In that area he could make her happy.

And he could keep her safe. If he had to guard her night and day, so be it. He would not allow this madman to touch her again.

Tearing his gaze away from her, he turned, went to the kitchen and called in.

"Morning, Malone," the desk officer said, way too perky for this godforsaken time of day. "Rise and shine."

Quentin wasn't in the mood for pleasantries. "Kiss my ass, Violet. What do you have?"

As the question passed his lips, Quentin knew and a sick feeling settled in the pit of his gut.

Another woman had been raped and killed. Another redhead.

Violet's next words confirmed that Malone had been right. A woman's body had been discovered that morning. Just off Esplanade Avenue and Decatur Street, near the river. Like Kent and Parker, she had been out partying with friends the night before. "It appears he suffocated her, just like the other two," the desk officer finished. "Walden and Johnson are on their way to the scene."

Quentin glanced at his watch. "That it?"

"Yeah...no, I almost forgot. The killer severed her right pinkie finger."

The words, their meaning, slammed into him. Quentin placed a hand on the counter for support. "What did you say?"

"The bastard cut off her pinkie finger. Can you believe that?"

A moment later, Quentin hung up the phone, hands

shaking. *Mother of God, how was he going to tell Anna?*

"There's a naked man in my kitchen. Quick, call the police."

Quentin turned to find her in the doorway, leaning against the jamb, wrapped in a silky, white robe. She looked soft and sleepy and far too vulnerable.

And she was smiling at him. In a way that made him feel ten feet tall—and scared as hell.

He forced a smile. "The naked man is the police."

"How convenient." She sauntered toward him, loosening her robe as she did. "Who says you can never find a cop when you need one?"

She reached him. Her robe parted and she slid her hands up his chest to his shoulders. He found his voice. "Don't, Anna." He caught her hands, curved his fingers around hers. "Don't."

Hurt crossed her features; she tried to step away. He stopped her, holding her tightly. "It's not you, it's—" He couldn't find the words and swore.

She lifted her gaze to his. The blood drained from her face. "What's happened?"

"I think you'd better sit—"

"No." She started to tremble. "Tell me."

So he did. Quietly, without fanfare or melodramatics.

When he'd finished, he pulled out a chair and she collapsed onto it, shaking. Pale.

"That was supposed to be me," she whispered. "Last night...he was here. He meant to—"

"We don't know that. We don't know anything yet."

"Why is this happening to me!" she cried. "It's been so long... Why won't he leave me alone!"

"It's not Kurt, Anna." Quentin brushed the hair away from her face, his touch gentle. "It's not."

"You're wrong." She looked at him, eyes wet with tears, wide with fright.

"No, Anna. Whoever launched himself over the side of that balcony was not only agile but in excellent physical condition. I have serious doubts that the man from your childhood, a man in his fifties or sixties now, could have done it."

"There's something I didn't tell you. He knew something only Kurt could. The FBI and police kept something from the public, something about that night... the one... Timmy died."

She struggled for an even breath, remembering. "That night... the night he killed Timmy, he... forced me to watch."

He'd heard that. A horror, but not the end of it. "Go on."

"When he had... finished with Timmy, he turned to me and he... smiled." She drew in a shuddering breath. "He smiled and said, 'Ready or not, here I come.' And then he did."

Quentin swallowed his revulsion. "But not with a pillow?"

"No. With wire cutters."

He hated that she had experienced such pain. He wanted to hold her close, protect her from her past and the memories that haunted her. But he knew he couldn't. Some demons could only be fought from within.

"I can't imagine how you survived. That you escaped is a miracle. You were only thirteen, for God's sake."

"I thought of Timmy," she said simply, cutting him off. "How could I give up when Timmy had endured so much more?"

"You're brave, Anna. And you're strong." He cupped her cheeks in his palms. "Stronger than you know."

That made her laugh. "I'm a total wimp. A chicken-shit of the highest caliber. Why do think I've been…hiding all these years?" Her voice thickened. "But he found me anyway."

"If he'd wanted to find you, he would have long before now."

"But I changed my name—"

"To your mother's maiden name," he interrupted gently. "Any half-competent P.I. could have located you in about an hour. It's not him, Anna."

"Then how—"

"Did he know what Kurt said that night? An incredible number of people have access to that information. People talk, cops, agents, family members. This crime is what, twenty-some years old? No one's guarding that information, Anna."

She searched his expression. "You…really believe that?"

"I do." He tightened his fingers on her face. "Look at me, Anna. I'll tell you what I believe. Someone is obsessed with you. Because of your books or your past or both. They've done their homework. And in this digital age, private information is far too easy to access. Until last night they were content to frighten you.''

"But they're not satisfied with that anymore.''

"No, they're not.''

She stood and placed her hand on his arm. "Why am I so hopeful that it's not Kurt who's after me? If it's not, it changes nothing. Is the monster I know so much worse than the monster I don't?''

"I'm going to catch this guy, Anna. I'm not going to let him hurt you.'' His beeper, on the counter by the phone, went off. Aware of the time passing, he swore. "I've got to go, Anna. I hate to but—''

"Go.'' She stepped away from him, curving her arms around her middle. "You've got a job to do.''

"But I'm not leaving you alone. Before I leave, I'll call the station and have a uniform sent over.''

She shook her head. "No. I don't want a stranger here. I'll call Dalton and Bill. They'll come.'' At his frown, she raised her eyebrows. "They're my friends, Malone. They wouldn't hurt me.''

If he had even a hint of proof that one or both of her neighbors were not what they seemed, he would argue with her. But he didn't. "I'm going to dress. Call them now, I won't leave until—''

"My baby-sitters arrive? Thanks.''

He ducked into the bedroom for his clothes, then the bathroom to quickly wash and brush his teeth, though all he had was Anna's toothpaste and his index finger.

When he emerged, Anna was dressed in a pair of khakis and a white turtleneck sweater. She'd combed her hair and pulled it back off her neck with a big tortoiseshell clip.

She wouldn't meet his gaze.

"Anna," he said softly, reaching out. "Please, don't be angry. I don't want to go, but—"

"I'm not angry. I'm not disappointed. You have a job to do."

He felt the distance growing between them. With it the cold. "Then look at me," he murmured. "I want to know you're okay with this."

"I can't. Because if I do, if I let you touch me, I'll fall apart." She pressed her lips together to stop their trembling. "I can't fall apart. I won't."

A knock sounded on the door, followed by Dalton's voice. "I'll call you when I know more," Quentin said as they moved toward it.

Dalton's and Bill's mouths dropped when they saw Quentin. They stared at him, for those few moments at a total loss for words. Dalton's cheeks grew pink and Bill shifted his gaze to Anna, then back to Quentin, eyes narrowed.

The man looked anything but happy to see him.

"Morning, fellas," Quentin murmured. He turned to Anna, acknowledging that he had never been as reluctant to report to a scene as he was at this moment. "I'll call later."

He bent and kissed her. As their lips brushed, his beeper sounded again. He knew it was the precinct, calling to see where he was. But still he held her. "Be careful today. If you need anything—"

"Go," she said, drawing away from him. Her lips trembled, and she pressed them together. "Find this guy. Stop him. Do it for me."

40

Tuesday, January 30
The French Quarter

Quentin made the scene last. He nodded to the other detectives as he wound his way to the victim. He stopped beside her, his heart lodging like a bowling ball in his throat.

Quentin struggled to breathe past it, to remain unaffected, professional. He couldn't, he acknowledged. Not this time. Because he looked at this woman and saw Anna instead.

The killer had meant it to be.

Quentin drew a deep, slow breath through his nose, using the oxygen to steady him. He didn't know that yet, not for sure. Maybe the killer had. Maybe not. He couldn't jump to conclusions. He needed to focus on the scene, its clues; he needed not to let his emotions rule his intellect.

Johnson ambled over. "Took your sweet time getting here, Malone."

"Kiss mine, Johnson."

The other detective grinned. "No thanks, I've got standards."

Quentin hooted at that. The other detective had notoriously bad taste in women. "What've we got?"

"Name's Jessica Jackson. She was twenty-one. Smart and pretty. A senior at Tulane."

Twenty-one. Shit. "Too young," Malone muttered. "Too damn young to die."

"No joke. This guy's really starting to piss me off." Johnson passed a hand over his face. "Walden's canvassing the area, knocking on doors. Maybe somebody will have seen or heard something."

Quentin glanced at the normally laconic detective. He looked tired. Frustrated. "You heard about the other attack last night?"

"Anna North? Yeah, I heard." He looked at Quentin. "MO doesn't fit. She was attacked in her home; she hadn't been out clubbing."

"She's a redhead. A week ago she was at Tipitina's, somebody followed her home. He was scared off."

The man narrowed his eyes. "It's worth looking into. Maybe he—"

"There's more, Johnson. I think our perp's changed his MO for her."

The other detective's eyebrows shot up. "How do you figure?"

"Anna North's missing her right pinkie finger."

That got him. He whistled under his breath. "And this vic is missing hers. The hard way."

Quentin squatted beside the victim. He moved his gaze over the body, then the scene, noting the differences between this one and the previous two.

Her bloodied right hand being the most obvious.

Quentin studied it, frowning. The killer hadn't done a neat job on the pinkie. He had hacked at it. The flesh around the wound was jagged and ripped. It looked as if he had sawed at it with a Swiss Army Knife or some other nonlethal implement.

He hadn't come prepared for this.

"Judging by the wound, the amount and color of the blood, it looks like he removed it postmortem," Johnson offered, squatting down beside him.

Quentin agreed. He moved his gaze to her face. She had been pretty. Real pretty. A natural redhead, a carrottop. Blue eyes. Nice features, real regular.

"He didn't do as neat a job on her as the others," Quentin murmured. "Look at the bruising on her face and neck." He indicated the matted hair and blood on the side of her head. "We haven't seen anything like this on the other vics."

"Think we're dealing with the same perp who did Kent and Parker?"

"My guess is yes," Quentin said. "But at this point that's what it is, a guess."

"It looks like she was raped."

"If this was the same guy, my thinking is he was upset about something. In a rage. Not as careful. Forced to change plans at the last minute."

"You're thinking he meant to kill Anna North. When that fell through, he found a replacement fast."

"And cut off her finger so she would symbolize Anna North."

Maybe they all symbolized Anna. "Yeah."

"So how'd he find a redheaded replacement so fast?"

Quentin drew his eyebrows together, pondering the question. "Maybe he didn't have to find one. Maybe he haunts the clubs. Zeros in on the women who hang out a lot. Makes a list. Learns their habits. When they're most often out, the places they frequent, where they park, their routes home."

"He's making a list and checking it twice," Johnson quipped, tone grim. "When North fell through, in a frenzy, he sought out one of the other women on his list."

Anna. He would be back for her.

As if reading his mind, Johnson murmured, "You think he'll move on?"

Quentin stood. He felt ill. "He wants Anna North. He's not happy that she got away."

"Let's put a uniform on her. If he goes for her, we'll have him."

Quentin nodded. "No chances," he muttered, then looked at Johnson. "I don't want to take any chances, not with this one."

41

Tuesday, January 30
Mid-city

Ben came to consciousness slowly. His head hurt. He ached all over. Uncomfortable, he shifted onto his side and pain shot through his chest. He gasped and opened his eyes.

Where was he?

He moved his gaze over the room, taking in the antiseptic white walls, the television mounted from the ceiling, the metal frame bed and chest of drawers.

He was in the hospital.

Ben brought a hand to his head, disoriented. *What…how had he ended up—*

"Morning, Dr. Walker." A nurse entered the room, wheeling a medicine cart. She smiled broadly at him. "Welcome back to the world of the living."

She crossed to the side of the bed and popped a disposable shield on the thermometer. He opened his mouth and she stuck it under his tongue. "I'm Nurse Abrams. How are we feeling this morning?"

He couldn't answer because of the thermometer, but she didn't seem to notice. Ben saw from her name tag that she was actually Beverly Abrams, an employee of Baptist-Mercy Hospital. She took his pulse, then blood pressure. She added the reading to his chart. The thermometer sounded; she plucked it from his mouth, checked the reading then noted it on his chart. "Normal," she said crisply. "Everything's normal. The doctor will be in soo—"

"Why am I here?"

She stopped what she was doing and looked back at him. "Excuse me?"

"If everything's normal, what am I doing here?"

"You don't remember what happened?"

"Obviously not. If I did—" Suddenly his head filled with what he did remember. The last thing he remembered.

You're falling in love with her.

She's going to die tonight.

Anna, dear God. Heart thundering, he threw back the bedclothes and sat up. His world spun and he fought to right it.

"What are you doing!" The nurse was beside him in a flash. She caught him gently by the shoulders. "You can't—"

"I have to get out of here. A friend…an accident."

"Yes," she said firmly, easing him back against the pillows. "You've been in an accident. You have several broken ribs and a concussion. You're not going anywhere until Dr. Wells says so."

Ben closed his eyes, too weak to argue. He brought a hand to his chest, to the tape and bandages. *An accident. He'd been in an accident.*

"What happened?" he asked. "I don't remember."

"You ran off the road. You had to be extricated

from your car. Dragged through a holly hedge. From what I hear you were lucky. It could've been a lot worse."

Worse. Anna. "I need today's newspaper," he murmured, voice thick. "A *Times-Picayune.*"

"I'll see what I can do."

"No." He caught her hand, squeezing her fingers. "Now. It's…wait, maybe you can tell me… Did anything bad happen last night?"

The nurse looked confused. "You were in an accident. I told you, you have a concussion."

"Not to me." He shook his head, though the movement hurt. "To my friend Anna North. Is she all right?"

The nurse frowned. "As far as I know, you were alone in the car. I could check—"

"Not my car. She was alone last night…I was going to see her."

"I think I'd better call the doctor."

"No, please." He tightened his fingers on hers, wishing he could more adequately express himself, but his brain felt scrambled, his tongue thick and slow. "The news this morning. I have to know, just tell me what happened last night. In the city. What happened while I was unconscious?"

He could tell by her expression that he was spooking her. She shook her head. "I don't know what you… They found another woman dead in the French Quarter. Is that the kind of news—"

He moaned and released her hand. "What was her name?" he asked, fighting a wave of dizziness. "Was it Anna?"

"I don't know." The nurse backed toward the door. "It's been all over the news, every station. But I don't recall her name."

Every station. Of course.

Ben grabbed the television remote from the bedside table, flipped on the set, then surfed the channels until he found what he sought: the twenty-four-hour local news.

"...In today's top story, another woman was found dead in the French Quarter. Jessica Jackson of River Ridge appears to be the third victim in a string of murders that have rocked the New Orleans area this month."

A picture of a pretty young woman in a high school graduation cap and gown flashed on the screen, and Ben nearly wept with relief. *Not Anna. Thank God. Not his Anna.*

"Good morning."

Ben dragged his gaze from the television screen. A small, neat-looking man in a white coat walked into the room. He wore a stethoscope around his neck.

"I'm Dr. Wells." The man stopped beside the bed and stuck out his hand. "I patched you up last night."

Ben shook his hand, wincing at the movement. "Thank you. I wish I could say I felt better."

"I'm a doctor, not a miracle worker." He opened Ben's chart. "You did a pretty good job on yourself, Dr. Walker. Besides four broken ribs and a concussion, you've got a bruised sternum and some vicious scratches. You needed a number of stitches."

Ben frowned. "I didn't go through the windshield, did I?"

"A holly hedge. The rescue guys had to cut you out of the car, you were smack-dab in the middle of thorn-central."

"Lucky me." Ben glanced at the TV. only to see they had moved on to another story. He needed to see Anna. Needed to see with his own eyes that she was safe. Unharmed. He would tell her about the message left on his windshield, then go to the police.

He looked back at the physician. "I have to get out of here, Doc. Can you give me my walking papers?"

The physician smiled slightly. "In good time. You were involved in a pretty nasty accident."

"So Nurse Abrams told me."

The doctor looked at him sharply. "You don't remember?"

"No."

"Nothing about the accident?"

"Nothing." Ben glanced at the clock, then back at the physician. "I was going to see a friend. She needed me, she...I never made it. Obviously."

"You were out cold when the paramedics arrived. In and out while I was working on you." He narrowed his eyes. "A concussion is nothing to take lightly."

Ben murmured that he understood and sat quietly while the man listened to his heart and questioned him about his head, his vision, his equilibrium.

Ben answered each question, lying only when necessary. "I feel fine, Dr. Wells." He forced a smile. "One hundred percent, A-okay. Can I get out of here now?"

"Within the hour, I suppose. You have someone at

home who can keep an eye on you? Make sure you take it easy, wake you up if you fall asleep?''

"I'll keep an eye on him, Doc.''

They turned toward the doorway. Detective Malone stood just inside the door. He looked like hell. The hair on the back of Ben's neck prickled.

"Hello, Ben.''

"Detective Malone, what brings you here?''

"You do.''

"Good news travels fast in this town.''

The detective sauntered into the room, stopping beside the bed. He turned to the physician. "Detective Quentin Malone, NOPD. Mind if I talk to your patient?''

"I think he's up to it.'' The doctor closed the chart and stood. "He might be confused, he suffered a pretty good blow to the head.'' He looked at Ben. "Take it easy today. No work. No driving. I was serious about a baby-sitter, by the way. Get one. Call me if you have any problems at all, headache, dizziness, excessive fatigue.''

"I'll do that.'' Ben held out a hand. "Thanks, Dr. Wells.''

He nodded at Malone. "Detective.''

When the man had exited the room, Malone faced Ben once more. "You called me last night. At the station. I'm curious why.''

"I did?''

"You left your name but no message. You don't remember?''

He brought a hand to his head. "I don't remember much about last ni—''

He bit the words back as a memory shot into his head. He was driving; it was dark. He was going too fast. He was panicked. Punching a number into his cell phone, not watching the road.

"I was trying to get Anna on the phone," he said softly, tentatively. "I couldn't get her. I was concerned about her—"

"Concerned?"

Ben blinked. "Panicked. Afraid for her. So I called you."

Malone dragged over a chair and sat down, his gaze intent. Unblinking. Again the hair at Ben's nape prickled.

"And why were you so worried about her?" Malone asked.

"Is Anna all right?"

"Physically, she's unharmed."

Ben's heart began to thrum. "What's that supposed to mean, Detective?"

"Let's talk about you first, Ben." He took a small spiral and pen from his jacket pocket. "What do you need to tell me?"

Ben brought a hand to his temple. It throbbed. He rubbed it softly, rhythmically, as he began to speak. "I visited my mother last night. She's a resident at the Crestwood Nursing Home. On Metairie Road. She has Alzheimer's."

"I'm sorry."

Ben inclined his head, then went on. "I left later than usual. She was upset. She thought someone had been by and threatened her. It took a while to calm her down."

Quentin's eyebrows shot up. "*Thought* she had been threatened?"

Ben looked at his hands, resting on the crisp white sheet, noticing the scratches on them. "My mother... gets confused. She watches TV, then gets real people and events confused with fictional ones."

"Go on."

"When I got to my car, there was a note tucked under my windshield wiper. I believe it was from the same person who sent me the book and left the photo of me and Anna."

"What did it say, Ben?"

Ben averted his gaze, uncomfortable, feeling exposed. His cheeks warmed. "That I was falling in love with her. And that...that she was going to die 'tonight.' Those were its exact words."

Malone straightened; his gaze sharpened. "It said that she was going to die last night?"

"Yes. I panicked. I called her from my car phone right away. Couldn't get her and tore out of there. Obviously, my attention wasn't on the road."

"You didn't think to call the French Quarter station?"

"I wasn't thinking. I reacted."

Malone glanced down at his spiral. "And was the note correct?" He lifted his gaze. "Are you falling in love with her?"

Ben stiffened. "That's personal, Detective."

"I think it's relevant." The detective looked him square in the eyes. "Are you?"

Ben met his gaze boldly. "Yes, I am."

Something, some strong emotion passed across the

detective's face and in that moment Ben realized he wasn't the only one who had strong feelings for Anna. Simultaneously, Ben felt indignant, possessive and threatened. "I'm the persistent type, Detective. I don't give up easily."

"No good adversary ever does." A smile touched the other man's mouth, then disappeared. "Do you still have the note?"

"It was in my car. I'm certain it's still there." A humorless laugh passed his lips. "Wherever that is."

"Any idea who left you that note?"

"The same person who left me the book is my guess. A patient, I believe. But which one, I don't know."

"Ever heard the name Adam Furst before?"

"No."

"You're certain? You don't have a patient by that name?"

"I'm positive."

"Any patient named Adam or Furst? Past or present?"

Ben thought a moment, then shook his head. "Why? Who is he?"

Malone ignored his question. "Last time we talked, you indicated you were attempting to narrow the list of potential suspects amongst your patients. You don't seem to have made much progress."

He stiffened. "It takes time, Detective. I can't simply accuse someone of something like this. I've eliminated all but a handful of my current patients as suspects. Within the week, barring appointment cancellations, I'll have put the remaining patients to the test."

"The test?" Quentin repeated. "And what test would that be, Dr. Walker?"

Ben explained about placing the book and note in plain view of his patients and his theory that the guilty party would not be able to ignore the items. "By the end of the week I expect to have a name for you."

"By the end of the week another woman could be dead. Perhaps you should try a bit harder? Or simply hand over your patient list and let us do our job?"

"You know I can't do that. It would be unethical of me to do so."

"And harboring a murderer is ethical?"

"Murderer? You're making a pretty big leap there, Detective. It seems to me the distance between a note left on a car's windshield and an actual murder is—"

"Anna was attacked last night. In her home."

Ben felt the words like a blow. The breath left his body and he struggled to find it again. "She's all...you said she was unharmed?"

"He was frightened off before he could do what he intended. She's shaken. Understandably so."

Ben leaned against the bed pillows. He felt ill. Felt that this was somehow his fault. Because he hadn't been able to reach Anna in time to stop this maniac; because he hadn't done more to discover which of his patients was responsible.

"There's more. A woman was raped and killed last ni—"

"In the French Quarter. I saw. On television." Ben

cleared his throat. "You don't think that murder had anything to do with... I mean—"

"She was a redhead, Dr. Walker. Another redhead. And he cut off her right pinkie finger." The detective paused, as if to allow time for his words to sink in. "Still think it would be unethical to hand over a list of your patients?"

42

Quentin angled his Bronco into one of the parking spots on the street in front of the Seventh District station. His tête-à-tête with Ben Walker had proved only mildly enlightening. The man had been genuinely distressed at the news of Anna's attack, deeply troubled both over the note that had been left on his windshield and the fact that one of his patients might be responsible.

Even so, he had refused to turn over his patient roster. Quentin cut his vehicle's engine. The doctor had insisted that if he knew which patient had left the notes, he would turn him in. But he didn't and claimed that in good conscience, he couldn't hand them all over.

It sounded like a load of crap to Quentin. For Quentin the issue was cut-and-dried. Somebody out there was killing women. There was a chance that same person wanted to hurt Anna. He needed to discover that person's identity and stop them. Code of ethics be damned.

Ben Walker was falling in love with Anna.

Quentin scowled and threw open the car door. The thought irritated the hell out of him. As did the question gnawing at the back of his brain—if it had been Ben at Anna's door last night, would he have been the one to share her bed?

He hated the question. But he couldn't completely erase it from his thoughts. Anna had been frightened. In shock. He had been there.

She had turned to him. For comfort. As a way to wash away the horror she had just experienced. Lord knew, he had seen enough cops do the same thing time again—with booze or babes or any of a dozen other diversions. He had done it himself.

Quentin slammed the door and hit the auto lock. Son-of-a-bitch. He had known making love with her would be a mistake before he had done it. But she had been so incredibly sexy. So vulnerable. Being strong and righteous had been beyond him.

He had wanted her from the first moment he'd seen her.

No doubt Ben Walker felt the same. A doctor. Quentin scowled. And what was he? A cop. A guy whose real dreams had always been beyond his capabilities.

"Detective Malone?"

Quentin turned. A couple of detectives he recognized from PID stood behind him. They held up their shields though they had to know he recognized them. It had been they who had questioned him about the events at Shannon's the night Nancy Kent died.

Quentin silently swore. The day had just taken a

trip south. He forced a smile. "Hi, fellas. What's up?"

Simmons, the shorter of the two, spoke first. "We need to ask you a few questions about your partner, Terry Landry."

"Really?" Quentin cocked an eyebrow. "I thought we'd been through all this already."

"All what, Detective?" Carter, the other detective, asked.

So this was the way it was going to go. "The events at Shannon's the night of the Kent murder."

"This morning we're interested in other events, Detective Malone."

Quentin leaned against his Bronco. He folded his arms across his chest. "Fire away."

"We hear Landry's having a hard time right now."

"You could say that, I suppose. He and his wife have separated." Quentin moved his gaze between the two. "But we talked about this the last time we got together."

"It's understandable then, that's he hitting the bottle pretty heavy."

Quentin stiffened slightly. "Is he? I hadn't noticed."

Simmons and Carter exchanged glances. "You haven't noticed him drinking...excessively?"

Quentin pushed away from the vehicle, annoyed. "Look, let's stop playing cat and mouse. If you're asking me if Terry has gone out and tied one on recently, yeah, he has. But he was off duty. It didn't affect his on-the-job performance or tarnish the sterling image of the NOPD."

"You've seen no change in his on-the-job performance?" Simmons asked.

"No," Quentin replied, leveling him with an unblinking stare. "None."

"It must be tough for him financially right now," Carter murmured. "What with having to support two households."

Quentin narrowed his eyes. "It'd be tough for any cop."

"He's talked to you about that?"

"Complained that money was tight, yeah."

"Yet he doesn't seem to be strapped for cash." This came from Simmons. "Does he, Detective?"

"I don't know what you mean."

"So, you haven't noticed Landry spending questionable amounts of money? Buying rounds of drinks? Tipping big?"

The fifty-dollar bill Terry had slipped Shannon. Son-of-a-bitch, this was bad. "No, I haven't." He looked Carter directly in the eyes. "Have you?"

The other detective ignored that. "Is there anything about Landry's behavior or performance you'd like to discuss with us?"

What the hell had his partner gotten himself into? Quentin worked to keep his unease from showing. "I told you, Terry's fine. Going through a tough time but hanging in there."

He moved his gaze between the two PID officers. "You want to tell me what's going on here?"

A small smile touched Simmons's mouth. "Thank you for your help, Detective Malone."

Carter's expression was not nearly so subtle. "We'll be in touch."

"I'll count on it," he muttered, watching the two officers walk away, then turned and crossed the sidewalk, moving toward the station house.

A couple of uniforms having a smoke on the front steps nodded in his direction and Quentin swore under his breath. How many of his fellow officers had witnessed his little chat with Carter and Simmons? Quite a few, he acknowledged, noticing the curious stares as he entered the building. Within the hour, word would have spread to everyone on the shift.

The PID boys had chosen that meeting place deliberately. They had wanted to alert everyone that something was gong on. That it either involved Quentin or someone close to him. They had wanted the Seventh on edge and Terry on notice—they were after his ass.

Damn. What did they have on his partner? What did they and the rest of the higher-ups know that he didn't? And how much trouble had he just gotten himself into by covering for his partner?

Quentin muttered an oath, angry at Simmons and Carter's tactics. Angry at Terry for being such a screwup. Angrier at himself for feeling the need to cover for the other man. To make excuses for him.

"Making excuses for Terry's bad behavior isn't helping him," Penny had said. *"It's not helping me or the kids."*

Quentin passed his aunt's office; noting that the door was closed. He considered ignoring protocol, barging in and demanding answers. As quickly as the thought registered, he discounted it. Mother's sister or not, he did that and she would make him sorry he'd been born.

He crossed to the coffeepot instead, poured a cup of the tar-black, burnt-smelling brew, then added a packet of sugar.

"Got a minute?" Terry asked from behind him.

Quentin glanced over his shoulder and forced an easy smile. Terry had seen him and the PID guys. And was stressing over it. Quentin saw it in the other man's eyes. "Sure. Just perfecting this cup of battery acid."

He tasted the drink, added another sugar, stirred the concoction then turned to face his friend. "What's up?"

"I saw them," Terry hissed, face red. "Those bastards from PID. What did they want?"

"Good morning to you, too, partner."

"Cut the crap. It's my ass hanging out there, I want to know what's going on."

Quentin glanced around them before replying. "First off, don't go getting paranoiac, because that's exactly what they want. Second, why don't you tell *me* what's going on? By virtue of my relationship with you, my ass's out there too, and I don't like it."

"I'm doing my job, that's what's going on. Dealing with my shitty life and keeping my nose to the grindstone."

Quentin looked his friend dead in the eyes. "They asked about your drinking, Terry. They asked about your finances."

"My finances?" His friend looked genuinely surprised. "What the hell? Here's a news flash, I'm flat broke."

"Give me a break." Quentin lowered his voice even more. "I saw, Terry. That fifty you slipped Shannon. If you're so broke, where'd that come from?"

"You think I'm on the take? Is that what they think? Is that what you told them?"

"I didn't tell them anything." He glanced over his shoulder. "I covered for you. Though I don't know why."

His friend looked relieved. Too relieved. "Because we're buddies," he said. "We look out for each other. We—"

Quentin made a sound of frustration. "That's over, Terry. Penny's right, my making excuses for you is not doing anybody any good. Especially you."

"Penny?" Hot color flooded the other man's face. "What are you doing talking to my wife?"

"You asked me to, remember?" Another officer started their way, coffee cup in hand, took a look at the two of them, turned and walked the other way. "Look, Terry, let's take this up another time. This isn't the time or pla—"

"That's bullshit. You talked to my wife and I want to know what she said. Is she running around? Who's she seeing?"

Quentin sighed. He had been dreading this conversation since seeing Penny more than a week ago. This scene had been inevitable; he might as well get it over with. "She's not running around, Terry. In fact, she said you were the one who owned that territory."

"And you believed her?"

"Yeah. I believed her."

Terry's expression turned ugly. "How come this is the first I'm hearing about your cozy little chat with my wife? You trying to hide something, partner? Like maybe that you're doing my wife?"

Quentin held on to his temper—barely. "I told you once before that Penny doesn't deserve that. And neither do I."

"What's the matter? The truth hurt?"

Quentin looked at the other man in disgust. "I'll tell you the truth, Terry. No way is Penny going to take you back, not until you get your act together. She thinks you're self-destructing and she doesn't want to be there, or for the kids to be there, when it happens. I didn't think you wanted to hear that, so I kept it to myself. Satisfied? I defended you, but right now I'm wondering why."

Terry fisted his fingers. "I should have known better. You don't send a fox into a chicken coop and not expect somebody to get eaten. Everybody knows about you and women. You nailing her, partner? Her and who else? That redheaded writer? Maybe you're doing them both at the same time?"

White-hot anger took Quentin's breath. He fought to keep it in check, fought not to lunge at the other man. "Keep Anna out of this."

A look of surprise crossed his friend's face, then one of understanding. "Anna, is it? We're on a first-name basis now? How sweet." He laughed, the sound nasty. "I see I was right, Malone scores again."

Quentin was shocked by the malevolence in the

other man's voice and words. Terry had been crude at times, sarcastic or bitter at others. But this was a man he didn't recognize. An ugly man. A mean one.

The man, no doubt, that Penny Landry had seen far too often.

Quentin leaned toward his partner, catching a whiff of alcohol as he did. "You're damn lucky I'm your friend and know what a hard time you're having, otherwise I'd beat the hell out of you right now. And you know what? You'd deserve it."

Terry swayed slightly, though he met Quentin's gaze evenly, his eyes bloodshot, raw-looking. "Better stay close to your new girlfriend, buddy. Because from what I hear, a murderer has his eyes on her as well."

Quentin sucked in a sharp breath, then counted to ten before responding. "I've had it with you, Terry," he said softly. "You got that?" He took a step closer, crowding the other man. "I'm not going to put up with your shit anymore and I'm not going to cover for it. I suggest you get your act together before you get yourself in some serious trouble."

43

Quentin stood in front of Anna's building for a full five minutes before the cold propelled him to her front steps. No, he corrected. Not the cold. The warmth. Her warmth.

It had been a hell of a day. Grim. Frustrating. In addition to Jessica Jackson's murder, his visit with the boys from PID and his falling-out with Terry, everyone at the Seventh District had been called on the carpet by Chief Pennington.

They weren't moving fast enough on the Kent, Parker and Jackson investigations, the NOPD chief had maintained. They weren't doing enough. Three murders in three weeks. This maniac was on a spree and O'Shay and her team were no closer to apprehending him than the morning after the Kent murder.

Quentin had jumped to all of their defense. He had told the man that if he thought he could do better, to go for it. They had left no stone unturned, had pursued every lead, real and imaginary. They had checked and rechecked for links between the victims. So far, all their work had led to nothing but one dead end after another.

The chief had been furious. But he'd backed off— after he had issued the detectives a warning: they were on the clock, they had better find and nail this killer. And they had better do it fast.

Through it all, Quentin had thought of Anna. About her predicament. About what had occurred between them the night before. He hadn't forgotten, not for a moment, that it could have been her laid out in the morgue instead of another young woman.

Ben Walker infuriated him. By refusing to share his patients' names, he could be harboring a killer. A man intent on killing the woman Ben professed to be falling in love with. What would it take to shake Walker loose of his sanctimonious ethics? Anna's death? Or a threat against his own life?

Quentin glanced toward Anna's windows. Her blinds were closed; light spilled through and around the edges. He had called her once during the day, to inform her that a uniform named laSalle had been assigned to watch over her. That had frightened her. Her fear had become anger when he had refused to discuss why, when he had refused to say more about the investigation than that they were following every lead.

They'd been on the phone a couple of minutes, tops. They hadn't broached what had happened between them the night before. They had hung up, a chasm growing between them.

He should end it here, Quentin acknowledged. He should walk away now. What did they have in com-

mon besides the frightening things happening to her?
Nothing else.

Liar. They had the sex.

*The spectacular, breath-stealing, brain-numbing
sex.*

Quentin closed his eyes, remembering. Dear Lord,
it had been out of this world. He had been like a horny
adolescent with her. Some sort of testosterone-
charged teenager.

He opened his eyes just as she walked past her
window, a slim shadow moving across her blind. Last
night, where had all that sexual energy come from?
Why did Anna North fit him like a glove, a glove that
had been fashioned just for him? Why her and no
other woman?

He wanted her now. Then again. All night long.

*God, he felt like such a shit. Like he was taking
advantage of her when she was most vulnerable.*

Quentin dragged his gaze from her window. She
didn't need this complication in her life right now.
She needed him to be dispassionate, analytical. Focused on finding and stopping the man who had been
terrorizing her, the man who meant her harm.

Not blinded by arousal. Not fatigued by nights
spent making love.

Go. Now. End it here.

He buzzed her apartment instead, waited a few moments then buzzed again. She answered, her voice
coming over the intercom.

"Yes? Who is it?"

"It's Quentin." Silence ensued. His gut tightened.
"Can I come up?"

"That depends. Have you come to replace laSalle as my guard dog? Or are you here to see me?"

"To see you." He paused. "We need to talk."

She hesitated a moment, then murmured, "I'll ring you in."

She did and he climbed the stairs to her apartment. Officer laSalle sat outside her door, a thermos of coffee at his feet, an open novel in his lap.

He looked up as Quentin cleared the landing. "Hello, Detective Malone."

"LaSalle." He crossed to the man. "It's been quiet?"

"As a tomb."

He indicated the novel. "I hope that book's not too good."

The man cleared his throat and closed the book. "No, sir. Not at all."

"Glad to hear it." Quentin glanced at his watch. "I'll stay with Ms. North for a couple hours if you want to grab some grub."

"I'll do that." The rookie stood, expression grateful. "I'll take a swing through the neighborhood while I'm out. Make sure everything's in order."

"Good idea. Enjoy your dinner."

Anna opened the door. Two spots of bright color dotted her cheeks. She watched as laSalle disappeared down the stairs, then turned to Quentin. "Slick," she murmured. "Getting rid of my baby-sitter that way. I'll have to remember that technique."

She wore straight-leg, soft-looking blue jeans and a bulky ivory sweater. She looked pale. Almost waiflike without makeup, her glorious hair pulled away from her face in a high, girlish ponytail.

She took his breath away.

"Don't even think about it." Quentin scowled. "He's here for your protection."

She crossed her arms over her chest. "And why are you here, Malone? For my protection?"

"You're angry."

"Shouldn't I be? You left here this morning with a promise to keep me informed. Instead, I get the party line from you and a baby-sitter at my door."

"I'm concerned for your safety. My captain is concerned. We're not taking any chances."

"The man from last night, he's going to come back for me, isn't he?" She tipped up her chin, working, he saw, to put on a brave face. "That's why laSalle's sitting outside my door."

He drew his eyebrows together, frustrated by her refusal to simply accept his assurances and NOPD protection. "We don't know for sure that he'll come back for you. But if he does, we'll be here."

"And?"

"And last night's murder may or may not be related to the previous two. There were some differences in the execution of this crime, including the removal of the woman's pinkie finger. This could be a copycat. I'd be inclined to consider that, but there are a few problems with that theory as well. The biggest being that we never publicly released the fact that the other two women were redheads."

Her bravado faded. She searched his expression,

hers suddenly, painfully anxious. "Do you have any…clues who—"

"No. I'm sorry, Anna."

She looked crestfallen and he made a sound of regret. "I'd hoped to have good news for you, but I don't."

She rubbed her arms, as if chilled. "Investigations like this aren't solved overnight."

Sometimes they're not solved at all. He looked away, then back at her. "Are you all right?" he asked softly, wanting to touch her but holding back. "I thought about you…today."

Her features softened and a ghost of a smile touched her mouth. "I'm okay." She opened the door wider. "Come in."

"You're sure?"

"I'm sure."

He stepped across the threshold; she closed the door behind them and locked it. "What's in the bag?" she asked.

He glanced at the brown paper sack he carried, realizing that he had forgotten about it. He held it out. "Chicken soup. For you."

She looked startled, then laughed. "You made me chicken soup?"

Quentin grinned at the thought. "I'm not trying to poison you. This is a container of my mother's chicken soup. She keeps all of our freezers stocked. Just in case. It's still frozen, by the way."

Anna took the bag. "*All* of your freezers?"

"I'm one of seven. The second boy and second oldest. Five of us are cops. As was my grandfather, my dad, three uncles and one aunt. I won't even go into my cousins."

"Oh my."

He grinned. "That's what everybody says."

She set the bag with its container of soup on her small entryway table. Awkward silence fell between them.

"How was your day?" he asked.

"Uncomfortable." She hugged herself. "I spent it looking over my shoulder. Jumping at every noise."

"You went out?"

"I was crawling the walls here. So this afternoon I...went into The Perfect Rose. Dalton needed me."

Quentin frowned. He understood that she couldn't hide in her apartment forever; even so, he disliked the thought of her out on the street alone. Especially so soon after that madman had attacked her. "You were careful?"

"Yes." As he opened his mouth to question her more, she held up a hand, stopping him. "Not to worry. Ben walked me there and Dalton walked me home. LaSalle never let me out of his sight. I was the safest woman in New Orleans."

At the mention of the psychologist, Quentin frowned. "Ben Walker was here?"

"Yes. He came to see me." She rubbed her arms, as if chilled. "He looked awful. That accident, how it happened... He said the two of you had spoken. And he...told me about the note left on his windshield. Told me it said—"

Her throat closed over the words and Quentin reached out to her. He cupped her face in his palms, forcing her to look directly into his eyes. "We're going to find this guy, Anna. *I'm* going to find him. I won't let him hurt you."

A half sob, half laugh bubbled to her lips. "Promise?"

He bent and brushed his mouth against hers. It trembled beneath his. "Yes," he murmured. "I promise."

With a small sound of relief, she brought her hands to his shoulders, her cheek to his chest. Silence engulfed them. Quentin looped his arms around her, but loosely, so she wouldn't know how frightened he was for her. Or how much she mattered to him.

After a moment, she tipped her face up to his. "That woman, the one who...died last night—"

"Jessica Jackson."

"Tell me about her."

"Anna—"

"Please." Her eyes filled with tears. "I want to know her. She died for me."

"You don't know that. We don't—"

"I know it." Her voice thickened, and she cleared her throat. "She was a redhead. He lopped off her right pinkie finger. She died the same night I was attacked, the same night someone left a note on Ben's windshield saying that I was going to die."

"The note said *she* was going to die, Anna. It didn't name you specifically, you or anyone else. He could have meant Jessica Jackson."

"You don't believe that. And neither do I. It's so obvious, Quentin."

He cupped her face in his palms once more.

"About the time I'm certain something is obvious, I'm wrong, Anna."

"Tell me about her."

He muttered an oath, even as he acquiesced. "Her name was Jessica Jackson. She was a student at Tulane and a bartender at the bar at the Omni Royal Orleans Hotel. She worked until eleven last night, then met some friends. They went out dancing. She was unmarried and had no children. She's survived by her parents and two sisters."

"How old?" Anna asked, voice trembling.

He hesitated. "Twenty-one."

Anna moaned. "I feel so bad for her. For her family. So guilty about what happened. So relieved it wasn't…me." She began to cry. "It's my fault she's dead. How am I going to live with that? How, Quentin?"

"Stop it, Anna." He caught her tears with his fingers. "You didn't kill her."

"But she died instead of me." She looked at him, eyes bright and wet. Full of despair. "Don't tell me it isn't so, because I know it is. In my heart, I know it's true."

He couldn't tell her otherwise, though he longed to.

He believed it to be true as well. And it shook him to his core.

He was growing to care for her. And someone wanted her dead. Someone who had killed before and would kill again.

Quentin bent and took her mouth with his. He kissed her, softly at first, then with growing urgency. Growing passion.

With a small, helpless-sounding cry, she looped her arms around his neck and pressed herself against him.

They made love there. In the entryway. He backed her up to the wall and lifted her onto him. She wrapped her legs around his hips and hung on tightly while he thrust into her.

It wasn't until after passion's frenzy that he realized she tasted of her tears. That her mouth trembled beneath his. Regret took his breath, and cradling her in his arms, he carried her to the bedroom. He laid her on the bed, then positioned himself beside her.

"I didn't mean for that to happen," he murmured. "Not like that."

"I'm not complaining."

He trailed his fingers tenderly over her face, stopping on the whisker burns on her jaw and the side of her neck. He swore. "I hurt you."

"You didn't."

"I'm sorry."

"Don't be." She laid her fingers against his mouth. A smile tugged at hers. "You're a nice man, Quentin Malone."

He laughed at that, the sound tight and humorless. "You think so? Some might call me an opportunistic son-of-a-bitch. Some might suggest I take advantage of women when they're most vulnerable."

"Really?" She arched her eyebrows. "And why don't I see it that way?"

"Because you've had a shock. Look, I show up at your door—"

"With chicken soup."

"And end up naked in your bed. Pretty slick."

"If I remember correctly, it was I who started this. Perhaps I'm the one who's opportunistic?"

He bent and rested his forehead against hers. "If that's the case, you can take advantage of me anytime."

"Promise?"

He opened his mouth to respond; her stomach growled loudly. She pressed a hand to it, cheeks pink.

Quentin smiled. "Have you eaten?"

"Not since breakfast, no." Her stomach rumbled again. She laughed. "Rumor has it your mother makes a pretty mean chicken soup."

"The best." He rolled off the bed. "Got any saltines?"

He held out his hand; she grasped it and he helped her up. "Yup. And if you promise to be a nice boy, I'll even pour you big glass of milk."

He grinned. "Depends, my dear, on what you mean by nice."

A short time later, they sat across from each other on her living-room floor, bowls of steaming chicken soup and an open package of crackers in front of them.

Anna took a spoonful of the savory soup, then looked up at him. "This is wonderful."

"Thanks." He smiled. "My mother's a great cook. When you have seven kids to feed, it's a plus."

"What's she like?"

"A dynamo. She's only five feet tall, but—"

"Five feet tall? You must be kidding."

"My dad's a big man. His dad and grandfather

were even bigger." Quentin took a spoonful of the soup, then wiped his mouth. "We all tower over her, my sisters, too. Even so, Mom's definitely the head of the family. While we were growing up, she wore a big leather belt around her waist, if we got out of line, watch out. A couple of times she couldn't get the belt off fast enough, so she came after us with a broom."

Anna smiled at the image. "Were you bad?"

"I was awful."

She plucked a soda cracker from the bag. "Tell me about your sisters and brothers."

"I have four brothers and two sisters. I'm second in the Malone lineup, which my older brother, John Jr., never lets me forget."

Anna leaned toward him, fascinated. Warmed by the affection in his tone, the way his eyes lit up while talking about his family. "I can't imagine having so many siblings. Tell me about them."

So he did. He described Percy as outgoing, Spencer as a hot dog. Shauna was a free spirit, Patrick more conservative than God and John Jr. was a big, over-stuffed teddy bear. His sister Mary was going through a tough time in her marriage and John Jr. was expecting his third child.

"All of us are cops except Patrick, who's an accountant, and Shauna, who's studying art in college. They're the black sheep of the Malone clan."

He went on to talk about his five nieces and nephews, his Aunt Patti, who was his captain at the Seventh and his various sisters- and brothers-in-law.

"What a nice family," Anna murmured, sounding as wistful as she felt.

"Most of the time. We fought like crazy when we were kids. Drove our folks nuts."

Anna glanced down at her bowl, saw that it was empty and snitched another soda cracker. "Did you always want to be a cop?" she asked.

"Being a cop chose me."

"Because of your family." She tilted her head, studying him. "What did you want to do instead?"

"Who said I wanted to do anything else?"

"Then you did want to be a police officer?"

"It's your turn to talk." He had finished his soup and pushed his bowl away. "Tell me what it was like growing up in Hollywood."

"Before the kidnapping, euphoric. After, it was... lonely."

"I'm sorry. That was a stupid question."

She lifted her shoulders. "Don't worry about it."

Awkward silence fell between them. After a moment, Anna stood. "Would you like some more soup?"

He followed her to her feet. "No thanks." He glanced at his watch. "LaSalle should be back any minute."

"Then you should go. People will talk."

"Let them. If you're okay with it, so am I."

She said she was and they collected their bowls, milk glasses, crackers and carried the items to the kitchen. After depositing the glasses and crackers on the counter, she took the bowls from him and carried them to the sink.

She turned on the water. "Ben told me you two were going to come up with a plan to discover which of his patients was behind the notes."

"Did he?"

At his tone, she looked over her shoulder at him. "You don't like him very much, do you?"

"I don't know him."

Anna turned off the water and faced him. She cocked an eyebrow. "So why the dislike? And don't deny it, I hear it in your voice."

"Maybe it's his ethics I don't like. Maybe it's that I want to catch a killer and he's more interested in protecting one."

"He won't turn over a list of his patients' names."

"That's right."

"And you think the name Adam's on it."

"I hope it is. Though I asked Ben and he said no. But it makes sense that all these events are related. The tapes and notes. Minnie's letters. Jaye's disappearance. The prosthetic finger. Your being followed. The attack on you last night."

"Jessica Jackson's murder. And those other two women as well." Tears burned her eyes. "Those people suffered because of me."

"Not because of you, Anna." He crossed to her, took her by the shoulders and turned her to face him. "You're the victim here. Not the perpetrator." He shook her lightly. "You're not."

"One of the victims," she corrected. "Just one."

Anna swallowed hard. "I've got to do something, Malone. I can't just sit in this apartment, kept safe by the NOPD, while women are dying. While Jaye is enduring God only knows what. Somehow this is my fault, Malone. I don't know what I did to cause this, but I have to do something to stop it.''

"You want to help? Get Ben to release that list of names. If there's not an Adam on it, I'll bet there'll be another name you recognize.''

"Like Kurt.''

"Or someone else in your life.''

She met his gaze evenly, in challenge. "If you're thinking Bill's or Dalton's name might be on that list, you're mistaken. Ben met them for the first time when he looked me up at The Perfect Rose.''

"You're sure of that?''

"Yes.'' She swung to face him. "Yes, dammit!''

For a moment they stared at one another, the air between them electric. Quentin swore. "This is my job, Anna. I look at facts. I consider opportunity and motive. Dalton and Bill have opportunity—''

"And no motive. They're my friends and I trust them completely.''

"And you probably have reason to. But consider this fact, Anna. In the great majority of violent crimes, the victim knows her attacker. I don't take that fact lightly. Neither should you.''

Anna hated that he could make her doubt her friends, even if only for a fraction of a second. "Do what you have to, Malone,'' she said. "That's fine. But I'm going to get that list from Ben. And you're going to see that you were wrong. Dead wrong.''

He crossed the kitchen in two strides. He pulled her against his chest and kissed her, deeply, with an edge of desperation.

She responded in kind, curling her fingers into his sweater, clutching him to her.

He broke the kiss. "Get the list, but then stay out of it, Anna," he said, voice gruff. "Let me and my guys do our jobs. This bastard would love for you to get involved. To get out there and make yourself vulnerable to him. Don't give him what he wants."

"You're wrong, Malone," she said, suddenly understanding her foe. What he wanted. What made him tick. "He wants me isolated and terrified. The way I was twenty-three years ago."

44

Wednesday, January 31
1:52 a.m.

"Minnie?" Jaye whispered. She sat up in bed and turned toward the door and the soft snuffling sound that had come from the other side. She hadn't heard from her friend since their captor had discovered them talking. Since he had forced Jaye to seal Anna's letter with a kiss.

Jaye had been worried sick about the other girl. Fearful that he had punished her for befriending Jaye. That he had hurt her. She had been afraid for Anna as well. Had she received the letter? What had she thought? Had she recognized the lip print as Jaye's?

It had been torture waiting and wondering, praying her friends were safe but so desperately afraid they were not. She had slept little in the past five days; she had paced and agonized, prayed and planned.

She had to get out of here. She had to save Minnie and warn Anna. There had to be a way.

The sound came again and Jaye scrambled off her cot. "Minnie? Is that you?"

"It's me."

Jaye made a sound of relief and tiptoed to the door

and knelt down in front of it, pressing her mouth close to the pet hatch. "I've been so worried about you. What did he do? Was it awful?"

"He was very angry." Tabitha mewed and Minnie shushed her. "I...I almost didn't come tonight. If he finds out I'm here... I'm so afraid, Jaye."

Rage welled up in Jaye. She squeezed her hands into fists. "I hate him," she said, tone low but fierce. "I hate him so much. For what he's done to us. And because of Anna. When I get out of here, I swear I'm going to make him pay. I promise I will."

"Don't say that, Jaye. He may be listening." Minnie sounded frightened. "You'll make him even angrier. He'll hurt you."

A part of her wanted to scream that she didn't care. She wanted to shout at the top of her lungs for him to come and get her, that she wasn't afraid of him.

But she had to think of Minnie. And Anna. She couldn't do anything that might endanger them. She wouldn't.

"Minnie?" Jaye pressed even closer to the door. "Do you know...is Anna...has he—" The question stuck in her throat. She couldn't utter it. As if saying the words aloud might make them come true.

They hung in the air anyway, taunting her.

Has he hurt Anna? Was she...alive?

"I think she's okay." Minnie paused and Jaye sensed that she was pausing to listen, to glance over her shoulder and make sure they were alone. When she spoke again, her voice was slightly muffled, as if she had pressed her mouth to the door. "The other night...he came in...he was upset. Something had gone wrong…it had to do with Anna. He was muttering to himself. He said some things…some bad things.''

Her voice trailed off and Jaye laid her hands on the door. "What, Minnie? What did he say? What bad things?''

For a moment the girl didn't respond, when she did, her voice shook. "He's going to move us, Jaye. I don't know where or when, but it has something to do with Anna. With hurting Anna.''

45

"**H**ey, partner. Got a minute?"

Quentin lifted his gaze. Terry stood at the entrance to the men's locker room, expression repentant. It had been twenty-four hours since their argument, and Terry had obviously come to his senses and cooled down.

Unmoved, Quentin slammed his locker and sat on the bench, back to the other man. "I'm a little busy right now."

Terry came into the room, stopping to stand in front of him. "I don't blame you for being angry."

Quentin ignored him. He bent, tied his running shoes, then stood. "I'm taking a run now, Terry. Excuse me."

"I acted like an ass."

"For starters. Like I said, I'm going for a run."

Quentin stepped over the bench and headed for the door.

"I'm sorry." Quentin stopped but didn't look back. "The things I said, they were wrong."

Quentin turned then, facing the other man. "They

stunk," he said flatly. "I didn't deserve them. Neither did Penny."

"I know, I—" He looked away. "I don't know what's happening to me, Malone. I feel like...it's all falling apart. Me. My life, the job. And I don't know how to stop it."

Quentin's anger at the other man evaporated. "You need help, Terry. You can't do this on your own."

"You mean a therapist."

"Yeah. The department has a—"

"No way." Terry sank onto the bench. "Word will get around. I don't want everybody knowing my business."

"You think they don't know now?" Quentin crossed to his friend. "You think they don't see? Come on, Terry, you're smarter than that."

Terry dropped his head into his hands. "I don't want to screw up anymore, Malone. I don't want to hurt anyone else."

"See the shrink. Do it, Terry. You need help."

His partner lifted his head; he looked at him. "Will you back me up, partner? If I do this, will you help me get Penny and my kids back?"

Quentin had serious doubts that anything Terry did would induce his wife to take him back, but he kept his opinion to himself. "Yeah, I'll back you up."

"Thank you." He slipped off his glasses and rubbed his eyes.

Quentin frowned, noticing for the first time that his partner was wearing glasses. "What's with the specs?"

"I got myself an eye infection from wearing my

contacts too long without changing them. My optometrist says no contacts for at least a month. Just another thing I'm screwing up at.''

"I saw his eyes, Malone. They were orange."

Colored contacts. Of course.

Quentin swore, run forgotten. He crossed to his locker and yanked it open. ''You got anything going right now?''

Terry shook his head. ''Why? What's up?''

''A research mission, but that's all I can say. You want to tag along anyway?''

''I'm with you, partner.''

Twenty minutes later, Quentin and Terry entered the Eyeware Showcase at the New Orleans Center. They crossed the carpeted showroom, heading toward the service counter. Quentin showed the young man behind the desk his shield and asked to speak with the manager.

''What's this all about?'' Terry asked while the man scurried into the back room to find his boss.

''A hunch,'' Quentin supplied. ''You'll see.''

Within moments, an elegantly dressed middle-aged woman emerged from the back. She crossed to the desk and smiled. She introduced herself as Pamela Bell. ''How can I help you, Detectives—''

''Malone and Landry,'' Quentin supplied. He held up his shield, as did Terry. ''I was hoping you could be of some help with an investigation we're working on.''

''I'll be happy to try.''

''I'm interested in learning about colored contact

lenses. Do they only come in the traditional colors like blue and green, or are they available in colors like red and orange?''

''Absolutely.'' She bent, rummaged under the counter for a moment, then emerged with a table-tent advertisement for colored contacts. It depicted models with eyes in various colors, from bright violet and Easter-egg blue to devil red.

''That's amazing,'' Quentin murmured. ''Creepy-looking.''

''We sell a lot of the bizarre colors around Hallow-een and Mardi Gras. The yellow, red and orange. Also to people who like to be different. You know what I mean.''

Quentin frowned. ''No, I don't.''

She glanced past Quentin, then returned her gaze to his. ''To those kids, you know, they call themselves Gothics. Also to…night people. The people into the alternative-music scene, the downtown clubs.''

Quentin nodded. Terry said nothing. ''Can anyone wear them?''

''Sure. But the effect is most startling on people with light eyes.''

''Do you know, Ms. Bell, are these contacts widely available in this area?''

''Certainly. They're a popular novelty item, espe-cially since the price has become so reasonable.''

Malone thanked the woman and he and Terry left the store, then the mall. ''You're awfully quiet,'' Quentin said as they crossed the parking lot.

''What can I say? It's difficult to comment on what I know nothing about.'' Terry glanced at him, then away. "And since you're not commenting, our little errand just now had something to do with the Kent, Parker and Jackson homicides."

"Maybe."

"Do you have a suspect?"

"No comment."

"I heard some talk, that your writer friend got a look at the guy. At his eyes. I heard they were some weird color."

Malone unlocked his Bronco, then glanced at his friend. "Interesting the things you can hear while hanging around the squad room. Got any opinions on that bit of information?"

They climbed into the SUV, buckled in and Malone started the engine. Terry looked at him. "Seems to me you might be on the right track. If the victim wasn't confused."

"She wasn't." Malone backed out of the parking space. "Why do you think our perp changed his eye color like that? What's his motivation."

"To be scarier. To intimidate." Terry shrugged. "Who knows."

"Or maybe he does it for himself, to make him feel more powerful. Not of this world."

"I can't imagine, buddy."

They drove back to the Seventh in silence, parting when they reached the station: Terry on another call, Malone to make some calls.

In the middle of his third, a memory hit Malone with the force of a freight train. For a New Year's Eve millennium party the year before, Terry had come dressed as Father Time. Only instead of the long white beard and flowing white robe, he'd spiked his spray-painted hair and dressed in biker gear. The effect had been like something out of that old futuristic movie, *Mad Max.*

Except for his eyes. They had been bright red.

Colored contacts.

Dammit, Terry, why didn't you say something?

Malone ended his conversation and hung up the phone. It meant nothing, he told himself. The manager of the Eyeware Showcase had said the colored contacts had become a popular novelty item.

So why hadn't Terry said something? He couldn't have just forgotten.

"Hey, partner."

Startled, Malone swung in his chair to fully face the door. "Terry! You're back."

"Cut-and-dried burglary. In and out in fifteen minutes. No clues, no suspects, no chance of catching the little weasels."

Malone forced himself to smile and lean casually back in his chair. "Bet the citizens didn't like hearing that."

He lifted a shoulder. "Jackass yuppies, what do they expect? You choose to live a couple of blocks from the projects, fancy renovations or not, you're gonna get hit. Period." He stretched and yawned. "What gives with you? When I walked in, you looked like you'd seen a ghost. You get another lead or something?"

"Nah. Just tired. It's been one mother of a day."

"Tell me about it."

Malone glanced at his watch, scrambling for a way

to ask the other man where he'd been two nights ago without tipping him as to why he was asking.

He cleared his throat, hating himself for his suspicions. And for what he was about to do. "What're you doing tonight? Going to Shannon's?"

Terry frowned. "I'd love to but I'm beat. I think I'm going to crash."

"No way." Malone smiled. "Not the Terror."

"I'm turning over a new leaf, man." He held up two fingers. "Scout's honor."

"I'll believe it when I see it." He grinned. "So, why are you so beat? Big night the last couple of nights?"

Terry stared at him a moment, a crease forming between his eyebrows. "Meaning what?"

"Just wondering if I missed a good party." Malone arched his eyebrows. "Why so defensive?"

"Last night I was with the kids." He made a face. "We went to Chuckie Cheese. The night before I hooked up with diMarco and Tarantino from the Fifth. We tipped a few." He dragged a hand through his hair, expression sheepish. "Man, can those two drink. I couldn't keep up."

"The Terror couldn't keep up?" Malone laughed, relieved. "There is hope for you."

As he walked away, he motioned for Malone to kiss his ass.

"Get some sleep," Quentin called after the other man. "You look like crap."

Terry flipped him off, then disappeared around the corner. Quentin forced himself to wait to the count of one hundred, then grabbed his jacket and punched out.

If he left now, made most of the lights and ran the ones he didn't, he should be able to catch diMarco and Tarantino before they checked out for the day.

Quentin caught the two detectives as they were on their way out of the station house door.

"Hey, Malone, what brings you out to God's country?"

"Figured I'd better check on my baby bro. Make sure he's staying out of trouble. Give him a little advice."

The two detectives hooted with amusement. "Good luck. That kid's a bigger hot dog than you are."

"I'll tell him you said so." He started off then stopped and glanced back. "Terry said the three of you tipped a few the other night."

"Put him under the table." Tarantino laughed. "Good Cajun boy like him, I couldn't believe it. What a lightweight."

"We had to carry him out," diMarco added.

"What bar was that?" Quentin asked with what he hoped was casual interest. He hoped the other two wouldn't hear the hint of desperation behind the question.

"Fast Freddy's on Bourbon."

Bourbon. In the French Quarter. "That's that new place. I haven't been there yet."

"The joint was packed. Great music, lots of chicks."

"Come out with us next time," Tarantino suggested. "We'll drink you under the table."

Quentin forced a laugh. "Fat chance of that."

"Nice talking to you, Malone." The two started

off, then diMarco stopped suddenly and looked back at Quentin. "Ask your partner how a guy with his reputation managed to get so stinking drunk when we never even saw him take a drink?"

46

Thursday, February 1
5:45 p.m.

Anna spent the next twenty-four hours doing what Malone thought she should: lying low, hiding out, allowing others to solve her problems for her. She paced the floor waiting for the phone to ring, jumped at every unexpected noise and agonized over Jaye and Minnie.

At the end of those hours, she came to a decision. She was done being a victim. With being a frightened little mouse to Kurt's cat. She had been doing that for twenty-three years. She was done with sitting back and waiting for Malone and his team to find and save Jaye. To save *her*.

The time had come to stop hiding. To take charge and *do* something. She was going to take Malone's suggestion and get a list of Ben's patients from him.

Only she wasn't going to ask. She wasn't going to try to wheedle or cajole the names out of him. Because he wouldn't give them to her voluntarily. She was certain of that.

Anna crossed to her apartment door and peeked out at laSalle. "Hey, Joe, you need anything?"

He smiled. "Nope. But thanks for asking."

"Who's replacing you tonight?"

"Morgan. At six."

"I'm going to wash my hair. So if I don't see you until tomorrow, have a great night off."

She ducked back into her apartment, locking the dead bolt behind her. She collected her portable phone and carried it to the bathroom, closed and locked the door behind her. She didn't know why she felt the need for subterfuge, for absolute privacy, but she did. She didn't want to chance anyone listening in on what she was about to say.

Guilty conscience. That's why. What she was about to do was pretty crummy. Especially since Ben had been nothing but good to her.

But she had to do this. And no one would be hurt, she reminded herself. Not even Ben. And someone— or several someones—might be helped. Most importantly Jaye and Minnie.

Taking a deep breath, Anna quickly dialed Ben's number. He answered almost immediately. "Ben," she murmured, feeling a pinch of guilt. "It's Anna."

"Anna, it's so good to hear from you."

At the pleasure in his voice, the pinch became a stab. She ignored it. "How are you feeling?"

"Sore. Plenty of aches and pains. But mostly I'm pissed for having been so stupid." He paused. "How are you feeling?"

"Okay. Not great."

"What can I do?"

"I'm glad you asked, because that's why I'm calling. For help."

"You've got it. Just ask."

"That fear group you told me about, is there still room in it for me?"

For several moments, he said nothing. Then he cleared his throat. "You've taken me by surprise."

"I have to do something, Ben. I can't go on this way, hiding in my apartment, jumping at every sound. I think the group might help."

"You have a genuine reason to be afraid now, Anna. In the group we deal with irrational fears. Things like—"

"My fear that after twenty-three years Kurt was going to come find and punish me for botching his kidnapping plan? Things like giving up the things I love, like my writing, to avoid being exposed to the public?"

"Yeah, things like that. But considering recent events in your life—"

"Please, Ben." She lowered her voice. "I'm tired of living this way. I need help."

He let out a long breath. "All right, Anna. We meet tonight. At seven. But I'll have to talk to the group before I let you participate. They have to give their okay."

"I'll wait in your office," she offered, feeling ill at her own duplicity. "For however long it takes."

"They're a good group of people," he went on. "I'd be surprised if they turn you away."

"Thank you, Ben." Anna heard the gratitude in her voice and acknowledged that it was authentic. She appreciated his friendship. She was glad he had come into her life.

She told him so.

"Grateful enough to go out for a drink with me after session?"

"I'd love to." She smiled. "It's a date, Ben."

Anna arrived at Ben's office fifteen minutes before seven. She was nervous. Her palms were sweating and she couldn't bring herself to meet the curious gazes of the other people in the waiting room. She felt like a fraud. An impostor. She feared that if she looked any of them in the eyes, they would be able to see right through her.

Same with Ben. He emerged from his office a couple of minutes before seven. He smiled and greeted his patients, then crossed to her. He caught her hands and smiled. "How are you?"

She forced herself to look him in the eyes. "Nervous." *At least that wasn't a lie.*

"It's going to be fine. Everyone in the group is nonthreatening and quite welcoming to newcomers." He motioned to the room to the right of his office. "That's where the group meets. You can wait here or in my office, wherever you think you'll feel most comfortable."

"Your office. If it's…okay?"

"Of course." He smiled warmly and turned to the ten men and women milling about or talking in small clusters. "The door's open. Go ahead and get comfortable, I'll be right in."

Ben escorted her to his office. Anna spotted the row of low, wooden files right away. The were located against the wall behind his desk.

"I'll be about fifteen minutes, maybe a few more," he said. "Don't worry about anything. It's all going to work out."

She promised she wouldn't, then watched as he exited the office, closing the door behind him. The second she heard it latch, she started for the files.

"Anna?"

She whirled to face him, cheeks hot. "Ben! That was quick."

He frowned. "What's wrong?"

She brought a hand to her chest. "You startled me, that's all. I've been so jumpy the last few days."

He shifted his gaze from her to his desk, then back to her, a small frown marring his forehead. *CIA, she was not.* She laughed lightly, nervously. "Have they made a decision already?"

His frown disappeared. "No, I just wanted to tell you, I'm really glad you're here. I think you're doing the right thing."

He wouldn't if he knew what she was really up to.

"Thanks, Ben. I appreciate you saying that."

This time, she waited a full two minutes after the door clicked shut behind him before moving toward the files. She felt awful about what she was about to do. But she had to do it. For Jaye.

She squatted down in front of them, grabbed the handle of the drawer on the far right and tugged.

It was locked!

Anna tried the other three drawers and found them locked as well. What did she do now?

The desk. Of course. She stood and crossed to it. Heart thundering, she opened the middle drawer first, rummaged through it, then moved on to the side drawers.

She found a daily journal, address book, pens, clips and a bunch of receipts. No keys.

Frustrated, she slid the last door shut, aware of time passing. She could try picking the locks, but the closest she had ever come to doing that was seeing James Bond do it in a movie.

Her gaze fell on the desktop. There, smack-dab in the middle sat a ring of keys.

She snatched them up, turned and hurried back to the files. With trembling fingers she tried the first key, then the second and third. The fourth did the trick—the latch turned, the drawer slid open.

Holding her breath, she flipped through the As, then Bs and Cs. She scanned each name, waiting for the one that jumped out at her. When those letters yielded nothing, she moved on, fingers flying over the neatly marked tabs. *Q. R. S.* Still nothing. No Kurt, no Adam or Peter. Nothing that struck a note of recognition in her.

Anna slid that drawer shut, glanced quickly over her shoulder, then turned her attention to the last seven letters of the alphabet. She scanned the names. *T. U.* From behind her came a sound, a footfall, the soft rasp of a knob being turned. It was too soon! She had yet to see the last few names. The door creaked. *V. W.*—

"Good news, Anna, the group agreed—"

She slid the drawer shut and jumped to her feet.

"What are you doing?"

She pasted on a smile, even as she fought to breathe normally. "What do you mean?"

A muscle in his face spasmed and angry color spotted his cheeks. "Were you in my files?"

"Don't be silly, Ben. I was simply...I...your diplomas..."

Her voice trailed off as he strode around the desk. She watched him, heart sinking. The key ring lay where she had left it—on the floor by the file drawers. Her heart sank. "I can explain."

He bent and snatched them up. A shudder rippled over him and he swung to face her. His anger transformed him from a kind and charming bumbler into a much more intimidating figure. She took a step back from him. "Please, Ben. Just let me explai—"

"Don't bother. I know what you were doing. A little detective work. You wanted to get a look at my patients' names." He took a step toward her. She saw that he was trembling with fury. "Isn't that right?"

She laced her fingers together. "I'm sorry, Ben. I was desperate."

"So, you used me. You used our friendship."

"Try to understand. I was—"

"Why should I listen to anything you have to say? You're a liar, Anna."

A liar. She recoiled from the word, the way he spat it at her. "I just thought, if I could see the names of your patients, I'd know. I'd recognize somebody. Or Kurt's name would be there and—"

"Didn't you think, even for a moment, that I would have told you or Detective Malone if I had a patient named Kurt?"

47

Thursday, February 1
7:20 p.m.

Quentin couldn't stop thinking about Ben Walker. Something about the man set his teeth on edge.

What was it?

In search of the answer, Quentin had pondered his reaction to the other man. He had replayed their two conversations in his head, looking for anything that didn't add up. Anything that would suggest the man was something other than what he seemed.

He had come up with squat. But still, something about the psychologist nagged at him. Something he had said or done.

Ben Walker was a key piece of this puzzle. Quentin just didn't know where that piece fit in relation to the whole.

Not yet. But he would.

The traffic light up ahead turned red. Quentin pulled his Bronco to a stop, flipped open his cell phone and punched in Anna's number. After five rings her machine picked up. Again. This was the third time he'd called her in the last hour.

Frowning, he dialed Morgan. "Morgan, Quentin Malone. Are you with Anna North?"

"Sure am. Sitting outside a doctor's office uptown."

"Dr. Ben Walker's office? On Constance Street?"

"That's the one. She's been in there thirty minutes. Said she would be a couple of hours, then was going out after. You want me to stick with her?"

Quentin told him he did, then hung up, frustrated. Irritated that he was jealous.

The light changed and he eased through the intersection, a thought jumping into his head. That day at the hospital, Walker had said he'd left his mother's nursing home late the night before. She had been upset, he'd said.

She had claimed a man had been in her room and had threatened her.

Quentin glanced over his left shoulder, then swung into the left lane and executed a U-turn at the crossover. Ben had said his mother was a resident at the Crestwood Nursing Home on Metairie Road. He was only a few minutes from there now.

Maybe he would just pay a little visit to Ben Walker's mother.

The nursing home was quiet. The dinner hour had come and gone, though visiting hours hadn't ended. The lobby television droned, tuned to a game show, the volume set at an ear-numbing level. A number of the home's residents sat circling the set, many of them in wheelchairs. One of them, a small silver-haired woman in a cherry-red robe, looked his way and winked as he passed. He winked back.

He crossed to the nurses' station, smiled and showed the woman his shield. "Detective Quentin Malone. I'm here to see one of your residents, a Mrs. Walker."

The nurse looked startled. "Louise Walker?"

"Dr. Benjamin Walker's mother."

"That's Louise. May I ask what this visit is in reference to?"

He could have refused or given her the standard "Police business," but didn't see the point. "Her son told me that she had been threatened. I'm checking it out for him."

"Oh, that." The nurse shook her head. "Louise gets confused. She watches these nighttime soaps and made-for-TV movies and confuses them with real life. Gets herself all riled up. But by all means, talk with her. It may reassure her to think the police are looking into the matter."

"So you don't think there's any truth to her claim?"

"Nope." She slid a registry across the counter. "I need you to sign in, please. Every visitor is required to do so."

"Anyone ever slip by?"

"I'm sure some do. But we're very careful."

"I'm sure you are." Quentin signed his name, who he was visiting and the purpose of his visit. While he had the registry, he scanned the names above his and on the previous couple of pages, looking for any he might recognize. The only one he did was Ben

Walker's. "Ben comes to see his mother often," he commented, sliding the book back.

"He's a devoted son," the nurse murmured, coming around the counter. "I wish more of the residents' children were as attentive. I'll show you to her room. Lucky for you, she's still up. She's a night owl, that one."

"I understand she has Alzheimer's?"

"That's right. This way."

"How lucid is she?" Quentin asked as they made their way down a long corridor, past mostly open doors. Most of the residents were awake, watching TV or reading. One sat in his wheelchair, toes tapping and fingers snapping to the music pouring out of his headphones.

The nurse stopped in front of one of the open doors, number twenty-six. She knocked on the door, then walked inside. Sure enough, Louise Walker, a wizened gray-haired woman, was watching television, transfixed by what appeared to be a schmaltzy courtroom drama.

"Louise," she said softly, "there's someone here to see you."

The woman dragged her pale gaze from the TV to stare at Quentin. "I don't know him," she said, frowning. "Why is he here?"

"He's a friend of Ben's. He's a detective with the police department. You two go ahead and talk, I'll be at my station if you need anything."

"You're a friend of my Ben's?"

"That's right. I'm Detective Quentin Malone with the NOPD."

He held up his shield and Louise Walker motioned him closer. As he moved farther into the room, he smelled cigarettes. In the way of those who had spent a lifetime smoking, the smell clung to her and everything in her room, though he knew from the sign posted at the home's entrance that this was a non-smoking facility. Her being a smoker surprised him because her son struck him as being so fastidious. The kind of person who abhorred smokers.

"I know he did it," she said as he neared her. "He's guilty as sin."

"Excuse me?"

"That awful Jack Crowley. Have you come to ask me about him?"

Quentin glanced at the television. A woman was pleading with "Jack," begging him "not to do it." He looked back at the old woman. "No, not about him," he said gently. "About the man who came to your room and threatened you."

Her expression changed. Suddenly she looked frightened. "Ben told you about him?"

"Yes. He said you were quite upset."

"No one believes me. Not even Ben." She lowered her voice. "They think I'm crazy."

"Can you tell me about this man?"

"I'm not crazy," she said, ignoring his question. Then she smiled. "I like it here, they're good to me."

"How many times has this man visited you?"

Her gaze seemed to refocus on him. "I don't know. Lots of times." Her chin quivered. "I don't like him. He's a bad man. Worse than Jack Crowley."

"Worse?" He pulled a chair over to the bed and

sat down, willing to play this out although it seemed pretty clear that Louise Walker's elevator no longer went all the way to the top floor. She seemed a sweet old lady, however, and maybe talking with her would ease her mind. "How could he be worse than Jack?"

"He's evil." Using the remote, she snapped off the television. The sudden quiet was disconcerting. "He…he frightens me."

"I'd like to help you," Quentin murmured. "But you must tell me everything you can about him."

"He means to hurt my Ben." She met Quentin's eyes, hers glassy. "He hates him."

Quentin frowned. "He threatened Ben? Not you?"

"He wants him dead."

"Why?"

She blinked, looking suddenly scattered. Confused. Quentin restated the question. "Why does he want Ben dead?"

"Because Ben's so much better than he is. Ben's a good boy. A good son. Adam is—"

Quentin's blood ran cold. "Did you say his name was—"

"Adam. The devil himself."

48

Quentin was unable to get much else out of Louise Walker. The more he questioned her, the more agitated and confused she became. The nurse suggested he come back in the morning. Louise would be more alert then, the woman maintained. Clearer.

Quentin agreed. Before leaving, he checked the registration book. He went all the way back to the previous fall without finding the name Adam.

Could the names be a coincidence, Louise Walker's claim of being threatened a delusion born of her illness? The nurse had admitted that visitors sometimes slipped by without signing in. Quentin imagined it wouldn't be that difficult for someone to do.

Could be a coincidence, Quentin admitted. If he believed in them. He didn't.

The minute Quentin slid into his Bronco, he dialed his captain at home. "Aunt Patti, it's Quentin."

"Nephew," she said warmly. "Tell me this is a personal call and not police business."

"Sorry, Aunt Patti. But when you hear what I have

to say, I think you'll be glad it is. We have what might be our first break in the French Quarter killings.''

"Go ahead," she said crisply, all business.

Quentin filled her in, reminding her of the letters Anna had received from Minnie, of Jaye's disappearance, who Ben Walker was and how he fit into the case and of the recent attack on Anna. "On a hunch, I paid a visit to Dr. Walker's mother, Louise Walker. Ben Walker had said something about her having been threatened, so I decided to check it out. Guess the name of the man who threatened her? Adam."

His aunt was silent a moment, as if mentally wrangling with all the pieces of the puzzle. "Those letters to Anna North, wasn't that the name of the box owner—"

"Bingo."

"Can she describe this man for a police artist?"

He heard her excitement. It sounded a lot like his. "I hope so. She's elderly and an Alzheimer's patient, but she seems positive about this Adam. I want to get the artist in there first thing in the morning."

"Do it. And get someone assigned to Louise Walker. I don't want to chance this guy showing up and us not being there."

Quentin wished her and his Uncle Sammy goodnight, then dialed the Seventh. "Brad," he greeted the officer on the desk. "Malone here. I just spoke with Captain O'Shay, we need a uniform assigned to a resident at the Crestwood Nursing Home. Name's Louise Walker."

"Can do," the man replied. "What's up?"

"She may be able to identify the French Quarter killer."

The desk officer whistled. "I'll get somebody over there, ASAP."

"Good. And line up a police artist for first thing in the a.m."

"To the same place?"

"You got it." Quentin glanced at his watch, thinking of Anna. And Ben, together. "Any calls tonight?"

"A woman called looking for you." The man paused. "She wouldn't leave her name, but I think it was Penny Landry."

"Penny? For me?"

"Yeah, for you. About half an hour ago." The desk officer paused again, then lowered his voice. "She sounded upset, Malone. She sounded really upset."

49

Quentin glanced at his watch, heart pounding. Fortunately, from his location on Metairie Road and Bonnabell Boulevard, Lakeview was a mere eight-minute drive. With siren and lights he could cut that time in half.

Quentin tore down the tree-lined streets, cherry lights flashing, the flashes of blue bouncing weirdly through the naked branches. He had tried calling Penny a half-dozen times on the way; each time he had gotten a busy signal.

Something was wrong. And it had to do with Terry. Penny wouldn't have called him otherwise.

He skidded to a stop in front of Landry's home, slammed out of his vehicle and ran up the walk. Although just after 9:00 p.m., the house was completely dark.

He rang the bell. Its chime echoed through the house. He waited but no sound of footsteps followed the bell.

She was home. Hiding from Terry.

He didn't know why he was so certain of that, but he was.

Quentin bypassed the bell and pounded on the door. "Penny! It's Malone!" He pounded again. "I'm here to help. Open up!"

From the other side of the door came a cry of relief, then the dead bolt sliding back. A moment later, the door opened and Penny fell sobbing into his arms.

He held her close while she cried. After a time her tears abated. But her trembling did not. Quentin stroked her hair, his heart in his throat. Finally, softly, he murmured, "It was Terry, wasn't it?"

She pressed her face to his chest and nodded.

"Are the kids all right?"

She nodded again. "They're…after, I sent them… next door. I didn't want them here…in case he… came back."

Dear Jesus. "What happened, Penny? Tell me so I can help."

She shuddered, working, he saw, to pull herself together. "He showed up here. He was drunk. Talking crazy. I could see that he…he was scaring the kids. So I…I asked him to leave. He went berserk."

Her lips began to tremble and she pressed them together for a moment, then began again. "He started screaming at me, saying these…awful things.

"I ran to our bedroom. He followed. He slammed the door behind us and locked it." She brought her hands to her face. "Thank God he did. I couldn't have stood it if Matti or Alex had seen…" Her tears welled once more; this time she fought them off. "We fought. He knocked me down, onto the bed—"

She choked on the words and Quentin held his breath, knowing what was coming but praying he was wrong. "What happened, Penny? Did he force himself on you?"

"He tried," she whispered. "He pushed my dress up and tore my panties off. The kids must have heard me crying and pleading with him. They started pounding on the door. Calling for me. Begging their daddy to…to st—stop."

Her words shuddered to a halt and Quentin tightened his arms around her, sickened by his partner's behavior. "What happened, Penny? Did he rape you?"

"No." She pressed her face to his chest. "The kids…that reached him. He started to…cry. And then he left."

For long moments, Quentin simply held her. Finally, she drew away from him. Her mascara had run, giving her owl eyes and creating dark blotches on his white shirt. She saw them and made a sound of dismay. "Look what I've done to your shirt. I'm so sorry. I—"

"It's nothing."

Tears welled in her eyes once more. "I wish I'd…I just wish… This sucks so bad." She met Quentin's gaze. "I loved him, I really did. But I don't know who he is anymore. He's not the man I married."

She drew in a shaking breath. "I'm afraid of him, Malone. I'm afraid for him. He could hurt someone. He was out of his head."

Quentin searched her expression, dismayed. "What do you think I should do, Penny? How can I help?"

"Find him. Talk to him. Maybe he'll listen to you." She started to cry again, this time silently, sadly. "He needs help. Please help him, Malone."

Quentin didn't have far to look. He found Terry at Shannon's, slumped at the bar, an untouched drink in front of him. Quentin crossed to the bar and sat beside him, signaling to Shannon that he didn't want anything.

Terry angled a glance his way, but didn't speak. Not at first. When he did, he sounded beaten. "Penny called you."

It wasn't a question; Quentin answered anyway. "Yes. She was hysterical."

Terry hung his head.

At least he didn't try to make an excuse for his behavior, Quentin thought. At least he wasn't so far gone that he didn't see that there was no excuse for what he'd done.

"What's going on with you, Terry?" he asked. "What's happening to you?"

"I don't know." His friend looked at him, eyes redrimmed, the expression in them tortured. "My life's turned to a nightmare. I can't sleep, I have no appetite. I'm angry all the time. At Penny. The job. Myself. Everything."

He looked away, then back. When he spoke, his voice was a hushed whisper. "Sometimes, this rage builds up inside me and I...I feel like it's eating me alive. Like soon there'll be nothing left of me but hatred and despair." He brought his hands to his face. "It's more alive than I am."

For a heartbeat of time Quentin couldn't speak. When he found his voice, he looked at the other man. "You've got to let go of the past, man. You've got to see that it was all bullshit, that the number your mother did on you was all bullshit. Get help, Terry. Get help before it's too late."

50

Friday, February 2
Noon

The doctor carefully probed Ben's side, his touch gentle but practiced. "This hurt?" he asked, applying the subtlest of pressure to his bandaged ribs.

Ben winced. "It's sore. But not unbearable."

"Good."

The doctor met his eyes. "And problems since the accident? Dizziness? Vertigo?"

"No, nothing like that. Just aches and pains. Trouble resting."

"That's to be expected. You were involved in a pretty nasty accident. Your injuries could have been much worse."

"I'm grateful somebody saw the accident and called 911. I drove by where it happened. I could have been trapped behind that hedge for a long time."

The doctor agreed. "And at that time of night, too. You were damn lucky."

Ben stood and pulled on his shirt. "It wasn't that late. What, a little after eleven?"

The physician looked at him. "You're kidding, right?"

Ben's fingers stilled on the buttons, a cold sensation slipping down his spine. "No. I left my mother's nursing home around eleven."

"Ben, you were wheeled in here at 3:00 a.m."

He stared at the other man, disbelieving. "You're mistaken."

"I'm not." The doctor frowned. "It's here, on your chart—3:13 a.m."

What had happened in the hours between eleven when he left Crestwood and three when he was admitted to the emergency room?

"Ben? Are you all right?"

He blinked and focused on the physician. "Fine." He forced an easy laugh. "I was just realizing that it was I who was mistaken. I fell asleep reading to my mother around eleven. I'm still confused about what happened that night."

"Considering, it's no wonder." The doctor smiled at him. "Call if you have any problems. You'll need to have those ribs checked again in two weeks. Your regular doctor can do it."

Ben thanked the man, then left the hospital. He found and climbed into his car, but made no move to start it. Instead, he brought the heels of his hands to his eyes, reviewing the events of the night of the accident, mentally retracing his steps. He had arrived at the nursing home around seven. He and his mother had eaten dinner together, he had wheeled her outside for a cigarette. Three cigarettes later they had returned to her room. They had watched a little TV, then she had gotten ready for bed. After he had tucked her in, he had picked up her copy of the latest Danielle Steel novel and begun reading to her.

He had fallen asleep while reading. When he had awakened, she had been frightened. A man had come into the room while he slept, she'd said. He had threatened her.

Ben dropped his hands and stared blindly out the side window, still recalling the events of that night. He had spoken with the nurses, checked the guest registry and helped them calm his mother. He had been upset about her increasing confusion. His head had begun to hurt. He'd gone to his car. There he had found the note. It had been just before finding the note that he had glanced at his watch. He frowned. At least he thought it had been.

Perhaps he had been mistaken about the time? Or perhaps he had looked at his watch when he had awakened from his nap, not when he left the nursing home?

But why was the last thing he remembered skidding out of the parking lot while trying to call Anna? What had happened between then and when another motorist had seen him run off the road, crash through an embankment of hedges and into a tree?

Ben began to shake, suddenly afraid. Of his episodes of lost time. Of the way he slept like the dead. Of his headaches. What was going on with him? Was he losing his mind? Had the doctors missed something? Something life-threatening?

Ben rested his forehead against the wheel, heart thundering. He was letting his imagination run away with him. It was just as his doctor had said—he suffered with headaches of such severity that he blacked out. They were caused by stress. Tension.

He'd certainly had enough of that lately. Stress caused in no small part by the fact that a madman was playing a deadly and dangerous game with him and Anna.

Anna. He thought back to Thursday night, to the moment he had discovered her rifling through his files. He had been so angry. So hurt. She had lied to him, had betrayed his trust in her, their friendship.

Now, in retrospect, he felt bad about feeling that way. About the things he had said to her. She was being terrorized. She had been attacked, someone she held dear was missing. She wanted answers. His patient list might hold them.

Hand it over.

He made a sound of denial. What was he thinking? He couldn't just turn over his patient list. Doing so was unethical. Police questioning could cause several of his patients severe emotional distress. Patients who trusted him with their fears and phobias, their innermost thoughts and feelings.

But women had died. More might yet die. Anna included. It seemed obvious that someone in his care was either responsible or otherwise involved. He had reached a dead end in his personal search for the guilty party. He had seen and tested all but a couple of his patients, and all had passed the test with flying colors. He was either missing something important or his plan of using psychology to trap Anna's stalker wasn't as clever as he had thought. Perhaps he could extract a promise from Malone, a promise not to approach anyone without good cause.

And maybe then, when this was all over, he and Anna could begin again.

Excitement rippled through him. A sense of purpose. His action might get this thing solved. Anna would be grateful and Malone would be of no further use to her. And a major portion of the stress in his life would be eliminated.

Ben started his car and shifted into gear. He would do it now, before he gave himself a chance to change his mind. Stop at the office, put together the list, then head over to the Seventh. He smiled to himself, imagining the look of surprise on Malone's face when he handed him the names.

Thirty-five minutes later, Ben entered the Seventh and crossed to the reception desk. He identified himself and asked for Malone.

"He's out," the desk officer said. "But his partner's here. Will he do?"

Ben hesitated a moment, then decided to go for it. He would miss Malone's expression when he handed over the list, but he sensed waiting would be a mistake. "He'll do."

"Name's Terry Landry." The man directed him to the squad room and to the right. "Landry's desk is fourth on the left. He's a tall guy with dark hair. He's wearing a Hawaiian shirt."

Ben thanked him and went in the direction the man had indicated. No one paid any attention to him as he made his way through the busy squad room. He caught sight of Landry, recognizing him by the bright blue, yellow and pink shirt. His back was turned; he appeared to be embroiled in an animated discussion with a fellow officer.

Ben started toward him. The detective turned.

Ben stopped cold. *Not Terry Landry. Rick Richardson. A mid-level pencil pusher for the Department of Recreation and Tourism.*

Rick was a patient of his. No, Ben corrected, not any longer. He had discontinued his sessions a couple of weeks back.

Ben did the math and his mouth went desert dry. He had last seen Rick around the time his keys had gone missing and the package containing Anna's book had appeared in his office.

Around the time the first redhead had been murdered.

His pulse racing, Ben reviewed the facts in his head: Richardson's dissatisfaction with his job—anger at the system, the pay, what he perceived as disrespect from those he worked to serve. His fury at his wife—for leaving him, for not understanding. His repressed rage toward his mother who had recently passed—for a lifetime of emotional abuse.

It all fit.

Ben turned on his heel and strode from the squad room, heart in his throat. He didn't think Rick—Terry, he corrected himself—had seen him. He prayed not. Because if what he feared was true, Terry Landry was not only deeply disturbed, he was a killer. He would not be pleased that Ben had uncovered his true identity.

Ben made it to his car, though his legs shook so badly he wondered how. Only after he was safely inside, the doors locked, did he dare glance back at the station house.

Terry Landry stood on the steps of the Seventh, hands on hips, head swiveling from left to right as if searching for someone.

"Son-of-a-bitch." Ben jammed the key into the ignition, twisted it and the engine roared to life. He hit the gas, tires spitting gravel as he pulled away from the curb, anxious to put as much distance between him and his former patient as quickly as possible.

Only after he had gone a half-dozen blocks with no sign of the detective following him did he breathe a sigh of relief. He glanced in his rearview mirror one last time, then flipped open his cell phone and dialed the Seventh. The desk officer answered, the same one he had spoken to only minutes ago.

"This Dr. Benjamin Walker," he said. "I need to reach Detective Quentin Malone. Tell him it's about the attack on Anna North. Tell him I have a name."

51

Friday, February 2
2:00 p.m.

Quentin parked in front of the Seventh District station. He cut the Bronco's engine but made no move to climb out. Instead, he sat, staring straight ahead, working to come to grips with the conversation he had just had with Ben Walker. With the contents of that brief conversation.

Under an assumed name, Terry had been a patient of Ben Walker's. He had dropped out of therapy about the time Anna had begun to be terrorized and Nancy Kent had died.

Quentin curved his fingers around the steering wheel, the weight of the evidence against his partner pressing in on him. Terry's public fight with Nancy Kent. The colored contacts. His friend's self-proclaimed rage. His attack on Penny. The unaccounted-for time at Shannon's.

The list went on.

Quentin muttered an oath. It was all circumstantial, every last bit of it. He could go to Terry. He owed him that much. Their years of friendship demanded it.

His friend would explain. He would have a logical explanation for everything.

Terry was not a murderer.

Quentin swore again. He couldn't do that. The badge demanded he go to his captain with what he had learned. His duty to Nancy Kent and the other two victims. His duty to Anna.

If Terry was innocent, he would be able to prove it. If he was innocent, they wouldn't find any physical evidence to support the circumstantial.

Quentin swung out of his vehicle and started for the station. He strode inside, ignoring the greetings of several of his fellow officers, his gaze fixed straight ahead. He reached his captain's office: she was inside, at her desk. She looked up when he knocked.

"We need to talk," he said.

She frowned and waved him inside. "Shut the door behind you, if you'd like."

He did, then crossed and sat heavily in the chair opposite her desk. "It's about the French Quarter homicides."

She folded her hands in front of her. "Go on."

He met her gaze, then looked away, muttering an oath.

"I find it helps if you just spit it out. The worse you have to say, the faster you should get it over with."

So he did. When he had finished, she didn't look surprised. Quentin narrowed his eyes. "What do you have on Terry? PID's been too interested in him not to have something more condemning than a drunken argument. I deserve to know."

"Let's talk about what you have first. This Dr. Walker is certain Landry is the same man who called himself Rick Richardson?"

"Absolutely."

"And you still believe that Anna North is the link between the victims and the killer? Because of the red hair?"

"And the last victim's severed pinkie. Yes."

His aunt arched an eyebrow. "Why the previous two victims? Why not go right for his primary target?"

Quentin felt ill. At the possibility that his friend may be responsible for three deaths. That he may have aided Terry in his crimes by supplying him with a false alibi. "He's been practicing. Working up to the main event. Taking his rage out on stand-ins. It wouldn't be the first time a killer's done that."

His aunt nodded, and he continued. "The night he attacked Anna, he might not have even meant to kill her. She said he was startled, but she didn't know by what. Maybe by nothing. Maybe that attack was foreplay. Maybe he's still getting off terrorizing her."

Quentin let out a deep breath. "In retracing the events of that night at Shannon's, I realized that I only thought I knew Terry's whereabouts the entire night. There was an hour or better after his fight with Nancy Kent that I lost sight of him. The bar was crowded, and I knew he had been drinking heavily. I just assumed he was there."

"Go on."

"The night of the Jackson murder, he was with

diMarco and Tarantino from the Fifth. In the French Quarter.''

''Another alibi,'' his aunt murmured.

''One with holes in it.'' Quentin rubbed his palms on his thighs. ''DiMarco mentioned that although Terry became stinking drunk, he never actually saw him take a drink.''

''Anything else?''

''The colored contacts. Terry wore them to a New Year's Eve party last year, yet played dumb when I was tracking down information about them.''

''You've been compiling quite a little list of evidence incriminating your partner. Any reason you haven't shared it with me before now?''

''Circumstantial evidence, Captain. And some of it pretty thin at that. Perhaps if you'd seen fit to include me in whatever it is that PID has on Terry, we could have put the pieces together sooner.''

She didn't argue. ''They didn't think you should know.''

''They questioned my loyalty.''

''It was logical that they would. Considering your relationship with Landry.''

He stiffened. ''Did you? Question my loyalty?''

A smile touched the corners of her mouth. ''I changed your diapers, Malone. I saw you take your first steps and your first communion. I know what you're made of. No, I never questioned your loyalty.''

Some of the tension eased from his neck and shoulders. ''So what is it? What does PID have on him?''

''From the Kent homicide. A blood-type match. We're still waiting for DNA on the semen.''

"Shit."

"It wasn't enough to move on. About thirty-eight percent of the people in the New Orleans metro area have O-positive blood. But paired with the argument Landry had with the deceased the night of her death, it was enough to keep him under an umbrella of suspicion."

"What's next?" he asked, though he already knew.

"Call PID. Get a search warrant for Landry's apartment, car and locker. Get him in here for questioning."

It was the last Quentin dreaded most. "I want to do it, Captain. I want to direct the interrogation."

"Malone, I don't think—"

"It's got to be my case now."

"But it's personal. I can't have you pulling back—"

"I won't, dammit." He balled his hands into fists. Angry. Disillusioned. Terry had been his friend. He had trusted him. "You bet it's personal. I stuck my neck out for him and if he did this thing, I want to nail him for it."

She thought a moment, then nodded. "Johnson needs to be with you. There can't be even a hint of impropriety here."

"You got it." He stood and crossed to the door. "You want me to call PID?"

"I'll do it," she replied, already reaching for the phone. "And Malone?"

He stopped and looked back at her. "Good job. I know this wasn't easy for you to do."

He gazed at her a moment, sick at heart, then nodded curtly. "I'm a cop. What else could I do?"

52

Two hours later, Quentin sat on a metal folding chair, facing Terry. His friend occupied an identical chair. Their knees almost touched. Malone had purposely placed the chairs close together: he wanted to heighten the other man's discomfort and give him nowhere to look but at him.

Considering his friend's strung-out appearance, Quentin figured it wasn't going to be too tough to rattle his cage. He was half there already.

"What's this all about, Malone?" Terry shifted his gaze to Johnson, who stood to the left, leaning against the wall, arms folded over his massive chest, then back to Malone. "Just how official is this official business?"

"It's serious, Terry."

"More PID bullshit, you mean?"

"Why do you say that?"

"Please, why else would I be here?" He looked directly at the video camera, not masking his disdain. "Do we have an audience today?"

"What do you think?"

Terry saluted the camera, then turned his attention back to Quentin. "Maybe I should lawyer up?"

"That's your right."

Terry relaxed back in his chair, working to present the picture of cocksure arrogance. Only the small twitch of his right eye gave him away. "Interrogate away, partner. I've got nothing to hide."

"Ever heard the name Benjamin Walker before?" Malone asked, going for the throat right away, not wanting to play it coy. "Dr. Benjamin Walker?"

"Sure." Terry shrugged. "He's the shrink friend of that novelist, Anna what's-her-name. What's he got to do with me?"

Quentin ignored his question. "You're aware that we believe he's somehow connected to the string of recent murders in and around the French Quarter?"

"Not really. As you know, I've been shut out of the case." Again, he looked at the video camera.

"So, you're saying that other than through this case, you don't know Dr. Walker?"

Quentin held his breath. *Don't be stupid, Terry. Don't try to lie your way out of this.*

"That's correct."

As the lie passed his partner's lips, the realization that Terry was hip deep in this rocked Quentin. One lie meant there were others, things he would jeopardize everything to keep hidden. Quentin masked his disillusionment in his friend. He tried another tack.

"Let's talk about contact lenses for a minute, Terry. Colored contact lenses. Weird colors."

"Like orange and red," Johnson supplied. "The kind somebody might wear to a costume party."

Terry lifted a shoulder. "So what? I wore colored contacts to a party. You heard the woman at that store, lots of people do."

"That's not what's bothering me." Quentin leaned forward; he lowered his voice. "That day, when we went out to the Eyeware Showcase, how come you didn't remind me about those contacts? How come you didn't make the connection?"

He grinned. "Hey, do I have to do everything for you? Besides, I figured you remembered about the contacts."

Quentin leaned back, sweeping his gaze over his friend. "Geez, if you had all the answers I needed, why would I have made that trip to the New Orleans Center?"

Terry stiffened. "I'm off that case. I figured you didn't want me involved."

"That's bullshit, partner."

"Take it or leave it, *partner*."

His snide emphasis on the last struck home, and Quentin narrowed his eyes. "Ever heard the name Rick Richardson before?"

Terry paled. Sweat beaded his upper lip. "Maybe."

"Maybe," Johnson repeated. "What's that mean, Terror?"

"It means maybe. That's a common name. I think I busted somebody by that name once."

Terry was lying. Convincingly, true. But not convincingly enough. "How about the name Adam Furst?" Quentin asked.

Terry drew his eyebrows together, as with thought. "Never."

"Where were you the night of Thursday, January eleventh and the early hours of January twelfth, the night Nancy Kent was murdered?"

"You know where I was. I was at Shannon's. With you."

"Where were you in the early hours of Friday, January nineteenth, the night Evelyn Parker was murdered?"

"Home, nursing a hangover." He made a face at the video camera. "As you boys already know."

"How about four nights ago, the night Jessica Jackson was murdered? The same night Anna North was attacked in her home?"

"Out with diMarco and Tarantino, from the Fifth."

"You visited a bar called Fast Freddie's on Bourbon?"

"Sounds familiar."

"Is that a yes or a no?"

"Yeah, it's a yes." He slouched back in his chair. "What's the big deal?"

"Jessica Jackson spent some time there that same night. The last night of her life."

"The place is hot right now. A party girl like her, I don't doubt she stopped in at Freddie's."

Quentin arched an eyebrow. "Jessica Jackson was a party girl?"

"You know what I meant. She liked to go out, to party."

"Or so you've heard." Quentin glanced at Johnson, then back at Terry, knowing it would unnerve the other man. "You like redheads, Terry?"

"Sure. They're okay."

Quentin arched his eyebrows. "Didn't you say just the other day that 'There was something about a redhead that got your motor running?' That's a quote, partner."

Terry shifted in his chair. "I might have said that."

"No, you did say it. About Anna North."

"I don't recall."

"Ever date a redhead?"

"I've dated a lot of women. I'm sure there were a few in there, I don't recall."

"So, you're saying you have?"

"Probably, yeah."

Quentin took a shot. "Your mother ever dye her hair, Terry? Was she ever a redhead?"

Terry launched to his feet. "You-son-of-a-bitch! I thought you were my friend."

An hour ago, those words from Terry would have made him feel disloyal. Not anymore. Not when Terry had sat across from him and lied—to him, Johnson, the officials watching on a monitor in another room. "You ever been in therapy, Terry? Or should I call you…Rick?"

"I want a lawyer. I'm not saying another word until then." He turned to the video camera. "You got that, you sons-of-bitches? Not another word."

53

Twenty-four hours later, Terry was arrested for the murder of Nancy Kent. He was also chief suspect in the deaths of Evelyn Parker and Jessica Jackson. Besides the overwhelming weight of circumstantial evidence and the blood-type match, investigators had found hair consistent with Nancy Kent's in his car and on his leather jacket. In addition, fibers consistent with the dress she had been wearing the night she died had also been found on his leather jacket. Both had been sent to the crime lab for analysis. The police felt confident that the test results would confirm what they believed to be true.

That Terry Landry was a murderer.

Quentin agreed to break the news to Penny, but refused to take part in the actual arrest. He hadn't wanted to see his former friend and partner cuffed and booked. Intellectually, he couldn't deny Terry's involvement. The facts spoke for themselves. But emotionally, he was having a hard time dealing with the facts. He couldn't believe Terry had done this. He wished to God he could.

Maybe then it wouldn't hurt so bad.

Quentin left the precinct and drove, no destination in mind. He maneuvered in and out of traffic, thoughts on Terry, remembering the man he had known and come to trust, wondering what had become of that man. Wondering when he had become a monster.

Dear God, who was to blame? Women were dead. His friend lost forever.

Quentin pulled his Bronco to the side of the road. He cut the engine and rested his forehead against the steering wheel, regret and self-recriminations tearing him apart. He could have saved those women. He could have saved Terry. If only he had seen what was happening.

Why hadn't he? He should have been able to. He was a detective, for God's sake. Why hadn't he?

Quentin lifted his gaze. And realized where he was. To whom he had run.

Anna.

He muttered an oath and looked away. What would a woman like her want with a man like him? His humorless laugh broke the quiet of the car. Stupid question. She wanted from him what he was best at. She might even call it love. For a while.

Quentin told himself to walk away, to cut his losses and go. He swung out of his vehicle instead and crossed to the apartment. The entrance gate was open and someone had also propped the building's outer door open with a brick. He pulled the door wider, strode through and up the stairs to her door.

She swung it open before he knocked. He saw by her expression that she had heard the news about

Terry. He suspected she had either learned it from laSalle when he had been called off guard detail or from the news.

Considering their relationship, he should have been the one to tell her.

"Anna," he managed to say, voice thick.

She held a hand out, gaze soft with understanding. He took it and she drew him inside, closing and locking the door behind them. She didn't speak. She led him from there to her bed, bringing him down to the mattress with her.

She cupped his face in her palms. "I'm sorry," she whispered. "So sorry."

Then she made love to him. She removed his clothes a piece at a time. She explored with hands and mouth, at times gently searching, at others demanding. She seemed to curl herself around him, accepting his pain as her own, shielding him against it. Telling him without words that she understood his hurt. His feelings of betrayal and disillusionment. His guilt.

He felt himself respond to her in a way that was foreign to him. Opening up. Giving himself to her, letting her lead. It was both freeing and frightening.

She brought him out of himself.

And into her. Until his body demanded he take charge, lead where she could not. Give what was beyond her power to simply take.

They went there together.

Afterward, they lay on their sides, facing each other on the bed, neither speaking. Moments ticked past, Quentin used them to study her. He noticed for the first time the flecks of violet in her green eyes, the sexy slope of her bottom lip, the wisps of hair that grew at her forehead and temple, baby fine and the color of fire.

It felt right to be her with her, he realized. Though they had only known each other a matter of weeks, he trusted her in a way he had never trusted a woman outside his family.

He had know Terry for ten years. He had trusted him completely.

That man had ceased to exist. If he had ever existed at all.

The breath shuddered past his lips and he rolled onto his back. The betrayal, the sense of loss, hurt more than anything he had ever experienced.

Anna laid a hand on his chest, over his heart. He turned and looked at her.

"Talk to me," she said softly. "Don't shut me out."

A knot formed in his throat and he closed his eyes and fought for control. It was as if she could read his mind. The realization didn't reassure and he tucked that truth away to examine later.

"I went to see Penny," he said after a moment, voice thick. "Terry's wife. She...it was pretty awful."

He let out a long breath, remembering. She had wept. For herself. For her children. In disbelief and despair.

"She wondered what she would tell the kids," he said finally. "How she could make this okay for them. There was nothing I could do to make it better for her. Or for them. Even if he's acquitted, they'll have to weather the publicity and the trial. People's cruel questions and gossip. They're just kids, they shouldn't have to go through that.''

''This isn't your fault. You didn't do this to them.''

''But I didn't do anything to help Terry. I knew he was drinking too much, that he was angry all the time. But I never imagined...a murderer? I still don't believe it.''

''Maybe he's not. Maybe it's all a mistake and—''

''They had enough to make the arrest, Anna.'' His voice was harsher than he intended and he softened it. ''An indictment looks certain.''

''Do they have...a lot of evidence?'' He heard doubt in her voice. And hope. The last gave her voice a youthful sound. One that tugged at his heart.

''Yeah, Anna. They've got a bucketful.''

A small breath rushed past her lips. Relief, he realized. That it was nearly over.

''What's next?''

''We wait for results from the crime lab. And we search for evidence that links him to the other two victims.''

''And to me.''

''Yes.'' He turned his face to the ceiling once more. Silence stretched between them.

She broke it first. ''Why me, Quentin?'' Her voice trembled slightly. ''Why does he hate me so much?''

''I don't know. He's not saying, so we're going to have to dig for it.''

''But what if—'' She paused as if uncertain exactly what she wanted to say. If she wanted to say it. ''What if he isn't the one who sent the videotape and notes to my friends? What if he isn't the one behind Minnie's letters and Jaye's disappearance?''

He turned to her once more. ''We believe he is, Anna. Think about it. Terry's the link between you and Ben Walker. Ben was always the wild card in this scenario. He didn't know you, so why did he receive the book and note urging him to tune in to E! that day? Somebody, a third person, was involving him. All along Ben thought it was one of his patients. He was right.''

She made a sound of anguish. ''But why?''

''Only Terry knows why. Soon we will, too. It takes time, Anna.''

She searched his gaze, the expression in hers both hopeful and devastated. ''Where's Jaye, Malone? I have this feeling…time's the one thing we don't have. We have to find her.''

''We're searching.'' Even as the words passed his lips, he knew it wasn't enough. Not for Anna's peace of mind, not for Jaye's safety. ''We'll find her, I promise we will.''

''But how?'' Her voice rose slightly. ''If he won't talk, what will you have to go on? What if she depends on him for food and water? What if days pass—''

''We search his apartment, his car, his past. We'll find her.'' Needing to touch her, he shifted onto his side and trailed his thumb along her cheek. ''I'm glad you're safe, Anna. I'm glad it's over for you.''

''Is it?'' she whispered, eyes bright with tears. ''How can it be over for me when Jaye's still God only knows where, alone and frightened? How can I feel safe?''

He had no response for her. The truth was, he wondered if she would ever feel safe again. In all likelihood, her quiet life had been altered forever.

''What are you going to do now?'' he asked, trailing his thumb along her jaw.

''Try to find another publisher. A new agent.'' A humorless laugh tripped off her lips. ''Try to write again.''

''I'm sorry he did this to you.''

''It's not your fault.''

''He was my friend.''

''It's not your fault,'' she said again. She reached for his hand and laced their fingers. ''Are you going to be all right?''

''I'm always all right.''

''Liar.''

At her soft challenge, he brought their joined hands to his mouth. ''Don't you know me, cher? Quentin Malone, jock, ladies' man and good ol' boy. Life's just one big party.''

''There's more to you than that.''

He saw reproach in her eyes. It made him feel small. And vulnerable. He didn't like the feeling.

He kissed her hand again, then released it and climbed out of bed. He began to dress.

''Too close for comfort?''

''It's not that.''

''No?''

''I need to get back. Crime and punishment calls.''

''I believe in you, Quentin.''

He didn't look at her. He yanked his polo shirt over his head, then went for his gun and shoulder holster. "I hope you're not a betting woman. You'll die broke."

He heard the bedclothes rustle, then the sound of her bare feet padding across the wooden floor. A moment later she was behind him, her arms circling his waist. She'd donned a robe and the fabric was silky and cool against his backside and legs. "I believe in you," she said again. "Talk to me. Tell me what you're thinking."

Sudden anger flared to life inside him. Not at her. At himself. He turned in her arms, facing her, wanting nothing more at that moment than to escape. "The only thing I've ever been known for, Anna, is my ability in the sack. It's nice to know I haven't lost my touch."

She didn't flinch. "Sorry to disappoint you, but the person I think you are has nothing to do with your sexual prowess."

"I have to go."

He moved to turn away, she reached up and cupped his face in her palms, forcing him to look at her. "You have so many good qualities. You're smart and honest. Moral and kind. Caring. Funny. Loyal."

"You make me sound like somebody's golden retriever. I don't want to be anybody's pet, Anna. Not even yours."

Her expression clouded and she took a step back from him. "Why are you angry? What did I say that was so wrong?"

He bent and retrieved his pants. "I shouldn't have come here today."

"But you did." She watched him, head tilted to the side, expression changing from perplexed to understanding. "What haven't you done that you wanted to?"

He finished fastening his trousers, then went to work on his belt. "I've got to go."

"Running away? From what, Malone? Me? Or the truth?"

"That's almost funny from the woman who's spent her whole life running away."

That one hit its mark. She took another step back, expression wounded. "What's going on here? Is this your way of saying, 'Thanks for the memories, babe, see you around sometime'?"

"We had a good time. I made you feel safe and you made me feel like a hero. Nobody got hurt and we both got off in the process. But you're safe now, so why don't we just leave it at that?"

She looked as if he had struck her. "You're right, it is time for you to go. I'll get your coat."

She strode to the living room and snatched his jacket off the arm of the couch. She tossed it at him. "Thanks for the good time."

"I never said this was forever, Anna."

"No, you didn't. So you certainly can't be held accountable, can you?" She crossed to the door and swung it open. "Go. I want you to leave."

Regret tasted bitter against his tongue. "Anna, I didn't mean to hurt you. I didn't want this to—"

"You wanted to push me away because I was getting too close. Well, you succeeded, Detective Malone. Congratulate yourself on a job well done.''

He stepped out into the hall and she followed him, pulling her robe tighter around her. ''And just for your information, I wasn't talking about forever. I just wanted a little honesty. But I guess that's something a big tough guy like you can't handle.''

54

Saturday, February 3
2:00 p.m.
Uptown

Ben unlocked the door to his inner office, stepped inside and crossed to the desk. He dropped the bouquet of flowers he carried into the trash can beside his desk, then settled heavily into his chair.

He had wanted to surprise Anna with flowers. Had wanted to celebrate with her Terry's arrest and the end to their ordeal. He had planned to ask her if they could start over—put the past behind them and give their romance another try.

Both the gate and outer door to her building had been open; he had gone up. And had seen them together. Anna and Quentin Malone, standing in the doorway to her apartment. It had been obvious what they had been doing this bright but chilly afternoon.

Ben closed his eyes and pictured the way Anna had looked, standing there, her silky robe clutched to her breasts, hair tousled, eyes luminous.

She had looked like a woman who had been making love.

Like a woman who was in love.

The depth to which that hurt shocked him. Ben groaned, the sound broken. He felt like such a fool. Like a total sap. He had suspected she had feelings for the detective, but he hadn't wanted to admit it was true. He had wanted to believe he had a chance to win her heart.

No, not wanted to believe—he had believed. When it came to self-deception, the human psyche could convince itself of almost anything. He had told himself that Anna was the one he had waited for, the one he would love and make a life with.

Fool.

He breathed deeply through his nose, battling the anger that rose up inside him, working to suppress the uncomfortable emotion. Working to suppress the headache lurking at the edges of his brain.

He was cold, he realized, shuddering. To-the-bone cold.

Ben shuddered again; his vision blurred. Then cleared. He blinked, disoriented. Unsettled by the prickly sensation on his forearms and the back of his neck.

He glanced quickly around him. Nothing had changed from the moment before—he was sitting in his office, at his desk. It was afternoon, around two. His head still hurt. He pushed his chair back and stood, intent on retrieving one of his migraine tablets. As he stood, a piece of paper fluttered to the floor.

He bent and picked it up. It was a note written to him in big, youthful-looking cursive.

Dear Ben,

You have to help. You're the only one who can. He means to hurt us. Read our journal and you'll know what to do.

Please, I don't want to die.

Ben reread the note three times. He brought a hand to his temple, headache creeping closer. The writer had dotted her "j" and "I" with a heart. Judging by that, he presumed the letter to have been written by a girl. By the quality of the handwriting, he figured her age to be between ten and thirteen, though he was certainly no expert.

But who was she? And why was she communicating with him? He frowned and moved his gaze over the room, looking for anything askance. He always kept his inner office locked. So, how had she gotten in?

Ben realized the answer to the last question first and his blood ran cold. His keys, the ones that had been stolen. He'd had his residence locks changed, but not those for his office.

Idiot.

His residence had been violated, so he'd had the locks changed. He'd never thought any further than what had been right in front of his nose.

Loser.

He ignored the negative voice in his head and instead worked to focus on the dilemma at hand. Perhaps the note had come from the daughter of a patient, the one who had stolen his keys.

But Terry Landry had been that patient. He was behind bars, so how could he pose a threat to anyone?

Unless Terry Landry was the wrong man.

A chill crept up Ben's spine. He shook his head, denying the thought. They had proof. Detective Johnson had told him so. Plenty of it.

Proof that linked Landry to Nancy Kent's murder. Not to Anna's stalker or Jaye's kidnapper.

It wasn't over, Ben realized, hands beginning to shake. Anna wasn't safe, none of them were. He had to call Anna and warn her. He should call the NOPD, he could speak with Detective Johnson. They needed to know what had happened. They would know what to do.

And it would begin all over again. They would start hanging around, asking questions, making demands. Hounding him.

Wait. He brought the heels of his hands to his eyes. He was jumping the gun. It could be a hoax. A sick joke.

Even as the thought registered, he rejected it. Who would know to play such a joke on him? Only someone familiar with the events of the past weeks. One of the detectives on the case. Anna herself or her friends Bill and Dalton.

He returned his gaze to the note. The girl had written: Read our journal and you'll know what to do.

A *journal?* She must have left it for him, he realized. But where? The most logical place would have been with the note. But it had been on his lap.

Under the desk.

Of course.

But it wasn't on the floor or under the chair. Next he tried the drawers—and came up empty.

He frowned. It was almost as if she had wanted to hide it. Though from whom, he hadn't a clue. He needed to put himself in her place. If he was a preteen girl, where would he hide his journal?

Attached to the underside of his desk.

The thought popped into his head and bending, he craned his neck to look at the underside of his desk. Sure enough, a plastic bag had been taped there.

Bingo.

Clever kid.

Ben detached the bag, then returned to his seat. He would bet the note had been on his chair and he hadn't noticed it when he came in because of his preoccupation with Anna. When he'd gone to stand, he had disturbed it, causing it to fall to the floor.

Taking a deep breath, he opened the bag and drew out the book, nothing more than a small notebook. The cover was tattered, the metal spiral crimped on the edges. At least three-quarters of the pages had been written on.

Ben's hands trembled slightly as he held the book. *In it, he would find the answers. The identity of Anna's tormentor. The part he played in this drama. The why.*

Finally, the why.

Leaning back in his chair, Ben began to read.

55

Sunday, February 4
2:00 a.m.

"Minnie!" Jaye cried, scrambling off her cot and to the door. "Is that you? Are you there?"

"I'm here," the other girl answered. "Are you okay?"

Jaye pressed closer to the door. "I'm really hungry. He hasn't brought me anything to eat in a long time."

"I know. I brought you something." Jaye heard the rustle and crackle of a paper wrapper being torn open. "A chocolate bar. I stole it from him while he was gone."

She slid it under the door and Jaye practically pounced on it. She wolfed down the first half, then savored the second.

When she had finished, she licked her fingers. Her stomach still burned with hunger, though not as hotly as before. "What's he up to?" she asked. "Is he trying to starve me to death?"

"I don't know what he's doing. I haven't heard him. And he's been careful not to let me out."

"But you're out now."

"I tricked him and escaped." She lowered her

voice to a shaky whisper. "I'm getting stronger, Jaye. I am. And I'm getting braver, learning his weaknesses. I'm not going to let him hurt you."

Jaye's eyes filled with tears. She was afraid, to her core frightened. Something had changed with their captor. Something more than his not bringing her food.

She sensed that all the pieces of his plan had come together. That she didn't have much time left. That none of them did. "Promise me, Minnie. Promise me you won't let him kill me."

"I promise. I won't let him hurt you or Anna." The other girl paused a moment. When she spoke, her voice quivered with emotion. "I love you, Jaye. You're my best friend."

56

Two evenings after Quentin walked out of her life, Anna found him waiting for her at the entrance gate. He was conversing with Alphonse Badeaux and feeding Mr. Bingle what looked to be pistachio nuts.

Her heart rate quickened. With anticipation. With hope. She'd feared she would never see him again. A part of her had been relieved. Quentin Malone frightened her. Because of the way he made her feel: awake and alive, protected. Because of the way she'd come to look forward to seeing him, to depend on seeing him, the way one simply depends on the sun rising and warming the earth.

But another part of her, the biggest part, had been devastated. For all the same reasons.

Alphonse stood when she approached. "Hello, Miss Anna. I was just keeping your friend here company."

"That he was," Quentin said, getting to his feet. "And quite good company he is."

"Thank you, Detective." The old man beamed at

him, then at her. "Glad to see a policeman in the neighborhood. They're good to have around."

Which was his sweet way of saying, "Don't blow it."

Too late. Maybe.

Or maybe not. Hopefully not.

She smiled. "I'll keep that in mind, Alphonse."

"You kids have a nice night." As if he had been following the conversation, Mr. Bingle got to his feet and ambled toward the curb, stopping and looking back at his master when he reached it.

Alphonse cleared his throat. "You ever get that bouquet of flowers, Miss Anna?"

She drew her eyebrow together. "What flowers?"

"The ones that nice doctor brought you. The other day." The old man's leathery cheeks took on a rosy hue. "Same afternoon Detective Malone here was visiting."

Anna frowned. *Ben was here that afternoon? Why hadn't he knocked? Why—*

Then a horrifying thought occurred to her. Thinking back she pictured standing in her doorway with Quentin, her in her robe. It would have looked like exactly what it had been.

"He left with the flowers, real sudden like. Didn't wave either, like he usually does. Looked upset." The older man cleared his throat. "None of my business, of course. Just wondered about those flowers, they were awful pretty."

Anna swallowed hard, embarrassed. "Thanks, Alphonse. I'll give him a call."

The old man nodded and started across the street,

bulldog by his side. Anna and Quentin watched until they'd made it safely across, then Quentin looked at her. "Sit with me a while?"

A lump formed in her throat. "Sure. It's a pretty evening, isn't it? Warming up. Finally."

She realized she was rambling and told herself to shut up and sit down. She did and he followed her lead. The concrete still held some of the day's warmth.

He held the bag of nuts out to her. "Pistachio?"

"Thanks." She scooped out a few of the nuts. "I love these."

"I figured you did."

She tilted her face up to his. "And why's that?"

"I peeked in your freezer, you had two kinds of ice cream. Pistachio and pistachio-fudge ribbon." One corner of his mouth lifted in a charming and boyish grin. "What can I say? I'm a detective."

"And I'm a writer. I was under the impression we'd already written the ending to this story."

"I didn't care much for that ending." He fell silent. The sun began to set. The sky became the fiery palette of a master artist. "I was wondering how you felt about rewrites?"

"Depends." She glanced at him. "They have to make sense to me."

He searched her gaze a moment, then dragged his away. "I wanted to be a lawyer. A prosecutor. I even imagined myself being the D.A."

"What happened?"

"I knew my limitations. Still do."

"That so?"

He met her eyes. "Stop that."

"What?"

"Responding to everything I say with a question. You sound like a goddamn shrink. And I don't want to be head-shrunk. Not today, anyway."

"Sorry. I guess I just don't know what limitations you're talking about."

His features tightened. "My friends used to say, 'Malone may not be the sharpest tool on the belt, but he's the biggest.' Or, 'That Malone, he's not the brightest bulb in the pack, but he sure can light up the night.'"

She sucked in a sharp breath, angry for him. "With friends like those, you didn't need enemies."

"I'm all brawn and no brain, Anna." He angled toward her. "I hardly got through high school. Squeaked by at the last moment. Rumor was, I slept with my English teacher to get a passing grade my senior year."

"And did you? Sleep with her?"

"Hell, no. She took pity on me and tutored me for two weeks so I would pass the exam."

"So you became a cop. You figured it would be easy. That you could do it without even breaking a sweat."

"Pretty much." He laced his fingers together. "I grew up around police work. Listening to my dad and uncles talk. It was expected that I'd follow in their footsteps."

"And you never told anybody what you really wanted to do with your life?"

"Until now, no."

She shifted her gaze to the darkening sky. "I'm not sure what to say."

He frowned. "Knowing your limitations is not chickening out."

"I didn't say you'd chickened out." She looked at him. "Is that the way you feel?"

"I like police work. I'm good at it."

"But it bores you." She searched his gaze, seeing the frustration in his eyes. The repressed anger. "You're angry. At me?"

"No. At—" He let out a short, sharp-sounding breath. "I settled, Anna. There, that's the truth. And I hate myself for it. Police work doesn't bore me, but it doesn't excite me. But here I am."

"It's not too late."

"It is." He dragged a hand through his hair. "I'm thirty-seven years old."

"Practically a babe."

"You're more stubborn than Badeaux's bulldog."

Her lips lifted. "I'm prettier, too."

"You got that right." He caught her hand and brought it to his mouth. "So, Anna, how do you feel about cops? How would you feel about being with one?"

"Depends on the cop."

"Yeah?"

"Yeah." She tightened her fingers over his. "There's this one cop I know, Irish, charming, a little too sure of himself in some areas, not sure enough in others. Him, I'd want to be with him if he were a ditchdigger. As long as that's what he wanted to be."

"Anna—"

"Settling is insidious, Malone. It'll eat at you. I don't want to wake up one morning next to a man who's fifty and hates himself."

They fell silent. Moments ticked past; the sun began its final descent. Anna leaned toward him. She cupped his face in her palms. "To my mind there's a big difference between a hormone-frenzied seventeen-year-old and a grown-up man driven to attain something he wants." She kissed him. "Think about it, Malone. That's all I ask."

57

Tuesday, February 6
8:50 a.m.

Anna arrived at Ben's office early the next morning. She had wanted to catch him before he became too involved in his day. And before too much more time had passed.

She had hurt Ben. She knew that without having spoken to him. A man didn't stop by unexpectedly with flowers unless he had strong feelings for a woman.

She felt bad about what he had seen. About how it must have hurt him.

Anna sighed and climbed out of her car. Although they hadn't been dating, they'd gone out a couple of times. And they'd had a good time; when he'd kissed her, she'd kissed him back.

Then Malone had come along. And blown thoughts of everyone else out of her head.

She owed Ben an explanation. An apology. She would like them to remain friends. That possibility, she knew, depended on how badly she had hurt him.

And there was only one way to find out.

She climbed his porch steps and crossed the outer

entrance to his office. She found it open and stepped inside. The bell above the door jangled, alerting him to her arrival.

The waiting room was empty; the door to his inner office ajar. Taking a deep breath, she crossed to it, tapped lightly in warning, then pushed it open.

Ben was sitting at his desk, its top stacked high with books. The heavy drapes were drawn; sunshine peeked around the edges. The halogen desk lamp provided the only other light in the room, resulting in an unnatural mix of bright highlights and deep shadows.

"Ben?"

He looked up and she made a sound of distress. He looked ill. His face was drawn, his complexion pasty.

She took several steps into the room. "Are you all right?"

He didn't speak and she closed the distance between them. As she neared him, she saw then that his eyes were red-rimmed and glassy, as if with fever. He looked as if he hadn't slept in a couple of days. "Ben...my God, what's happened?"

He blinked several times, then wetted his lips. "I stopped by your apartment the other day. I wanted...I saw you with Quentin Malone."

"I know." She looked away, then forced her gaze back to his. "One of my neighbors saw you and I...I wanted to talk to you about it."

"Are you in love with him?"

Good question. One she didn't know the answer to. "I have...feelings for him. Strong feelings."

He tipped his face toward the ceiling, a shudder rippling over him. "I should hope so," he said softly, returning his gaze to hers. "Since you're *fucking* him."

She made a sound of shock and took an involuntary step backward. "I don't think it's necessary to use that kind of lang—"

"Don't tell me what's necessary!" He brought his fist crashing down on the desktop with such force the lamp flickered. "Weren't you fucking him that day? Maybe if I had just been a bit more insistent, you would have fucked me t—"

"Stop it!" Anna brought a hand to her mouth, shocked that Ben could say these things to her. "I'm sorry if I hurt you. I didn't mean to. I didn't mean to become involved with Quentin, either. It just... happened. I don't know what else I can say to you. Goodbye, Ben."

She turned on her heel and crossed quickly to the door, anxious to be away from him. Even so, when she reached it she glanced back. And found him slumped forward, head in his hands.

Something wasn't right here. He was ill, sick with a fever. He never would have spoken to her that way otherwise. She had spent enough time with him to know that.

"Ben?"

He lifted his head; he looked devastated. "I could have...fallen in love with you, Anna. I halfway did. And I thought you...I thought you felt the same."

"I'm sorry, Ben." She held out a hand. "I didn't mean for this thing to happen between me and Malone. It just did."

"Is that supposed to make me feel better?"

He brought a hand to his forehead; she saw that it trembled. She made a sound of concern and moved cautiously toward him. She stopped a couple of feet from the desk. "You don't look good, Ben. I think you're sick. I think you have a fever."

He gazed blankly at her and she held out a hand once more. "You have a fever, Ben." She kept her voice low, gentle. "Why don't you go lie down? I could get you a fever reducer and something cold to drink. I could call your physician for you."

For a second he looked as though he would capitulate, then he shook his head. "I can't…a patient…I need to…help."

"But you're ill, Ben. You need—"

The phone rang. He hesitated a moment, then answered it. She could tell immediately that the call was from a patient. He glanced at her, then swiveled in his chair so that his back faced her.

She lowered her gaze, realizing suddenly that it was more than Ben's physical appearance that had changed. His desk was covered with books, medical journals and papers. She scanned the titles, they included ones on schizophrenia, disassociation and post-traumatic stress syndrome. Some of them looked dog-eared, some new.

Anna shifted her gaze to take in the office in general. It, too, looked a jumble. It looked as if he had been working around the clock here, not even leaving to eat or sleep.

He'd said a patient needed his help. Which patient? What could be of such urgency that he would work while ill?

Anna inched closer. A notebook lay open in front
of him. She craned her neck in an attempt to read
what it said. She could only make out a few words;
it appeared to be a plea for help.

She drew her eyebrows together. The writing was
uneven, at times an almost unreadable scrawl, at others a precise pinched cursive. The margins contained
doodles, some of them sweet, others frightening.

The drawings had come from a troubled soul.

The patient Ben sought to help.

"You just can't help yourself, can you?"

Anna looked up, embarrassed. Ben had ended his
call and had caught her snooping. Again.

Heat flooded her cheeks. "I'm sorry. I...you're
right. I couldn't help my...I'm a writer. And I'm concerned about you."

He closed the journal. "I'd like you to leave,
Anna."

"I'm sorry," she said again, straightening. She
took a step from the desk. "Won't you at least agree
to let me call a doct—"

"Get out."

"Ben, please. I don't want us to part this way.
You're not well, Perhaps if you got some rest—"

He shivered; his features sharpened. "Perhaps
what? If I get some rest I won't be furious with you?
You shared your goodies with that bimbo cop, Anna.
Do you know how much that disgusts me? Can you
imagine how sickened I was to see you there, half-
dressed and slobbering all over him? Like some cheap
slut."

Her breath caught. She took a step backward. "If

that's the way you want it, Ben. I'd hoped we could be friends. I see now that's not possible.''

He shuddered and rubbed his arms. ''Don't go, Anna. I'm sorry. I'm under so much pressure. This patient…it's bad, Anna. If I could tell you about it, I know you'd understand. Please don't—''

''You're not well and I suggest you see a doctor.'' She reached the door and looked back at him. ''I can't help you. Goodbye, Ben.''

58

Across town at central lockup, Quentin waited for Terry. His former partner had requested to see him. And he had come, not because of their history. But for Anna. In the hopes that he could coerce information out of his former friend that Johnson and the others had been unable to.

Time was running out for Jaye Arcenaux.

Quentin glanced at his watch, then continued pacing the small room. It was empty save for a metal table and two folding chairs. The table was bolted to the floor; the walls and door were made of reinforced steel. The room's only light was provided by a single fluorescent tube, secured under a steel-mesh housing. A viewing window had been cut out of the three-inch-thick door, a barred opening not big enough for even Houdini to shimmy through.

He flexed his fingers, anxious to begin. Dreading beginning. He had purposely removed himself from the case. He had been worried his anger at Terry would cloud his objectivity.

And as the days had passed, that anger had not

dimmed. If anything, it burned brighter than before. Hotter.

At the sound of a key in the lock, Quentin swung to face the door. The guard appeared. Then Terry. His once-dashing friend shuffled in, unshaven and unkempt, wrists and ankles manacled. He didn't meet Quentin's eyes, simply crossed to one of the chairs and sat down.

"Just holler if you need me," the guard said, already closing the door.

Quentin nodded, then sat. Terry lifted his gaze. Quentin met it. For several moments, neither man spoke. They simply considered each other, accused and accuser. Betrayer and betrayed.

Quentin broke the silence first. "Orange isn't your color," he murmured, referring to Terry's jail-issue jumpsuit. "You look like shit."

One corner of Terry's mouth lifted in a mimicry of his former cocksure grin. "Yeah? Well, they were all out of the Brooks Brothers navy pinstripe."

Always the joker. Quentin stiffened. "What do you want, Terry?"

He looked away, sobering. "How's Penny?"

"Do you really care?"

Hot color flew to the other man's face. "Yes, dammit! How is she?"

Quentin leaned forward. "How do you think? Devastated. Humiliated. Worried about the kids and how this will affect them."

"I...miss them."

His former partner's voice thickened and Quentin hardened himself to the way that made him feel. "But are you sorry, Terry? Are you sorry you did this to them?''

''Yes. But not for the reasons you think.'' Terry brought his hands to the table, the manacles clanging against its top. ''Why did you have to go to O'Shay? Why didn't you come to me first?''

''I had a job to do. I did it.''

Terry made a sound of bitterness. ''Duty before friendship, right?''

''Our friendship ended with your lies.''

''I could have explained.''

Quentin shook his head. ''Sorry, partner, this is one situation you couldn't have talked your way out of. The evidence speaks for itself.''

''It doesn't. That's just it, I...I need your help, Malone.''

Anger took his breath. How like Terry to simply assume others should help him. To assume that Quentin would rush to his rescue, even with the weight of the evidence against him. Even after all his lies.

''No,'' Quentin replied, tone caustic. ''Jaye Arcenaux needs my help. Minnie needs my help. You want to tell me where they are?'' He leaned toward the other man. ''You help me, maybe I can help you.''

''You really believe I did this.'' Terry swore. ''I thought that maybe, because I hadn't seen you—''

''That I bought into your bullshit? Give me a break.'' He made a sound of disgust. ''Help me, Terry. I'll see what I can do for you.''

''I can't.'' He fisted his fingers. ''I don't know where they are. I didn't do this.''

Quentin pushed away from the table, so violently

his chair crashed to the floor. "Call me when you're ready to tell the truth."

"I didn't do it!" Terry scrambled to his feet. "That's the truth! I swear it is!"

Quentin crossed to the door, glancing back at his former friend when he reached it. "Then I'm sure the evidence will bear that statement out. The DNA will come back and you'll be home free."

Quentin saw that Terry's throat worked, as if he fought strong emotion. When he faced Quentin once more, his eyes were bright with tears. "It won't," he said thickly. "That's the problem." He sank back to his seat and dropped his head into his hands. "The DNA...it won't."

Quentin froze. The hair on his forearms and the back of his neck stood up. "Maybe you'd better clarify that."

Terry lifted his head. He met Quentin's gaze, the expression in his tortured. "I was having an affair with Nancy Kent. I had been for...months. It was Nancy who had been keeping me in fifties, courtesy of her fat divorce settlement. I thought I had it made.

"It wasn't a romance." A strangled laugh slipped past his lips. "Far from it. We were fucking each other. And it was great. At first."

He looked away. "That night at Shannon's, she was playing with me. Making me pay for standing her up the night before. Treating me like a leper."

His face took on a faraway expression. "I was furious with her. For teasing me. For embarrassing me in front of everyone. For coming on to every guy but me." He blinked, his expression clearing. "I'd had too much to drink. She played into that. And it got...ugly.''

Quentin arched an eyebrow, unmoved. "The fight."

"Yes." Terry wetted his lips. "But it didn't end there. Afterward, I watched her. I couldn't help myself. I was like a hungry dog hunting a juicy bone. She knew it, too. And liked it. That's the way she was."

He shifted in his seat. "She slipped out the back entrance. I followed her. And we...we screwed. Right there. Up against the wall. She liked it like that. Dangerous. Kind of rough."

Quentin thought of Penny. He thought of Matti and Alex, Terry's kids. He felt ill. "And that's it? Your whole sordid tale of woe?"

"When she turned up dead, I panicked. She and I had fought publicly. I hadn't used protection, so I knew they'd find my DNA and God only knew what other trace evidence on her. That's why I kept quiet. I knew how it'd look if I came clean. I couldn't say anything. Don't you see, Malone? I was screwed."

Quentin schooled his features to neutrality. "Who knew you and Nancy Kent were having an affair?"

"No one. We were very careful."

Quentin made a sound of disbelief. "You just lost me, partner. Big time. Discretion was never one of your strong suits. No way you could have kept this a secret. Not from me. Not from the other guys."

"But I did! We became involved before she was divorced." Desperation crept into his tone. "If anyone had found out, her settlement would have been jeopardized.''

''So, no one knew? Not even Penny?''

''No! Especially not Penny. Dear God, I'd hurt her enough already.'' His eyes grew bright. ''I wasn't proud of what I was doing to her. In fact, I hated myself for it.''

Quentin found that comment interesting, but stored it away for later. ''Where did you first meet Nancy Kent?''

''In the Quarter. At a club.''

''Which one?''

''Fritz the Cat. I think.''

''You think?'' He arched an eyebrow. ''Seems to me that would be something you'd remember.''

''I'd been to a lot of clubs that night. I'd been drinking.''

''That excuse is starting to sound patented, Terror. Want to rethink it?''

''It's true! I swear to God!''

Quentin ignored that. If he had a buck for every time some perp ''swore to God,'' he would be bloody rich. ''Was anyone with you?''

''No.''

Quentin folded his hands in front of him, hoping it would hide the way they shook. Hoping it would keep him from using them to pummel the other man. Terry made him sick. ''And what about Dr. Walker? Why were you seeing him in secret?''

''I didn't want anyone to know. Not even you or Penny.'' He leaned forward, expression earnest as a choirboy's. "I knew it'd get around. I didn't want to take anybody's shit."

"But why use an alias with the doctor?"

"I thought it was safer."

"And then you up and quit?" Quentin snapped his fingers. "Just like that?"

"Penny left me. I figured, what was the point of continuing?"

"You have an answer for everything, don't you?"

"It's all true!"

"It's all bullshit," Quentin countered, pushing away from the door. "How long did it take you to come up with this story, Terry?"

"It's true, I swear! They won't find any evidence that links me with the other two victims. Or to Anna. No DNA, no—"

"Evelyn Parker wasn't raped."

"But Jessica Jackson was." He got to his feet, movements clumsy because of his bound ankles. "Why would I terrorize Anna North? I don't even know her!"

"You tell me."

"I'm an adulterer, not a murderer! You've got to believe me!"

Disgusted, Quentin swept his gaze over the other man. "Your story's awfully convenient, Terror. And like every quickly constructed, half-baked story by every-guilty-as-sin asshole trying to get off, it lacks substantiation."

"You can get it for me." He reached out with his shackled hands. "You're the best, Malone. You can ask around, find someone who saw Nancy and I together before that night at Shannon's.''

"And why would I want to waste my time like that? I think you're lying, Terry."

"Because you care about Anna North. Because you're smart enough to realize that if there's a chance it wasn't me, then whoever's after her is still out there.''

59

Tuesday, February 6
11:30 p.m.

That night Jaye's captor brought her food. A feast. A Big Mac and large order of french fries. A tall glass of ice-cold chocolate milk. She awakened to the smell of it, her empty, aching stomach propelling her off the cot and across the room.

Jaye fell on the food, gobbling it down hungrily, eating so fast she nearly choked. As she stuffed the fries into her mouth, it occurred to her that this might be her last meal. Like a prisoner on death row, she was being treated to her favorites.

She ate anyway, hating how grateful she was for his crumbs, hating him for knowing she would be.

She consumed the milk last, slurping as she drank, taking in every drop though she felt as if she was going to burst. Only then did she realize how odd she felt, light-headed and prickly, the way she had the time she had sneaked three of her foster father's beers from the cooler on his fishing boat.

The plastic cup slipped from her fingers. It hit the floor and rolled to the door. The room spun and she moaned.

A soft, deep laugh came from the other side of the door. "Did you enjoy your meal, Jaye?"

Him. His voice. A cry of terror passed her lips. She tried to stand but found she couldn't.

He laughed again. "Were you terribly hungry? I think you were. I wanted you to be." He paused. "So you wouldn't question what you were eating. So you wouldn't look too closely at it."

Dear God. He had poisoned her. She got to her knees, then dragged herself to her feet, holding on to the door frame for support. The room wobbled. She began to sweat.

"I've come to take you bye-bye."

She heard the key in the lock. A moment later the door swung open. And he filled it. He wore a Mardi Gras mask, the flesh-colored featureless ones the krewe riders preferred. He was dressed in black.

She whimpered and pressed closer to the door.

"Do I frighten you? Is this the way you pictured me?" She sensed his smile. "What does evil look like, little Jaye?"

Minnie, where are you? Jaye clutched the door frame for support, legs rubbery, hands growing slippery with sweat. *You promised you wouldn't let him hurt me.*

He stepped back from the door, then returned, dragging a large, sturdy-looking cardboard box. A mover's box, she realized. One more than big enough to hide a body in. A strangled sound of fear slipped past her lips.

"I know you've been missing your friend Anna."

He opened the flaps of the box. "But don't worry, you'll be seeing her soon."

"No," she whispered. "No!" Summoning up the last of her strength, she lunged at him.

He caught her easily, chuckling at her efforts. She twisted and kicked, her movements weak, less than feeble. He held her pinned to his chest until whatever drug he had given her had consumed not only her strength but her body's ability to follow the commands of her brain. Then he let her go. The floor rushed up to meet her. Her head snapped against the linoleum.

Jaye gazed up at him, her vision blurring, growing dark around the edges. She moved her mouth in a prayer, though it sounded only in her head. She prayed for God to protect Minnie and Anna.

60

Wednesday, February 7
10:00 a.m.

Quentin couldn't put aside his conversation with Terry. His former partner's parting words about Anna ate at him. Because they were true. Because they scared the hell out of him.

If Terry wasn't the one after Anna, then he was still out there. And she was still in danger.

If. In this situation, that one little word packed a big swing. On one side, life. On the other, death.

Quentin swiveled in his chair so that his back faced the squad room. He closed his eyes. Terry could be manipulating him. He probably was. Criminals did it all the time.

But what if he wasn't?

He couldn't take the chance.

Quentin pushed away from his desk and crossed to his captain's open door. He tapped on it and she looked up. "Got a minute?" he asked.

She waved him in and he crossed to stand directly in front of her desk. He got right to the point. "I'm having some doubts that Terry's our guy."

Her eyebrows shot up but she said nothing.

"I went to see him yesterday. At his request. He claimed he was having an affair with Nancy Kent. That they had sex that night, but that he didn't kill her."

"Tidy. Does he have any proof?"

"He wants me to find some."

"Why is this the first I'm hearing about it?"

"I needed some time to put it all together in my head."

"And?"

"I didn't buy it, not at first. But now..." With a sound of frustration, he crossed to the window that looked out at the squad room, then swung back to the captain. "Now, I don't know what I believe. But if Terry's telling the truth, a killer's still on the street. And Anna North's still in danger."

She frowned and rubbed her temple. "The chief's not going to like this."

"He's not going to like another victim showing up even more." Quentin returned to her desk, laid his palms on it and looked her directly in the eyes. "Let me make a few calls. We'll keep it quiet. See if I can substantiate Terry's story. If I can, we go bigger, more public. If I can't, we drop it."

She agreed and Quentin began by paying a call on Penny Landry. They stood on the front porch of her Lakeview home, the sun working to fight its way through the crisp, cold air. She looked tired. Stressed-out. His heart went out to her. He would love to offer her hope that this nightmare would end soon, but he couldn't. Not yet.

He inquired about her and the kids; she about Terry

and the investigation. Then he got to the point. "Penny, a couple of weeks ago you told me that running around had always been Terry's territory. What did you mean?"

She looked taken aback by the question. "You know. His drinking and carousing. He was the original party boy." Her mouth thinned. "I married him anyway. I was young and smitten. Stupid."

He understood her anger. Her regret and bitterness. He felt himself another victim of Terry's charm.

If Terry had committed these horrible acts.

If. That word again. Back to torment him.

"I'm sorry." She pushed the wisps of hair that had escaped her ponytail away from her face. "I must sound so bitter."

He laid a hand on her shoulder. "Don't apologize. I feel betrayed, too. I'm angry."

"Thanks, Malone." She covered his hand with her own. Tears sparkled in her eyes. "I always liked you."

He smiled, squeezed her fingers and dropped his hand. "I always liked you, too, Penny."

She tilted her face up to the flat blue sky, then looked back at him, expression suddenly wistful. "I'm thinking of moving back to Lafayette. My folks and sisters are there. It'll be better for the kids."

Quentin nodded. "It sounds like a good plan. If I can help in any way, let me know."

"I will." She smiled. "I'll probably need another strong back on moving day."

"You got it." He glanced toward the street and his Bronco, then back at her. "Penny, I have to ask you something. And I need an honest answer. It's important." He paused, waiting for her full attention. "Was Terry having an affair?"

She hesitated, pink climbing into her cheeks. When she answered, she didn't quite meet his eyes. "I don't have any proof, but I...I think so. In my heart, I know he was." Her voice thickened. "With all I'd put up with from him...I wasn't going to put up with infidelity, too."

"Did you confront him?"

She shook her head. "I feel sort of stupid about it, but after everything, I guess I didn't want to know for sure. And I didn't think I could bear it if he lied to me." She sighed. "Instead, I asked him to leave."

Quentin digested that information. "This is crucial, Penny. Do you think you could get any proof? Receipts for hotel rooms, records of calls? Anything like that?"

Her expression clouded. "I'm not...sure. I could try but...why do you need this, Malone?"

"I just do, Penny. Could you trust me for now?"

She said she could, and minutes later Quentin was on the road again. His next stop was Ben Walker's office uptown. It seemed to Quentin that if anyone besides Penny knew for certain that Terry had been having an affair, it would be his therapist. Quentin hoped the doctor would talk.

He arrived at the therapist's just before noon. Although midday, the office door was locked tight. He walked across the porch to the residence. After both ringing the bell and knocking, he tried the door.

It was unlocked. Glancing over his shoulder, he

pushed it the rest of the way open and slipped inside. The place had been ransacked: furniture toppled, paintings ripped off walls and drawers emptied.

Muttering an oath, Quentin unsheathed his weapon. As quietly as he could, he made his way from room to room. Broken glass crackled beneath his feet. From the back of the home came the sounds of a radio, tuned in to a top-forty station.

He fully expected to find the doctor home.

And quite dead.

Quentin reached the doctor's bedroom, located at the very back of the house. There, as he had in every other room of the house, he found devastation. But no sign of Ben Walker, no sign that he had been physically harmed.

The clock radio lay on the floor, housing cracked but still plugged into the wall and playing. Quentin stared at it, working to sort out his thoughts. To organize them into a plan of action. It seemed obvious now that Terry wasn't their guy. He wasn't the patient who had involved Ben in Anna's life. It had been another.

One who seemed to be fitting together the last pieces of his scheme. Eliminating the components that were no longer necessary. Like Ben Walker.

Quentin thought of Anna and his heart began to race. Time was running out. For her. For Jaye. He needed Walker's files. He needed those names. To hell with legal channels, he was going to get them.

Quentin headed next door. He opened the door the old-fashioned way, by breaking one of the sidelight windows, reaching inside and unlocking the dead bolt.

He slipped inside. The waiting room hadn't been disturbed. Save for the ticking of a clock, the office was deathly quiet. Stifling hot. A sour smell hung in the air.

The hair on the back of his neck prickled. Unsheathing his weapon, Quentin made his way further into the room. Dead ahead lay a closed door. He opened it. The room inside resembled a kind of living room, with comfortable-looking chairs set up in a circle. It was in the same condition as the waiting room.

Quentin moved on. A bathroom. A kitchenette. He found the last door locked.

Walker's inner office. Pay dirt.

He kicked it open.

The smell hit him in a nauseating wave. Like human waste and rotting food. He brought a hand to his nose. A large mirror lay faceup on the floor, its shattered surface covered by spidery veinlike lines. Someone had emptied their bowels in its center.

Mother of God. This just got better and better.

After a quick scan of the room, Quentin holstered his gun and stepped around the mirror, going for the file cabinet.

He found the drawers unlocked. He slid them open one at a time and flipped through the files, searching the names, looking for Adam Furst. He stopped on the name Rick Richardson. *Terry's file.* He removed it, stood and tucked it under his jacket and into the back waistband of his jeans.

Time to call this nightmare in. And to call Anna. He had to warn her.

His beeper sounded before he could.

"We've got a possible homicide," the desk officer informed him when he answered. "Crestwood Nursing Home. One of your witnesses. Louise Walker."

Quentin's blood went cold. "I'm on my way."

61

Wednesday, February 7
12:30 p.m.

Across town, Anna arrived home, arms loaded with fruit and vegetables from the Farmer's Market and bunches of three-day-old flowers from The Perfect Rose. She called a greeting to Alphonse and Mr. Bingle, loitering on their porch across the street, then made her way through the courtyard gate. She saw that the outer door had been propped open with a brick—again—and she frowned.

She suspected the kids on four were the ones who had been doing it, although she hadn't actually caught them. They were kids, they didn't understand the danger. But they needed to be made aware of the danger. Perhaps she would speak to their parents. Or let Dalton take care of it.

She thought of Dalton and her frown deepened. He had been on edge when she'd stopped by for the flowers. Flushed and jumpy. He had repeatedly glanced at his watch and had asked her the same question three times. Then he'd insisted she take some of the Sterling roses.

And he never parted with those.

Something was up with her friend. Probably a fight with Bill, she decided as she slipped into the building. It had happened before. The hallway and stairwell were cold. No doubt because the door had been left open. She shivered and trotted up the stairs. She had just enough time to get the flowers in water, her purchases put away and eat a sandwich before having to relieve Dalton at The Perfect Rose.

She unlocked her apartment door and went straight to work. She arranged the flowers in a vase, then began unpacking her produce. The pears and tomatoes went in a ripening bowl on the counter, the apples, cucumbers and bell peppers into the fridge.

Cradling the items against her chest with her right arm, she opened the refrigerator. Her heart stopped. A scream rose in her throat and one by one, the fruit and vegetables dropped to the floor.

On a dessert plate topped with a heart-shaped paper doily sat a bloodied, severed finger. A pinkie.

Anna fought back her scream. She brought a shaking hand to her chest, fighting for calm. Mustering fury. She wasn't going to fall for this sick gag, not again.

Pressing her lips together, she leaned forward. An odor emanated from the finger, sickly sweet and sour at the same time. Natural and chemical. She brought a hand to her nose. The nail bed had a bluish tint. The severed edge was discolored, the rust-colored material around it crusty.

Real. The finger was real.

It wasn't over.

Anna sprang back from the refrigerator, stomach hurtling to her throat.

Her phone rang.

She swung toward it, heart thundering. She saw that her message light was blinking. The phone rang again. She stared at it, a chill of premonition racing up her spine.

Don't answer it. Call Malone.

It rang a third time. And a fourth.

She leaped for it, ripping it off its cradle. "Yes?"

"Hello, Harlow."

Her legs went weak. She grabbed the counter for support.

Kurt.

He laughed. "No nice hello for an old friend?"

She closed her eyes. "What do you want?"

"A little appreciation maybe. I went to a great deal of trouble acquiring that gift."

She brought a trembling hand to her mouth. *Dear God. That woman. That poor…woman.*

"I did it for you. I did all of them for you."

She fought hysteria. Fought falling completely apart. That's what he wanted; she wouldn't give it to him. "Why? You wanted me, why not just come and—"

"Get you?" he supplied. "I could have, certainly. But every wonderful meal is enhanced by an appetizer. The first course is simply a teaser, a sensory awakener for the main meal."

"You're insane."

He made a clucking sound with his tongue, admonishing her. "That's not a very nice thing to say, dear Harlow. I thought you'd think me so clever. After all, I've managed to have you all jumping through hoops. You, the police, Ben. Even my little Minnie.''

Ben. Minnie. Dear Lord. ''What have you done with Jaye?''

''I wondered when you would get around to asking. She's with me, of course. But I believe you knew that.''

''Is she...is she—''

''Alive?'' She heard the smile in his voice. ''Yes, quite. And I assume you'd like her to stay that way?''

Anna stiffened. ''You assume correctly.''

For a moment he was silent. When he spoke she realized by the anger in his tone that she had surprised him. He hadn't expected her to be brave. He didn't like it. ''Did you learn from your parents' mistakes, Harlow?''

''I don't know what you mean.''

''Don't be coy, you know exactly what I'm asking. Did your parents' mistakes teach you anything?''

''What do you want?''

''If you contact the authorities, Jaye will die. If you fail to follow my instructions to the letter, Jaye will die. Do you understand?''

Anna went light-headed with fear. She curled her fingers around the receiver, fighting it. Fighting him. ''Yes,'' she murmured evenly. ''But I don't have...anything. What ransom could you want? I have no money, no jewelry—''

''I want you, my dear. The price for Jaye Arcenaux's life is Harlow Anastasia Grail's.''

62

Anna hung up the phone, grabbed her purse and ran for the door. She didn't consider not complying with Kurt's demands, even though she knew he intended to kill her. She was trading her own life for Jaye's. It was a trade she was willing to make.

This was her nightmare, not Jaye's.

She had come full circle.

Anna glanced at her watch. She didn't have much time. Kurt had given her a mere twenty minutes to arrive at her first stop—a pay phone at the Shell service station just off the I-10 West expressway in Metairie. If she was late, he'd warned, Jaye would pay the price.

A finger. Her right pinkie first. He had arranged ten stops, all tightly timed. One for each of her friend's fingers.

She wouldn't be late, Anna vowed. She would not.

Anna exited her apartment. When she paused to lock the door, a hysterical laugh bubbled to her lips. What did it matter if she was robbed? She would most likely be dead in a matter of hours anyway.

Leaving the door unlocked, she raced for the stairs, running down them, aware of every moment that passed. At the bottom of the stairs she ran headlong into Bill. Her friend caught her arms to steady her.

"Hey, Anna, where's the fire?"

"Let me go!" She wrenched herself free. "I've got to go!"

"Wait!" Bill grabbed her arms again, expression alarmed. "My God, Anna, what's wrong? What's happen—"

"Please...Jaye needs me. I can't be late... He'll hurt her if I don't...he'll kill her!"

The blood drained from her friend's face. "I'm calling the police."

This time it was she who held him fast. "No! Please, you mustn't. He'll kill her. Promise me you won't."

"I can't. I—"

"I'll be all right. Please, for Jaye."

He looked terrified. "Okay, Anna. I promise I—"

"Thank you." She stood on tiptoe and pressed a kiss to his cheek. "Tell Dalton I said goodbye."

63

Wednesday, February 7
12:50 p.m.

Quentin stared down at Louise Walker's face, frozen in death. She appeared to have been smothered. Judging by her fixed lividity and the stage of rigor mortis, she had been dead six to eight hours. That meant she had been murdered sometime the night before. The nurses hadn't discovered she'd passed until after breakfast, assuming at first that the woman had simply decided to sleep in. When they realized she was gone, they'd thought she'd died in her sleep, the victim of a quiet heart attack.

The blood and other debris under her fingernails suggested otherwise.

"He likely used one of her bed pillows," Quentin murmured, straightening. "She tried to claw herself free. Judging by the amount of matter under her fingernails, he's going to be pretty torn up."

He swung to face the first officer. "Make sure the evidence collection guys get scrapings from both hands. I want them taken here and back at the lab."

Quentin turned to the two nurses, huddling just inside the doorway. One had been on duty the night before, the other was the one who had discovered Louise dead this morning. "Have you notified her son?" he asked.

The morning-shift nurse answered. "We tried. We...I called and left messages at his home and office."

Quentin nodded. He didn't expect Ben Walker would be returning any of those calls, but he didn't say that. Right now, a crime scene crew was at the doctor's place, sifting through the destruction, looking for evidence.

"Who could have done this?" the night nurse cried. "How did they get in and why...her? She was just a sweet old lady."

Why her? Somebody was cleaning up loose ends. Louise Walker had been one of those ends.

"We'll find that out, I promise you. Did Mrs. Walker have any unexpected visitors last night?"

She shook her head. "No."

"Was there anyone suspicious in the facility? Anyone you didn't recognize from previous visits?"

The night nurse shook her head again. "No, no one like that. It was a quiet night."

Quentin frowned. "No visitors at all?"

The nurse hesitated. "Her son was in, of course. But no one else."

The hair on the back of Quentin's neck prickled. "Ben Walker was in? What time?"

"It was late. Well past visiting hours, but I let him in anyway. He was here for several hours and left after his mother had fallen asleep."

That would mean Ben Walker had been the last person to see his mother alive.

Son-of-a-bitch.

The blood began to pound in his head. He thought suddenly of the photo of Anna and Ben at the Café du Monde. "Are you certain it was her son?"

The nurse flushed. "Yes, of cour...well, I think so. He was acting strangely, not like himself, but I figured he'd had a bad day. Nobody's perky all the time."

Quentin frowned, surprised by her answer. Confused by it. He had thrown out the question, expecting her to vehemently insist the man had been Ben Walker.

But she hadn't. So either Adam looked enough liked Ben to be mistaken for him or they were one and the same person.

He struggled to put the pieces together, to make them fit. What had Louise Walker said the other night? She had called Adam "The bad one. The devil himself."

"I'd like to see the guest registry now please."

While the one nurse hurried to get it, Quentin continued to question the other nurse. "Do you know, did Louise Walker have another son?"

The woman frowned. "Not that I know of. She never mentioned one and the only pictures of her family I ever saw were of her Ben."

The nurse returned. She handed him the registry, open to the previous evening. Quentin found Ben's name, then flipped back in the book until he found the doctor's name again.

The signatures didn't match.

Mother of God, that was it.

Quentin started toward the door, eyes on the other officer. "Get Captain O'Shay on the phone now, fill her in. And I need Detectives Johnson and Walden down here, ASAP. I'll be available by cell and beeper."

The officer frowned. "But where should I tell them you've—"

"Anna North's apartment. This guy's taking care of loose ends before starting the main event. And my guess is Louise Walker was his last one."

Six minutes later, Quentin screeched to a stop in front of Anna's apartment building. In those six minutes, he had tried to call her a dozen times. He had tried her apartment and The Perfect Rose; he had gotten a recording at both numbers.

He refused to speculate as to what that might mean. If he did, he might lose it. And he couldn't afford that, not now.

He jumped out of the Bronco and headed for her apartment at a dead run, weapon out.

"Detective!"

Quentin swung in the direction of the call. Alphonse Badeaux was hurrying across the street, frantically waving his arms. Mr. Bingle loped along beside him.

Quentin holstered his gun, then waved him back. "Alphonse, I don't have time—"

"It's about Miss Anna! I'm afraid something bad's happened to her." He cleared the sidewalk. "That man was here this morning! I saw him and didn't...I should have done something. I should have warned her.''

"What man? Who was here?"

He struggled to catch his breath. "The one who looks like Doc Walker."

Quentin focused his full attention on the other man. "What do you mean 'looks like Doc Walker'?"

"He's been here before. At first I thought it was Anna's friend, the doctor. But today I got a good look at him. He'd gone into the building so I moseyed over for a chat, you know. Was going to tell him that Miss Anna had gone to the Farmer's Market.

"Met him on the steps. Right there." He pointed. "He just looked at me. Made me feel real cold. Chilled to the bone, you know what I mean?"

Quentin swallowed hard. He did know. And he couldn't contemplate that Anna might be with him.

Quentin glanced at Anna's apartment, then back at the old man, impatience pulling at him. "Go on."

"He had these...gouges on the back of his hands. Real nasty-looking. You know, like someone or something had—"

"Clawed him?"

The man nodded. "Something's not right with that one. His eyes...they were flat."

"But it wasn't Ben Walker?" he asked. "You're sure?"

The man's expression clouded. "I wouldn't be but...it couldn't have been him. Bingle liked the doc, but this one...he wouldn't come near him. Growled, real deep, and hung back. Like that man was a devil or somethin' else. Somethin' real bad."

After advising Alphonse to go home and stay inside, Quentin entered Anna's building. He made his way up the stairs to her apartment, weapon out and ready. His heart stopped when he saw her door was cracked open.

"Anna!" he called, nudging the door the rest of the way open with the barrel of his gun. "Anna, it's Quentin."

A shuffling sound came from the kitchen and Quentin pivoted in the direction. "Come out where I can see you with your hands up! I have a weapon and I will use it."

Dalton and Bill appeared in the kitchen doorway, hands above their heads. "Don't shoot!" they cried in unison. "It's only us."

"Where is she? Where's Anna?"

"We tried to call—"

"They said you were out. We didn't know what to do!"

"I saw her earlier today, I was distracted..." Dalton wrung his hands. "Bill and I had argued, but still, she seemed fine...and now she's...gone. Bill tried to stop her, but he couldn't."

"Gone?" Quentin repeated, going cold with dread. He holstered his gun. "Gone where?"

"I don't know!" Bill cried. "She was talking crazy...she said Jaye was in danger. That he would hurt Jaye if she didn't go. That he would kill her. She had to do exactly what he said, she made me promise not to call you."

"He did anyway," Dalton inserted. "I convinced him he had to."

He was too late. Dear God, he was too late.

"She left her apartment unlocked." Bill's voice shook. "We shouldn't have come in but..."

Dalton took over. "There's something you've...he left her another finger, Detective Malone. But this one, it looks real."

It was.

Quentin studied the severed appendage, mouth dry, heart fast. It was a woman's pinkie, most probably it had belonged to Jessica Jackson. It was in a partial state of decomposition, decomposition that had been slowed by immersion in formaldehyde.

He brought the heels of his hands to his eyes. Bill had described Anna as nearly hysterical. She had to go, she'd said. She had to do exactly as "he" said or Jaye would be killed.

The bastard was using Jaye as a way to lure Anna into his trap. He had known that to save Jaye, Anna would do anything he asked.

It had all been one big game.

Quentin dropped his hands. What did he do now? How did he find her? He had talked to his captain; evidence teams had been sent to the nursing home, Ben Walker's home and office and were on the way here. He had called in the last number registered on Anna's caller ID and was awaiting word on that.

He fisted his fingers. It wasn't enough. Every minute that passed brought her closer to a madman.

His cell phone rang. He snapped it open. It was Johnson. "What do you have?"

"Phone number's registered to one Adam Furst."

"Got an address?"

They did. It was the Madisonville apartment that he and Anna had visited. "No good. Been there. He vacated weeks ago."

"I've got more, Malone. Talked to the Atlanta PD. Seems early last year in separate incidents, two women turned up dead after nights out on the town. Both were raped, then smothered. No arrests, no suspects."

"And both were redheads."

"You got it. And guess who lived in Atlanta during that time?"

"Dr. Benjamin Walker."

"Bingo."

Quentin frowned. *Who were they dealing with? One person or look-alikes?* "Johnson, check something out for me. That photo of Ben Walker and Anna North at the Café du Monde, see if you can get somebody in the know to verify its authenticity for me."

"Sure. What're you thinking?"

"That it would have been difficult for Ben to have photographed himself with Anna. We might be dealing with a look-alike."

"A good-twin, bad-twin scenario?"

"Yeah, maybe."

"I'll get right on it. Here's Captain O'Shay."

His aunt came on the line. She sounded excited. "Call just came in for you. A kid, she was sobbing. Said it was an emergency. Said you had to help. That 'he' was going to hurt Anna and Jaye. Made me promise to get this message to you."

Quentin tightened his grip on the phone, fighting

the panic that had him by the throat. "She give you a name?"

"Name was Minnie. Sound familiar?"

She knew it did. "Where was she?"

"A service station and marina. She didn't know where, but she gave us the pay phone number. She's in Manchac, Malone."

"Manchac, Louisiana? The fishing village up toward Hammond?"

"The very one."

He looked at his watch, mentally calculating Anna's arrival time and what his own would be. He swore and started for the door. "Any idea what the land-speed record is to Manchac from the French Quarter?"

"No clue. But break it anyway, Malone."

64

After stopping at a half-dozen locations to receive further instructions from Kurt, Anna arrived at her final destination—a fishing camp located in Manchac, a small community an hour north of New Orleans. Situated on Lake Maurepas and surrounded by swamps, the area was home to shrimpers, fishermen and a number of rustic hunting and fishing camps.

As directed, Anna had parked her car at the end of the unmarked dirt road about a mile past the only sign of civilization for miles, Smiley's service station and full-service marina. Also as instructed, she had left the keys in it and started up the road on foot.

Up ahead, through the dense cover of cypress and oak trees, she could just glimpse a building.

A quiver of uncertainty moved through her. *This was it. The end of the line.*

After twenty-three years, she was about to come face-to-face with her past.

Anna glanced behind her and saw that her car was no longer visible. She let out a long breath, allowing herself her first moment of pure terror since telling

Bill goodbye. And her last, she promised herself. Anna rubbed her damp palms against her thighs. Kurt wanted her to be afraid. He wanted her terrified and begging for mercy. She was here to save Jaye, but she would not give him the pleasure of watching her fall apart.

She scanned her surroundings. The road had been carved out of the swamp. Other than by water, it provided the only way in or out. She suspected that up ahead lay more of the same. Step off the road and within moments she would be knee deep in snakes, alligators and God only knew what else.

She shuddered and rubbed her arms. Was she doing the right thing? He had wanted her alone and helpless, with no avenue for escape. He had promised to free Jaye, but what guarantee did she have that he would keep his word?

She understood suddenly some of the agony of indecision her parents must have suffered. Their response to Kurt's demands hadn't been about the money, she realized. It had been about not knowing which way offered their daughter the greater chance of survival.

The truth of that took her breath. She felt a small, wounded part of herself begin to heal. The truth was, she had always wondered if the money had been more important to them than she.

Anna swallowed her hesitation. She had lived the consequences of noncompliance. Timmy had died. She believed Kurt when he said he would take each of Jaye's fingers, then her life.

This avenue offered Jaye her best chance of survival.

She had to take it.

Heart pounding, Anna made her way up the driveway. Shells crunched beneath her feet, insects buzzed in her ears and a bird screamed overhead. Too soon the structure appeared before her. Like most of the camps built in and along the south Louisiana swamps and bayous, this one had been built on pilings to accommodate the ebb and flow of water. It was crude, little more than a shanty, with a makeshift front porch and screens for windows.

Taking a deep breath, Anna climbed the rickety front steps and crossed to the door. Unlatched, she pushed it cautiously open. The room was empty save for a large cardboard box at its center.

A coffin-shaped box. *Dear God, no.* Anna brought a hand to her mouth to hold back her whimper of fear. She took one halting step forward, then another.

She reached the box. Whispering a prayer, Anna worked open one of the top flaps, then another. She peered inside.

A cry spilled off her lips. Jaye was folded up inside the box, gagged, hands and feet bound. "Jaye," she whispered. Her friend didn't move. Anna bent and touched her. She was warm, her skin soft, pliant. Her chest moved in and out with her shallow breathing.

She was alive. Thank God.

The girl shifted suddenly, the movement slight. It was accompanied by a muffled sound, like a moan.

"Jaye," Anna said again, shaking her. "Wake up. Please. We've got to go."

Her friend opened her eyes. For one moment, she stared at Anna, her gaze dark with terror. A moment later the fear disappeared and her eyes filled with tears.

Anna's lips lifted, her own eyes brimming. "I've got to get you out of here," she said softly, voice thick. "Come on, we can do it together."

Anna managed to get Jaye to her feet. She freed her hands, then feet. Jaye ripped off her gag, then fell sobbing into Anna's arms.

"I didn't think I'd ever see you again!" she cried. "It was so awful. I was so scared."

"I know, sweetheart." Anna held her friend close. She stroked her hair and back, hungry to reassure herself that she was unharmed. "I was so frightened for you. I knew you didn't run away. I knew it."

"Are the police here? Did they get—"

"No police. Just me."

Jaye's eyes widened. "But they…got him. Right? They—"

"No." Anna caught her friend's hands, squeezing them tightly. "He told me he would kill you if I didn't come. He said he would kill you if I contacted the police."

"No." A moan slipped past Jaye's lips. "He's not going to let us escape. He hates you, Anna. I don't know why, but—"

"I do. It's the man who kidnapped me twenty-three years ago. He intends to finish what he started." She sucked in a deep breath. "I'm so sorry I got you into this. But I'm going to get you out, I promise."

She tugged on Jaye's hand. "My car's about a mile

up the road. There's a service station just beyond that. We can make it, Jaye. We can.''

"Not without Minnie. I can't leave her."

"Where is she?"

"I don't know. I thought... We haven't spoken since the night he moved us.''

"Let's look. If she's here, we'll find her."

But they didn't. A search of the cabin's other two rooms revealed no sign that the other girl had ever been there.

Jaye started to cry. "What's he done with her? I can't go without her, Anna. I won't!''

From somewhere behind the cabin came the sound of an outboard motor. Anna caught Jaye's shoulders, forcing her to look her in the eyes. "She wasn't a part of this, Jaye. Not really. He wanted me. He needed you to get to me. But Minnie's been with him a long time. He's hidden her somewhere, but she's safe. If we can get to the police, they'll find her. Please," she finished, tightening her grip, the sound of the motor drawing closer, "we have to go. We can't help her if we don't get the police."

The rumble of the motor stopped abruptly. A moment later, Anna heard the sound of feet pounding on the dock. She grabbed Jaye's hand and they sprinted for the door. They ran through it and down the stairs.

Jaye was having trouble keeping up. She stumbled once, then again. Anna caught her arm, steadying her.

A high, thin scream broke the silence. Jaye stopped and swung back toward the cabin. "Minnie? Minnie!''

"Run, Jaye!" a girl shouted. "Don't stop! Run for the road, the police will come. I called them, I—"

The girl's words ended abruptly, as if she had been forcibly silenced. A cry of denial ripped past Jaye's lips and she started for the cabin.

Anna grabbed her arm, stopping her. "Jaye, no! You can't—"

"I can't leave her!" Her friend wrenched her arm free. "I won't!"

She started to run. Anna caught her easily. "I'll go back. Not you, Jaye. Go for the road—"

"But I promised I wouldn't leave her!" Tears streamed down her friend's cheeks. "We promised each other we wouldn't let him—"

"I'll go. I won't let him hurt her." She shook her friend. "It's me he wants, not you. Get the police, Jaye. It's the only way."

Jaye hesitated a moment more, then nodded. Anna hugged her, eyes flooding with tears. "I love you, Jaye. Be careful. Promise."

She hugged her back. "I promise. You, too."

Anna had to force herself to let go, to take a step back. "Go," she said, giving Jaye a gentle nudge. "Get the police."

They parted. Anna took one last glance over her shoulder, then hurried toward the cabin. A prayer played repeatedly in her head. That Jaye escaped. For Minnie's safety. That she could find the strength to do this.

Dear God, she was afraid.

Heart in her throat, she climbed the stairs, her every instinct warning her to flee. To join Jaye at the road.

She couldn't do that. She couldn't leave Minnie alone. She had promised Jaye; she knew what it was to be alone and at the mercy of a madman.

Anna reached the door and pushed it open. She stepped inside. She saw that the room was empty and took another step in.

The door snapped shut behind her.

"Hello, Harlow. Welcome to your nightmare."

She whirled around. A sound of shock, of disbelief, slipped past her lips. She had expected to see Kurt standing behind her.

Instead, she came face-to-face with Ben. And he had a gun.

She shook her head. It couldn't be. Not Ben. Not sweet, funny Ben.

He trained the gun on her chest. "I see by your expression that you expected someone else. Someone named Kurt."

She opened her mouth to respond, but found she couldn't and closed it again.

"I suppose a formal introduction is in order." He smiled, the curving of his lips obscene. "Adam Furst, at your service."

She fought to get a grip on her fear, on her disbelief. She found her voice, though it trembled when she spoke. "All along...everything...it was you, Ben?"

"Ben? That wimp? That...*nothing?*" He made a sound of disgust. "'I love you, Anna,'" he mocked the other man. "'Please don't tell me it's over.' He makes me sick."

Anna wetted her lips, dropping her gaze to the gun,

then returning it to his. She could see the difference in the two men, now that she looked closely. Adam's features were harder than Ben's, his eyes colder. He held himself differently as well. This was an aggressive man. An angry one.

"You and Ben, you're...twins?"

His mouth thinned with fury. "Stupid bitch, don't make that mistake again. I'm no part of Ben. We're nothing alike. Nothing!"

She took a step backward. "Where's Minnie? What have you done with her?"

At the mention of the girl, his expression changed from one of fury to self-satisfaction. "Our little Minnie's a pain in my ass most of the time, but she certainly came in handy. Did you like her letters?"

"You made her write them."

"Yes."

"You sent the tapes to my family and friends. You kidnapped Jaye. You...killed those other women."

"Yes and yes. Ingenious, I know."

He was so proud of himself. "Not ingenious. Sick." She curved her hands into fists. "You're sick and evil. I feel sorry for you."

Furious color flooded his face. Whatever button she had pushed was a hot one. Fear shot through her, and she took another step back.

"He said that. The bastard. He's dead now."

"So kill me." She forced the fear out of her voice. "Get it over with."

The breath shuddered past his lips. "A quick death? I don't think so, Harlow. That wouldn't be good enough for you."

"You want me to suffer. To be afraid."

"That's right." He took a step toward her, expression twisted with hate. "And I want you to keep suffering. Before it's over, I want you to wish you were dead. The way I wished it."

The door behind him eased open. *The police. Jaye had gotten through.* Anna struggled to keep her gaze trained on him; if she didn't, if she let the hope show on her face, she would give them away.

"But why?" she asked, inching backward again. "Why do you hate me so much? What have I ever done to you?"

"Bitch! Betrayer!" The words exploded from him. "You have no idea what real fear is. Real fear is lying in bed at night and waiting for him to come. Because you know he will. He always does. But for what? That's the question. Sometimes it's to inflict physical pain. Other times it's for sex. Sometimes he simply comes for your tears. For your pleas for mercy. It's a game, you see. Our pain and humiliation is his pleasure. The greater ours, the greater his."

Anna brought a hand to her mouth, sickened by what this man had been forced to endure, most probably as a young child. "I'm sorry," she whispered. "I am. But I don't know what this has to do with—"

"I took that for him," he went on as if she hadn't spoken. "For all of them. Because of you. You and that old bitch—"

Behind him, the door flew open.

Not the police, Anna realized, a cry ripping past

her lips. Jaye. She hadn't run, she hadn't gone for help.

The girl leaped at Adam's back, attaching herself to him, digging her nails into his shoulders. He howled and stumbled, the gun slipped from his grasp. It hit the floor.

Anna dived for it; he kicked it beyond her grasp. He swung sideways, freeing himself of Jaye. She careened backward, slamming into the wall, her head snapping back against it.

"Jaye!" Anna cried, swinging toward her friend. "No!"

"I'm oka— The gun!"

Anna scrambled for it. Too late, Adam got it first. He curved his hands around the grip, rolled then leaped to his feet, the weapon aimed at Anna.

Jaye launched herself at him once more. "What have you done with Minnie!" she screamed. "If you've hurt her, I'll—"

This time, she didn't get ahold of him. He caught her easily, pinning her to his chest. She fought like a tiger, kicking and cursing him. "If you've hurt her, I'll kill you! I swear I will."

Adam laughed. "I see that," he murmured. "I'm really scared."

"Minnie!" she screamed. "Minnie, where are you!"

Suddenly, Adam released Jaye. A violent shudder racked his body; he looked away, then back. Anna caught her breath. His face was changed, softer-looking, more open and younger. He curled his arms

around his middle, hunching into himself, as if trying
to make himself as small as possible.

"I'm here, Jaye," he said, voice a girlish whisper.
"I'm here. He hasn't hurt me."

Anna froze. Jaye scooted backward, her expression
horrified. "Mi—Minnie?"

Adam held his hand out, gun dangling from it. His
eyes filled with tears. "You'd be so proud of me,
Jaye. I was so afraid, but I did it. I called Detective
Malone, the one Ben told me about. He's coming with
the police, he—"

Another shudder racked Adam's body. With it, he
transformed again. His face and stance altered. The
softness and insecurity disappeared, replaced by fury.
Fury fueled by hatred.

Anna struggled to make sense of what she had just
seen. She glanced at Jaye. Her friend sat on the floor,
back pressed to the wall, eyes wide with terror. With
disbelief.

*Adam and Minnie were the same person. But how
could that be? How—*

"You like boating, Harlow? Or are you afraid of
the water? You used to be, a long time ago. Remember? You were afraid of all the slimy, slithery things
hiding in the dark."

She had been afraid of the water, a long time ago.
But how did he know that?

She shook her head. "I don't know what you're
talking about."

He grinned. Something about the way his lips
stretched over his teeth made her shudder. "Liar."

He glanced at Jaye. "Get to your feet. We're going for a little ride, the three of us."

"No!" Anna took a step toward him, hand out. "Please, let her go. She has nothing to do with this."

"The way we had nothing to do with you? She comes."

"Please, you promised." Desperation crept into her tone. "You said if I followed your instructions, you'd let her go."

"That's the thing about promises, princess. They're only as good as the person who makes them. You of all people should understand that."

"No, I don't understand. Why are you doing this? Why—"

"Would you prefer I shoot her now?" He cocked the weapon. "I don't have a problem with that."

"No!" Anna threw herself in front of Jaye. He pulled the trigger. The gunshot reverberated through the cabin. The bullet whizzed by her head, hitting the wall, splintering it.

"Now then," he murmured, "it's time to go."

65

Minnie's call had come from a marina named Smiley's, located just off the old Manchac Bridge, only a couple of minutes up ahead. Quentin flexed his fingers on the steering wheel. He had made great time, just under thirty minutes.

It had felt like an eternity.

His captain had called him with directions to the marina while en route. She had contacted the local police; they would be waiting for him when he arrived. Johnson had returned from the computer imaging center before they had hung up: the photo of Ben and Anna was a work of fiction. It had been generated by computer, using several different images.

Quentin swore. Ben had created the image to divert suspicion from himself. Why hadn't he checked the photo's authenticity before?

Quentin reached Smiley's. As his aunt had promised, the local boys were waiting for him. Quentin slammed out of his vehicle and strode toward the ranking officer. "Detective Quentin Malone, NOPD."

"Davy Pierce, sheriff's deputy." They shook

hands. "Your captain filled us in. We're ready to help in any way we can."

"Thanks, Deputy Pierce. I appreciate that."

The man smiled. "Call me Davy. We're pretty informal around here."

Quentin returned his tense smile. "I'll do that. What do you have so far?"

"Not much. We found Anna North's car a mile up the road. No sign of her. Keys were in it."

"Shit," Quentin muttered. "The attendant see—"

"Negative. Didn't even see her drive by."

"Where is he?"

"Come on. I'll introduce you." They started across the parking lot, the shell gravel crunching under their feet and coating the toes of their shoes with a fine white dust. "His name's Sal St. Augustine. He's lived here all his life. If anybody can help you, he can."

Sal turned out to be a wizened old man with sunbrowned skin the texture of alligator hide. His deeply set blue eyes seemed to miss nothing as he studied Quentin. "What can I do for you?" he asked.

"Looking for a woman, red hair, real attractive. She was driving a white Toyota Camry—"

"The one Davy and his boys found parked up the road." He shook his head. "Didn't see her. I must have been servicing a boat." He indicated the dock behind the building. "I'm the only station around these parts. I stay pretty busy."

Quentin couldn't quite hide his frustration. "How about a young girl, eleven or twelve years old? She made a call from your pay phone. About an hour ago."

Sal removed his baseball cap and scratched his balding head. "Don't recall no young girl either. Man used the phone. Weird guy. Real quiet."

Quentin narrowed his eyes. "What did he look like?"

"Dark hair. Kind of curly." Sal slipped the cap back on, tugging it low on his forehead to protect his eyes from the fierce sun. "Thin. Pale."

"Pale," Quentin repeated. "He wearing a hat?"

Sal squinted in thought. "Nope."

That basic description fit Ben Walker and the man Louise Walker had described for the police artist. He glanced at Davy. "Get one of your guys to give my captain a call. Ask her to fax over the computer-enhanced sketch of Adam Furst and the photo of Ben Walker."

"You got it." While Davy did that, Quentin turned his attention back to Sal. "This guy, you ever seen him before?"

"Handful of times in the past couple of weeks, never before that. He's not from around here, that's for sure."

"He's gone now?"

"Left the way he came. By boat." He pointed. "I filled him up 'fore he went."

Quentin turned toward the water, squinting in thought. Fishermen had skin the color of Sal's and Davy's. They were a hardy breed with a healthy respect for the sun. So what was a thin, pale, hatless guy doing filling up a boat in an area used almost exclusively by fishermen?

Quentin waved the other detective over. "This is our guy. I know it."

Sal spoke up. "There're a couple of camps close by. Owners rent them out."

"Where?"

He pointed up the waterway. "Only two ways in or out. Boat and the road out front. It dead-ends about three miles up."

But the water didn't dead-end. Lake Maurepas fed into dozens of bayous and other small tributaries, many navigable. Many of which snaked their way through land that could be traversed by foot.

The son-of-a-bitch planned to escape by boat.

Quentin looked at Davy. "He's going by water."

"Boats are on their way. Just in case, let's set up a roadblock out front. I'll get a team of uniforms to check out those camps."

"Warn your men to use extreme caution," Quentin murmured, gaze still on the water. "This guy's a killer."

Within five minutes the sheriff's department's three powerboats had arrived and two teams of deputies had been assembled to search the camps. Quentin chose to go by boat; he believed that avenue would provide the best chance of getting his hands on Adam. And of saving Anna.

As he and the Manchac deputies boarded the powerboats, a fisherman pulled up to the dock for fueling. His was a small flat-bottom boat fitted with a Yamaha outboard motor. The aluminum pirogue-style boat had been designed to navigate through the shallow, vegetation-choked waters of the swamp and bayous.

Quentin drew his eyebrows together. *If he was about to do what Ben Walker planned, he would want to do it in the deserted backwaters, away from the view of others. He would want to leave the bodies where they would never be found, where, after the alligators had finished with them, there would be little left to find.*

And then he would walk away.

"Sal!" he shouted. The other man looked over and Quentin indicated the small craft. "That the kind of boat our guy had?"

With a nod, Sal indicated it was. Quentin hopped off the speedboat and back onto the dock.

"Malone," Davy shouted over the roar of the engines, "what are you doing?"

"Change of plans. I've found another means of transportation."

66

Wednesday, February 7
4:10 p.m.

Anna held herself erectly on the pirogue's bench seat. An insect buzzed next to her ear and she swatted at it with her bound hands. Beside her, Jaye trembled and wept quietly. They didn't speak.

Adam had bound her and Jaye together by their right and left ankles, respectively. He had secured their wrists individually, palms pressed together. If they escaped him or the boat capsized, they would have a minimal chance of surviving.

He had thought through every detail of his plan carefully, Anna realized. The boat and location. The way they had been bound. How he planned to kill them. No doubt his escape route as well.

Even so, Anna refused to consider what Adam's plans for them might be or how the creatures that inhabited the swamp might be involved in those plans. She refused to give in to her fear.

Fear would strangle her, she knew. It would choke off any chance she had to outwit this monster. If she gave in, she would be signing a death warrant not only for herself, but Jaye as well.

The outboard motor hummed as it propelled the craft down the winding, dark waterway. Little sun got through the branches of the huge cypress and live oaks trees. Anna shivered as the cold, damp air worked its way through her clothing to her flesh, chilling her to her core.

Up ahead, a snake dropped from the branch of a cypress tree and slithered toward the bank of the bayou. Anna shifted her gaze to Adam. "Why are you doing this?" she asked evenly. "What have we ever done to you?"

"Why?" he repeated. "Because I want Harlow Grail to know the terror we knew. The horror. I want little princess Harlow to know what it is to be alone, to be abandoned and left for dead."

"Left for dead?" she repeated. "I don't understand."

"Think, Harlow. You know who we are. You abandoned us though you promised you wouldn't. You're a liar."

A denial sprang to her lips; she never uttered it. She brought a hand to her mouth. "Timmy?" she whispered. "You can't be…you can't mean… Timmy?"

Once again his teeth stretched over his lips in an obscene attempt at a smile. "But I do, princess. Little Timmy Price."

Anna made a sound of disbelief. Her hands began to shake. "Timmy's dead. He's been dead a long time. Kurt killed him. He killed him right in front of my eyes."

"He would have died," Adam murmured. "But the

old bitch wanted a little boy. She wanted to be a mommy.''

"I don't believe you. You're a monster. You'd say anything to—''

"While Kurt was performing surgery on your hand, the old bitch revived him. She'd worked in a hospital, she knew CPR.'' Adam leaned forward, face twisted with hate. "He was alive when you left him behind.''

Despair choked her. She struggled to understand, to make sense of what he was saying. "You're the liar!'' she cried. "He was dead! He was!''

"No. You abandoned him. You promised to take care of him, but you left him behind. You left him with Kurt.''

Timmy had been alive. She shook her head against the horror of it, tears spilling over. "I thought he was dead. I didn't...I never would have—''

"No one came for him, Harlow. Not ever. Even though he waited and prayed. He believed you'd come back. But you didn't.''

No one had come because she had told everyone Timmy was dead.

It couldn't be true. She didn't want to believe it.

But she did, and it hurt almost more than she could bear. Anna gazed at him through her tears, searching for a glimpse of the boy she had known and loved. The sweet, curly-haired cherub who had followed her around.

"Timmy?'' she managed to say. "Is it really you?''

Anger seemed to explode from Adam. Beside her, Jaye whimpered and leaned closer to Anna's side. "Timmy? I'm not Timmy. That sniveling little wimp.

He wanted his mommy. He wanted Harlow. He couldn't take it. So I stepped in. I'm the strong one." He thumped his chest with the butt of his gun. "Me. I took everything Kurt dished out."

Anna struggled to understand, to make sense of what he was telling her. Suddenly she remembered a conversation she and Ben had had, that night at the Café du Monde. He'd talked about his work, his book. He had discussed the toll childhood trauma took on the psyche, about the ways that trauma manifested itself in adult personality.

The ultimate expression of that being the fracturing of the psyche into separate and distinct personalities.

Anna searched her memory for exactly what he had said. That such fracturing occurred as a way for the psyche to protect itself. That it was seen in adults who had experienced repeated, sadistic abuse in early childhood. He'd said that the various personalities performed specific functions for the host personality.

Adam had taken Kurt's abuse.

"You took it from Kurt," she said softly, voice quivering. "So what about Ben? What did he…take, if you handled Kurt?"

"Ben got all the glory, the prick. He got to be mommy's good boy. He got the fancy education and the accolades." Adam's lips twisted in a sneer. "He was so pathetic, he didn't even see that it was me paving the way for him. Making it all possible. I was the one who took the heat, the one who made everything all right. He thought he was the only one."

Ben hadn't been aware he was a multiple. He hadn't known about Adam or his plans. She didn't know why that made her feel so much better, but it did.

He waved the gun at her. "I was the one who finally took care of Kurt. That's right, *me*. All these years you've been afraid of him, he's been maggot food. Today I offed the old bitch. Now it's little Harlow's turn."

"Evening the score?"

"Damn right," he said proudly. "The great Savannah Grail was easy to trick. I played on her vanity and guilt and she handed her daughter over without a second thought. Ben's mother, the addled old fool, always did my bidding. I moved her to New Orleans, knowing Ben would follow, knowing he would think her slipping further into her disease. Ben played along, reacting just as I predicted at every turn. So did Minnie. I controlled them all."

"Really?" Anna arched an eyebrow. "Seems to me Minnie threw you a few curves."

"That Minnie's a real pip. Surprised the hell out of me, going to Ben the way she did. Then calling that detective. But I can't stay too angry with her, she's helped me out over the years. Especially when Kurt brought those friends of his around. They were a real friendly bunch, if you know what I mean. She helped me out by taking—"

"Don't talk about her!" Jaye said suddenly, voice high and quivering. "You don't deserve to even know her!"

He turned his flat gaze on Jaye. "You're a lot of trouble, you know that? I'd like you to shut the fuck up."

He delivered the words in a conversational tone, as if simply commenting on the weather. Frightened for her friend, Anna brought his attention back to her.

"So, Ben didn't know about you. Or Minnie. Or…me."

He adjusted the boat's prop as they eased into shallower water. "Give the lady a gold star."

Anna felt ill. She imagined the horrors Timmy had been forced to endure, abuse horrific enough to cause his psyche to fracture in an attempt at self-preservation.

"What about Timmy?" she asked. "Where is he now?"

Adam's lips lifted into a thin smile. "Gone."

"Gone," she repeated. "I don't understand."

He snorted, impatient. "We're almost there, I don't want to talk anymore."

Anna ignored him. "He can't be gone. Because you're part of him."

"Shut up."

"Timmy," she said. "It's Harlow. Are you there?"

"Shut up," he said again, voice rising.

"I'm so sorry, I didn't know. They told me you were dead." She leaned forward, voice quivering with emotion, tears choking her. "I would have come for you, we all would have. I loved you." The tears welled in her eyes, blurring her vision. "Your mother…your real mother loved you, too. She died a few years back, but she mourned your loss until that day. She missed you…so much."

Adam shuddered and twitched. His rage seemed to slip away, his features became soft, childlike, his body language that of one who was small and lost. In that split second, Anna glimpsed the boy she had known. She saw Timmy.

As quickly as he had appeared, he was gone. Replaced again by Adam.

Anna fought grief and focused instead on what she had just witnessed. On how it had happened.

The switch from one personality to another occurred in the blink of an eye. They were proceeded by a twitch or a shudder, but one that was natural, nearly seamless. Unless one looked for it.

She could get the gun away during one of the switches. If she could move quickly enough.

Adam seemed to be tiring. She wondered at the cost in mental energy to keep the other two suppressed. Because if they existed in a state of coconsciousness, which she vaguely remembered having read about, then Minnie and Ben were aware of what was happening.

And if they were, they would try to stop Adam. She believed that.

He cut the motor. Instead of silence, she heard the sound of another boat in the distance. Adam glanced over his shoulder, then back at them. "That's nothing. A fisherman."

"How can you be so sure?"

He ignored her and motioned with the gun. "Stand up."

Jaye began to cry. Anna stiffened her spine. "No."

"Stand up or I'll shoot you where you sit."

He meant what he said and Anna stood, bringing Jaye up with her. The boat rocked, and Anna tried to steady Jaye. The sound of the other boat drew grew louder.

"I chose this little spot because it's a favorite with the alligators. Lots of nests in the spring and summer." He chuckled and motioned with his revolver. "See that big boy over there? Handsome devil, isn't he? I bet he's twenty feet. Looks hungry, too."

Anna fought falling apart. "Let Jaye go. I don't care what you do to me, but she's the innocent—"

"An...na..." The voice ebbed and retreated on the chill, damp air. "Ja...ye..."

Quentin. Anna almost sobbed with relief. "We're here!" she shouted. "We're here!"

"Shut your mouth! Shut—"

"Quentin!" she screamed again. "Come quick! Come qui—"

Adam laughed suddenly, the sound high and wild. He cocked the gun. "Go ahead, shout. Scream your fucking head off. It's too late, Harlow Grail. You're already dead."

67

Wednesday, February 7
4:30 p.m.

From a place above and outside himself, Ben watched in horror as Adam leveled the gun on Anna's chest. He fought to free himself, but Adam was too strong. He refused let him out.

Stop! Leave them alone! Do you hear me? Let me out!

Adam could hear him, he knew. In the past few days he had taken a crash course in being a multiple. He had managed to get the hang of coconsciousness, had learned how to tune in to the voices in his head, had learned how to facilitate a switch.

He owed it all to Minnie. She had contacted him through the journal. Through it she had explained who—and what—he was.

Adam Furst. Minnie. Benjamin Walker. He was all of them.

Or rather, they were all part of the boy who had been Timmy.

He had been horrified. Despairing. But after the first shock had worn off, he had been unable to deny it was true. He understood now the headaches. The moments of lost time. Why he slept like the dead. The missing pieces of his past. His mother's confusion. The many times he had been recognized by people he didn't know.

All the pieces fit. Each of them a classic symptom of disassociative identity disorder. Dear Jesus, how could he not have seen it? He was a psychologist, for God's sake. He had observed patients who had suffered with DID.

If only Minnie had come to him sooner. Those women wouldn't have died. He wouldn't have allowed it.

We can do it together. Minnie's voice. *We can save them.*

He and Minnie had made their own plan. They had agreed that working together was the only way to stop Adam. They would wait for the right moment. And when it came, whoever managed to get free would do it. No hesitation.

Now!

He heard Minnie and strained to be free. He shouted at Adam, he kicked and clawed and demanded to be let out. Minnie did the same.

Adam weakened; Minnie slipped out.

No hesitation, Minnie. Do it.

Ben watched as she turned the gun on herself. "You're my best friend, Jaye. I won't let him hurt you."

Then she pulled the trigger.

68

Eight weeks later
The French Quarter

Spring had come to New Orleans. Though the winter of 2001 had gone on record as the city's coldest ever, the azaleas had bloomed as if on cue, the trees had budded out, becoming green as if by magic.

Anna breathed deeply of the warm, fragrant air and caught Quentin's hand, curling her fingers around his. They had brunched with Jaye and the entire Malone clan on Jackson Square, enjoying not only the day and each other's company, but watching the parade of wide-eyed tourists as well.

In a way, Anna had felt like one of them. Every day, she was wide-eyed at the wonder of living without fear. Without the constant weight of it at her back and at the edges of her consciousness. She supposed that one day she would forget to be awed and thankful, but not yet. Not for a very long time.

The last of Quentin's family bid them farewell, and now Jaye was getting ready to leave. The girl kissed Anna's cheek. "I've got to run. Fran's taking me to the mall. There's a big sale at Abercrombie's."

Anna smiled, pleased by Jaye's obvious happiness.

"You and your foster mom are getting along well these days."

Jaye lifted a shoulder, expression wicked. "She's not so bad. She hasn't sacrificed any small animals in weeks now."

Fran Clausen had wept with joy when Jaye had been returned to her. She had begged the girl's forgiveness for having believed she'd run away. Her tears had meant the world to Jaye, and in a show of real maturity, Jaye had not only forgiven her, but accepted some of the responsibility for the couple's attitude. Jaye's past history of bolting had warranted it.

Her kidnapping ordeal had left Jaye a changed girl. She was more accepting of herself and others, easygoing in a way she had never been. It was as if almost dying had given her a sense of how precious life was. How good.

"Love you, kiddo," Anna murmured, giving her a quick hug. "Have fun."

Anna watched the girl walk away. She tucked her arm through Quentin's. "It's so quiet now."

Quentin glanced down at her with one of his quick-silver smiles. "Blessedly so. My family can be a little overwhelming when attempted all at once."

Anna laughed. "I adore them, individually and taken as a whole. You're a lucky guy, you know that?"

He stopped and met her eyes. "Lucky I found you."

Tears stung her eyes. Ones of joy. And of sadness. Because joy brought thoughts of Timmy. Some nights she awoke dreaming of him; in them he was alive and happy. The way he had been as a young child.

He was happy now, she believed that. He was with his mother, his real mother. Finally and forever.

Anna stood on tiptoe and kissed Quentin. "Thank you, Detective Malone. I feel mighty lucky, too."

They began to walk. "I went to see Terry today," he said.

"How's he doing?"

"Not great. He's taking Penny's move to Lafayette hard. But the therapy seems to be doing him good. It's going to be a long haul, though." Affection warmed his tone. "But Terry's never done anything the easy way."

She squeezed his arm. "I know it helps that you're there for him."

"We all are, Aunt Patti, too. She checks in on him every day. She's made it clear that when he's ready, she wants him back at work."

They walked in silence a while; Quentin broke it first. "So, hotshot, how's the new book coming?"

He had taken to calling her that ever since three major publishers had gotten into a bidding war over her next book. The competition had sent the amount of the offer into the stratosphere. Her new publisher had no doubt about the book earning out the advance—because of her past, they expected interest in her book to be overwhelming. They were already talking about her tour and she had barely begun writing the story.

Anna tilted her face up to his. "Great. And my new editor's a dream to work with."

She shook her head, amazed at herself. When she toured, she would be on television and radio answering questions about herself and her past. She would be in front of the public, exposed and vulnerable to any nutcase who might be lurking about.

And she wasn't afraid.

She had promised herself she would never be afraid again. That she would never again hide from life. Life was about taking chances, facing the good...and the bad. It was about birth and death and everything in between.

Her apartment building came into view up ahead. She elbowed Quentin. "Besides, who's the hotshot here? I'm not the one who was accepted into Tulane's law school."

He laughed and shook his head. "I still can't believe it. Quentin Malone, future shark in a suit." His smile faded. "If I can cut it."

"You can." She stopped and turned toward him. "I believe in you."

"Yeah?" He cupped her face in his palms, a smile tugging at the corners of his mouth.

"Yeah."

He kissed her then. Deeply. Passionately.

She kissed him back the same way.

"Good to see you kids out and about."

Alphonse Badeaux and Mr. Bingle stood behind them, dog and master both grinning from ear to ear. Anna's cheeks warmed. "Alphonse! I didn't know you were there."

Malone held out a hand. "Good to see you again, Alphonse. How are you and Bingle doing today?"

They shook hands. "Can't complain. Not on a day as pretty as this."

Anna reached down and scratched the bulldog behind the ears. "Come up for an iced tea sometime. I've got some biscuits for Mr. Bingle, too. The ones he likes."

"That's mighty kind of you, Miss Anna," he murmured. "I'll do that. By the way, a package came for you today. Around eleven this morning. Just thought you'd want to know."

A feeling of déjà vu settled over her. Anna glanced toward her building, then back at her neighbor. "Did the deliveryman toss it over the gate?"

"Nope. Took it up. Door was propped open again." He cleared his throat. "You might want to speak to those kids from four about it. Not that it's any of my business, of course."

Anna thanked him, said goodbye and she and Quentin entered the building. They climbed the stairs to the second floor. As her neighbor had warned her she would, she found a package propped against the door.

Wrapped in brown paper, it was about the size and shape of a videocassette.

What if it wasn't over? What if it was never over?

Quentin looked at her in concern. "Are you okay?"

She hiked up her chin. "Fine. Absolutely okay." Anna let out a long breath, marched across the hall and picked it up. The package looked as if it had been run over by a truck; the paper was dirty and torn, the box half crushed.

It was from Ben.

She lifted her gaze to Malone's, her hands beginning to shake. "This can't be."

Quentin bent his head and read the label, then met her eyes. "There's only one way to find out."

She ripped the package open. And found two journals. The one she had seen on Ben's desk that afternoon all those weeks ago and another, only partially full.

He had attached a note. She read it aloud:

Dearest Anna,

If you are reading this, I will have been successful in my attempt to stop Adam. And I am most probably dead.

Read and understand.

Yours,
Ben

So she did. Curled up on the corner of her couch, she began. Documented in the one notebook was a story of abuse, rage and despair, a testament not only of the depths to which the human spirit could sink but of its will to survive. The other spiral contained the story of a man's struggle to understand and come to grips with parts of himself and his past.

Both stories were told through individual narrations, drawings and conversations between the three personalities, the handwriting and voice of each dramatically different, a physical testament to Adam's rage, Minnie's fear and Ben's desperation.

Anna learned that Timmy, unable to cope, had essentially ceased to exist and had "gone to sleep" deep inside himself. Adam had emerged first. Then Ben and Minnie. The three had taken over Timmy's life and consciousness, each performing a specific role, each with their own strengths, weaknesses, past and memories.

Anna learned how Minnie's love for Jaye had forced her to overcome her fear and contact Ben through the journal. Faced with the proof of the journal, Ben had been unable to deny what he was, though he had wanted to. Instead, he had set out to wrest control from Adam. To heal them. To integrate them into a whole.

It had been too late. There hadn't been enough time.

Afterward, Quentin held Anna while she cried. "I'll never forget," Anna whispered. "Not Timmy. Not Ben or Minnie. I'll never forget what they did for me."

"I know, sweetheart," he murmured, holding her close. "I'm so sorry."

She lifted her face to his, vision blurred with tears. "Children are a gift. They should be cherished. Protected. They—" She bit the words back. "I'm not going to let this go, Malone. I can do…something. Through my writing…I've got to do something."

For a moment he was silent, then his expression softened. "I love you, Harlow Anastasia Grail."

His words moved over her like a healing balm. And in that moment she knew without a shadow of a doubt who she was.

She would never hide from that person again.

A gripping novel of psychological suspense
from the bestselling author of *Sacred Trust*

MEG O'BRIEN

GATHERING
LIES

Six women have come to Thornberry, a writers' colony on a tiny
island off the coast of Seattle, each hoping to work on her own
writing at this secluded resort. But they have also come to hide.
Each harbors her own secret—until a devastating earthquake
shatters the haven these women have found. Suddenly the resort
is partly in ruin, communication has been cut off from the
mainland and the women are forced to rely on each other for
basic survival.

Then a man washes up on shore. Is he the salvation they've
been looking for...or an even greater threat to their survival?

Available April 2001, wherever paperbacks are sold!

The spellbinding story of a man and woman who journey through hell to arrive at a place in their hearts that offers the promise of heaven.

THE DEVIL'S OWN

In a terrifying race to save nine children from the threat of war-torn Central America, Kerry Bishop prepared for the fight of her life. But she wasn't prepared for a passion almost as dangerous as the mission she had undertaken.

Dependent on a stranger, Kerry refused to let unexpected desire complicate their mission. Survival was all they could think about. But if they succeeded, what then?

NEW YORK TIMES BESTSELLING AUTHOR

SANDRA BROWN

Available March 2001
wherever hardcovers are sold!

MIRA®

Harmless prank...or murder?

HELEN R. MYERS

DEAD END

When Brette Barry finds a bloody handprint on a Dead End, she's certain it's a harmless Halloween prank. But when she sends her son over to clean it up, the handprint is gone...and a teenager is missing.

Brette suspects her vindictive neighbors, the Pughs, are involved. The local sheriff is convinced the troubled teen has likely run away again...but he's also suspicious of Sam Knight, Brette's suddenly attentive new neighbor.

Brette can't deny her own doubts about the mysterious man—or her attraction to him. And

> "Ms. Myers gives readers an incredible depth of storytelling."
> —Romantic Times

her feelings grow even more conflicted, the truth murkier, when the missing teen reappears, only to confide that they've been searching for the wrong person. *Tracie Pugh* is missing, and the last person to see her alive...was Sam.

ERICA SPINDLER

66551	ALL FALL DOWN	__ $5.99 U.S.	__ $6.99 CAN.
66497	CAUSE FOR ALARM	__ $5.99 U.S.	__ $6.99 CAN.
66415	SHOCKING PINK	__ $5.99 U.S.	__ $6.99 CAN.
66042	RED	__ $4.99 U.S.	__ $5.50 CAN.
66071	FORBIDDEN FRUIT	__ $5.99 U.S.	__ $6.50 CAN.
66275	CHANCES ARE	__ $5.50 U.S.	__ $6.50 CAN.

(limited quantities available)

TOTAL AMOUNT	$_____
POSTAGE & HANDLING	$_____
($1.00 for one book; 50¢ for each additional)	
APPLICABLE TAXES*	$_____
TOTAL PAYABLE	$_____

(check or money order—please do not send cash)

To order, complete this form and send it, along with a check or money order for the total above, payable to MIRA Books®, to: **In the U.S.:** 3010 Walden Avenue, P.O. Box 9077, Buffalo, NY 14269-9077; **In Canada:** P.O. Box 636, Fort Erie, Ontario L2A 5X3.

Name:_____
Address:_____ City:_____
State/Prov.:_____ Zip/Postal Code:_____
Account Number (if applicable):_____
075 CSAS

*New York residents remit applicable sales taxes.
Canadian residents remit applicable GST and provincial taxes.

MIRA®